"Stayed in from recess to read it . . . **CAN'T WAIT FOR NEXT ONE!**"
—Zac A., age 9, Hood River, Ore.

"*Hilo* was **SO GREAT** I couldn't stop reading until I'd finished it. I want to read the next one **NOW!**"
—Jack A., age 10, Brooklyn

"I love all the funny parts—it's just **'OUTSTANDING!'** And his **SILVER UNDERPANTS** are hilarious."
—Bennett S., age 5, Spokane

"**I LOVE** this book because it is **EXCITING** and **FUNNY.**"
—Nate A., age 8, Brooklyn

"My big brother and I fight over this book. **I CAN'T WAIT** for the second one so we can both read a Hilo book at the same time."
—Nory V., age 8, Montclair, N.J.

"**FANTASTIC. EVERY SINGLE THING ABOUT THIS . . . IS TERRIFIC.**"
—Boingboing.net

"**HIGH ENERGY** and **HILARIOUS**!"
—Gene Luen Yang, winner of the Printz Award

"*Hilo* is **REALLY, REALLY FUNNY.** It has a **LOT OF LAUGHS.** The raccoon is the funniest. It made me feel really happy!"
—Theo M., age 7, Miami, Fla.

"**ACTION-PACKED** and **AMAZING FUN.**"
—Brad Meltzer, THE FIFTH ASSASSIN

"*Hilo* is loads of **SLAPSTICK FUN!**"
—Dan Santat, winner of the Caldecott Medal

READ ALL THE HILO BOOKS!

HILO #1 THE BOY WHO CRASHED TO EARTH

HILO #2 SAVING THE WHOLE WIDE WORLD

HILO #3 THE GREAT BIG BOOM

HILO #4 WAKING THE MONSTERS

HILO #5 THEN EVERYTHING WENT WRONG

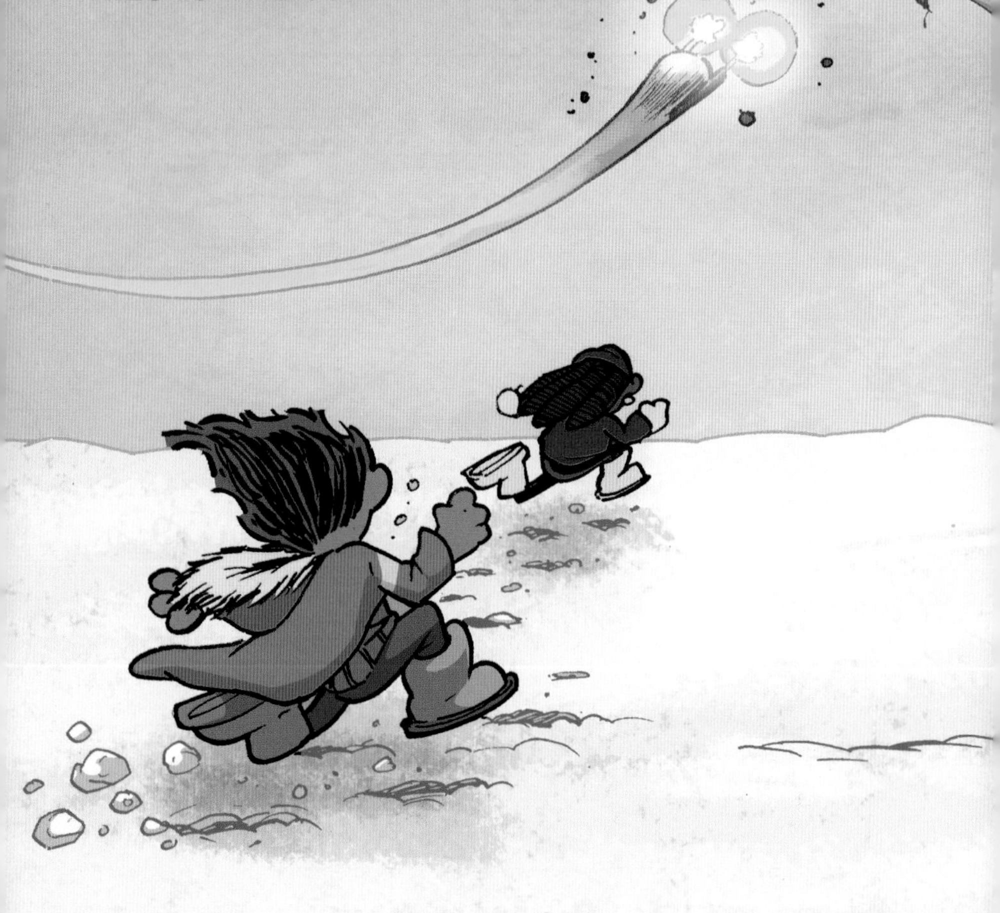

BOOK 2

HiLo

SAVING THE WHOLE WIDE WORLD

BY JUDD WINICK
COLOR BY GUY MAJOR

RANDOM HOUSE 🏠 NEW YORK

Visit us on the Web! randomhousekids.com
Educators and librarians, for a variety of teaching tools, visit us at RHTeachersLibrarians.com
Library of Congress Cataloging-in-Publication Data
Winick, Judd, author, illustrator.
Hilo: saving the whole wide world / Judd Winick. — First edition.
p. cm. — (Hilo ; book 2)
Summary: Hilo and his friends must save the world from monsters from another dimension.
ISBN 978-0-385-38623-4 (trade) — ISBN 978-0-385-38624-1 (lib. bdg.) — ISBN 978-0-385-38625-8 (ebook)
1. Graphic novels. [1. Graphic novels. 2. Robots—Fiction. 3. Extraterrestrial beings—Fiction.
4. Friendship—Fiction. 5. Monsters—Fiction. 6. Science fiction.] I. Title.
PZ7.7.W57Hh 2016 741.5'973—dc23 2015001395
MANUFACTURED IN CHINA
13
Book design by John Sazaklis
First Edition

For Pam

CHAPTER 1

A LITTLE WEIRD

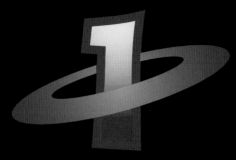

I'LL TRY TO EXPLAIN, BUT IT WAS A LITTLE WEIRD.

MY NAME IS **DANIEL JACKSON LIM**, BUT EVERYONE CALLS ME **D.J.** AND I WASN'T GOOD AT ANYTHING.

THEN A BOY FELL FROM THE SKY.

BOOM

BUT HE **WASN'T** A BOY.

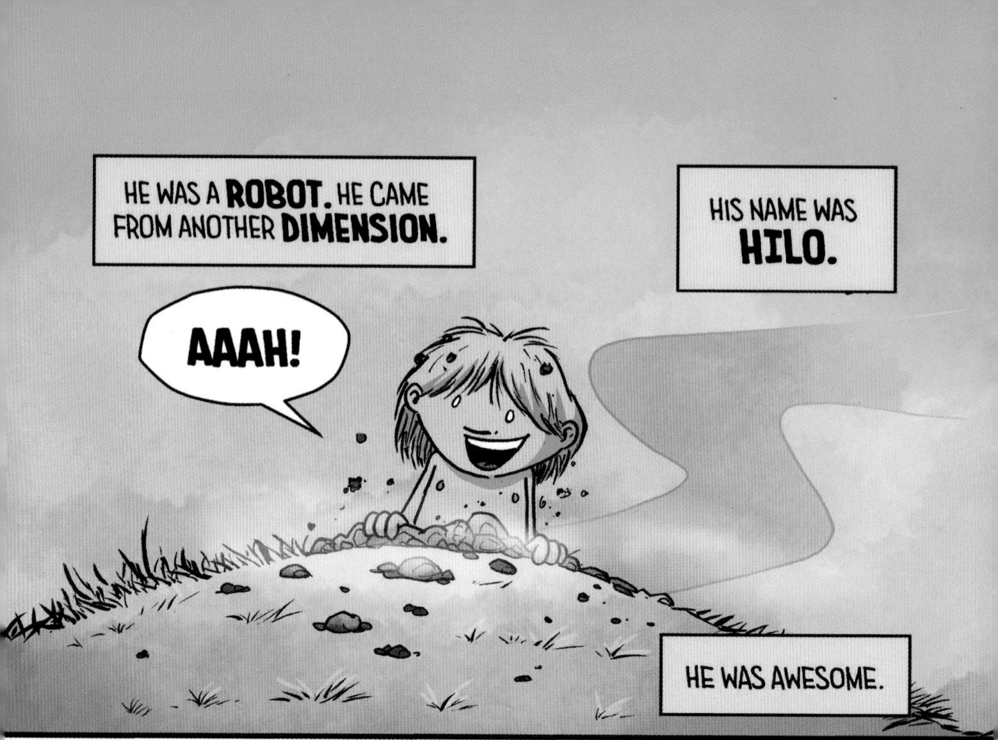
HE WAS A **ROBOT.** HE CAME FROM ANOTHER **DIMENSION.**
HIS NAME WAS **HILO.**
AAAH!
HE WAS AWESOME.

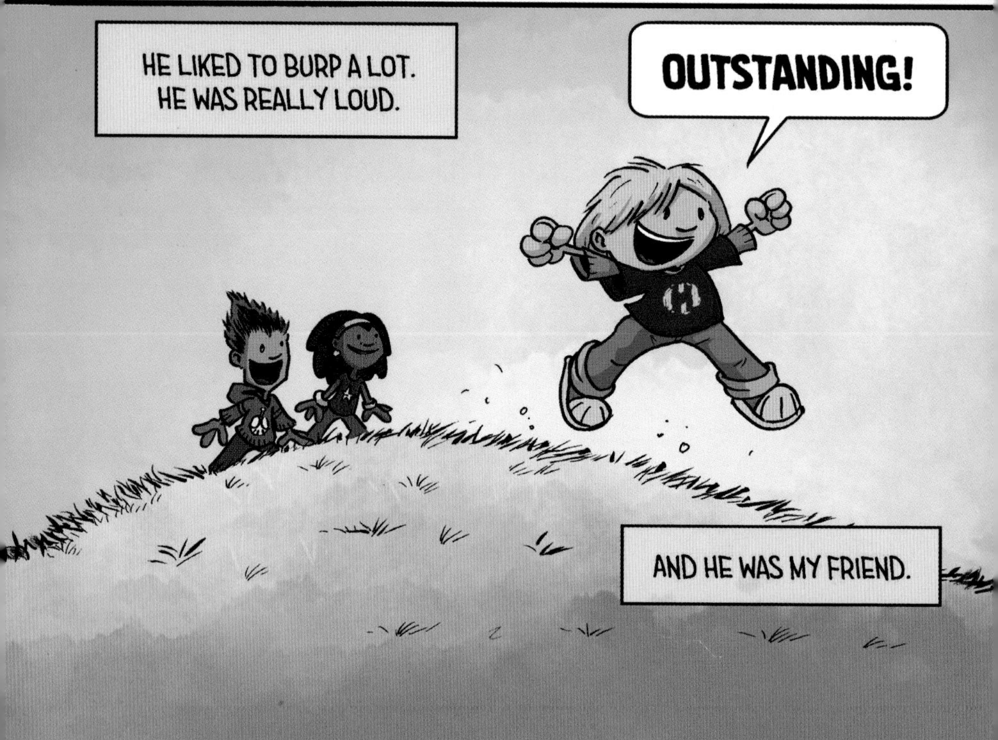
HE LIKED TO BURP A LOT. HE WAS REALLY LOUD.
OUTSTANDING!
AND HE WAS MY FRIEND.

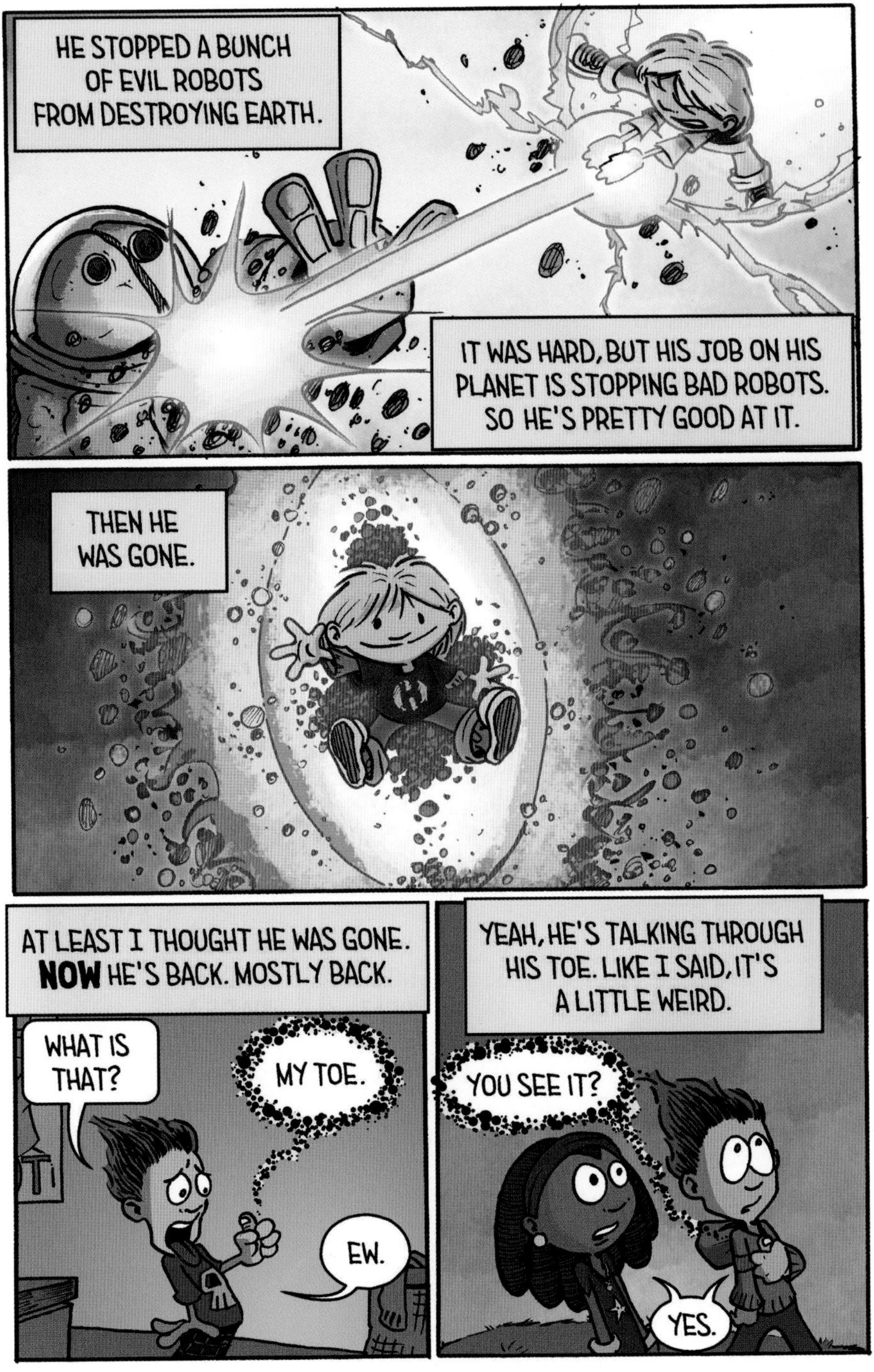
HE STOPPED A BUNCH OF EVIL ROBOTS FROM DESTROYING EARTH.
IT WAS HARD, BUT HIS JOB ON HIS PLANET IS STOPPING BAD ROBOTS. SO HE'S PRETTY GOOD AT IT.
THEN HE WAS GONE.
AT LEAST I THOUGHT HE WAS GONE. **NOW** HE'S BACK. MOSTLY BACK.
WHAT IS THAT?
MY TOE.
EW.
YEAH, HE'S TALKING THROUGH HIS TOE. LIKE I SAID, IT'S A LITTLE WEIRD.
YOU SEE IT?
YES.

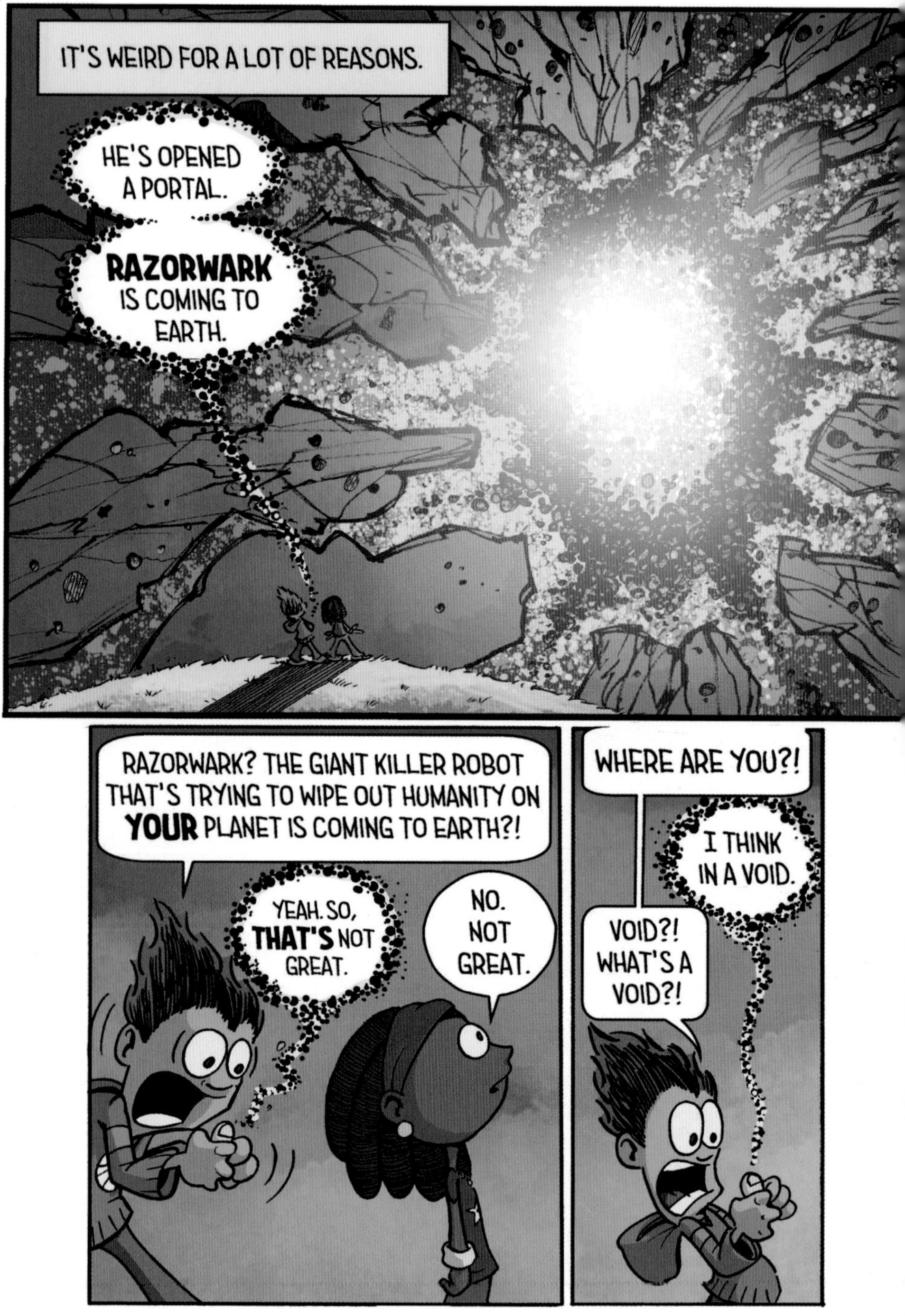

IT'S WEIRD FOR A LOT OF REASONS.
HE'S OPENED A PORTAL.
RAZORWARK IS COMING TO EARTH.
RAZORWARK? THE GIANT KILLER ROBOT THAT'S TRYING TO WIPE OUT HUMANITY ON YOUR PLANET IS COMING TO EARTH?!
YEAH. SO, THAT'S NOT GREAT.
NO. NOT GREAT.
WHERE ARE YOU?!
I THINK IN A VOID.
VOID?! WHAT'S A VOID?!

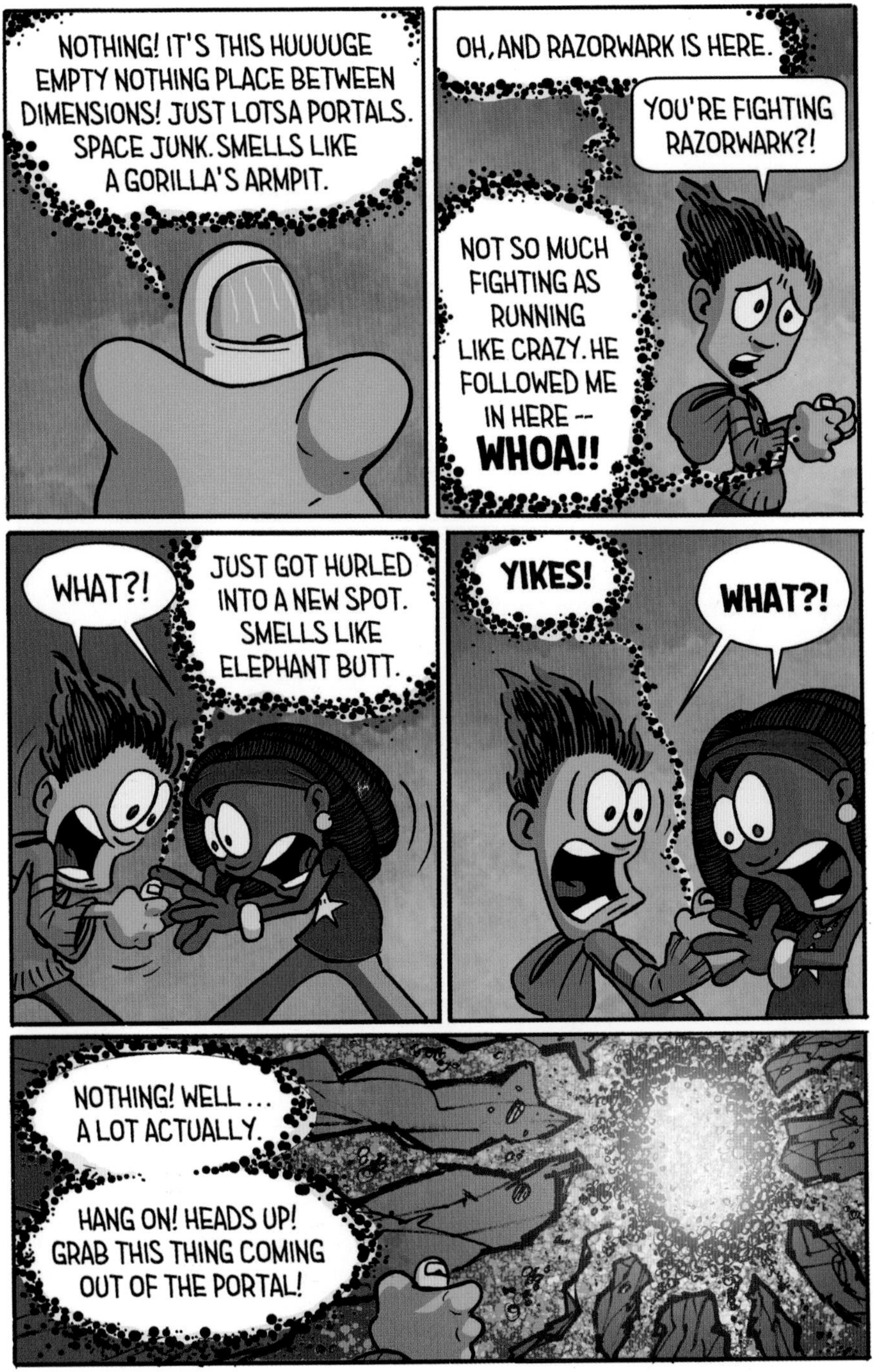
NOTHING! IT'S THIS HUUUUGE EMPTY NOTHING PLACE BETWEEN DIMENSIONS! JUST LOTSA PORTALS. SPACE JUNK. SMELLS LIKE A GORILLA'S ARMPIT.
OH, AND RAZORWARK IS HERE.
YOU'RE FIGHTING RAZORWARK?!
NOT SO MUCH FIGHTING AS RUNNING LIKE CRAZY. HE FOLLOWED ME IN HERE -- WHOA!!
WHAT?!
JUST GOT HURLED INTO A NEW SPOT. SMELLS LIKE ELEPHANT BUTT.
YIKES!
WHAT?!
NOTHING! WELL ... A LOT ACTUALLY.
HANG ON! HEADS UP! GRAB THIS THING COMING OUT OF THE PORTAL!

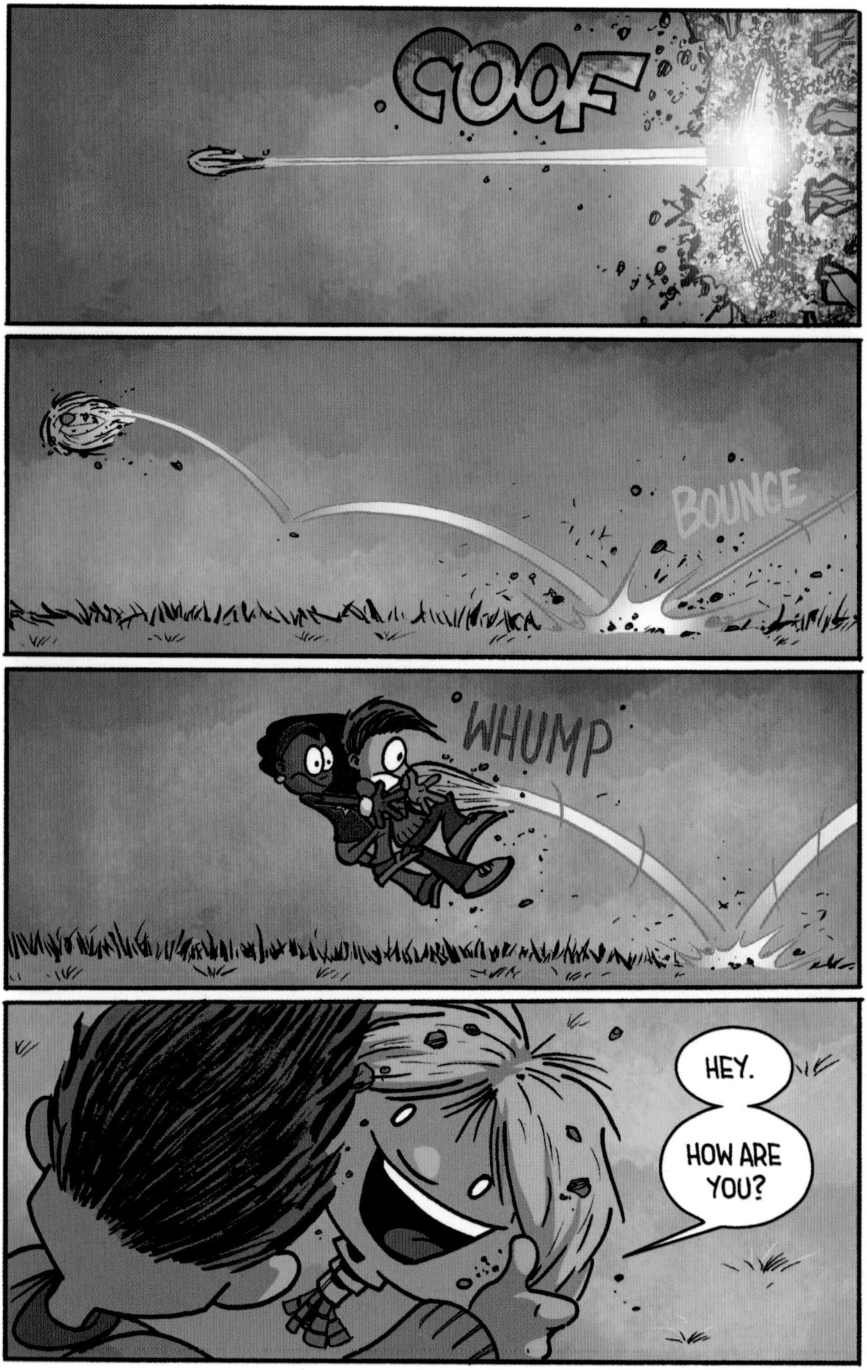
COOF
BOUNCE
WHUMP
HEY.
HOW ARE YOU?

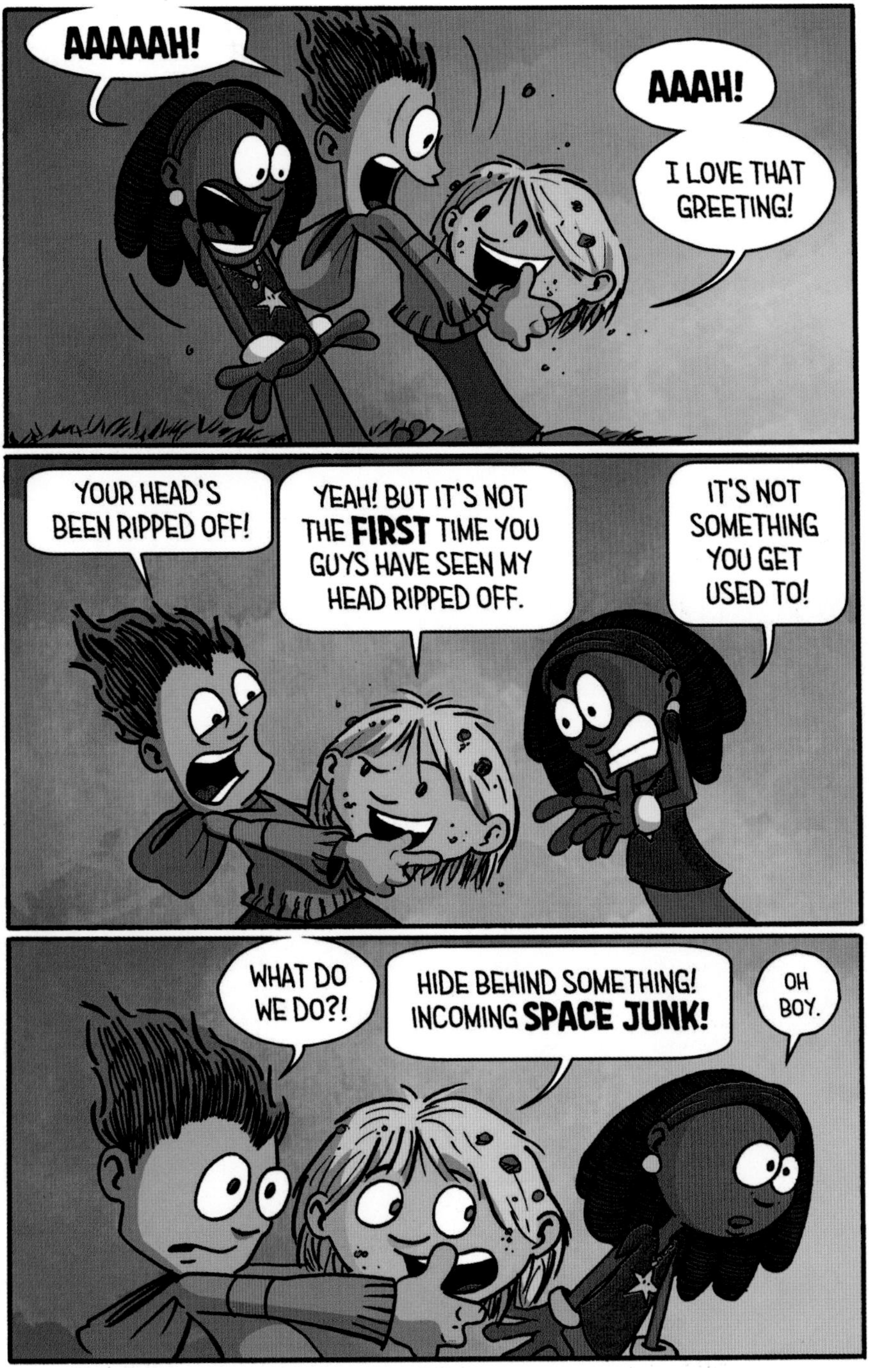
AAAAAH!
AAAH!
I LOVE THAT GREETING!
YOUR HEAD'S BEEN RIPPED OFF!
YEAH! BUT IT'S NOT THE **FIRST** TIME YOU GUYS HAVE SEEN MY HEAD RIPPED OFF.
IT'S NOT SOMETHING YOU GET USED TO!
WHAT DO WE DO?!
HIDE BEHIND SOMETHING! INCOMING **SPACE JUNK!**
OH BOY.

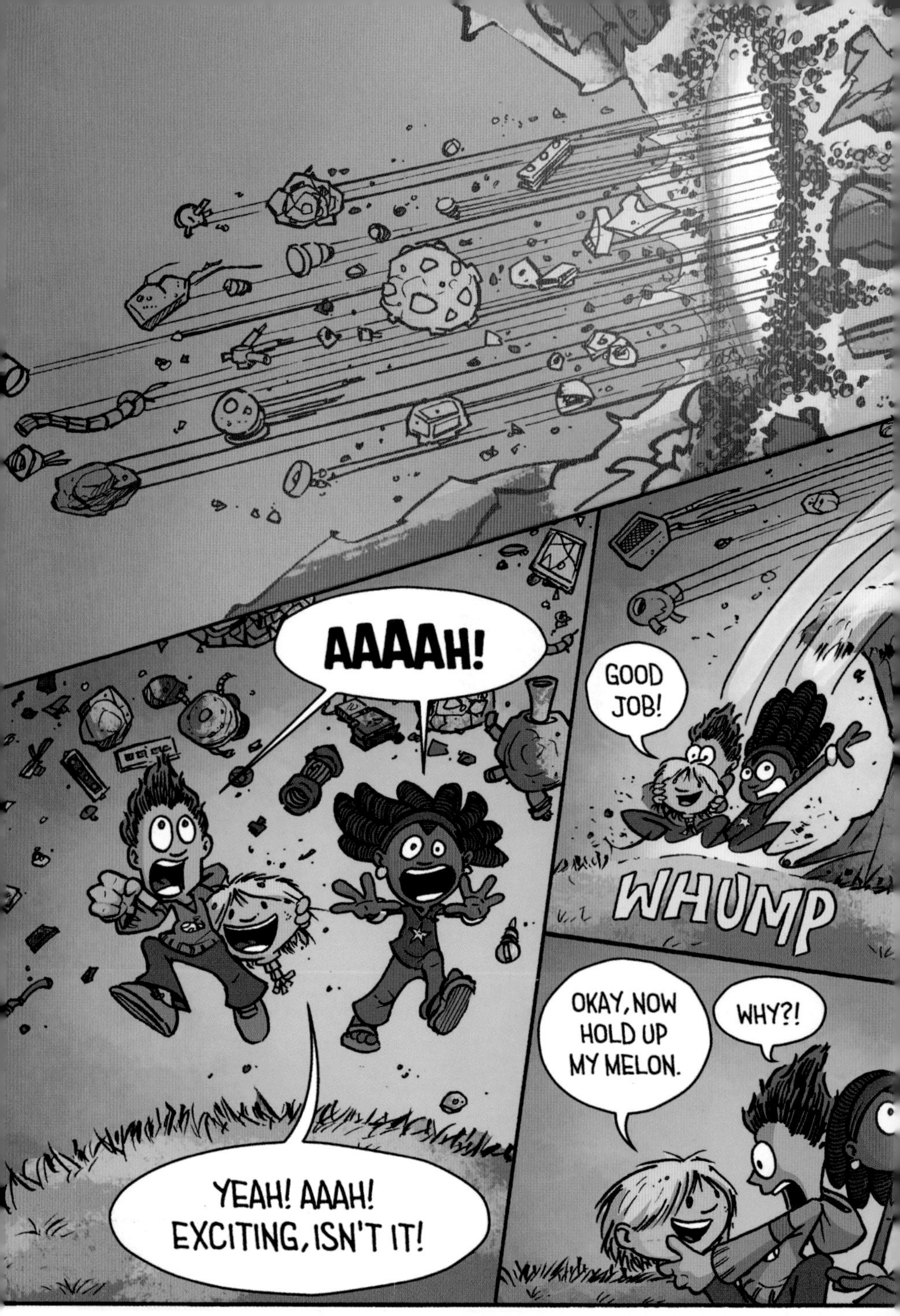
AAAAH!
YEAH! AAAH! EXCITING, ISN'T IT!
GOOD JOB!
WHUMP
OKAY, NOW HOLD UP MY MELON.
WHY?!

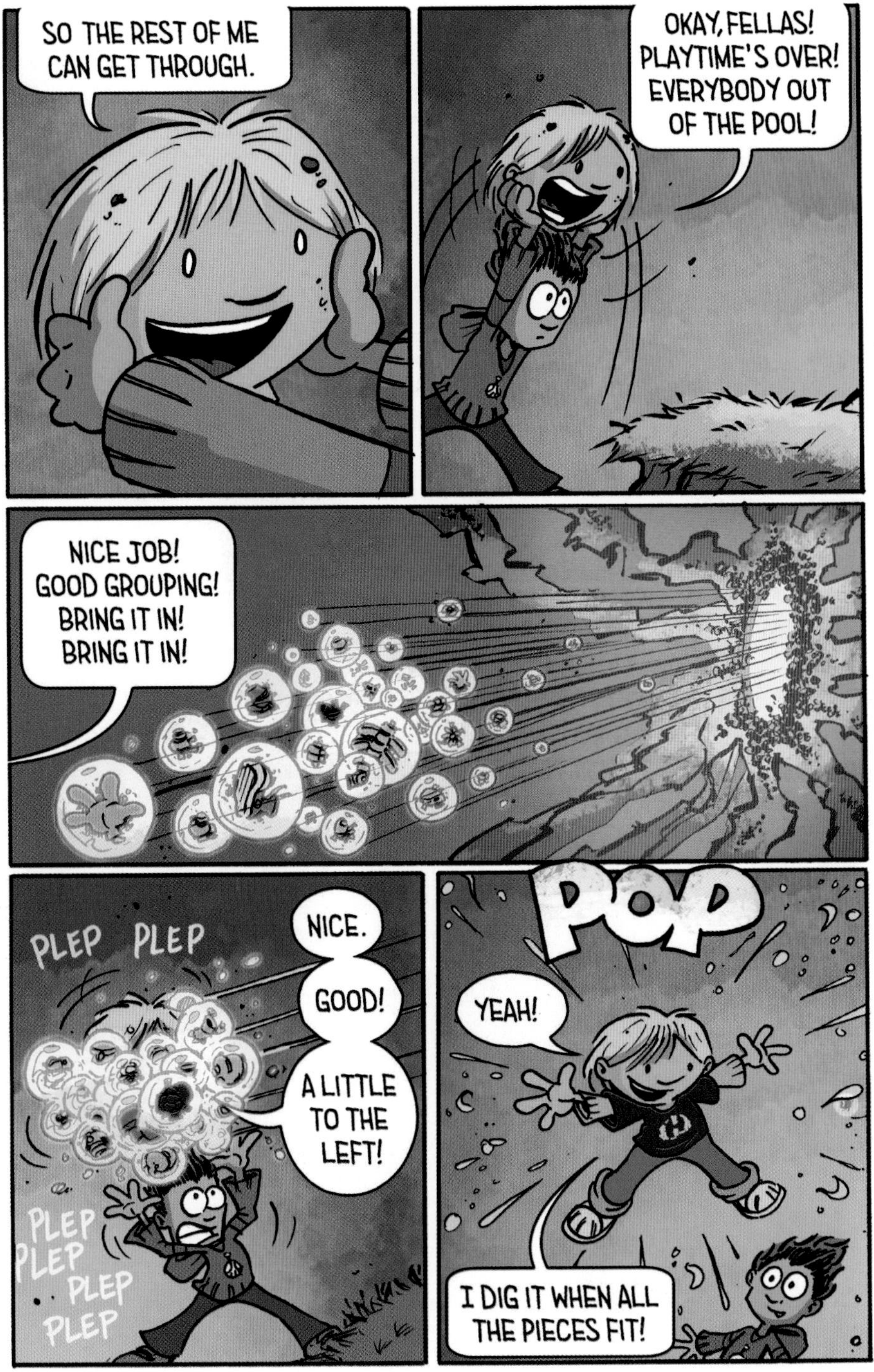
SO THE REST OF ME CAN GET THROUGH.
OKAY, FELLAS! PLAYTIME'S OVER! EVERYBODY OUT OF THE POOL!
NICE JOB! GOOD GROUPING! BRING IT IN! BRING IT IN!
PLEP PLEP
NICE.
GOOD!
A LITTLE TO THE LEFT!
PLEP PLEP PLEP PLEP
POP
YEAH!
I DIG IT WHEN ALL THE PIECES FIT!

HOW DO I LOOK? TALLER? I WAS HOPING FOR TALLER.

HILO! SOMETHING'S HAPPENING!

RIGHT! THE PORTAL!

Y'SEE, I LURED RAZORWARK INTO THIS LIMBO.

LURED. ISN'T IT A GREAT WORD? **LURED :** *VERB, PAST TENSE.* TO TEMPT A PERSON OR ANIMAL TO DO SOMETHING OR GO SOMEWHERE. I --

HILO!

YES! RIGHT! I LURED HIM INTO THE VOID AND NOW HE'S STUCK THERE! WE JUST HAVE TO WAIT FOR THE PORTAL TO EXPLODE AND SEAL HIM IN.

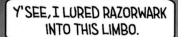

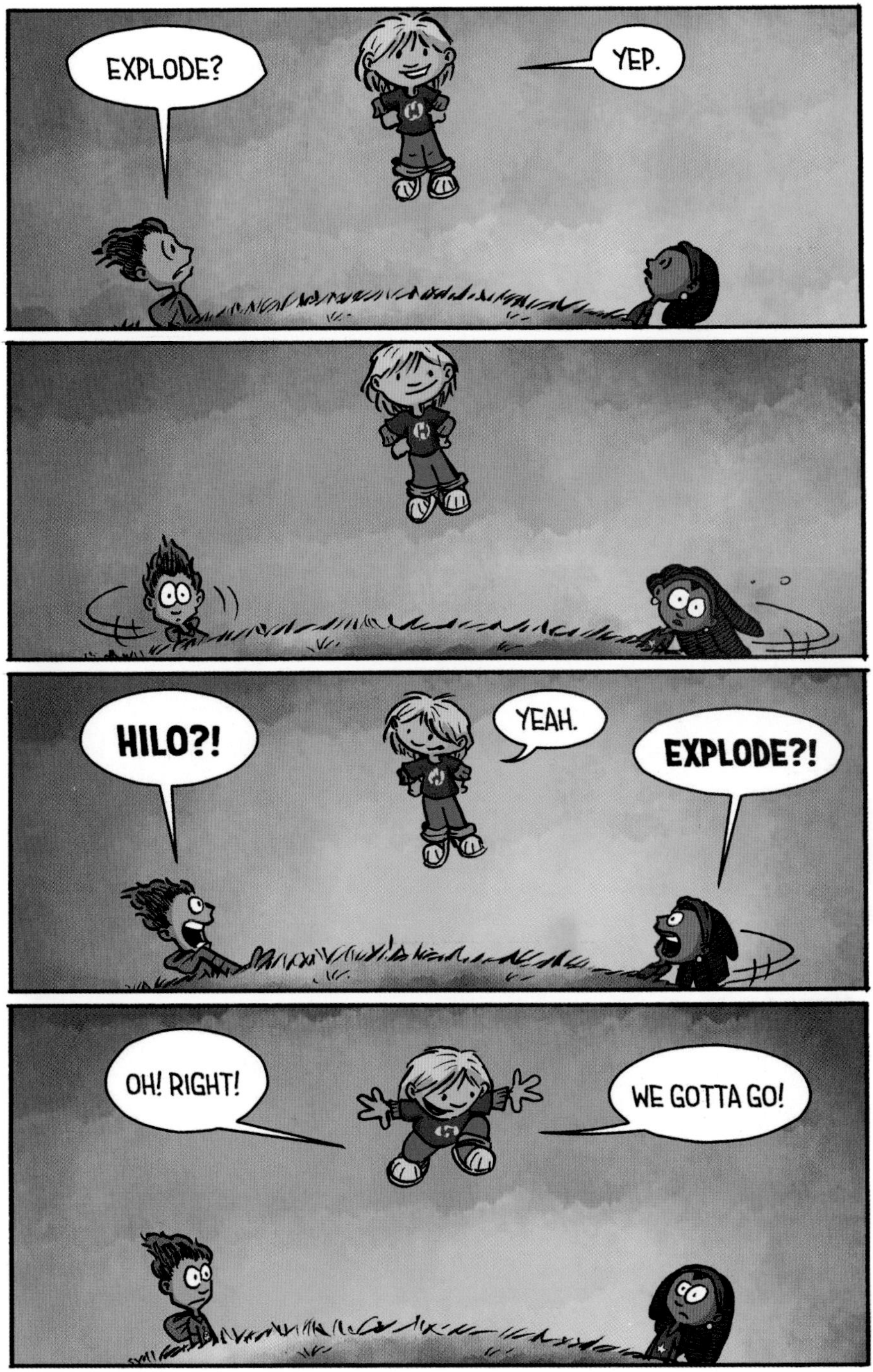

EXPLODE?
YEP.
HILO?!
YEAH.
EXPLODE?!
OH! RIGHT!
WE GOTTA GO!

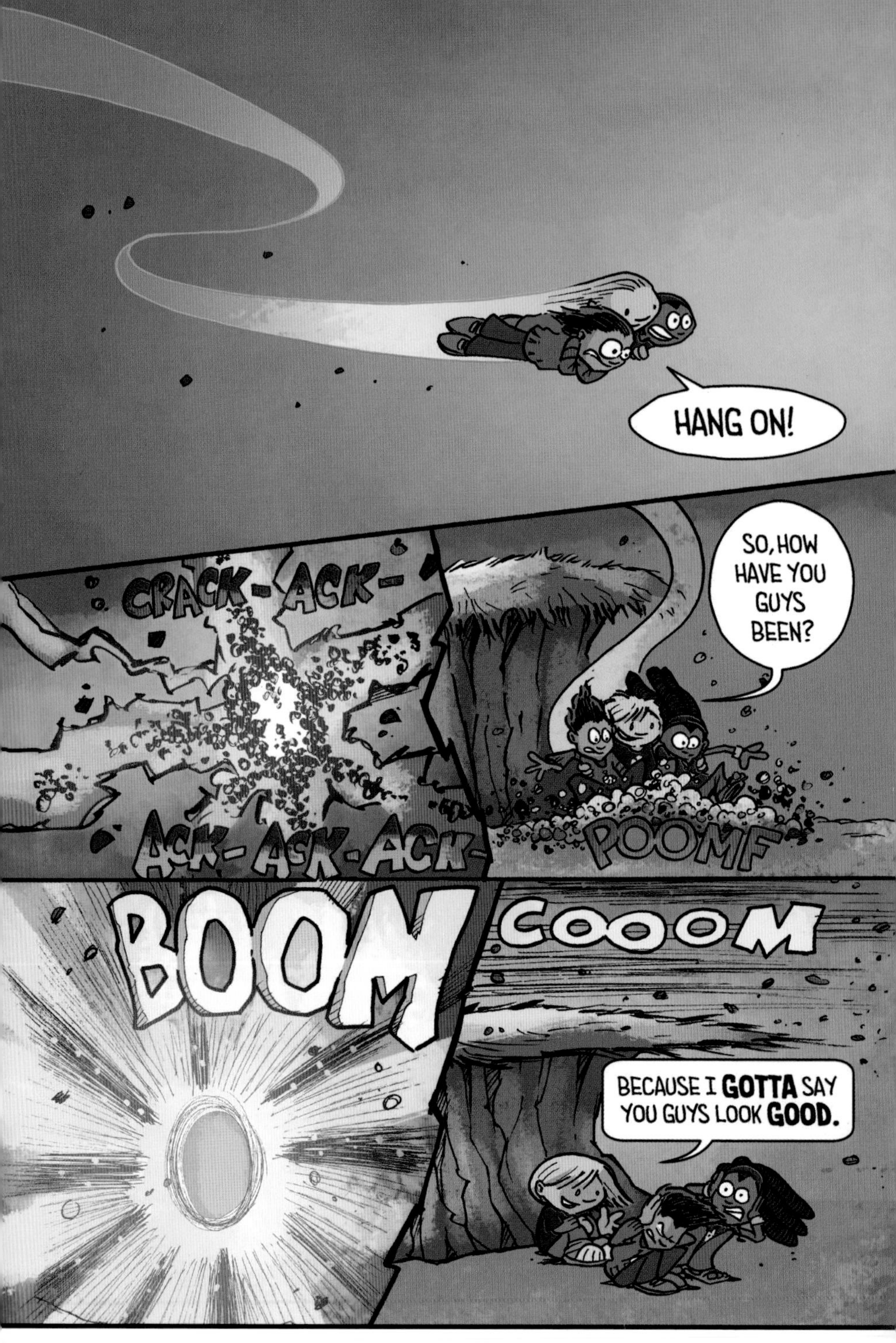
HANG ON!
CRACK-ACK-
ACK-ACK-ACK-
SO, HOW HAVE YOU GUYS BEEN?
POOMF
BOOM
COOOM
BECAUSE I **GOTTA** SAY YOU GUYS LOOK **GOOD.**

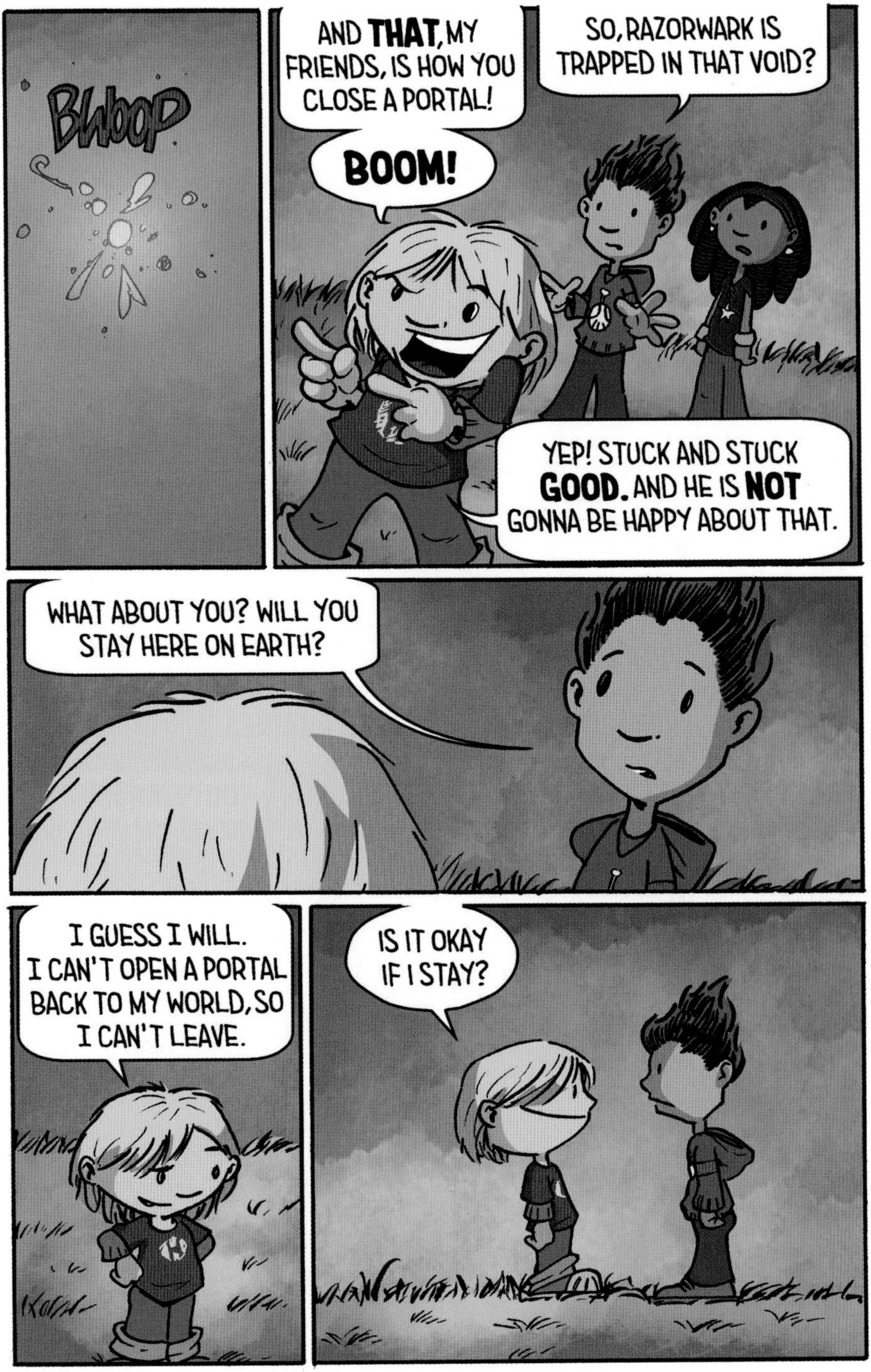
Bwoop
AND **THAT**, MY FRIENDS, IS HOW YOU CLOSE A PORTAL!
BOOM!
SO, RAZORWARK IS TRAPPED IN THAT VOID?
YEP! STUCK AND STUCK **GOOD.** AND HE IS **NOT** GONNA BE HAPPY ABOUT THAT.
WHAT ABOUT YOU? WILL YOU STAY HERE ON EARTH?
I GUESS I WILL. I CAN'T OPEN A PORTAL BACK TO MY WORLD, SO I CAN'T LEAVE.
IS IT OKAY IF I STAY?

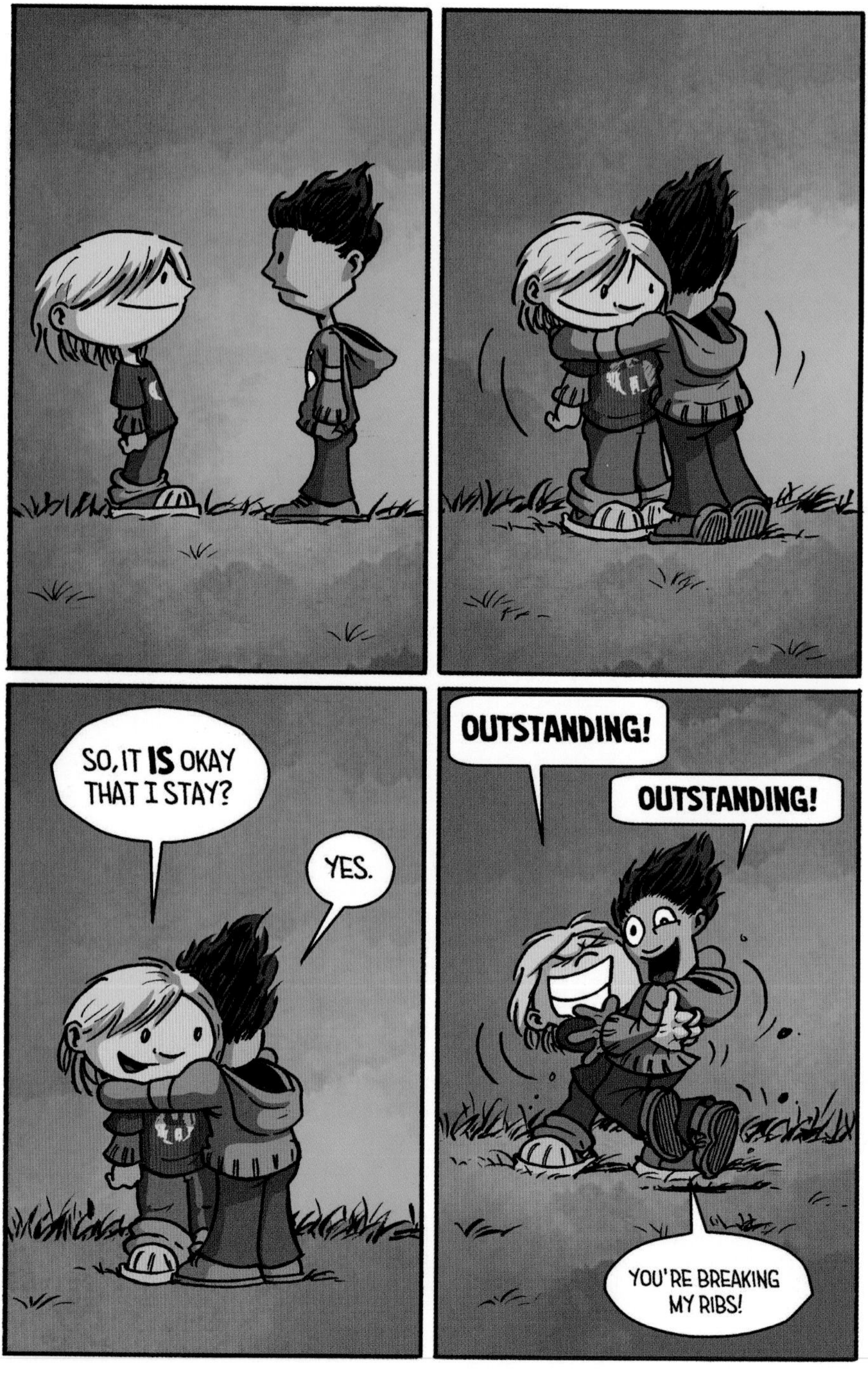
SO, IT **IS** OKAY THAT I STAY?
YES.
OUTSTANDING!
OUTSTANDING!
YOU'RE BREAKING MY RIBS!

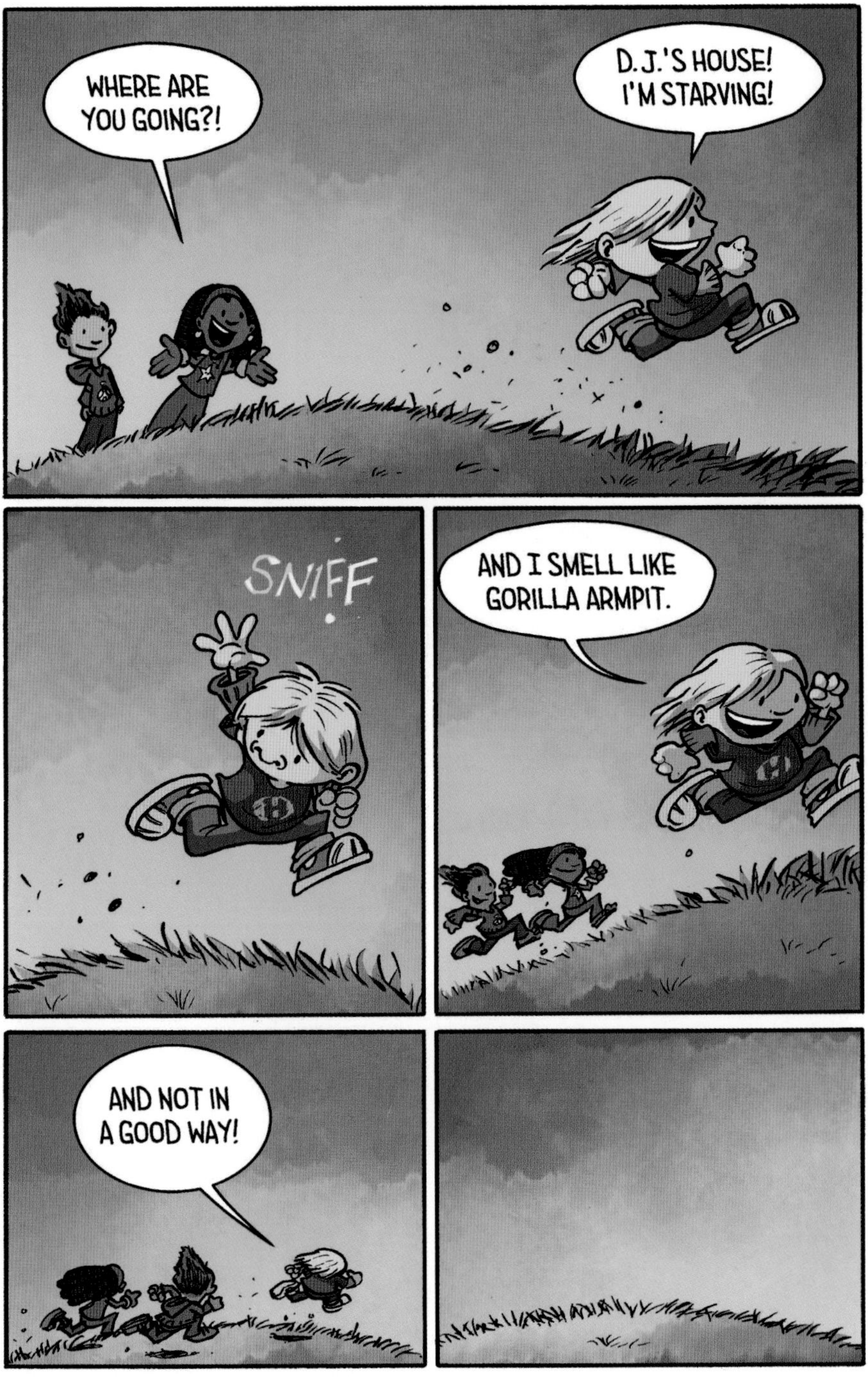
WHERE ARE YOU GOING?!
D. J.'S HOUSE! I'M STARVING!
SNIFF
AND I SMELL LIKE GORILLA ARMPIT.
AND NOT IN A GOOD WAY!

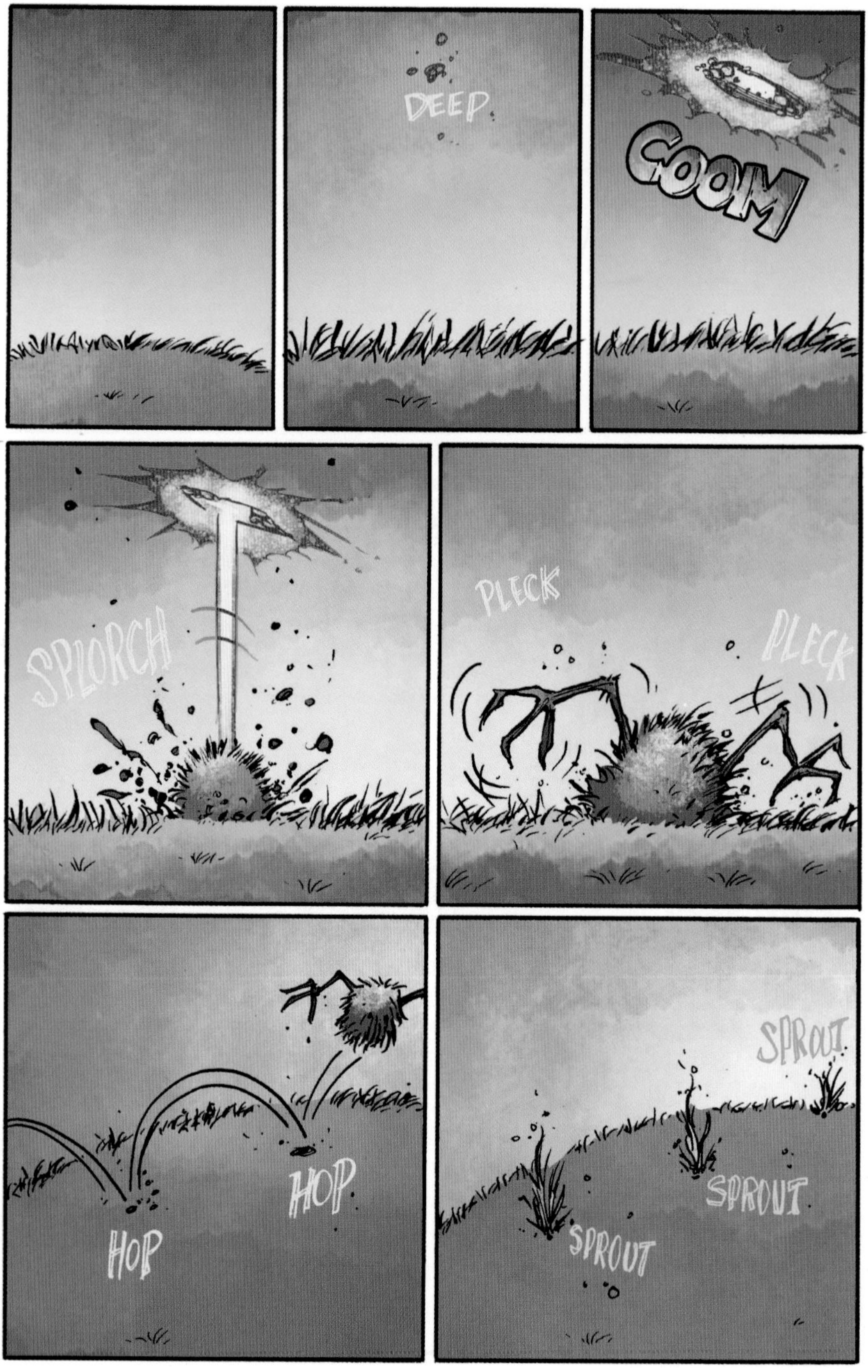
DEEP
COOM
SPLORCH
PLECK
PLECK
HOP
HOP
SPROUT
SPROUT
SPROUT

CHAPTER 2

KNOCK KNOCK

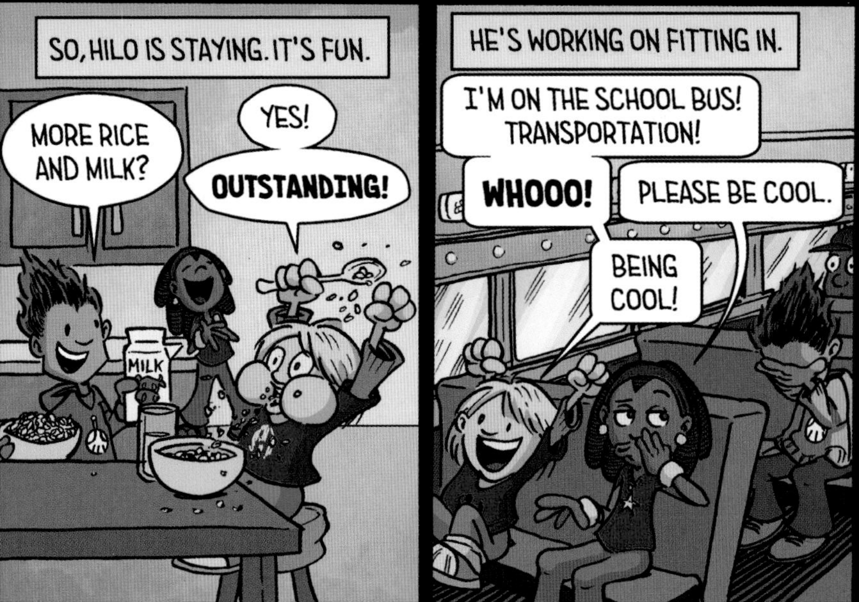

SO, HILO IS STAYING. IT'S FUN.
MORE RICE AND MILK?
YES!
OUTSTANDING!
MILK
HE'S WORKING ON FITTING IN.
I'M ON THE SCHOOL BUS! TRANSPORTATION!
WHOOO!
PLEASE BE COOL.
BEING COOL!

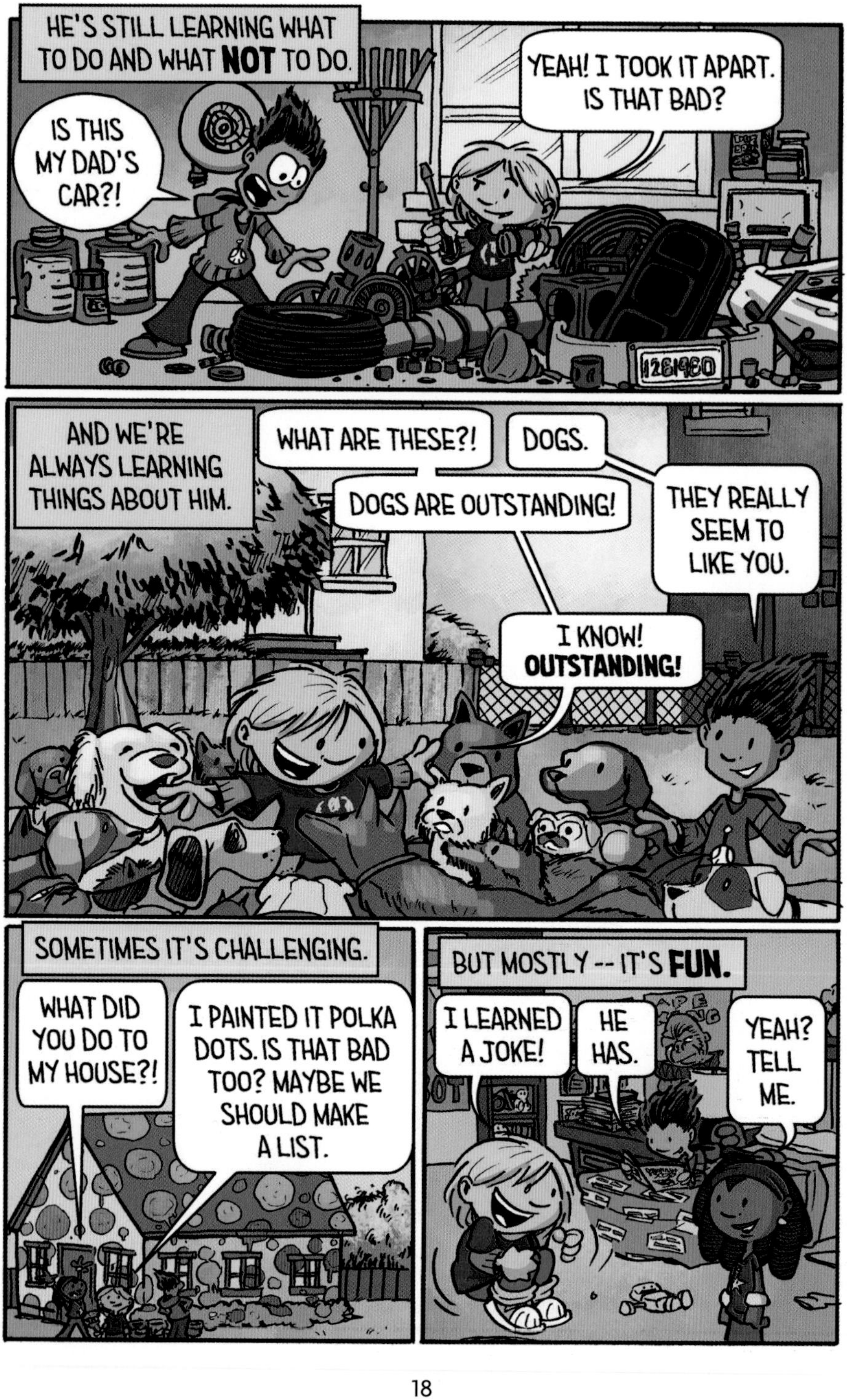
HE'S STILL LEARNING WHAT TO DO AND WHAT **NOT** TO DO.
IS THIS MY DAD'S CAR?!
YEAH! I TOOK IT APART. IS THAT BAD?
1281980
AND WE'RE ALWAYS LEARNING THINGS ABOUT HIM.
WHAT ARE THESE?!
DOGS.
DOGS ARE OUTSTANDING!
THEY REALLY SEEM TO LIKE YOU.
I KNOW! **OUTSTANDING!**
SOMETIMES IT'S CHALLENGING.
WHAT DID YOU DO TO MY HOUSE?!
I PAINTED IT POLKA DOTS. IS THAT BAD TOO? MAYBE WE SHOULD MAKE A LIST.
BUT MOSTLY -- IT'S **FUN.**
I LEARNED A JOKE!
HE HAS.
YEAH? TELL ME.

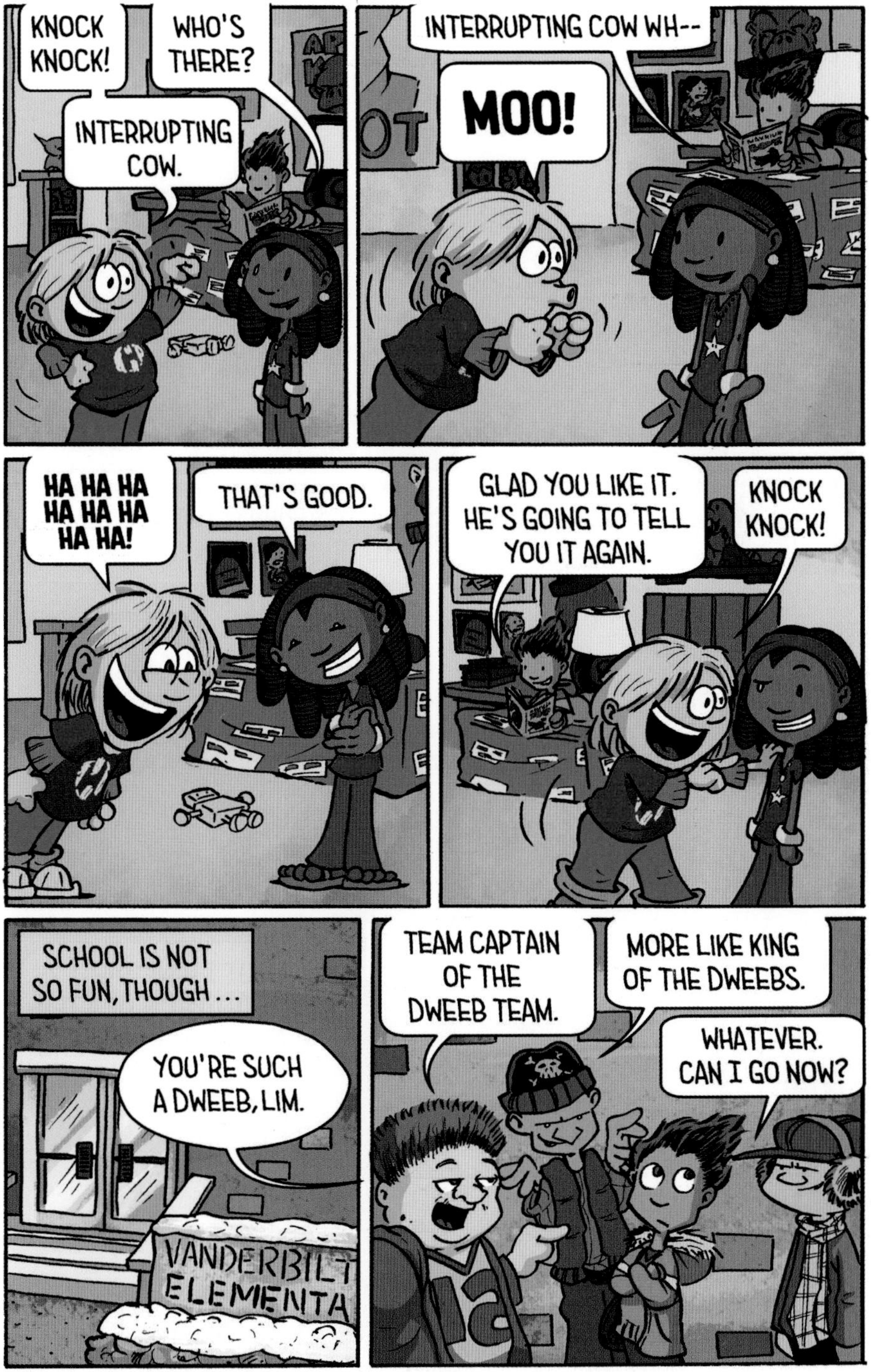
KNOCK KNOCK!
WHO'S THERE?
INTERRUPTING COW.
INTERRUPTING COW WH--
MOO!
HA HA HA HA HA HA HA HA!
THAT'S GOOD.
GLAD YOU LIKE IT. HE'S GOING TO TELL YOU IT AGAIN.
KNOCK KNOCK!
SCHOOL IS NOT SO FUN, THOUGH . . .
YOU'RE SUCH A DWEEB, LIM.
VANDERBILT ELEMENTA
TEAM CAPTAIN OF THE DWEEB TEAM.
MORE LIKE KING OF THE DWEEBS.
WHATEVER. CAN I GO NOW?

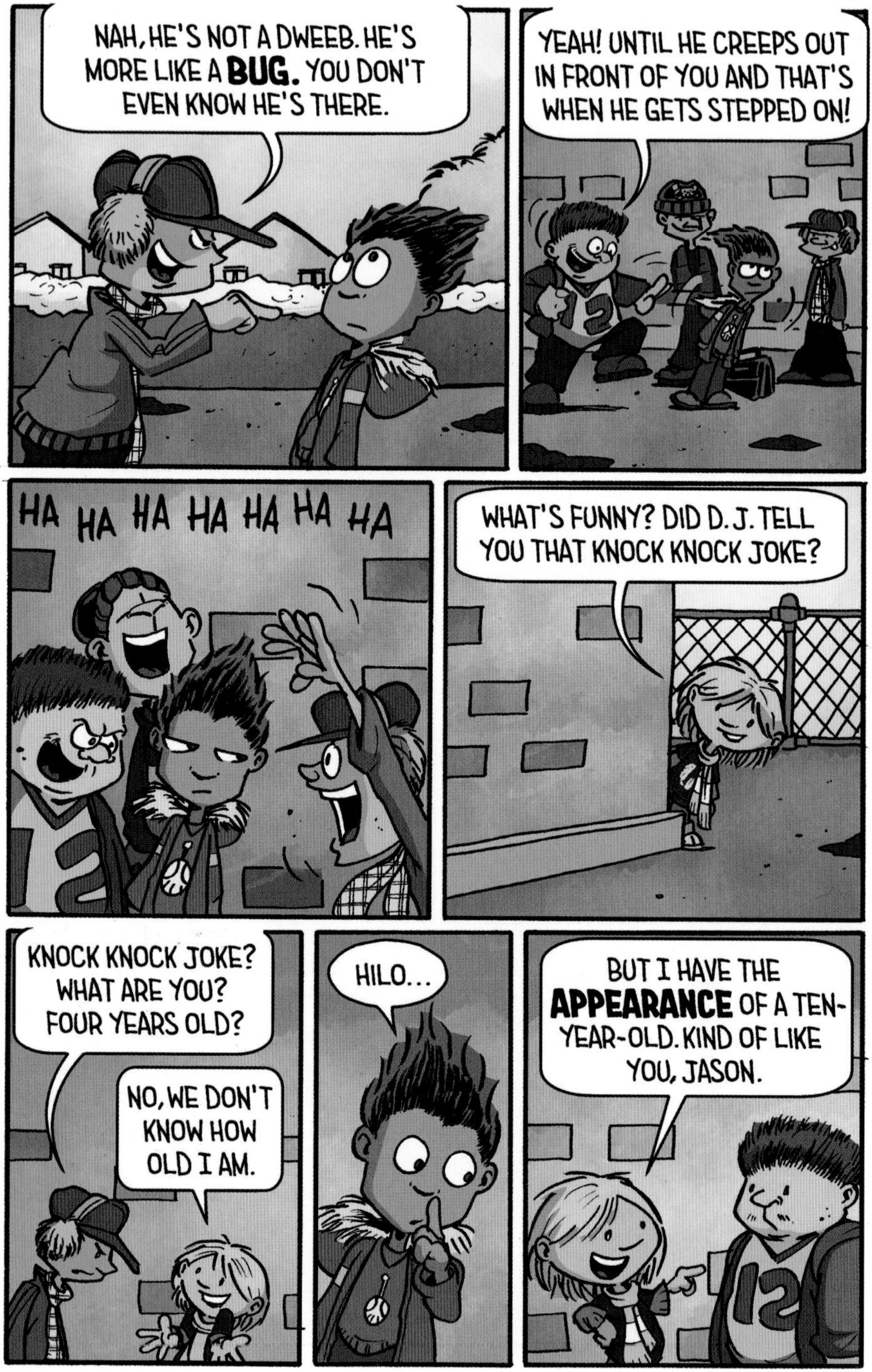
NAH, HE'S NOT A DWEEB. HE'S MORE LIKE A **BUG.** YOU DON'T EVEN KNOW HE'S THERE.
YEAH! UNTIL HE CREEPS OUT IN FRONT OF YOU AND THAT'S WHEN HE GETS STEPPED ON!
HA HA HA HA HA HA HA
WHAT'S FUNNY? DID D. J. TELL YOU THAT KNOCK KNOCK JOKE?
KNOCK KNOCK JOKE? WHAT ARE YOU? FOUR YEARS OLD?
NO, WE DON'T KNOW HOW OLD I AM.
HILO...
BUT I HAVE THE **APPEARANCE** OF A TEN-YEAR-OLD. KIND OF LIKE YOU, JASON.

YOU LOOK LIKE YOU'RE THIRTEEN BUT YOU'RE ONLY ELEVEN. WHICH MUST BE HARD IF PEOPLE EXPECT YOU TO ACT THIRTEEN AND YOU'RE NOT VERY SMART. EVEN FOR AN ELEVEN-YEAR-OLD.

YOU CALLING ME STUPID?

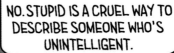

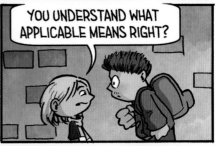

NO. STUPID IS A CRUEL WAY TO DESCRIBE SOMEONE WHO'S UNINTELLIGENT.

BUT ITS USAGE IS APPLICABLE.

YOU UNDERSTAND WHAT APPLICABLE MEANS RIGHT?

OH NO.

"OH NO"? WHAT? YOU GONNA HIT ME, DORK?

NO. NOT ME.

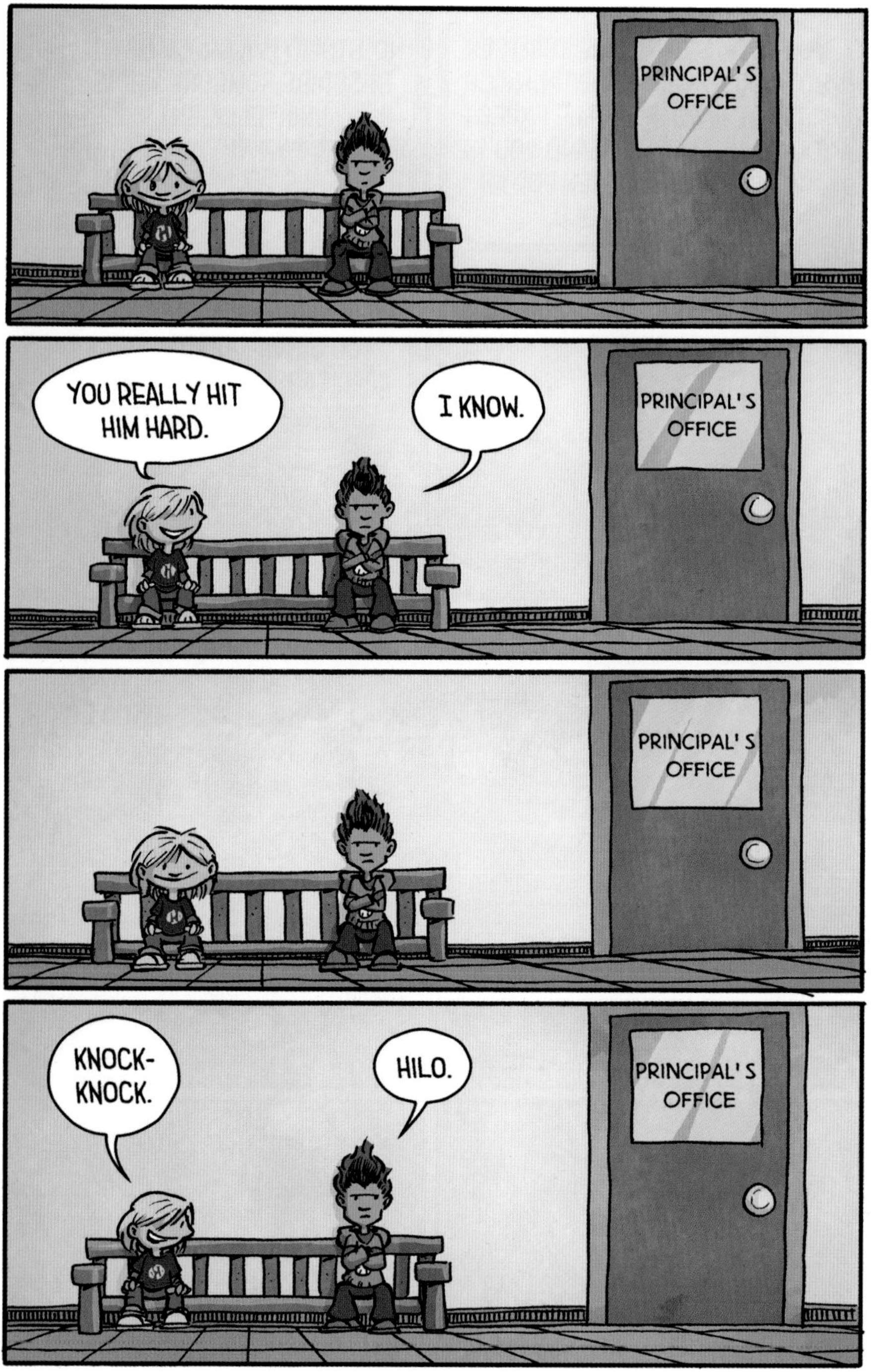
PRINCIPAL'S OFFICE
YOU REALLY HIT HIM HARD.
I KNOW.
PRINCIPAL'S OFFICE
PRINCIPAL'S OFFICE
KNOCK-KNOCK.
HILO.
PRINCIPAL'S OFFICE

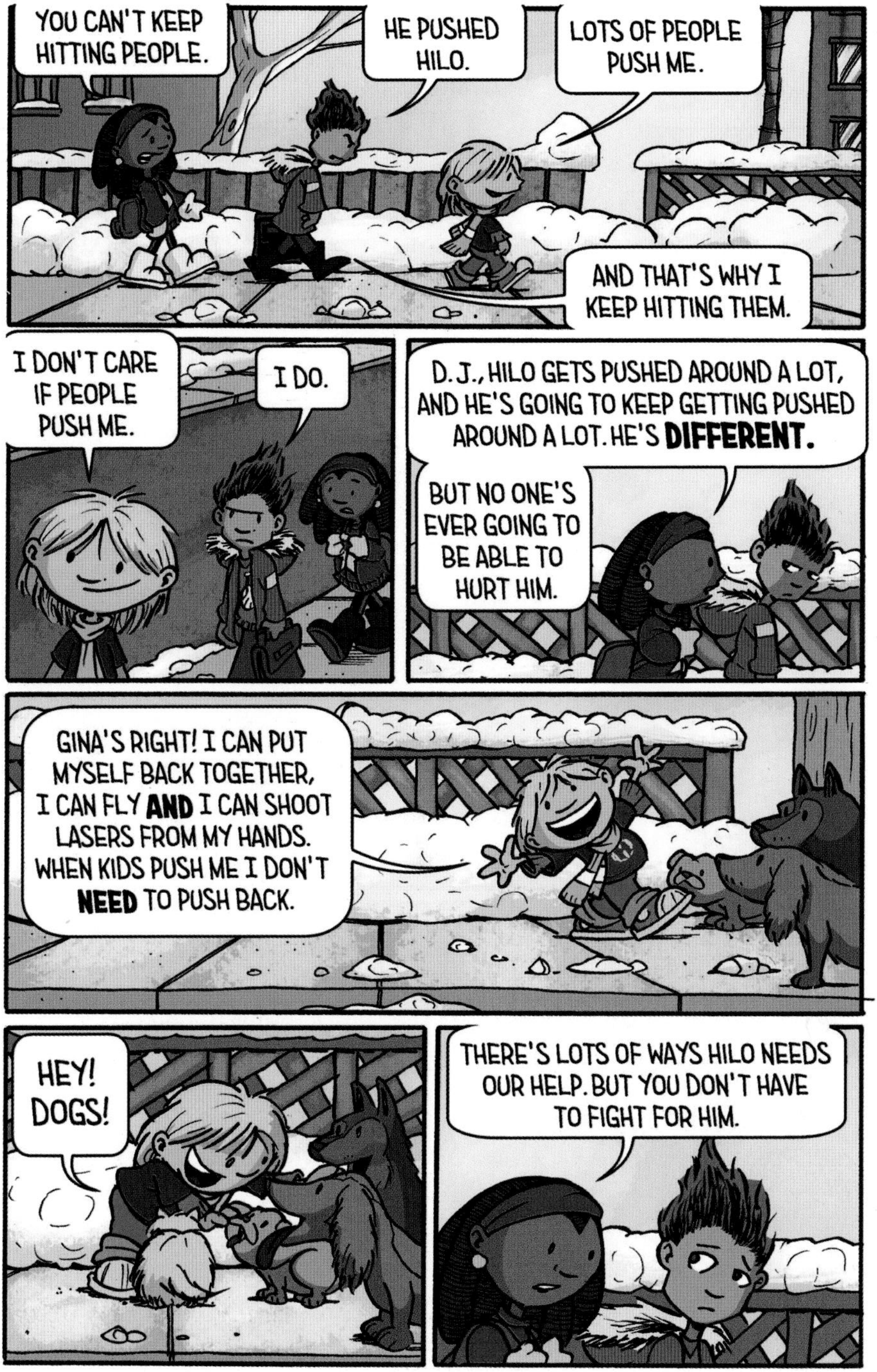
YOU CAN'T KEEP HITTING PEOPLE.
HE PUSHED HILO.
LOTS OF PEOPLE PUSH ME.
AND THAT'S WHY I KEEP HITTING THEM.
I DON'T CARE IF PEOPLE PUSH ME.
I DO.
D. J., HILO GETS PUSHED AROUND A LOT, AND HE'S GOING TO KEEP GETTING PUSHED AROUND A LOT. HE'S **DIFFERENT.**
BUT NO ONE'S EVER GOING TO BE ABLE TO HURT HIM.
GINA'S RIGHT! I CAN PUT MYSELF BACK TOGETHER, I CAN FLY **AND** I CAN SHOOT LASERS FROM MY HANDS. WHEN KIDS PUSH ME I DON'T **NEED** TO PUSH BACK.
HEY! DOGS!
THERE'S LOTS OF WAYS HILO NEEDS OUR HELP. BUT YOU DON'T HAVE TO FIGHT FOR HIM.

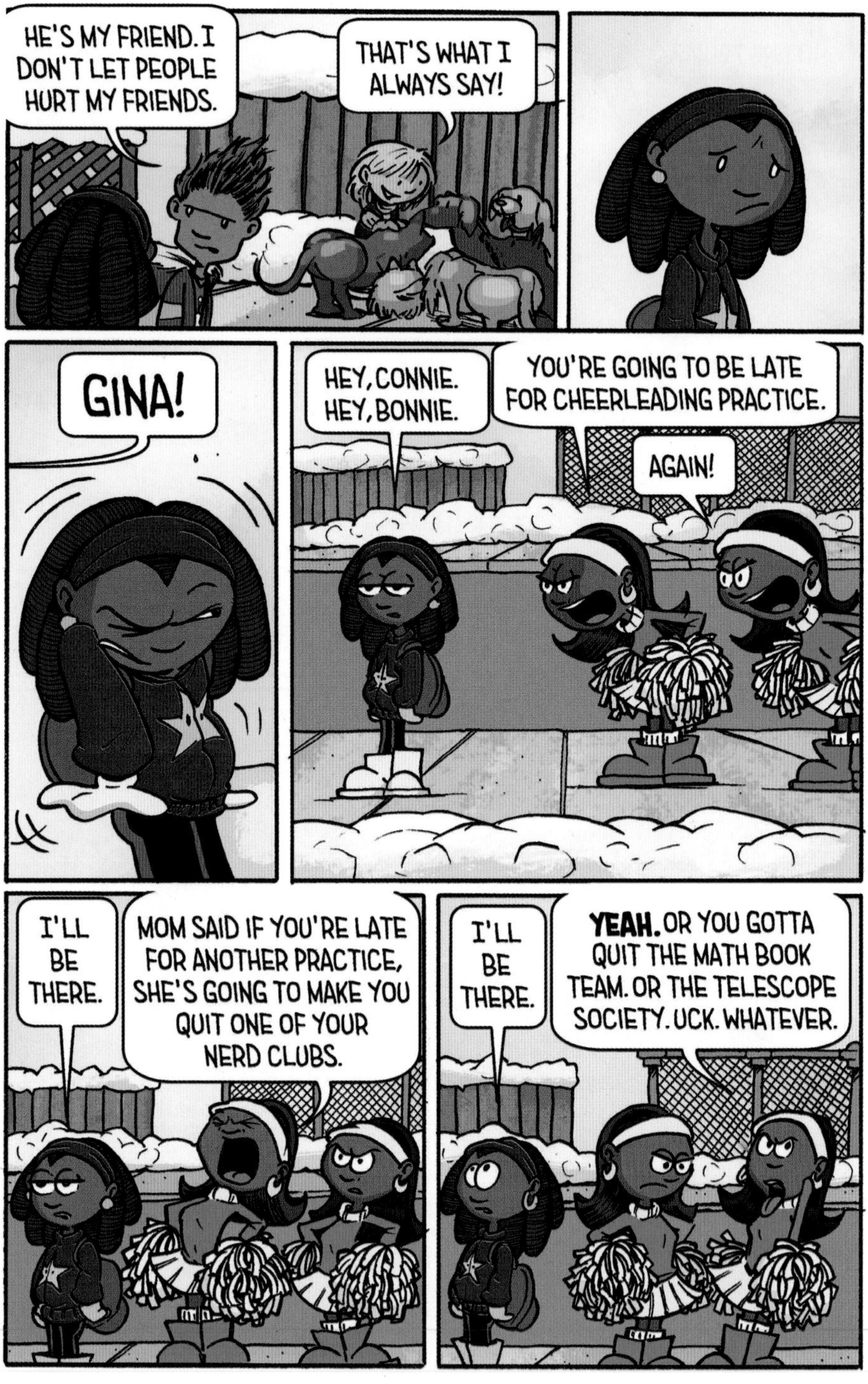

HE'S MY FRIEND. I DON'T LET PEOPLE HURT MY FRIENDS.
THAT'S WHAT I ALWAYS SAY!
GINA!
HEY, CONNIE. HEY, BONNIE.
YOU'RE GOING TO BE LATE FOR CHEERLEADING PRACTICE.
AGAIN!
I'LL BE THERE.
MOM SAID IF YOU'RE LATE FOR ANOTHER PRACTICE, SHE'S GOING TO MAKE YOU QUIT ONE OF YOUR NERD CLUBS.
I'LL BE THERE.
YEAH. OR YOU GOTTA QUIT THE MATH BOOK TEAM. OR THE TELESCOPE SOCIETY. UCK. WHATEVER.

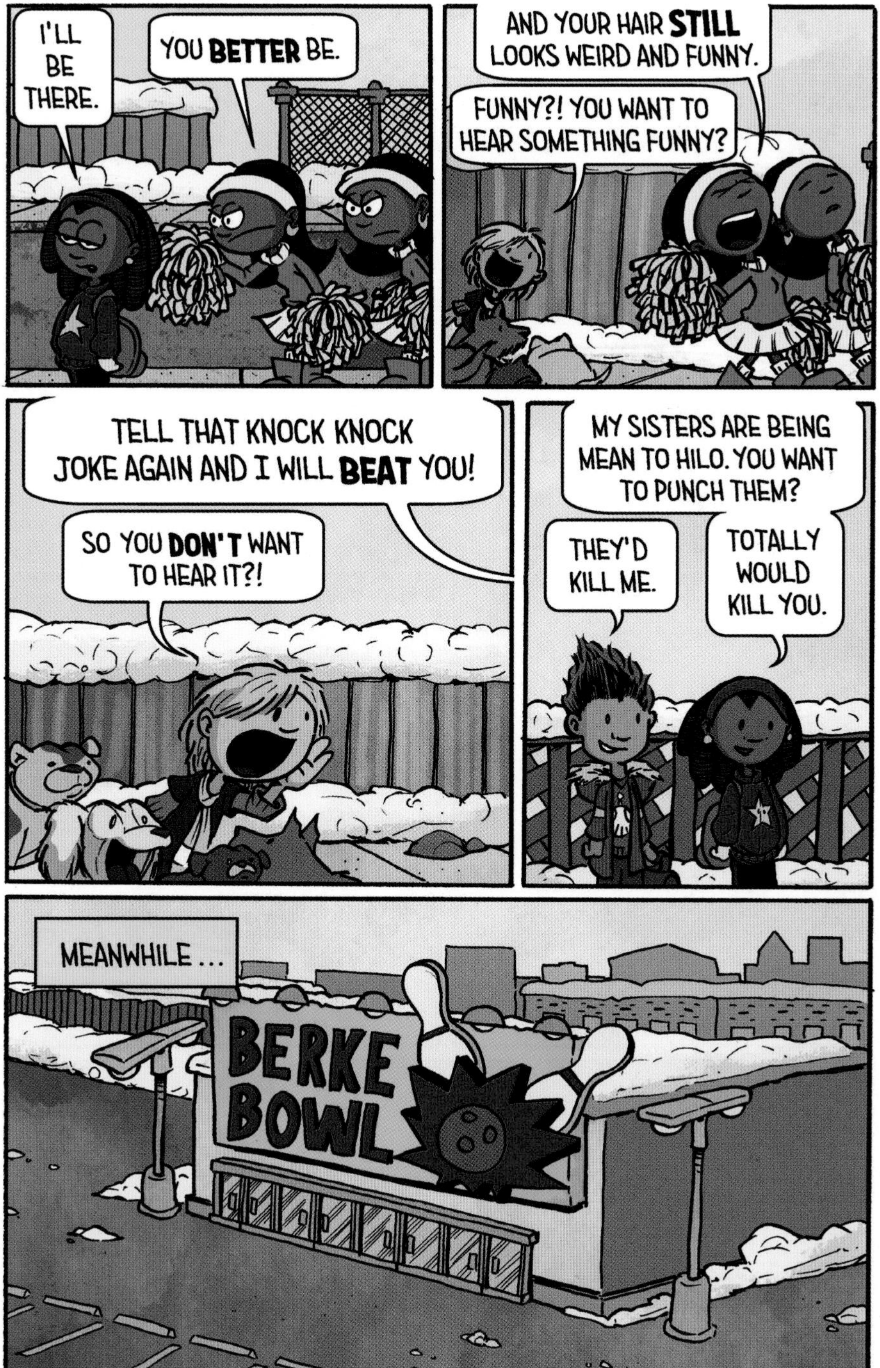
I'LL BE THERE.
YOU **BETTER** BE.
AND YOUR HAIR **STILL** LOOKS WEIRD AND FUNNY.
FUNNY?! YOU WANT TO HEAR SOMETHING FUNNY?
TELL THAT KNOCK KNOCK JOKE AGAIN AND I WILL **BEAT** YOU!
SO YOU **DON'T** WANT TO HEAR IT?!
MY SISTERS ARE BEING MEAN TO HILO. YOU WANT TO PUNCH THEM?
THEY'D KILL ME.
TOTALLY WOULD KILL YOU.
MEANWHILE . . .
BERKE BOWL

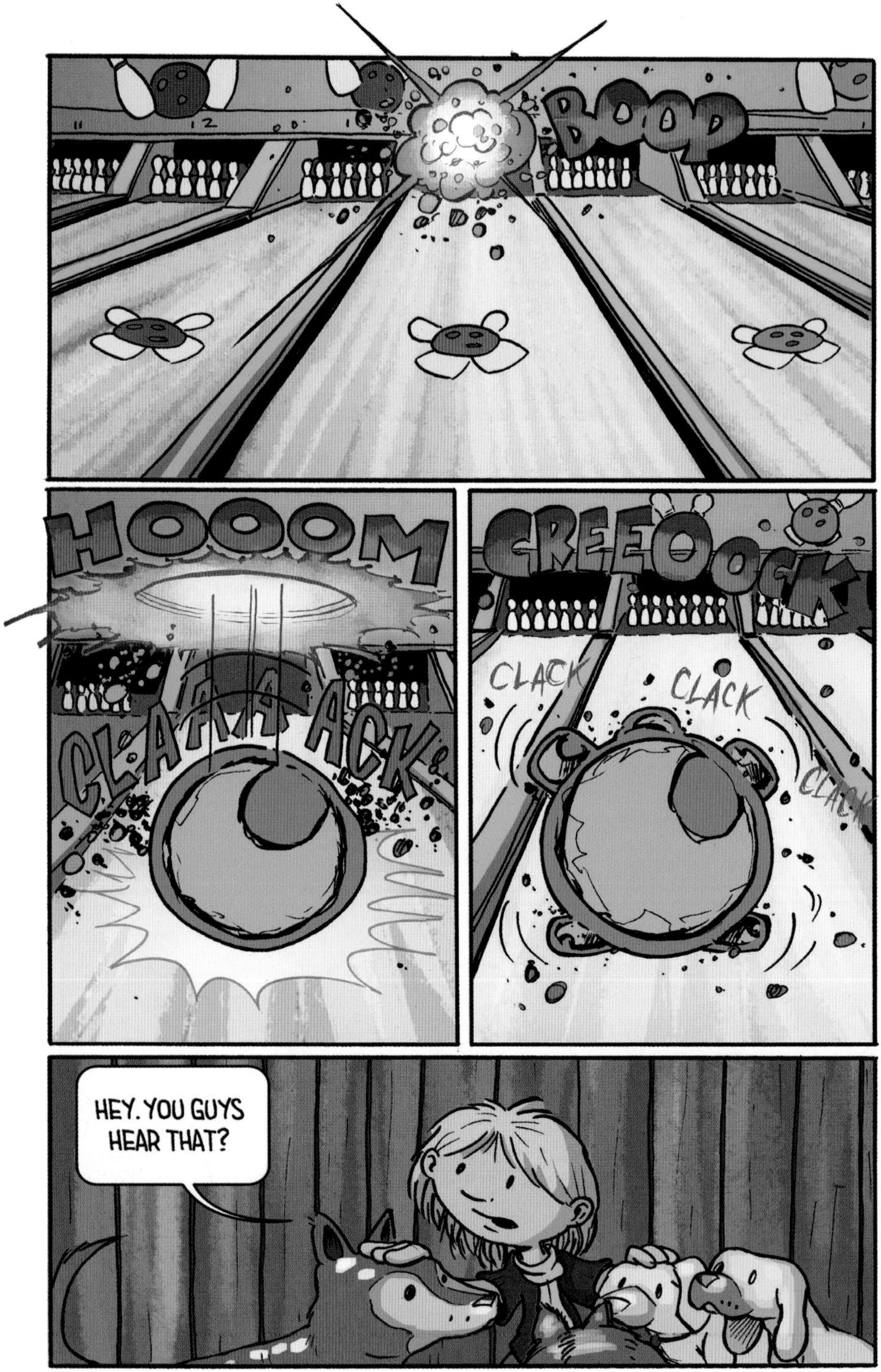
BOOP
HOOOM
CLAAAACK
CREEOOCK
CLACK
CLACK
HEY. YOU GUYS HEAR THAT?

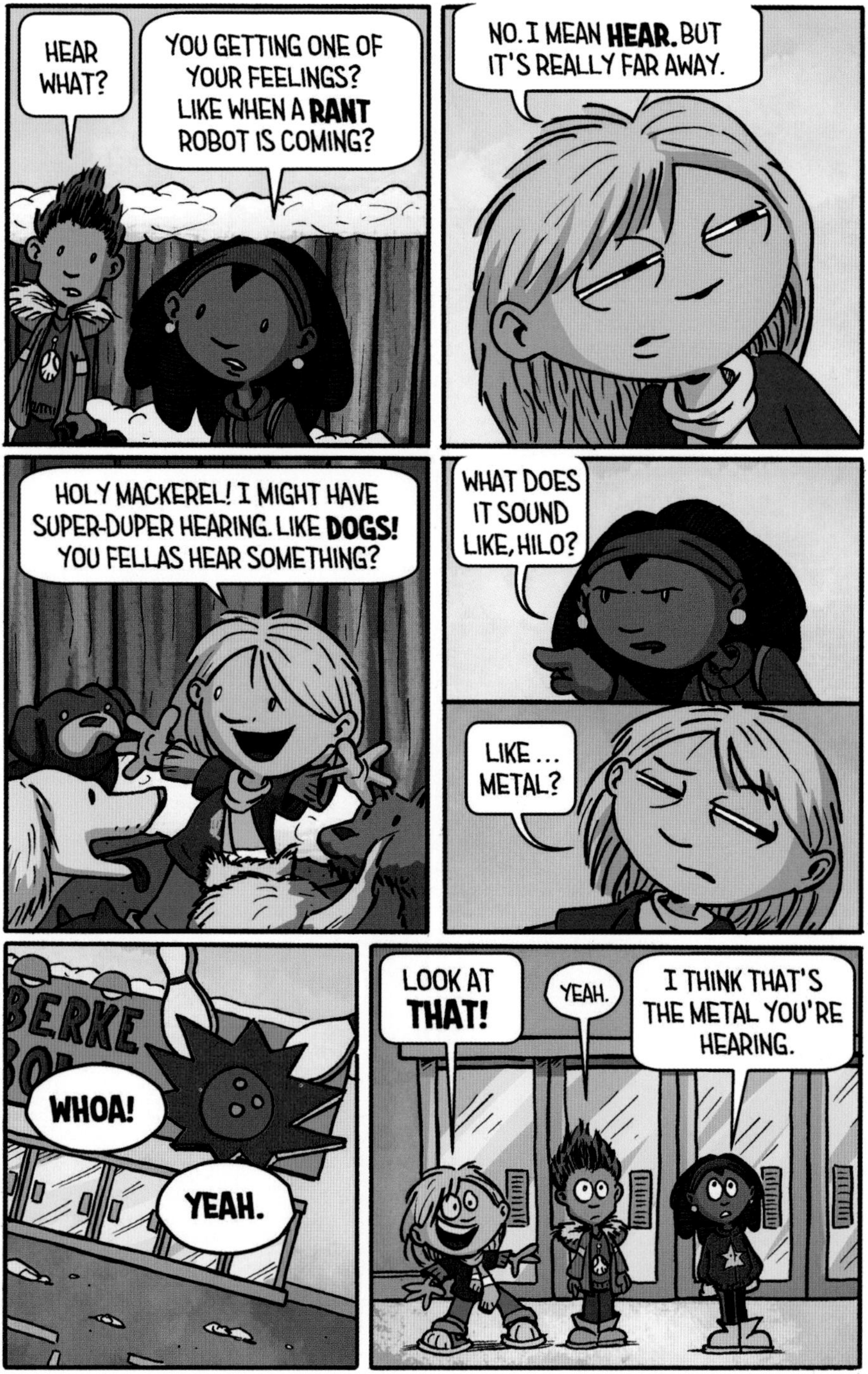
HEAR WHAT?
YOU GETTING ONE OF YOUR FEELINGS? LIKE WHEN A **RANT** ROBOT IS COMING?
NO. I MEAN **HEAR.** BUT IT'S REALLY FAR AWAY.
HOLY MACKEREL! I MIGHT HAVE SUPER-DUPER HEARING. LIKE **DOGS!** YOU FELLAS HEAR SOMETHING?
WHAT DOES IT SOUND LIKE, HILO?
LIKE . . . METAL?
BERKE
WHOA!
YEAH.
LOOK AT **THAT!**
YEAH.
I THINK THAT'S THE METAL YOU'RE HEARING.

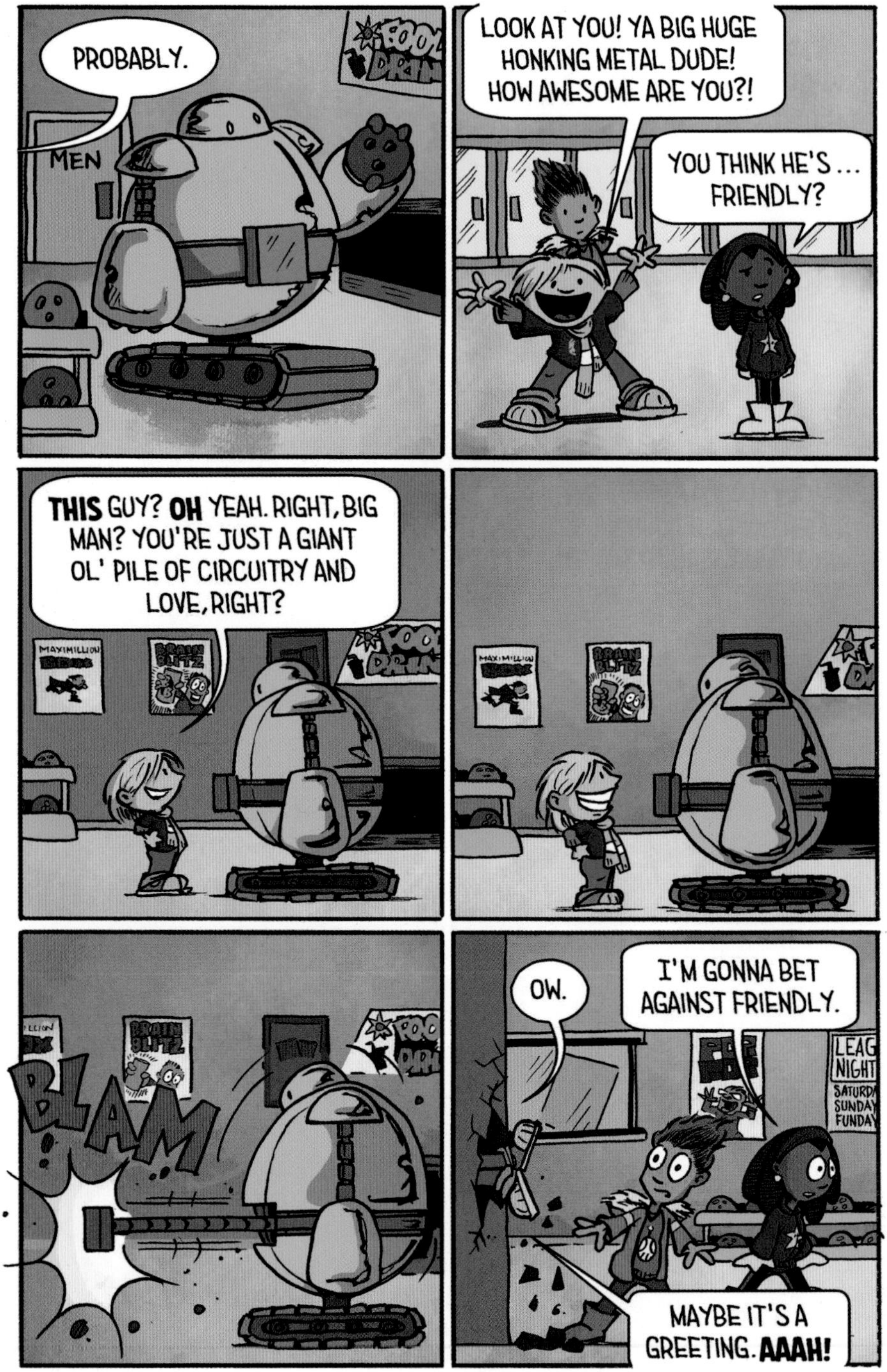
PROBABLY.
MEN
LOOK AT YOU! YA BIG HUGE HONKING METAL DUDE! HOW AWESOME ARE YOU?!
YOU THINK HE'S . . . FRIENDLY?
THIS GUY? **OH** YEAH. RIGHT, BIG MAN? YOU'RE JUST A GIANT OL' PILE OF CIRCUITRY AND LOVE, RIGHT?
BLAM
OW.
I'M GONNA BET AGAINST FRIENDLY.
MAYBE IT'S A GREETING. **AAAH!**

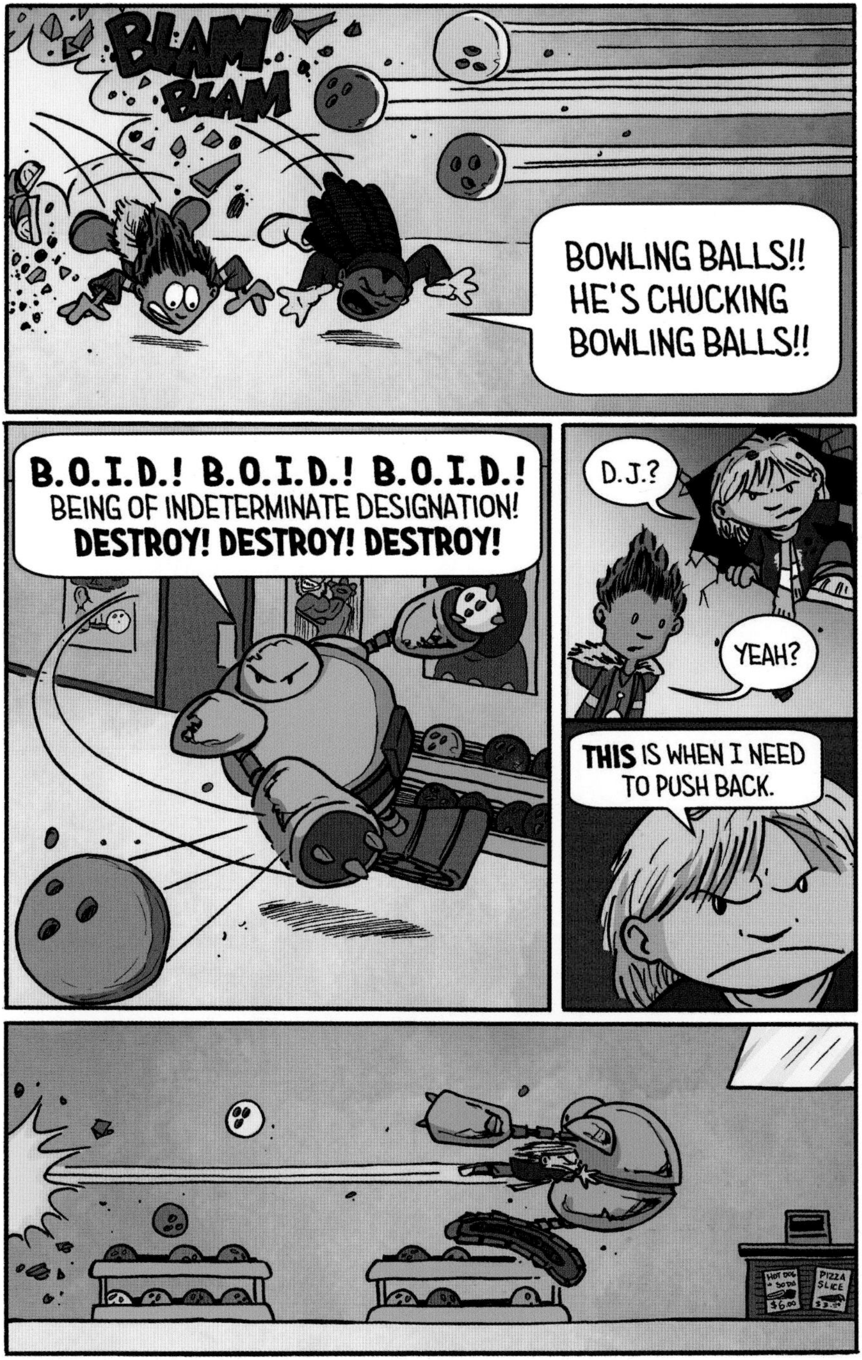
BLAM
BLAM
BOWLING BALLS!! HE'S CHUCKING BOWLING BALLS!!
B.O.I.D.! B.O.I.D.! B.O.I.D.! BEING OF INDETERMINATE DESIGNATION! DESTROY! DESTROY! DESTROY!
D.J.?
YEAH?
THIS IS WHEN I NEED TO PUSH BACK.
HOT DOG + SODA $6.00
PIZZA SLICE

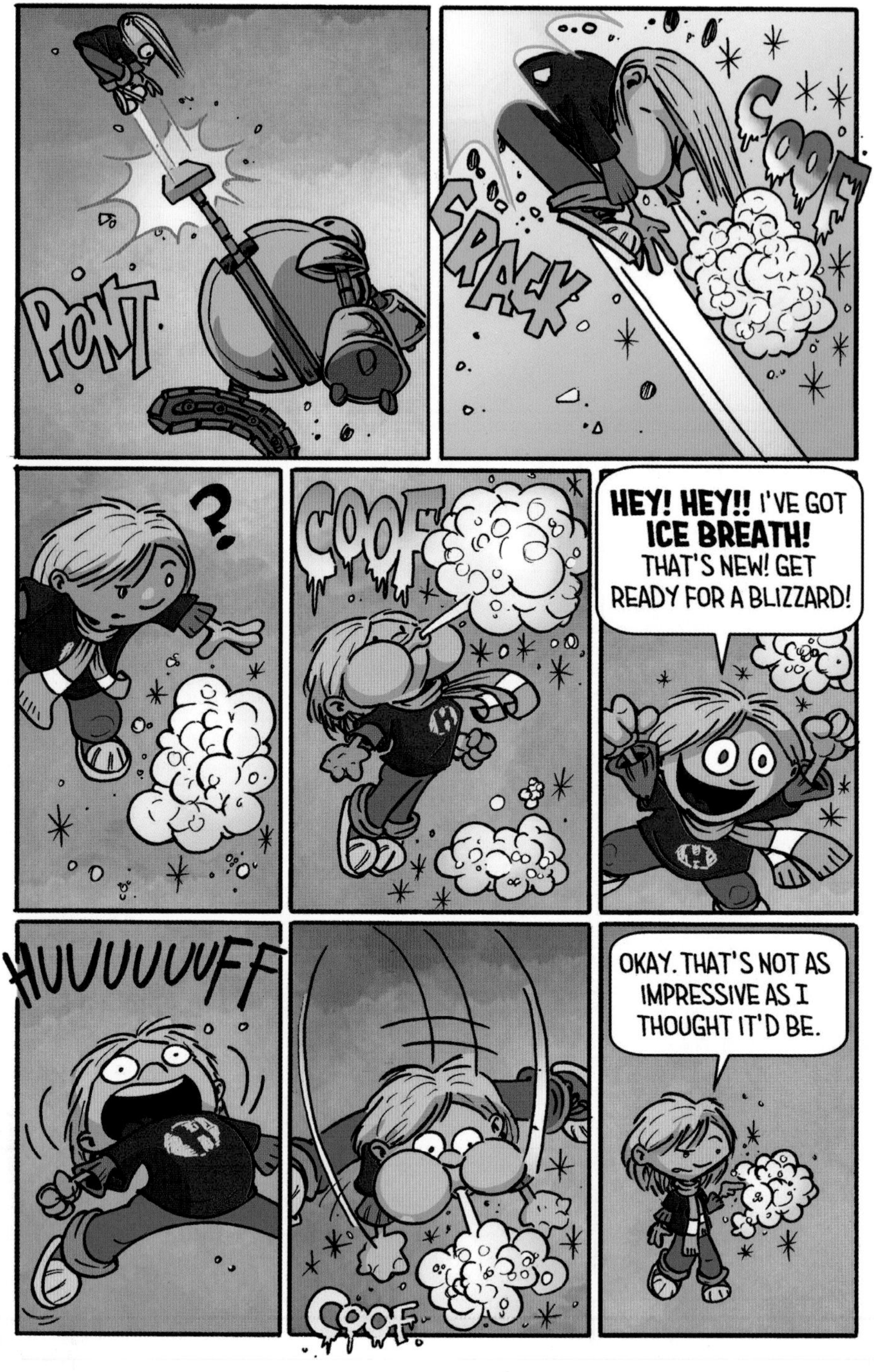
PONT
CRACK
COOF
COOF
HEY! HEY!! I'VE GOT ICE BREATH! THAT'S NEW! GET READY FOR A BLIZZARD!
HUUUUUUFF
COOF
OKAY. THAT'S NOT AS IMPRESSIVE AS I THOUGHT IT'D BE.

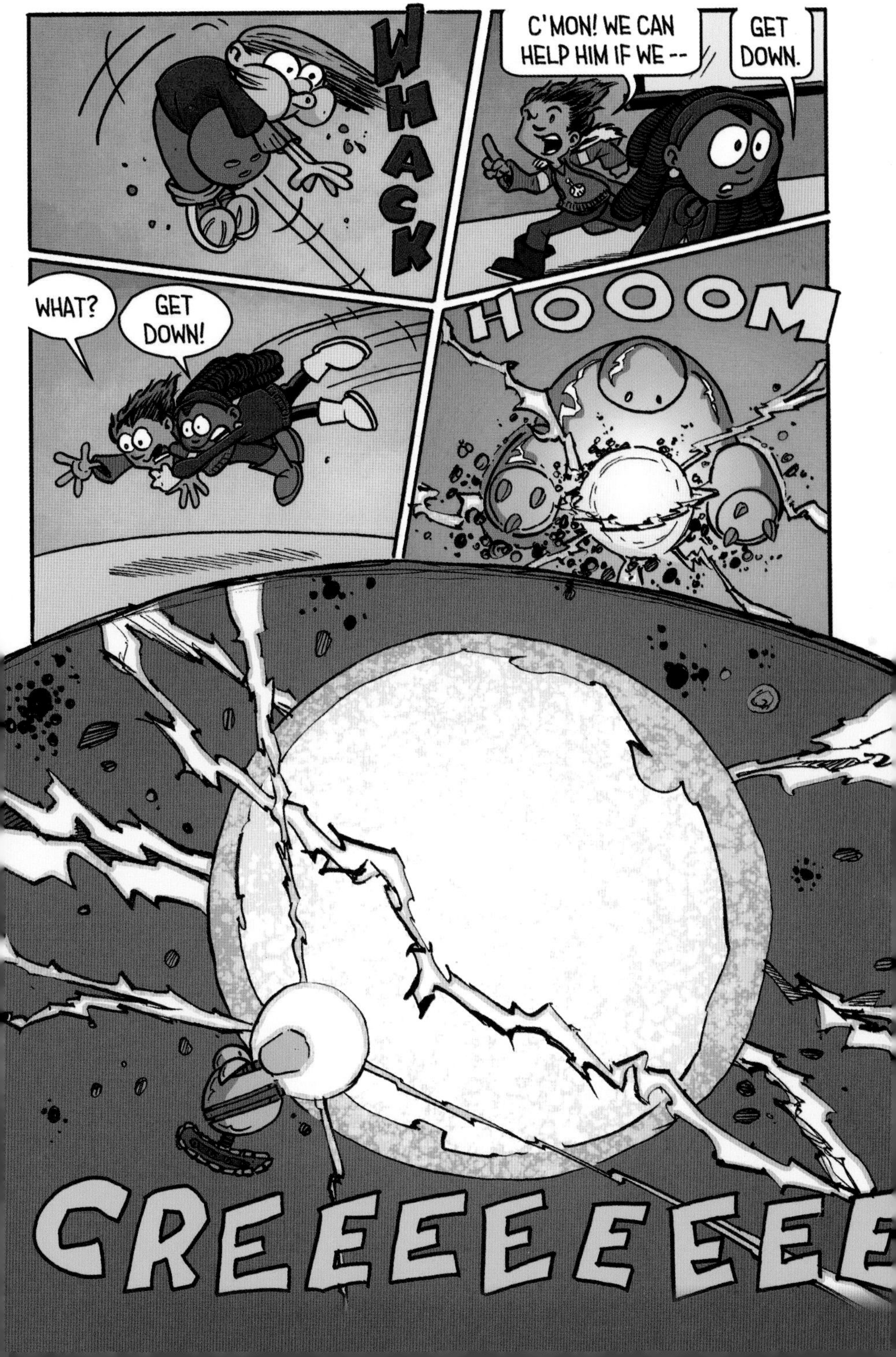
WHACK
C'MON! WE CAN HELP HIM IF WE --
GET DOWN.
WHAT?
GET DOWN!
HOOOM
CREEEEEEEE

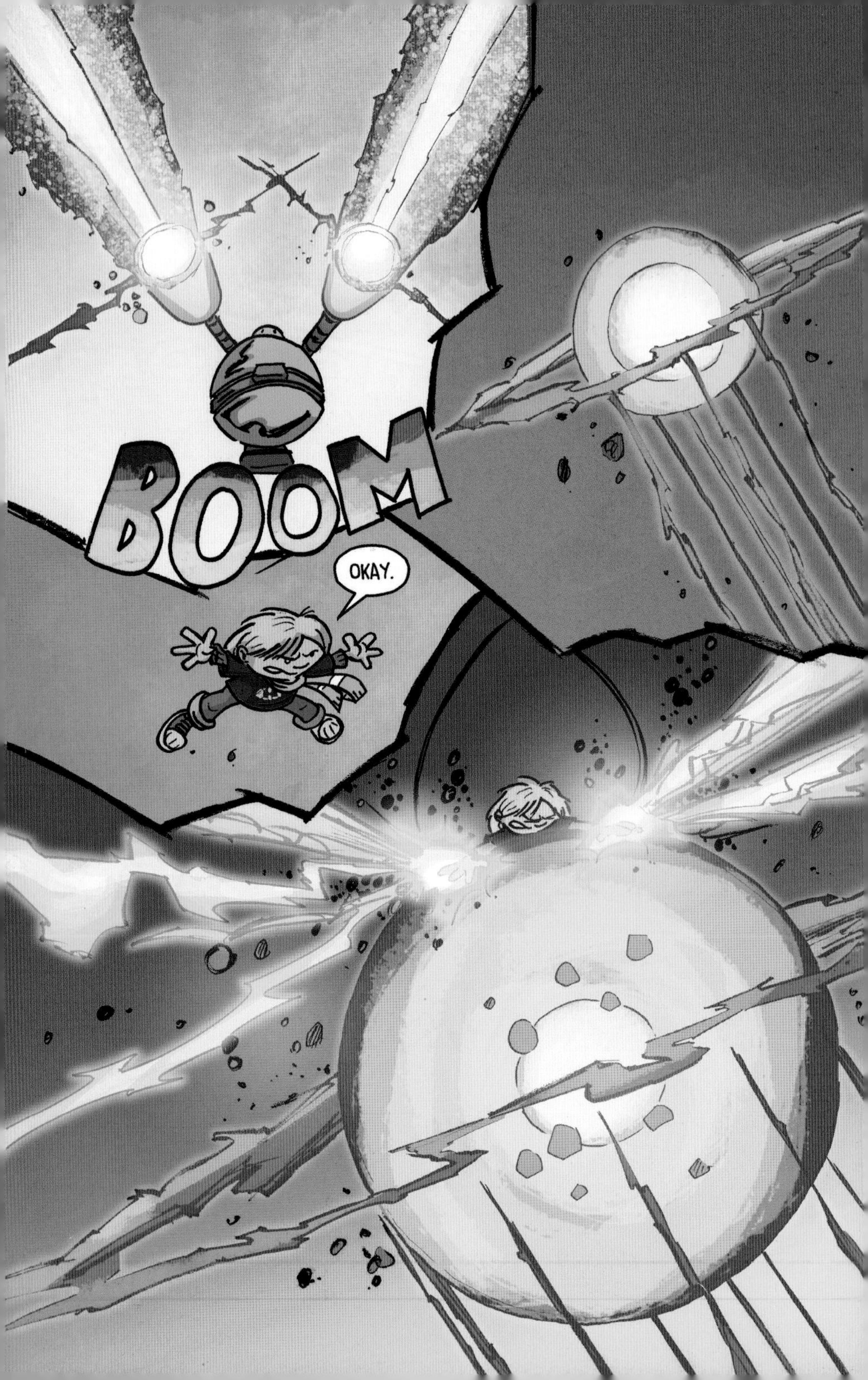
BOOM
OKAY.

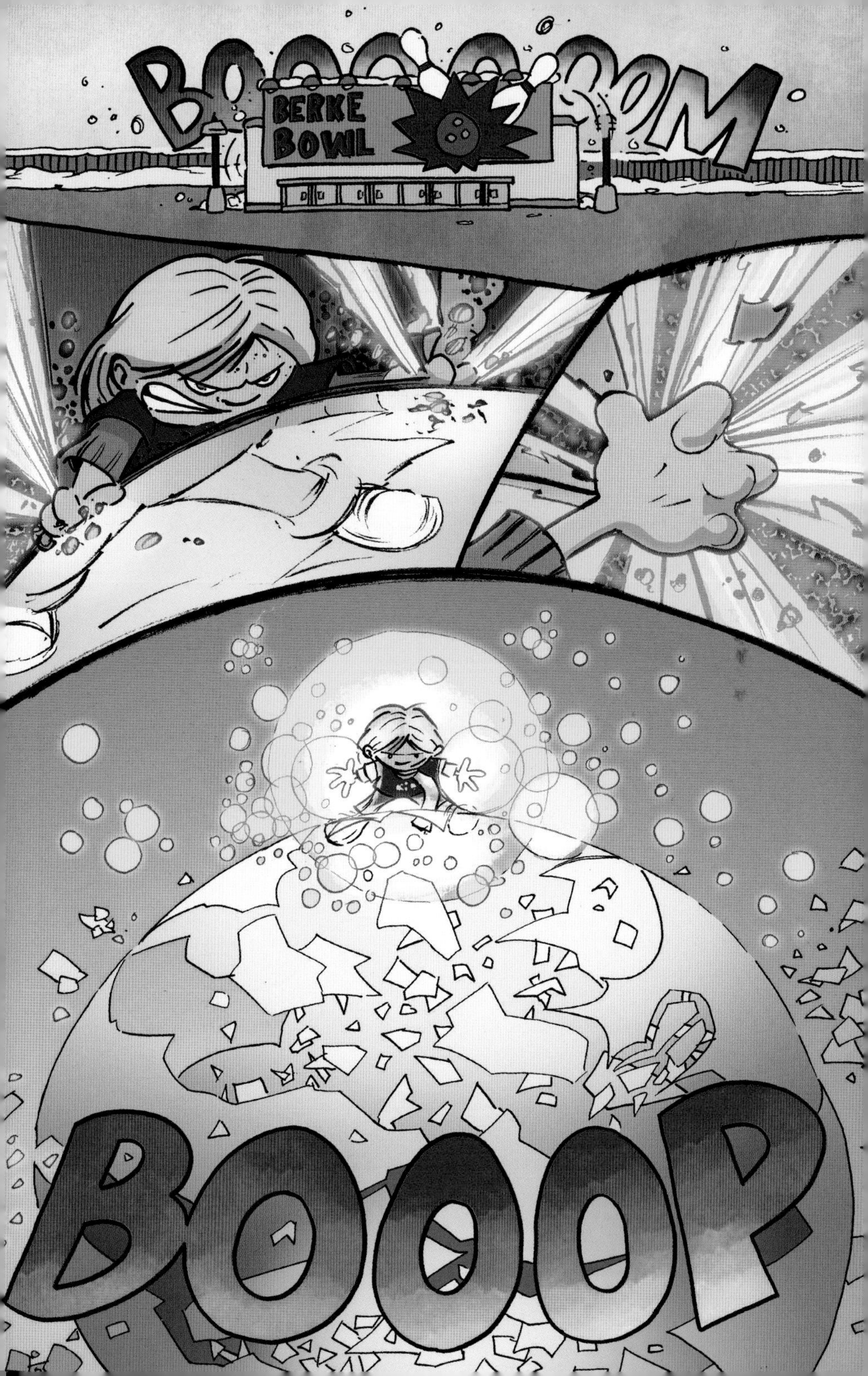
BOOOOOOOM
BERKE BOWL
BOOOP

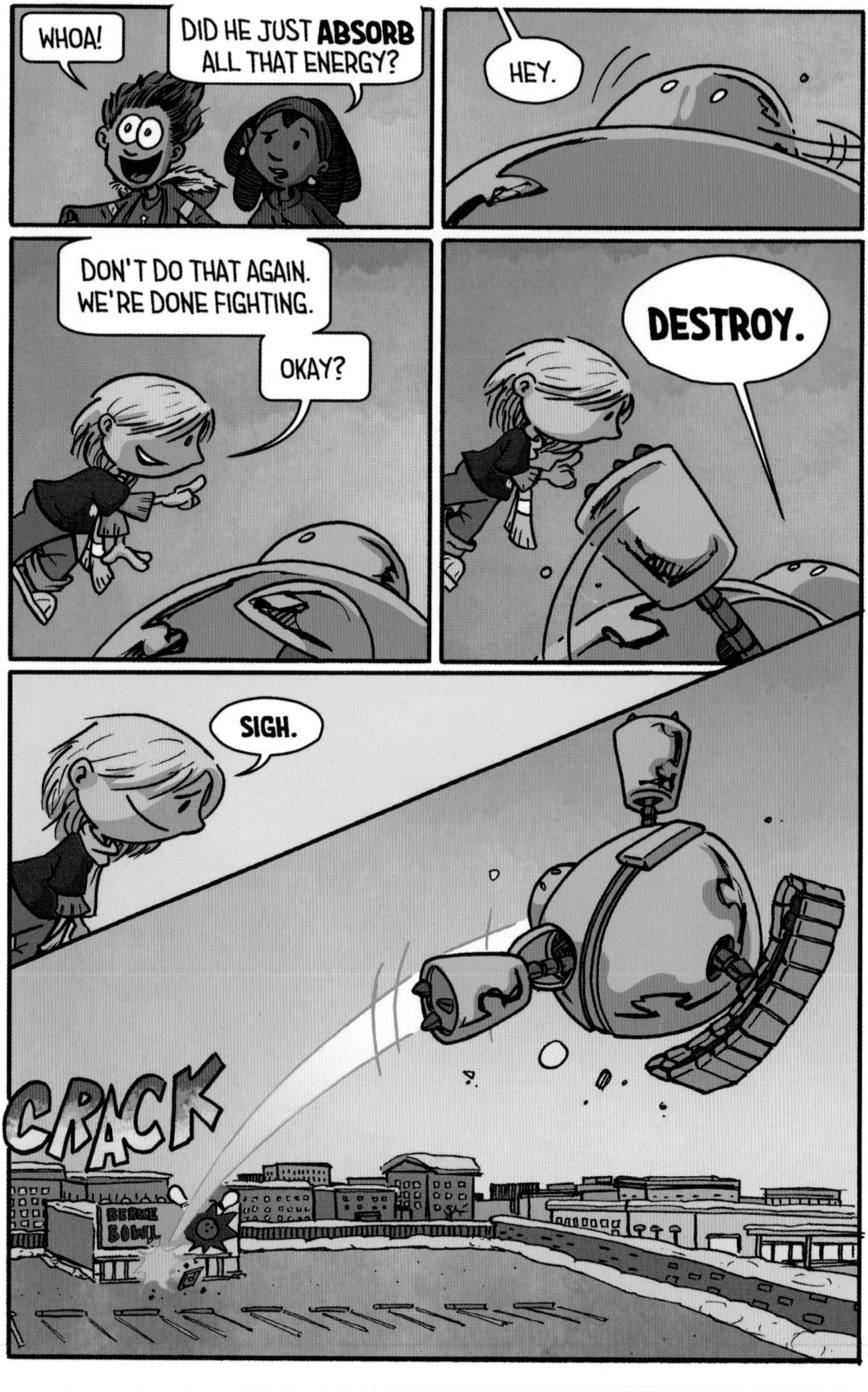
WHOA!
DID HE JUST **ABSORB** ALL THAT ENERGY?
HEY.
DON'T DO THAT AGAIN. WE'RE DONE FIGHTING.
OKAY?
DESTROY.
SIGH.
CRACK
BERKE BOWL

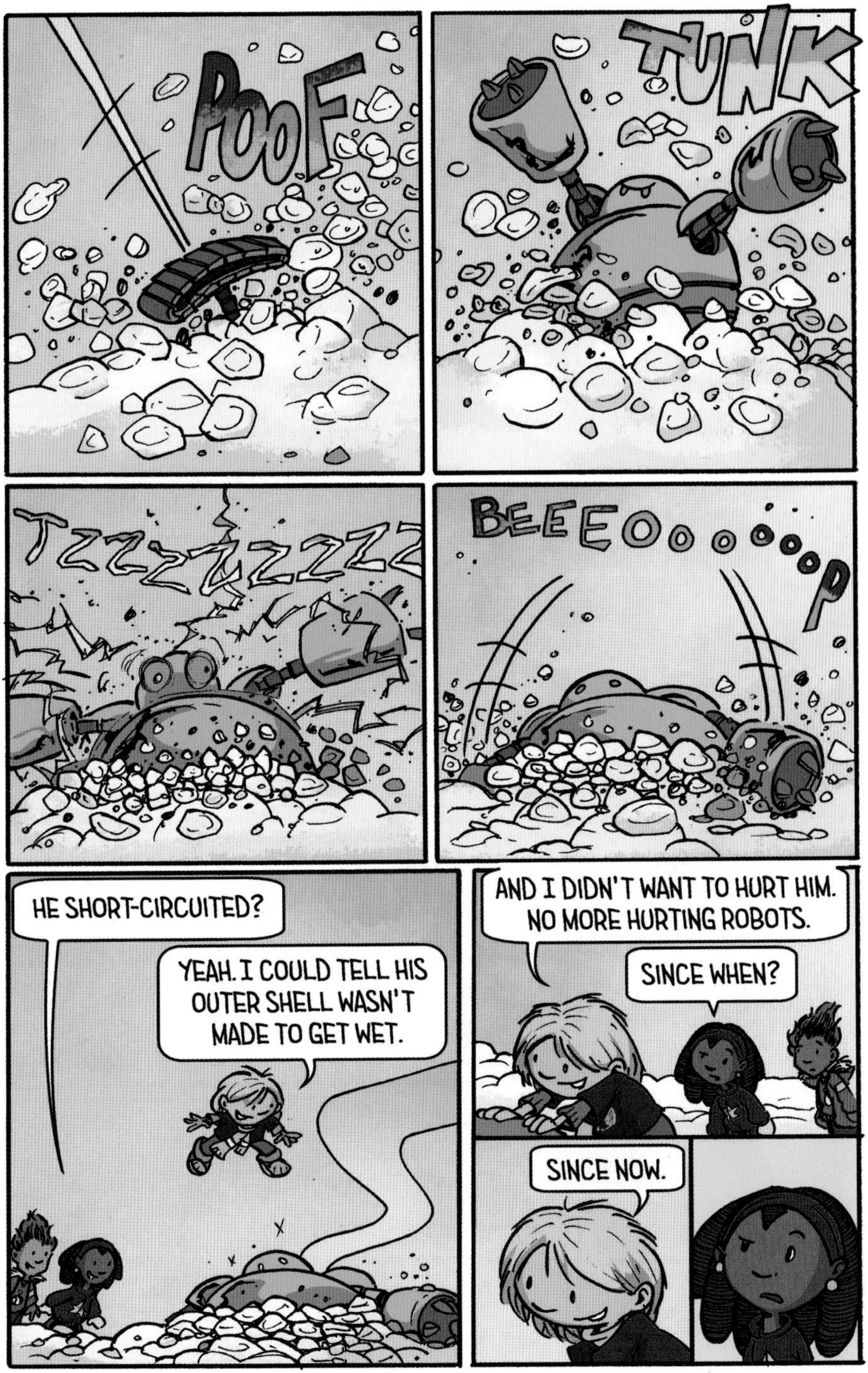
POOF
TUNK
TZZZZZZZZZ
BEEEOoooooP
HE SHORT-CIRCUITED?
YEAH. I COULD TELL HIS OUTER SHELL WASN'T MADE TO GET WET.
AND I DIDN'T WANT TO HURT HIM. NO MORE HURTING ROBOTS.
SINCE WHEN?
SINCE NOW.

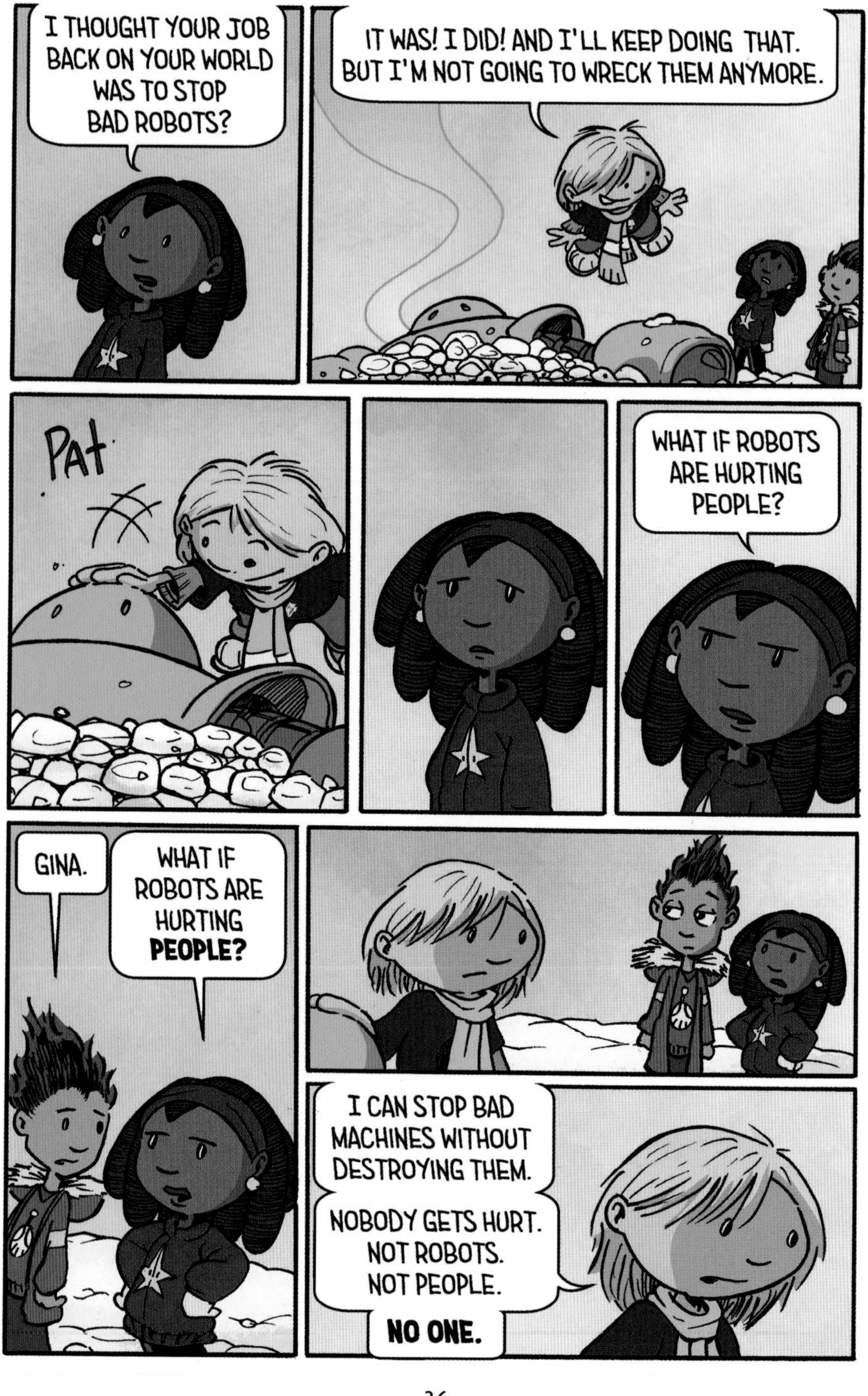
I THOUGHT YOUR JOB BACK ON YOUR WORLD WAS TO STOP BAD ROBOTS?
IT WAS! I DID! AND I'LL KEEP DOING THAT. BUT I'M NOT GOING TO WRECK THEM ANYMORE.
PAT
WHAT IF ROBOTS ARE HURTING PEOPLE?
GINA.
WHAT IF ROBOTS ARE HURTING **PEOPLE?**
I CAN STOP BAD MACHINES WITHOUT DESTROYING THEM.
NOBODY GETS HURT. NOT ROBOTS. NOT PEOPLE.
NO ONE.

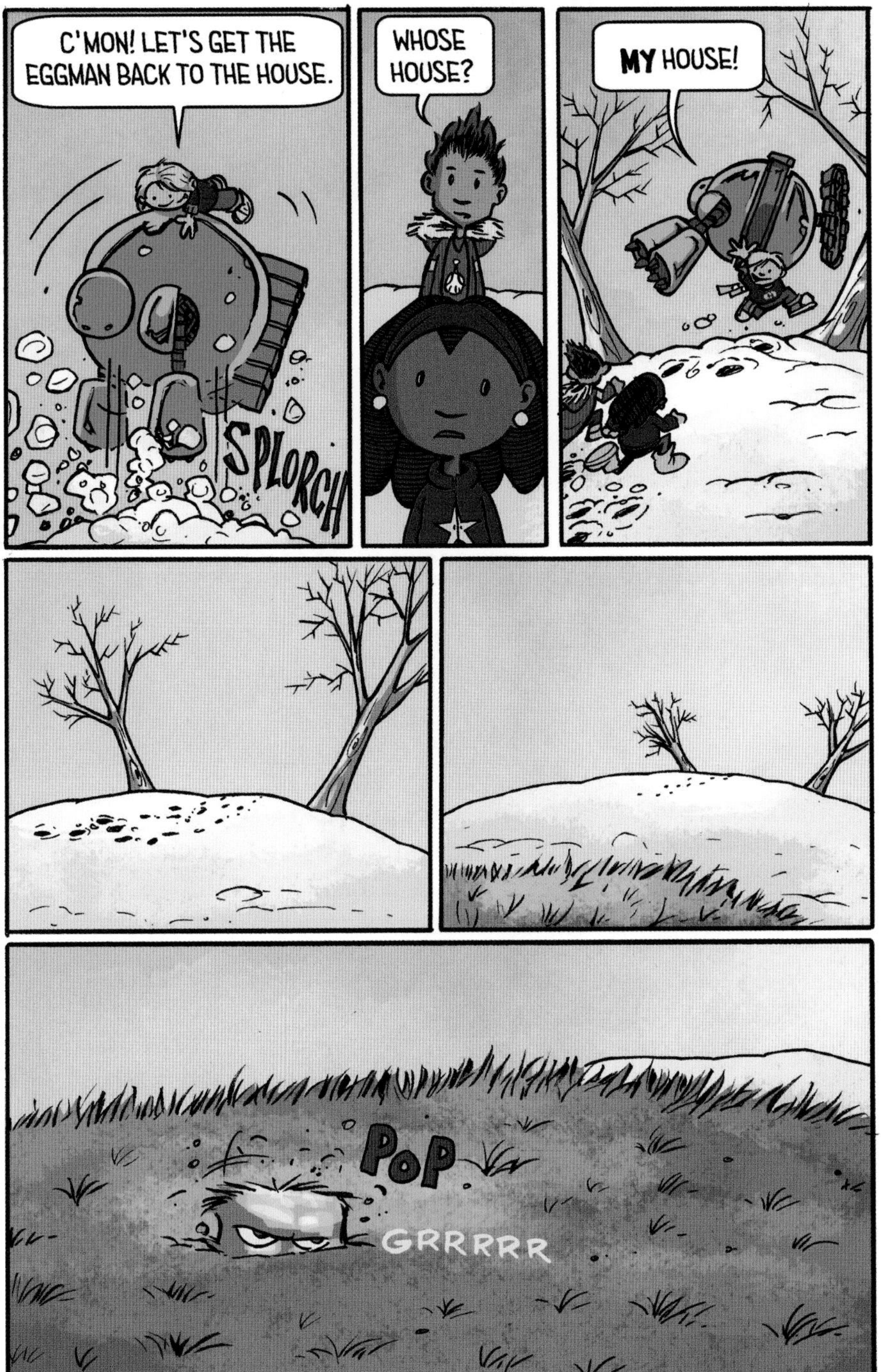
C'MON! LET'S GET THE EGGMAN BACK TO THE HOUSE.
SPLORCH
WHOSE HOUSE?
MY HOUSE!
POP
GRRRRR

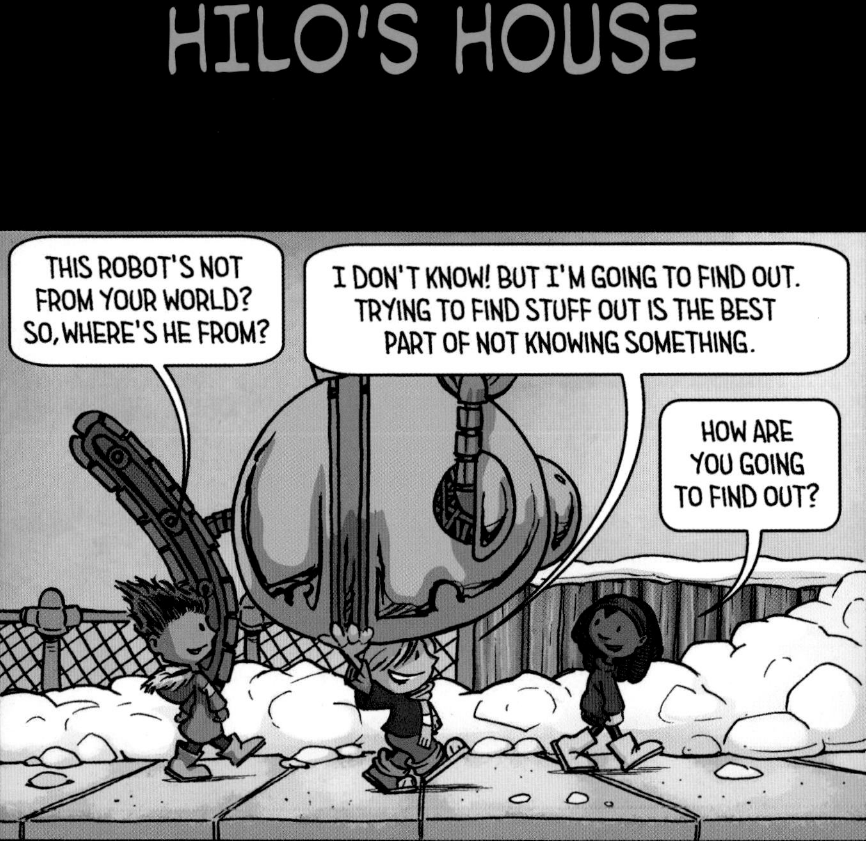
HILO'S HOUSE
THIS ROBOT'S NOT FROM YOUR WORLD? SO, WHERE'S HE FROM?
I DON'T KNOW! BUT I'M GOING TO FIND OUT. TRYING TO FIND STUFF OUT IS THE BEST PART OF NOT KNOWING SOMETHING.
HOW ARE YOU GOING TO FIND OUT?

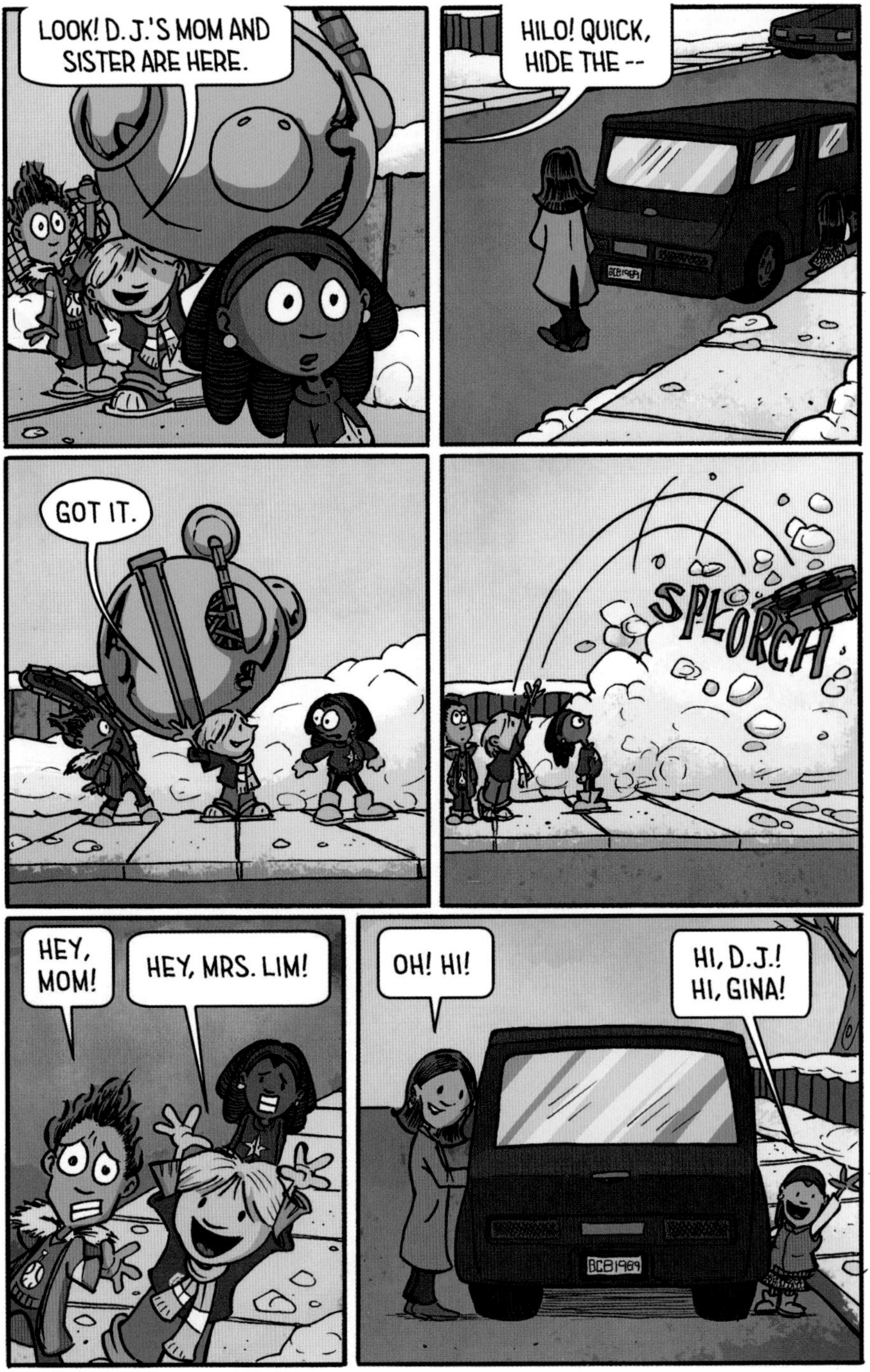

LOOK! D. J.'S MOM AND SISTER ARE HERE.
HILO! QUICK, HIDE THE --
GOT IT.
SPLORCH
HEY, MOM!
HEY, MRS. LIM!
OH! HI!
HI, D.J.! HI, GINA!

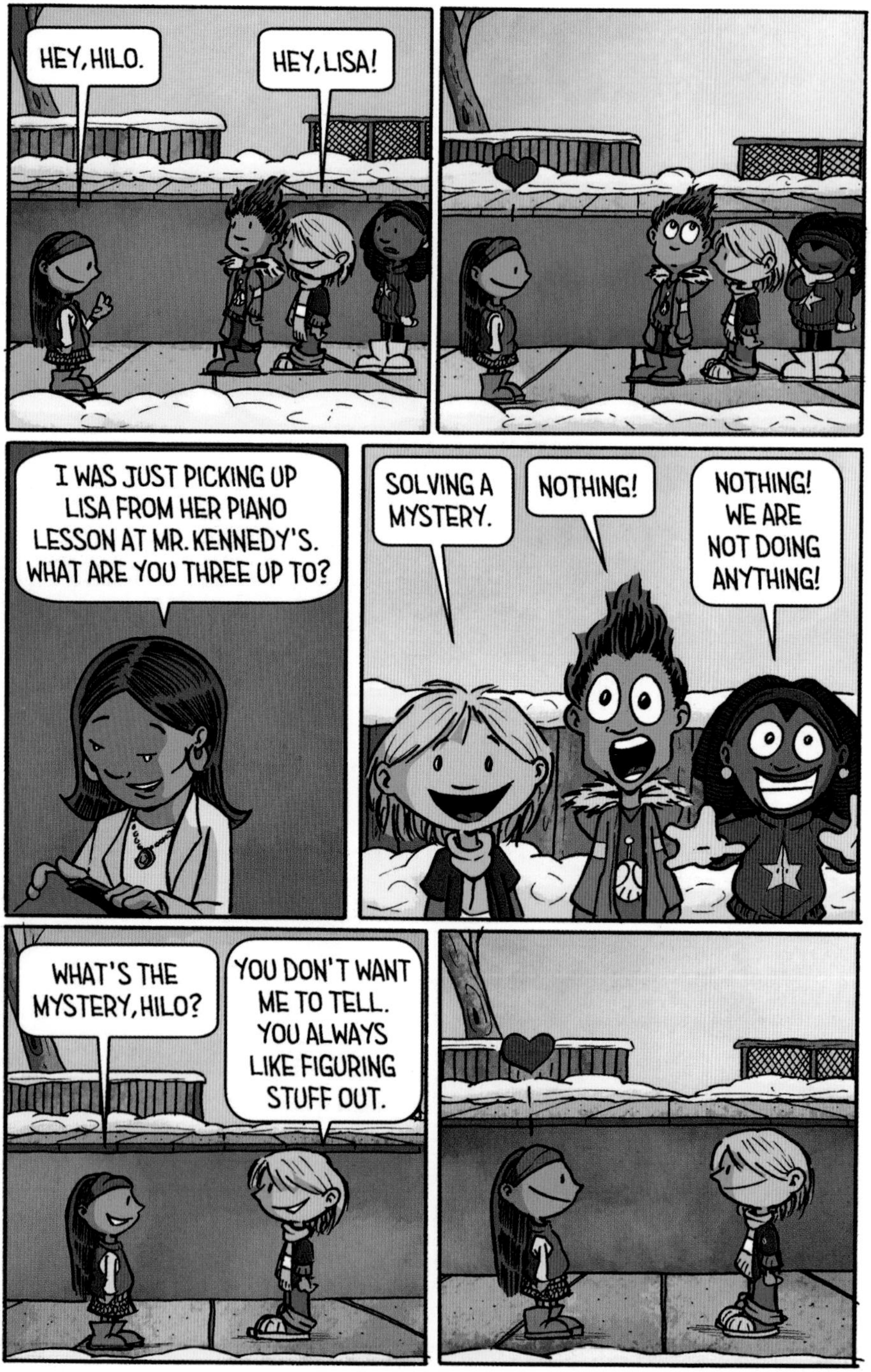

HEY, HILO.
HEY, LISA!
I WAS JUST PICKING UP LISA FROM HER PIANO LESSON AT MR. KENNEDY'S. WHAT ARE YOU THREE UP TO?
SOLVING A MYSTERY.
NOTHING!
NOTHING! WE ARE NOT DOING ANYTHING!
WHAT'S THE MYSTERY, HILO?
YOU DON'T WANT ME TO TELL. YOU ALWAYS LIKE FIGURING STUFF OUT.

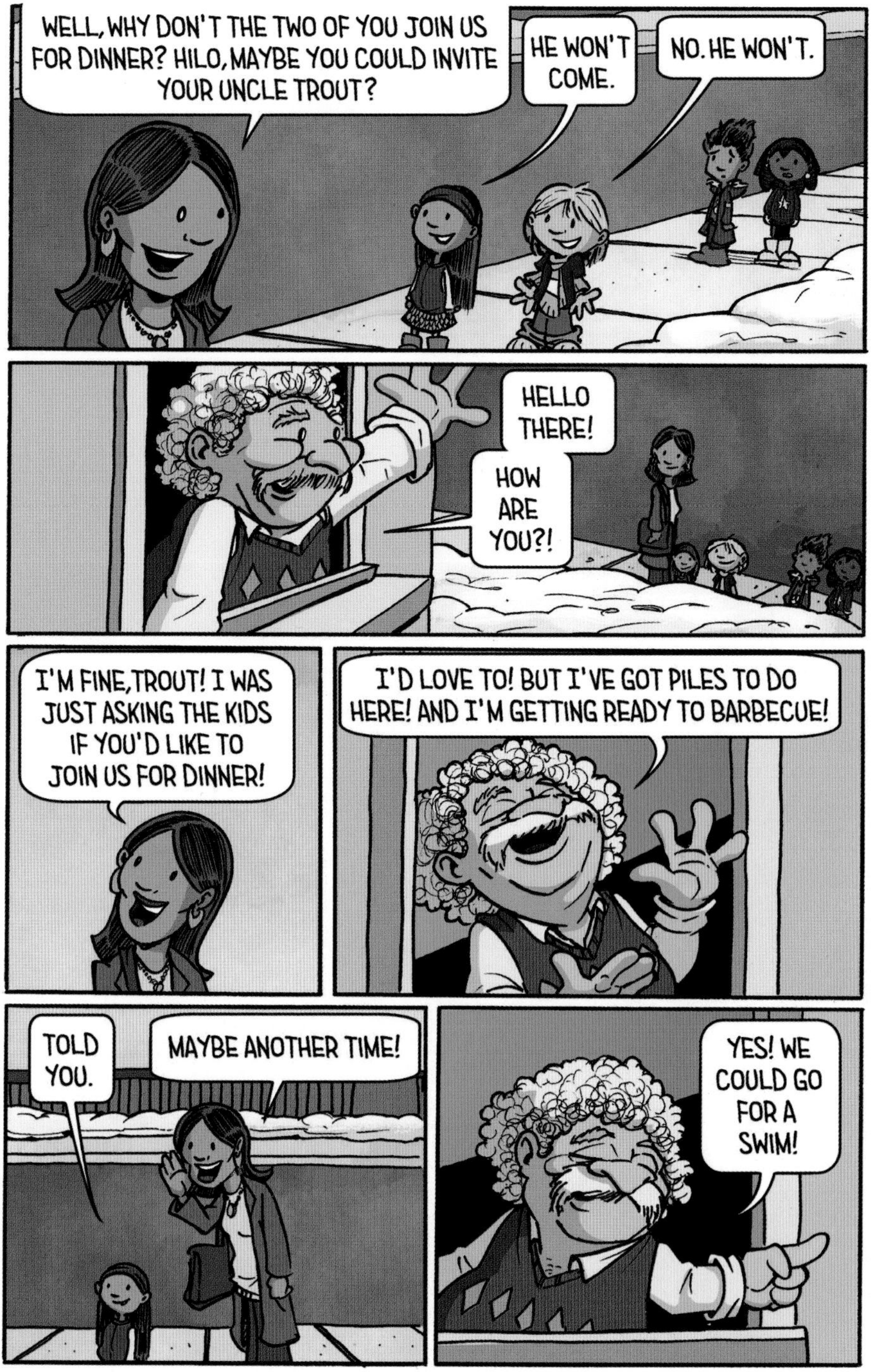
WELL, WHY DON'T THE TWO OF YOU JOIN US FOR DINNER? HILO, MAYBE YOU COULD INVITE YOUR UNCLE TROUT?
HE WON'T COME.
NO. HE WON'T.
HELLO THERE!
HOW ARE YOU?!
I'M FINE, TROUT! I WAS JUST ASKING THE KIDS IF YOU'D LIKE TO JOIN US FOR DINNER!
I'D LOVE TO! BUT I'VE GOT PILES TO DO HERE! AND I'M GETTING READY TO BARBECUE!
TOLD YOU.
MAYBE ANOTHER TIME!
YES! WE COULD GO FOR A SWIM!

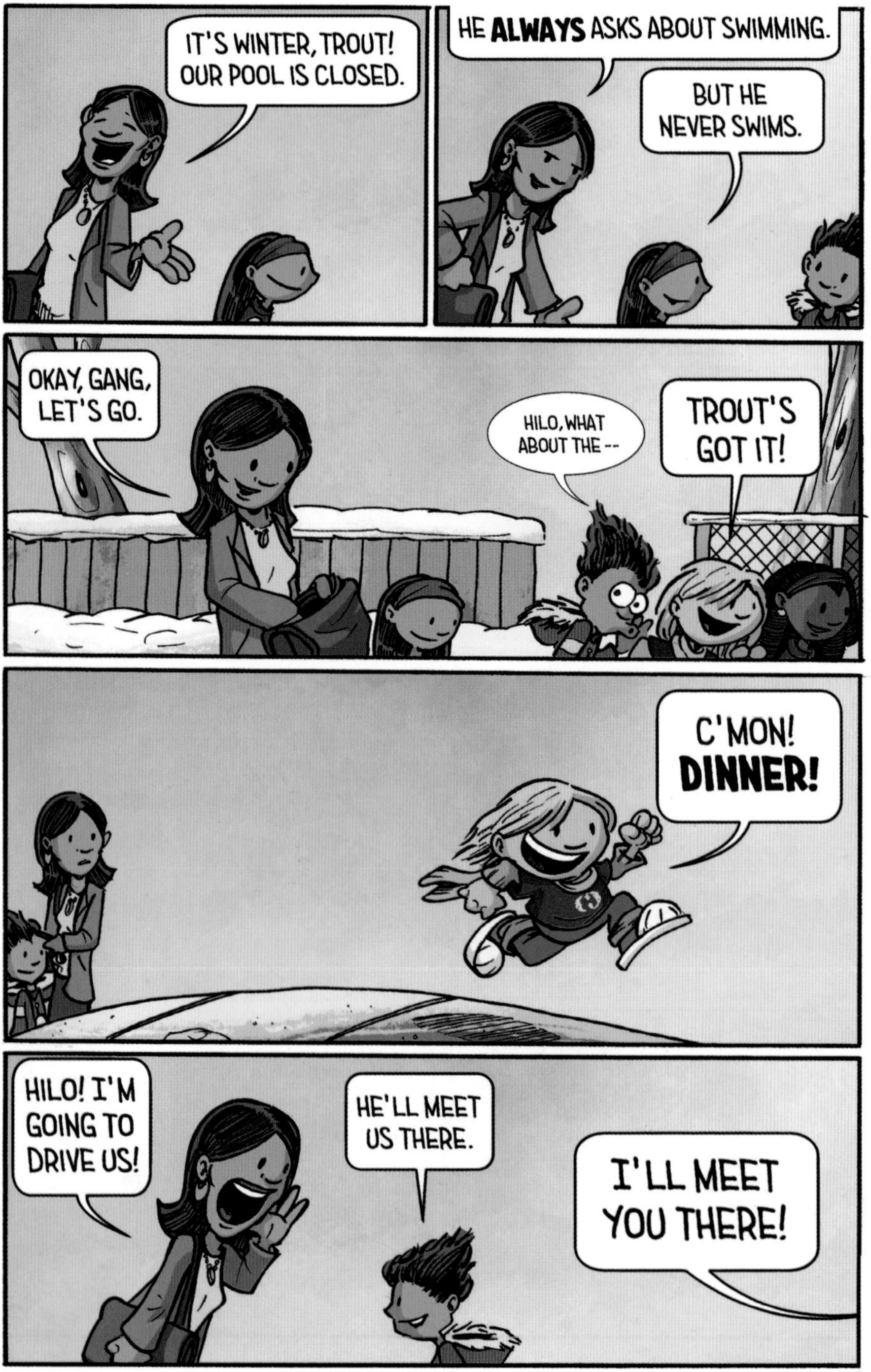
IT'S WINTER, TROUT! OUR POOL IS CLOSED.
HE **ALWAYS** ASKS ABOUT SWIMMING.
BUT HE NEVER SWIMS.
OKAY, GANG, LET'S GO.
HILO, WHAT ABOUT THE --
TROUT'S GOT IT!
C'MON! **DINNER!**
HILO! I'M GOING TO DRIVE US!
HE'LL MEET US THERE.
I'LL MEET YOU THERE!

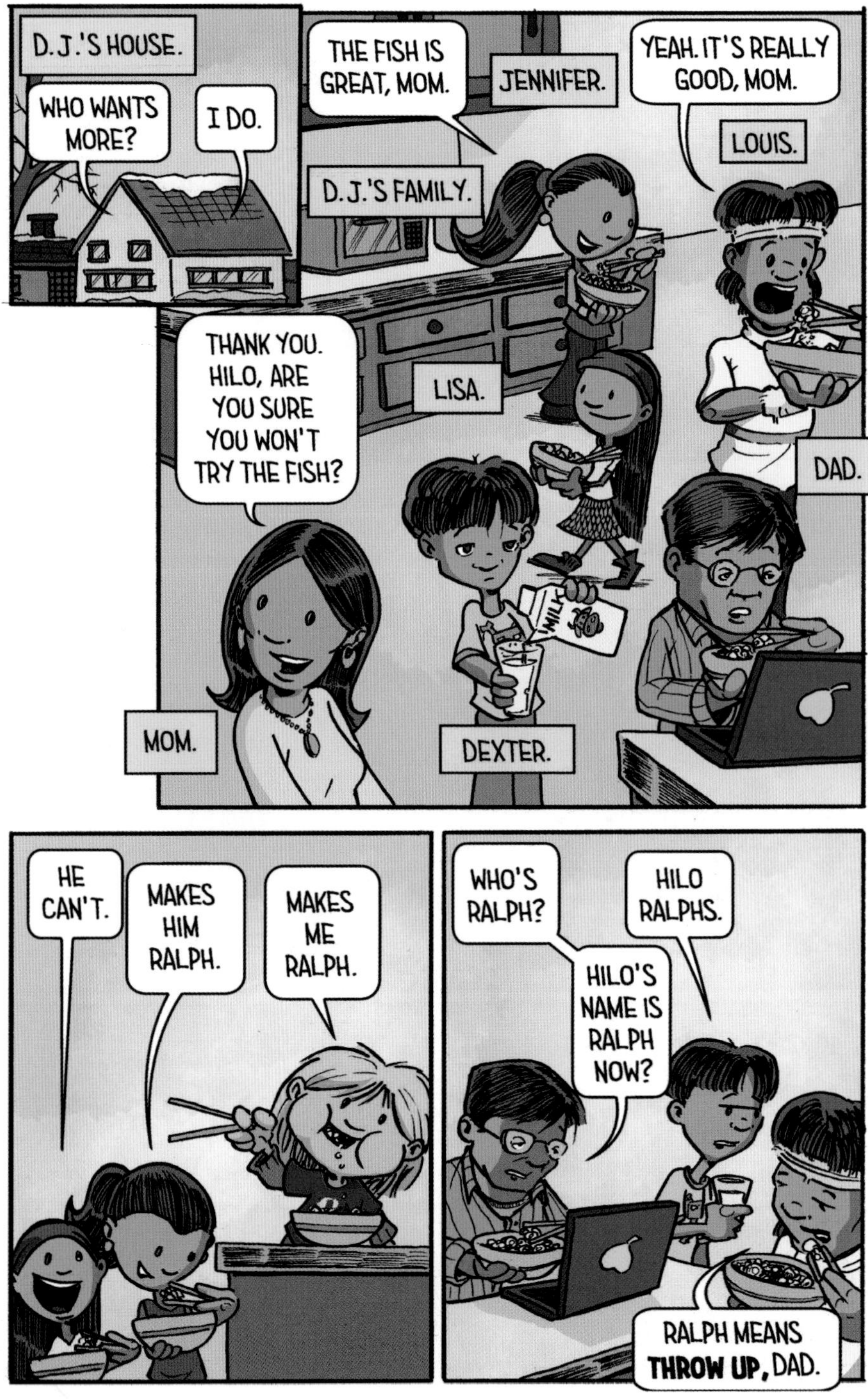
D.J.'S HOUSE.
WHO WANTS MORE?
I DO.
THE FISH IS GREAT, MOM.
JENNIFER.
YEAH. IT'S REALLY GOOD, MOM.
LOUIS.
D.J.'S FAMILY.
THANK YOU. HILO, ARE YOU SURE YOU WON'T TRY THE FISH?
LISA.
DAD.
MILK
MOM.
DEXTER.
HE CAN'T.
MAKES HIM RALPH.
MAKES ME RALPH.
WHO'S RALPH?
HILO RALPHS.
HILO'S NAME IS RALPH NOW?
RALPH MEANS **THROW UP,** DAD.

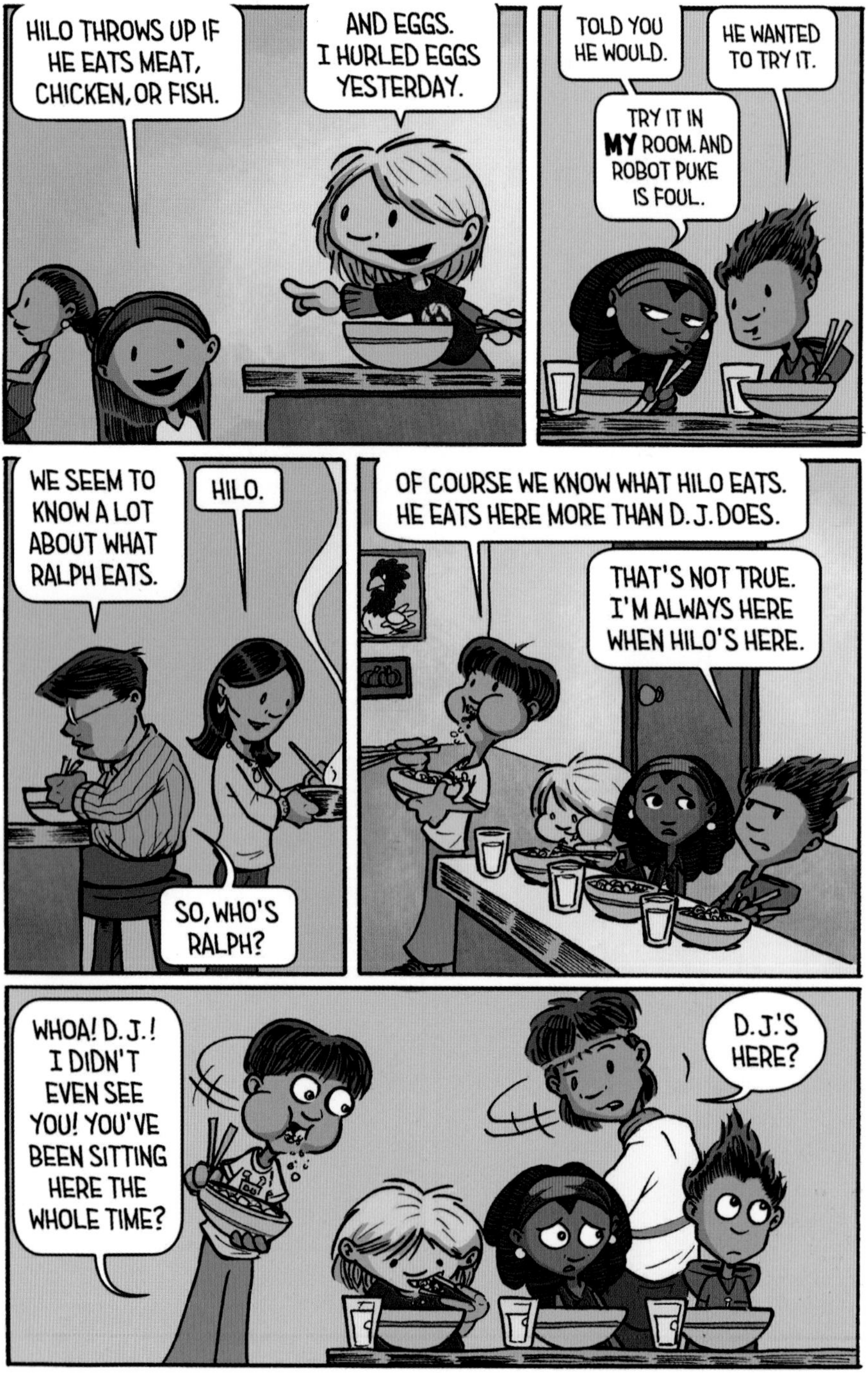
HILO THROWS UP IF HE EATS MEAT, CHICKEN, OR FISH.
AND EGGS. I HURLED EGGS YESTERDAY.
TOLD YOU HE WOULD.
HE WANTED TO TRY IT.
TRY IT IN MY ROOM. AND ROBOT PUKE IS FOUL.
WE SEEM TO KNOW A LOT ABOUT WHAT RALPH EATS.
HILO.
SO, WHO'S RALPH?
OF COURSE WE KNOW WHAT HILO EATS. HE EATS HERE MORE THAN D. J. DOES.
THAT'S NOT TRUE. I'M ALWAYS HERE WHEN HILO'S HERE.
WHOA! D. J.! I DIDN'T EVEN SEE YOU! YOU'VE BEEN SITTING HERE THE WHOLE TIME?
D. J.'S HERE?

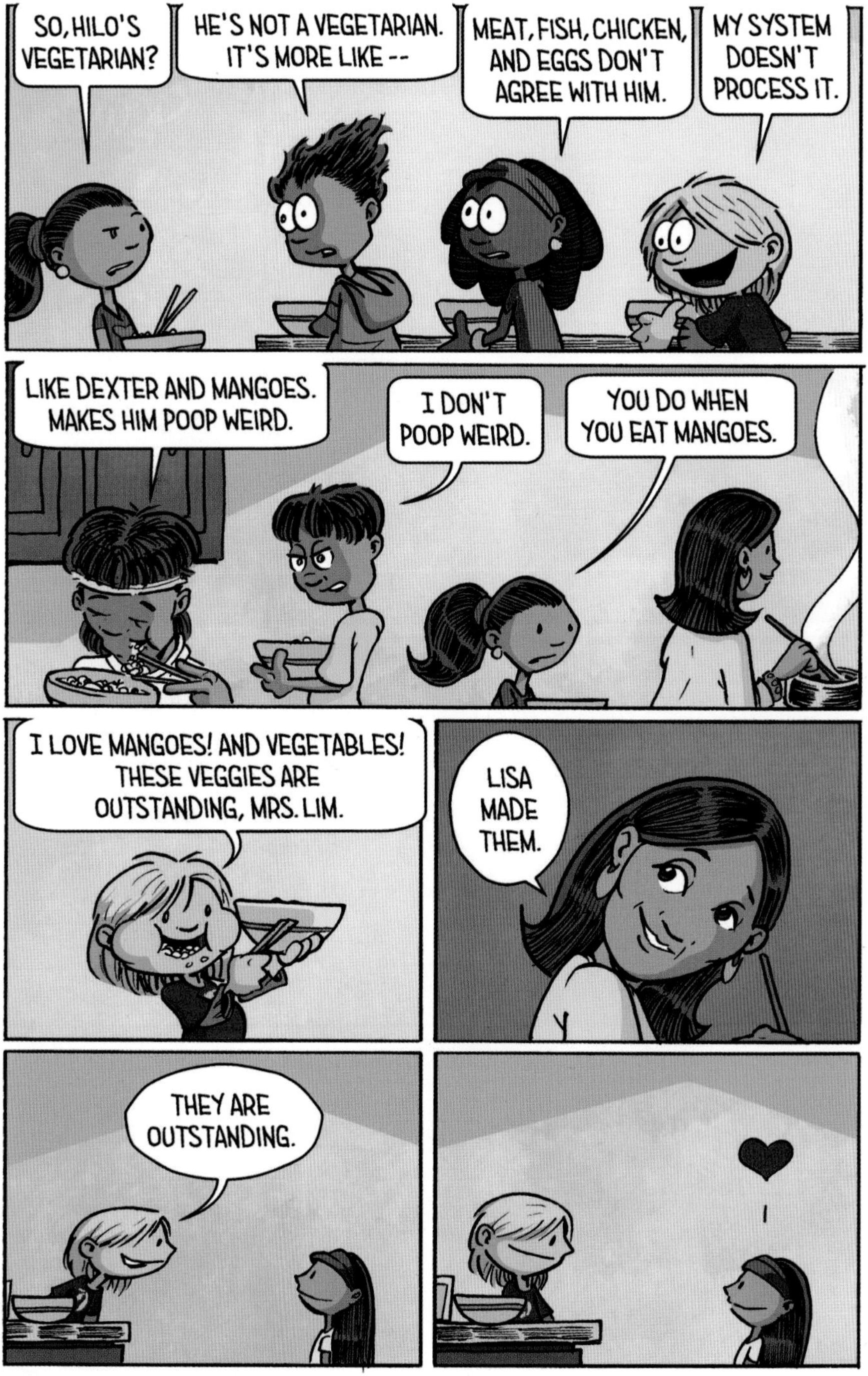
SO, HILO'S VEGETARIAN?
HE'S NOT A VEGETARIAN. IT'S MORE LIKE --
MEAT, FISH, CHICKEN, AND EGGS DON'T AGREE WITH HIM.
MY SYSTEM DOESN'T PROCESS IT.
LIKE DEXTER AND MANGOES. MAKES HIM POOP WEIRD.
I DON'T POOP WEIRD.
YOU DO WHEN YOU EAT MANGOES.
I LOVE MANGOES! AND VEGETABLES! THESE VEGGIES ARE OUTSTANDING, MRS. LIM.
LISA MADE THEM.
THEY ARE OUTSTANDING.

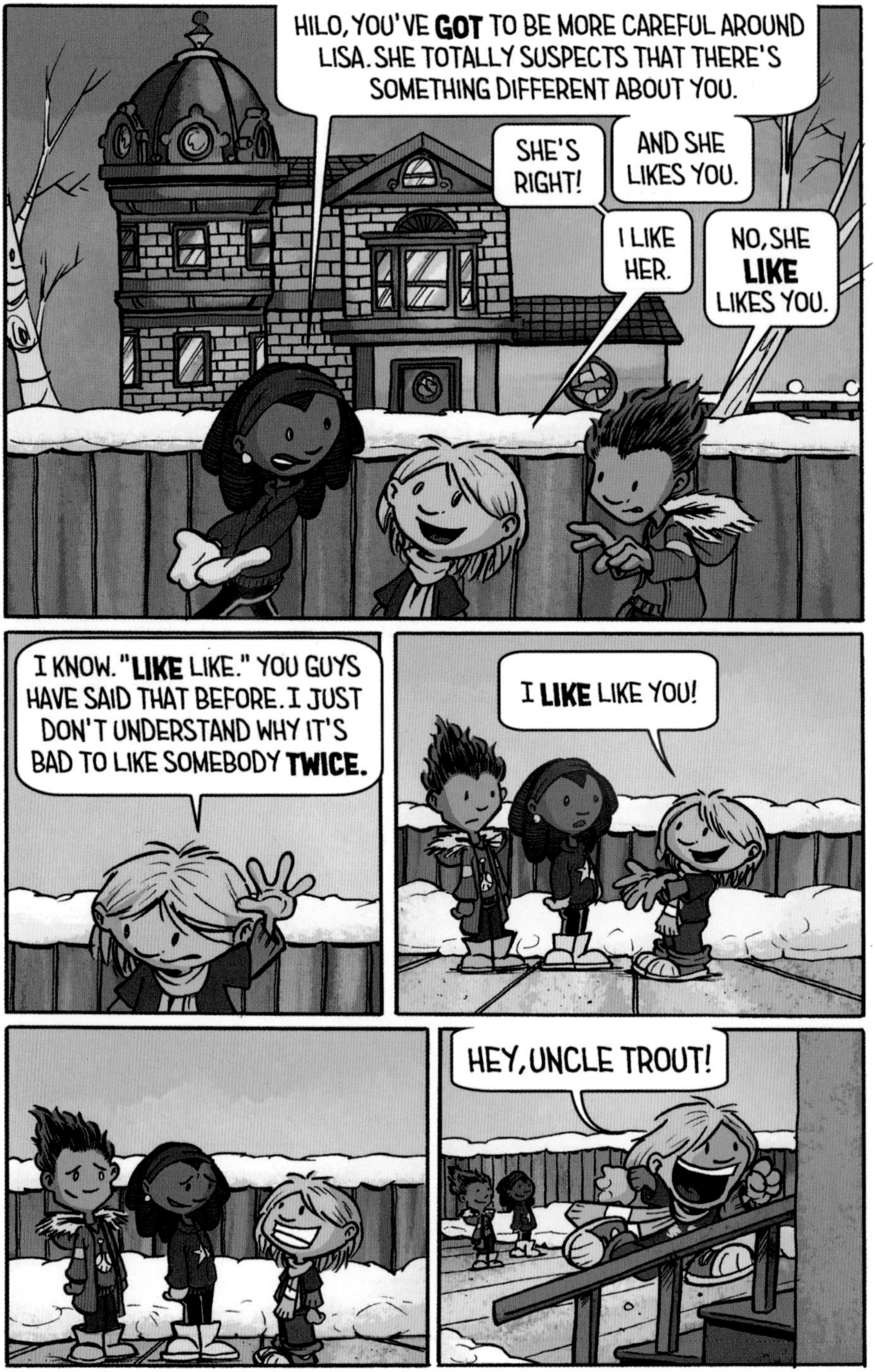
HILO, YOU'VE **GOT** TO BE MORE CAREFUL AROUND LISA. SHE TOTALLY SUSPECTS THAT THERE'S SOMETHING DIFFERENT ABOUT YOU.
SHE'S RIGHT!
AND SHE LIKES YOU.
I LIKE HER.
NO, SHE **LIKE** LIKES YOU.
I KNOW. "**LIKE** LIKE." YOU GUYS HAVE SAID THAT BEFORE. I JUST DON'T UNDERSTAND WHY IT'S BAD TO LIKE SOMEBODY **TWICE.**
I **LIKE** LIKE YOU!
HEY, UNCLE TROUT!

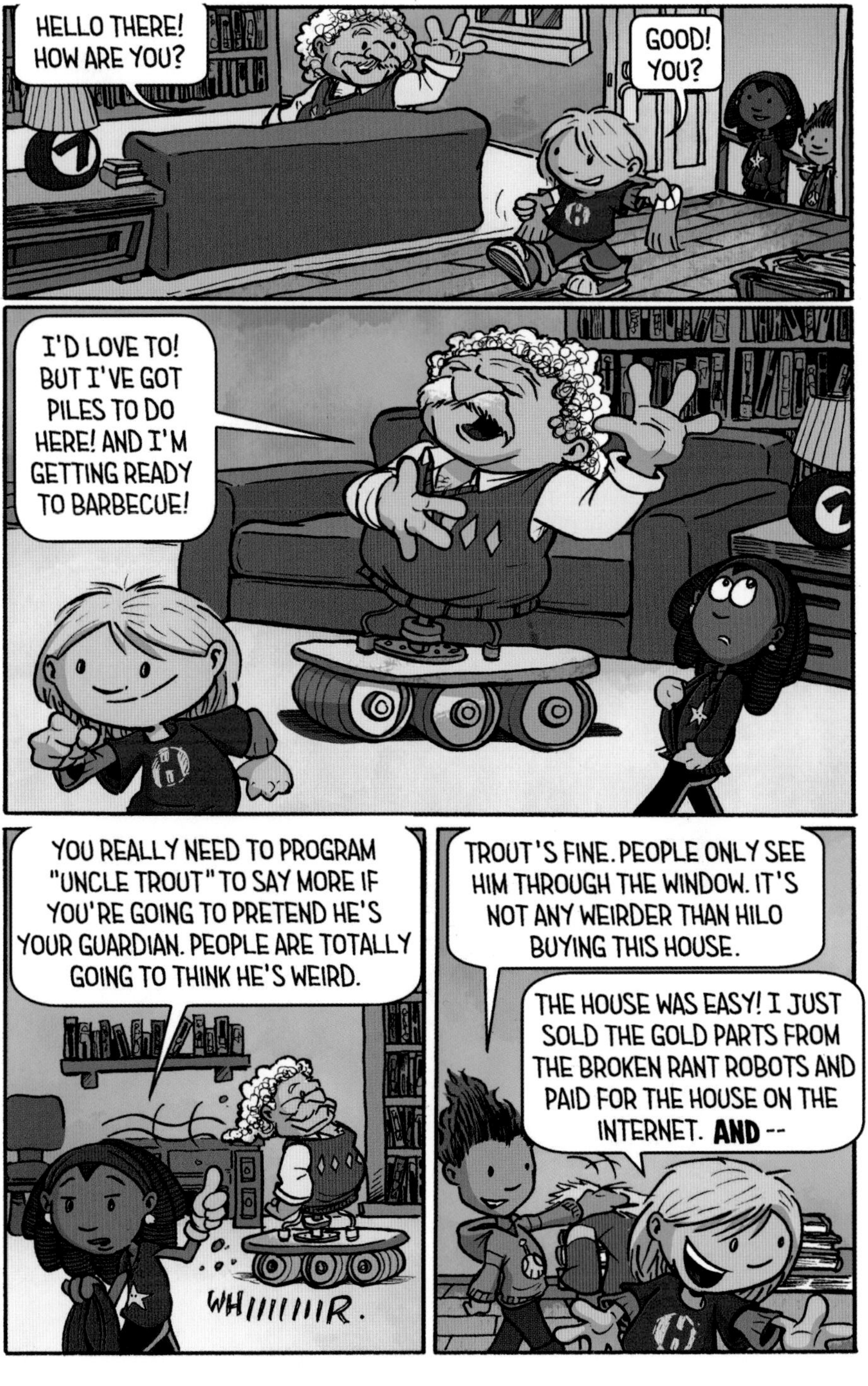
HELLO THERE! HOW ARE YOU?
GOOD! YOU?
I'D LOVE TO! BUT I'VE GOT PILES TO DO HERE! AND I'M GETTING READY TO BARBECUE!
YOU REALLY NEED TO PROGRAM "UNCLE TROUT" TO SAY MORE IF YOU'RE GOING TO PRETEND HE'S YOUR GUARDIAN. PEOPLE ARE TOTALLY GOING TO THINK HE'S WEIRD.
WHIIIIIIR.
TROUT'S FINE. PEOPLE ONLY SEE HIM THROUGH THE WINDOW. IT'S NOT ANY WEIRDER THAN HILO BUYING THIS HOUSE.
THE HOUSE WAS EASY! I JUST SOLD THE GOLD PARTS FROM THE BROKEN RANT ROBOTS AND PAID FOR THE HOUSE ON THE INTERNET. **AND** --

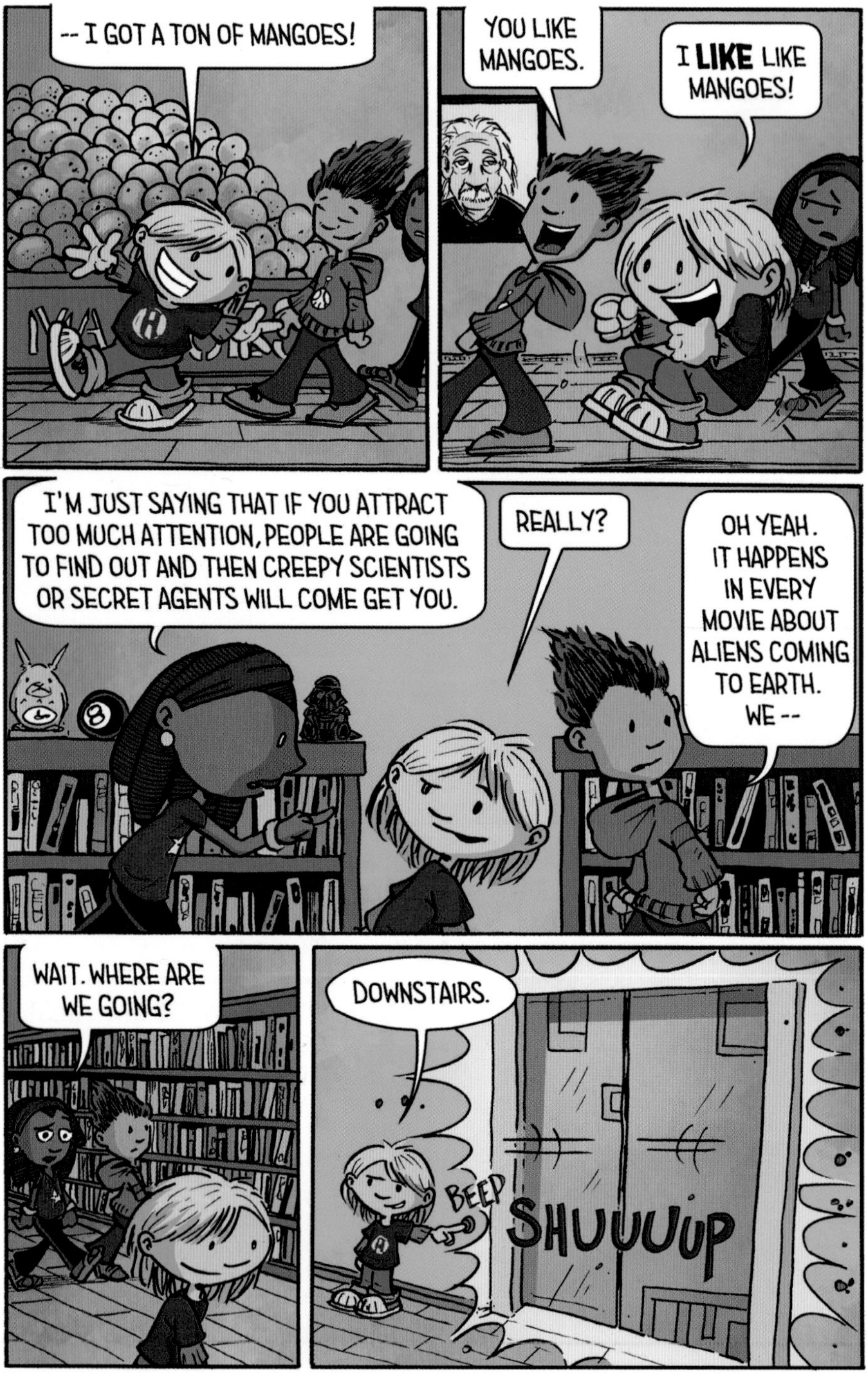
-- I GOT A TON OF MANGOES!
YOU LIKE MANGOES.
I **LIKE** LIKE MANGOES!
I'M JUST SAYING THAT IF YOU ATTRACT TOO MUCH ATTENTION, PEOPLE ARE GOING TO FIND OUT AND THEN CREEPY SCIENTISTS OR SECRET AGENTS WILL COME GET YOU.
REALLY?
OH YEAH. IT HAPPENS IN EVERY MOVIE ABOUT ALIENS COMING TO EARTH. WE --
WAIT. WHERE ARE WE GOING?
DOWNSTAIRS.
BEEP
SHUUUUP

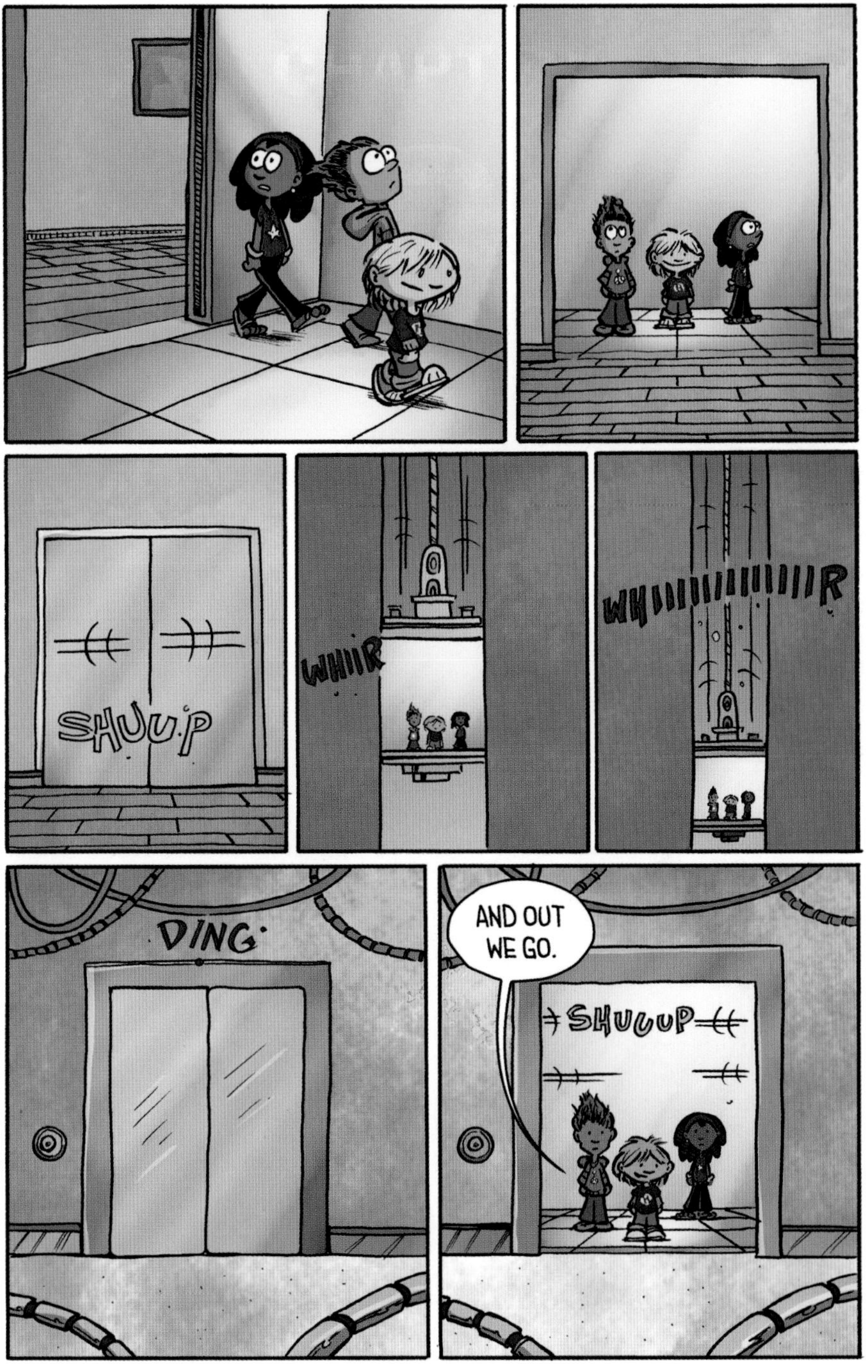
SHUUP
WHIIR
WHIIIIIIIIIIIIIIR
DING
AND OUT WE GO.
SHUUUP

CHAPTER 4

AND OUT WE GO

HOLY MACKEREL!
YEAH. **BIG** HOLY MACKEREL.
WHY A BIG HOLY MACKEREL?
THIS.
THIS?

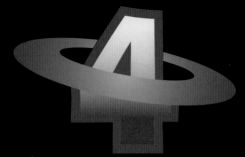

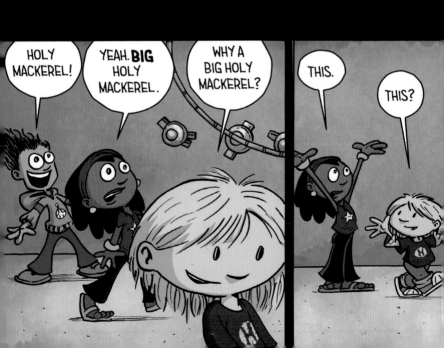

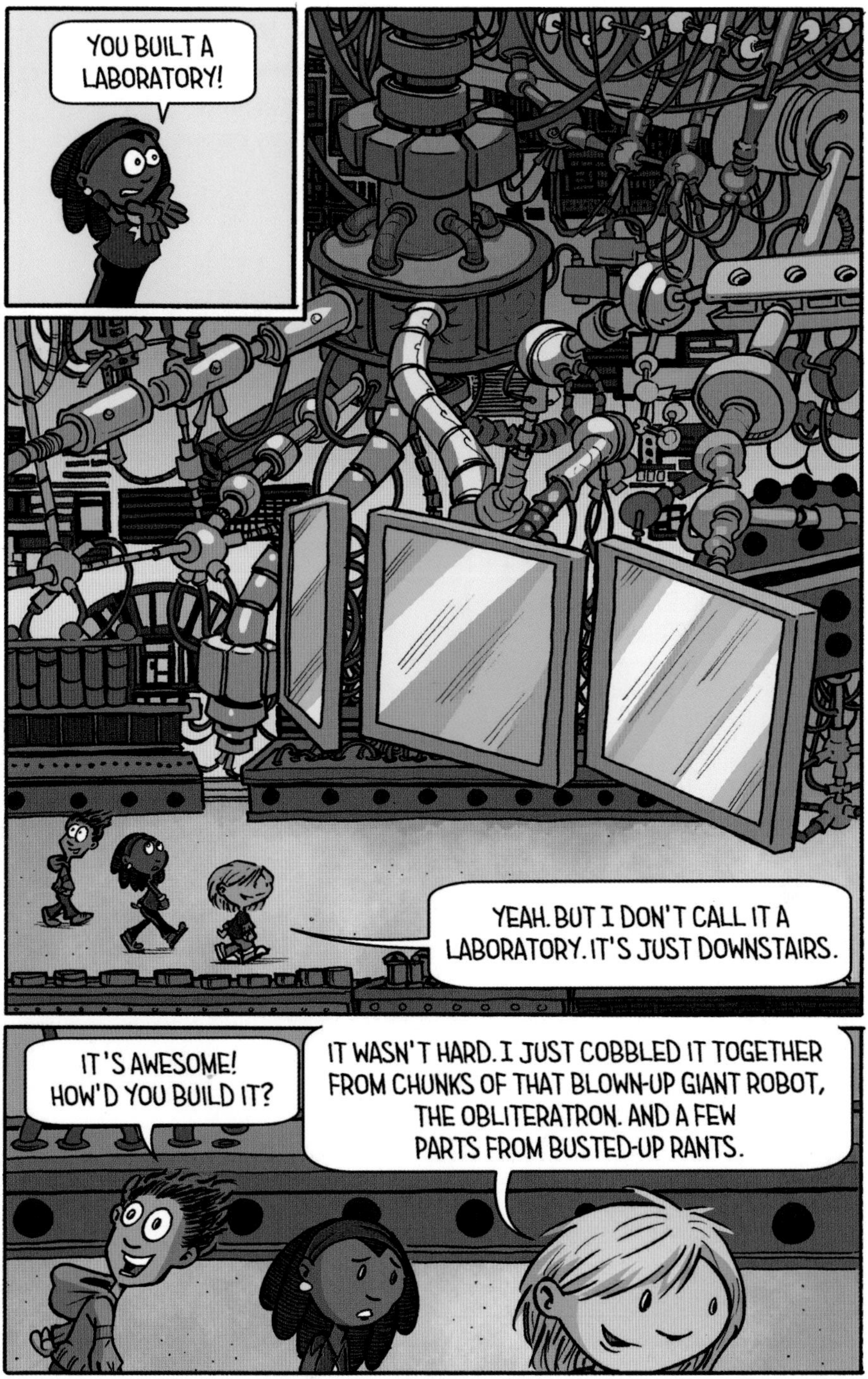
YOU BUILT A LABORATORY!
YEAH. BUT I DON'T CALL IT A LABORATORY. IT'S JUST DOWNSTAIRS.
IT'S AWESOME! HOW'D YOU BUILD IT?
IT WASN'T HARD. I JUST COBBLED IT TOGETHER FROM CHUNKS OF THAT BLOWN-UP GIANT ROBOT, THE OBLITERATRON. AND A FEW PARTS FROM BUSTED-UP RANTS.

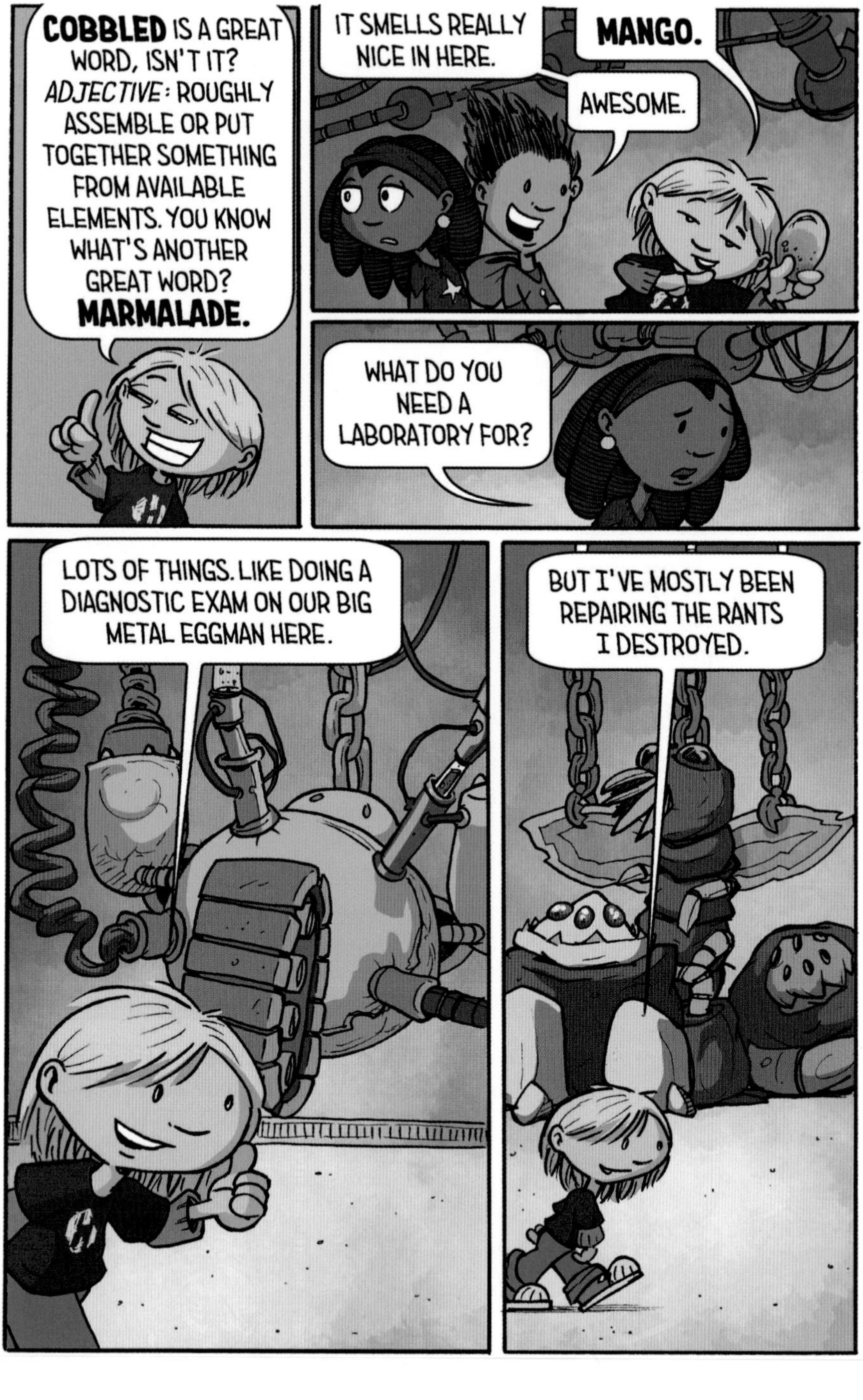
COBBLED IS A GREAT WORD, ISN'T IT? ADJECTIVE: ROUGHLY ASSEMBLE OR PUT TOGETHER SOMETHING FROM AVAILABLE ELEMENTS. YOU KNOW WHAT'S ANOTHER GREAT WORD? MARMALADE.
IT SMELLS REALLY NICE IN HERE.
MANGO.
AWESOME.
WHAT DO YOU NEED A LABORATORY FOR?
LOTS OF THINGS. LIKE DOING A DIAGNOSTIC EXAM ON OUR BIG METAL EGGMAN HERE.
BUT I'VE MOSTLY BEEN REPAIRING THE RANTS I DESTROYED.

THE RANTS! THEY WERE THE ROBOTS RAZORWARK SENT TO DESTROY EARTH!

I NEED ANSWERS, AND THEY PROBABLY HAVE THEM.

ANSWERS ABOUT WHAT?

ME.

AND **RAZORWARK.**

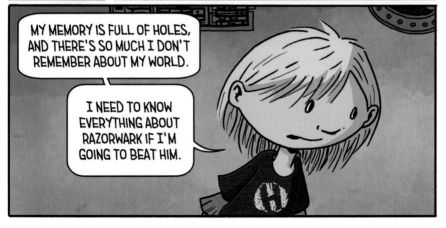

MY MEMORY IS FULL OF HOLES, AND THERE'S SO MUCH I DON'T REMEMBER ABOUT MY WORLD.

I NEED TO KNOW EVERYTHING ABOUT RAZORWARK IF I'M GOING TO BEAT HIM.

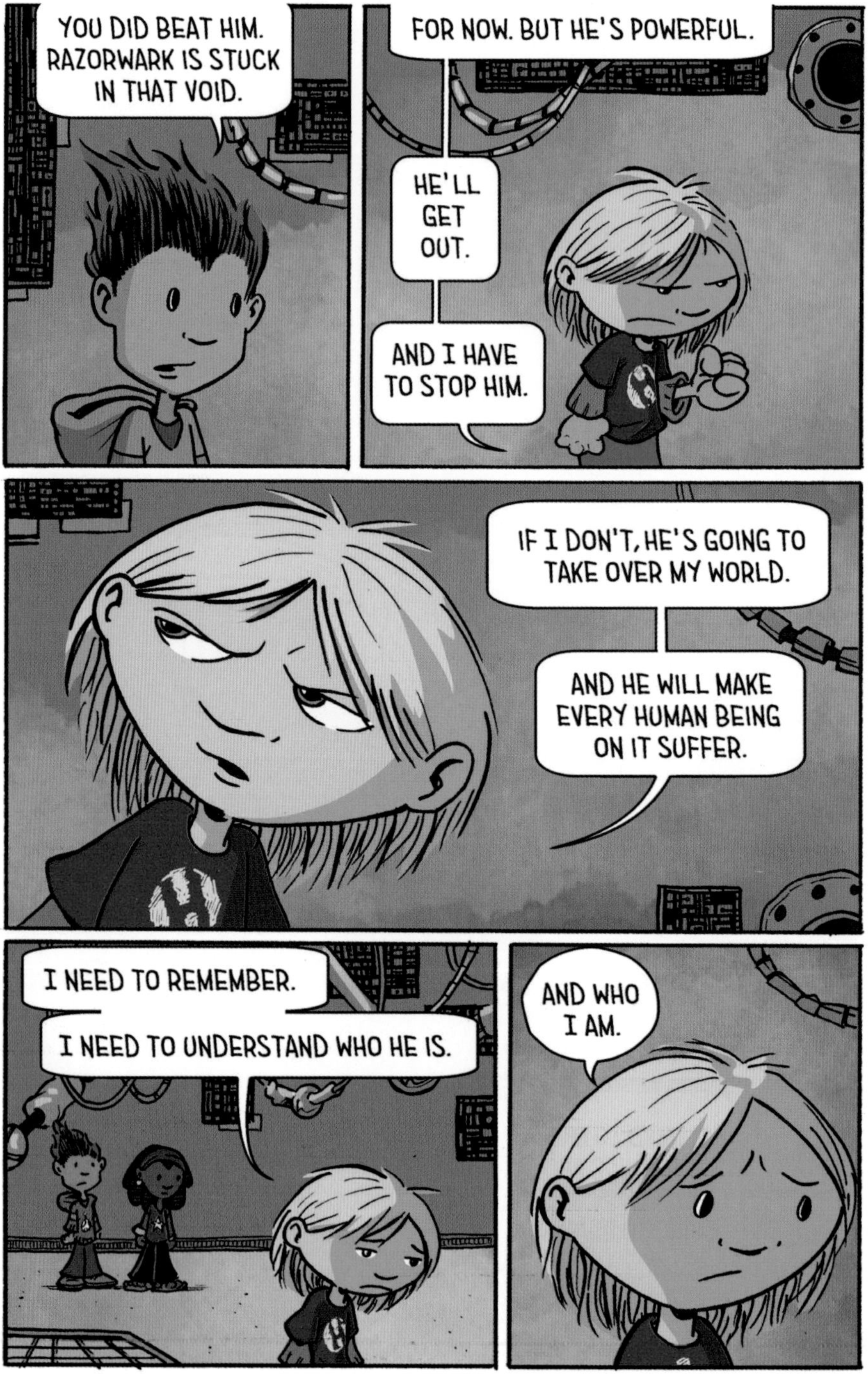
YOU DID BEAT HIM. RAZORWARK IS STUCK IN THAT VOID.
FOR NOW. BUT HE'S POWERFUL.
HE'LL GET OUT.
AND I HAVE TO STOP HIM.
IF I DON'T, HE'S GOING TO TAKE OVER MY WORLD.
AND HE WILL MAKE EVERY HUMAN BEING ON IT SUFFER.
I NEED TO REMEMBER.
I NEED TO UNDERSTAND WHO HE IS.
AND WHO I AM.

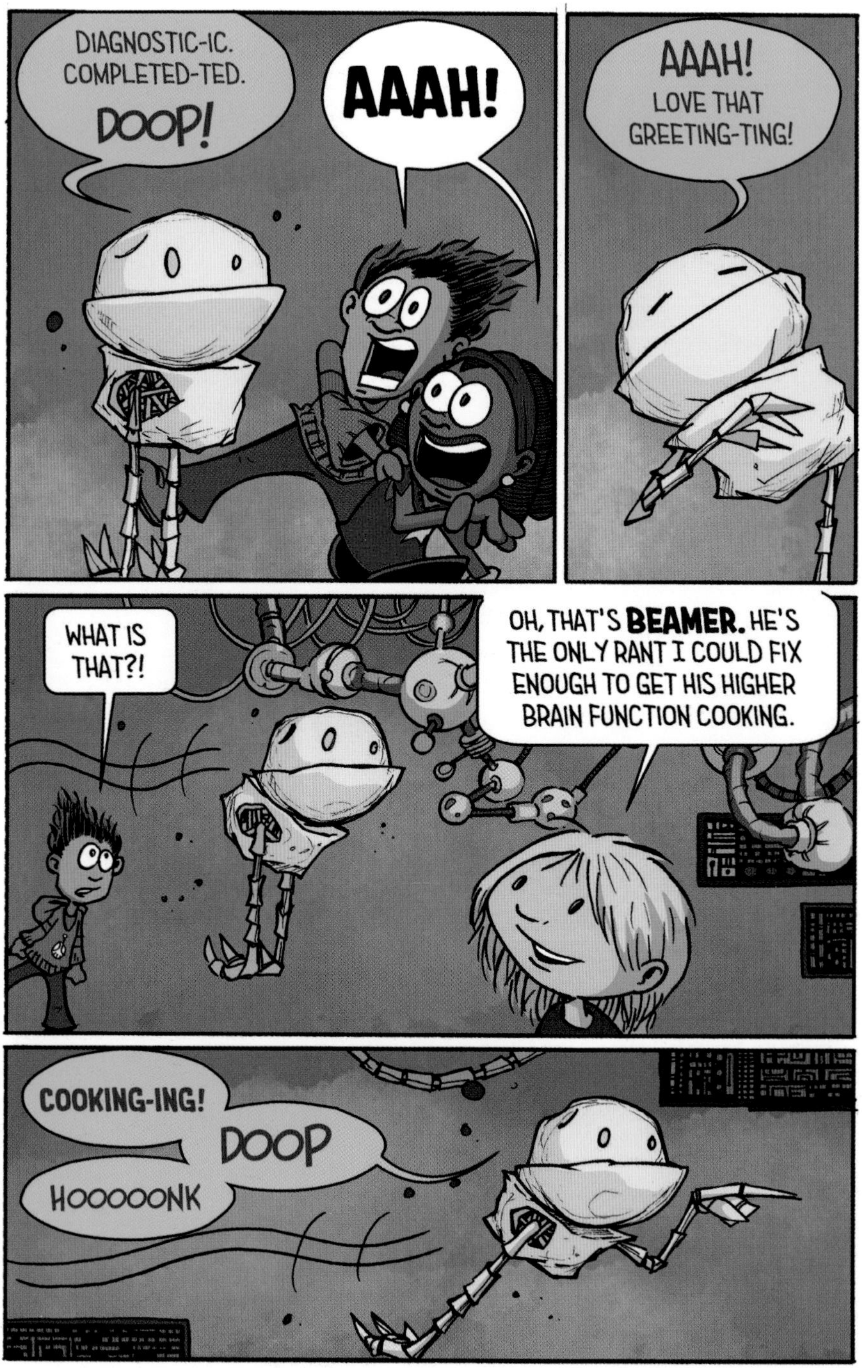
DIAGNOSTIC-IC. COMPLETED-TED. DOOP!
AAAH!
AAAH! LOVE THAT GREETING-TING!
WHAT IS THAT?!
OH, THAT'S BEAMER. HE'S THE ONLY RANT I COULD FIX ENOUGH TO GET HIS HIGHER BRAIN FUNCTION COOKING.
COOKING-ING!
DOOP
HOOOOONK

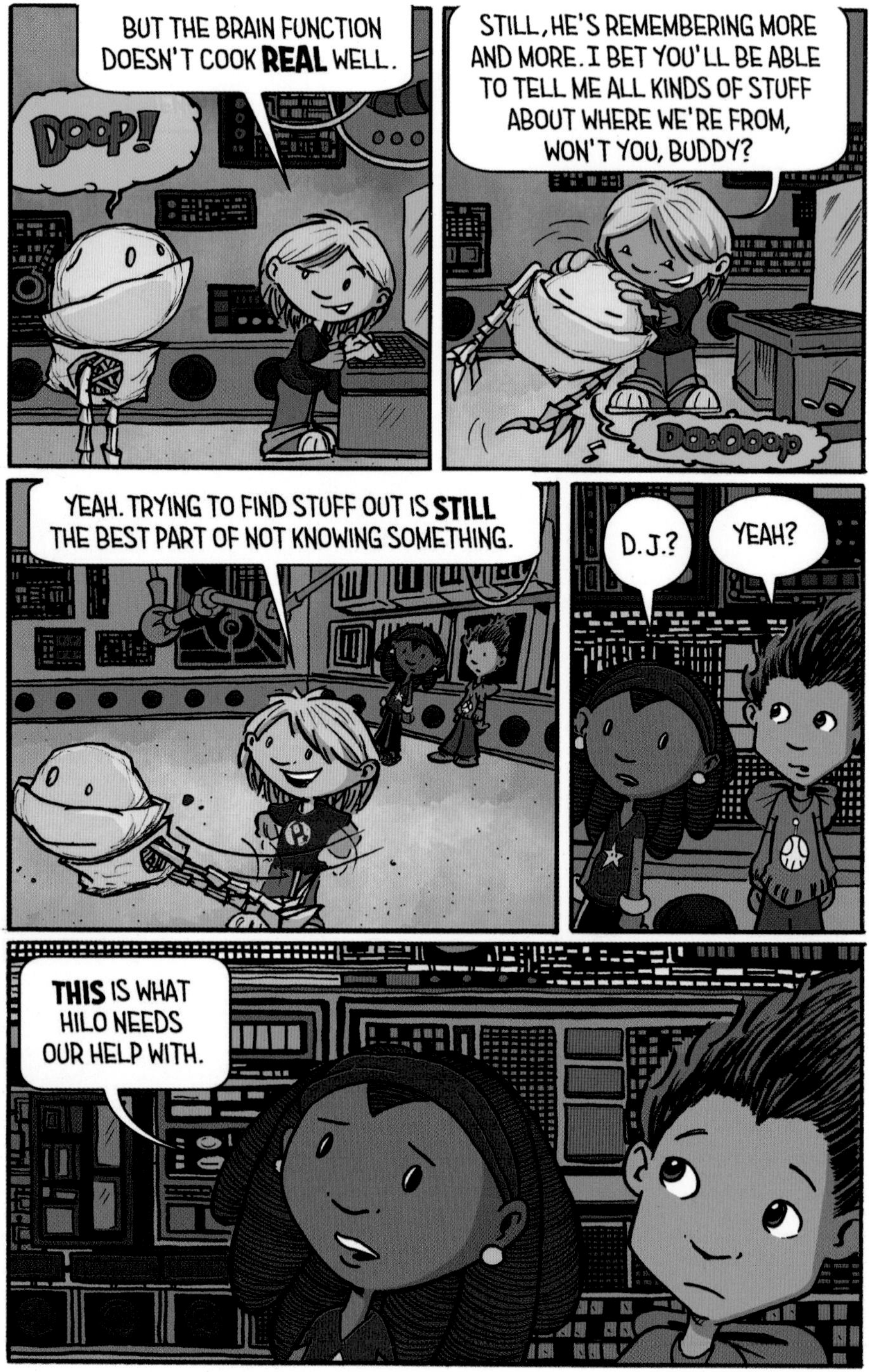
BUT THE BRAIN FUNCTION DOESN'T COOK **REAL** WELL.
DOOP!
STILL, HE'S REMEMBERING MORE AND MORE. I BET YOU'LL BE ABLE TO TELL ME ALL KINDS OF STUFF ABOUT WHERE WE'RE FROM, WON'T YOU, BUDDY?
DOoDOOP
YEAH. TRYING TO FIND STUFF OUT IS **STILL** THE BEST PART OF NOT KNOWING SOMETHING.
D.J.?
YEAH?
THIS IS WHAT HILO NEEDS OUR HELP WITH.

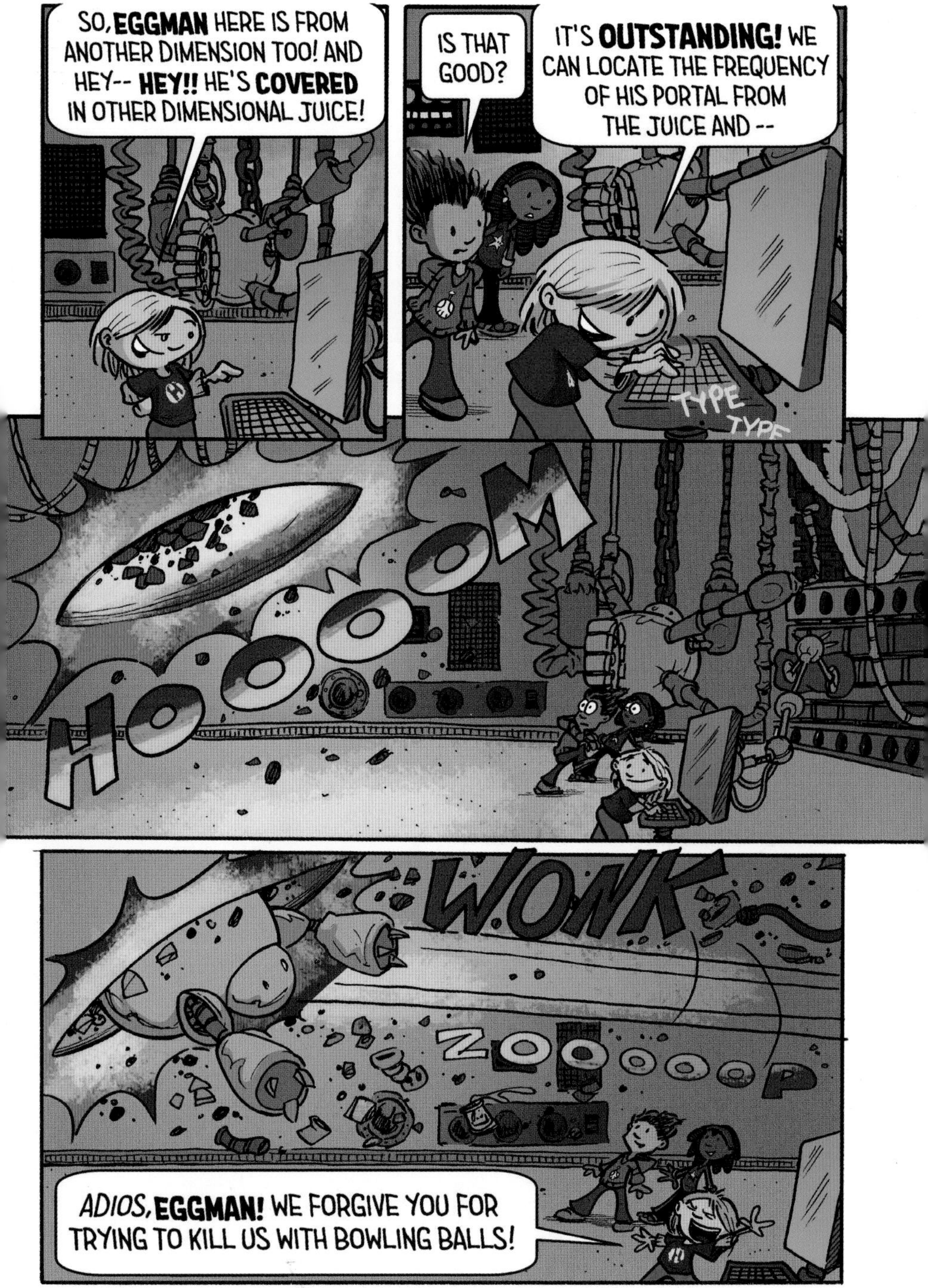
SO, EGGMAN HERE IS FROM ANOTHER DIMENSION TOO! AND HEY-- HEY!! HE'S COVERED IN OTHER DIMENSIONAL JUICE!
IS THAT GOOD?
IT'S OUTSTANDING! WE CAN LOCATE THE FREQUENCY OF HIS PORTAL FROM THE JUICE AND --
TYPE
TYPE
HOOOOOOM
WONK
ZOOOOOOP
ADIOS, EGGMAN! WE FORGIVE YOU FOR TRYING TO KILL US WITH BOWLING BALLS!

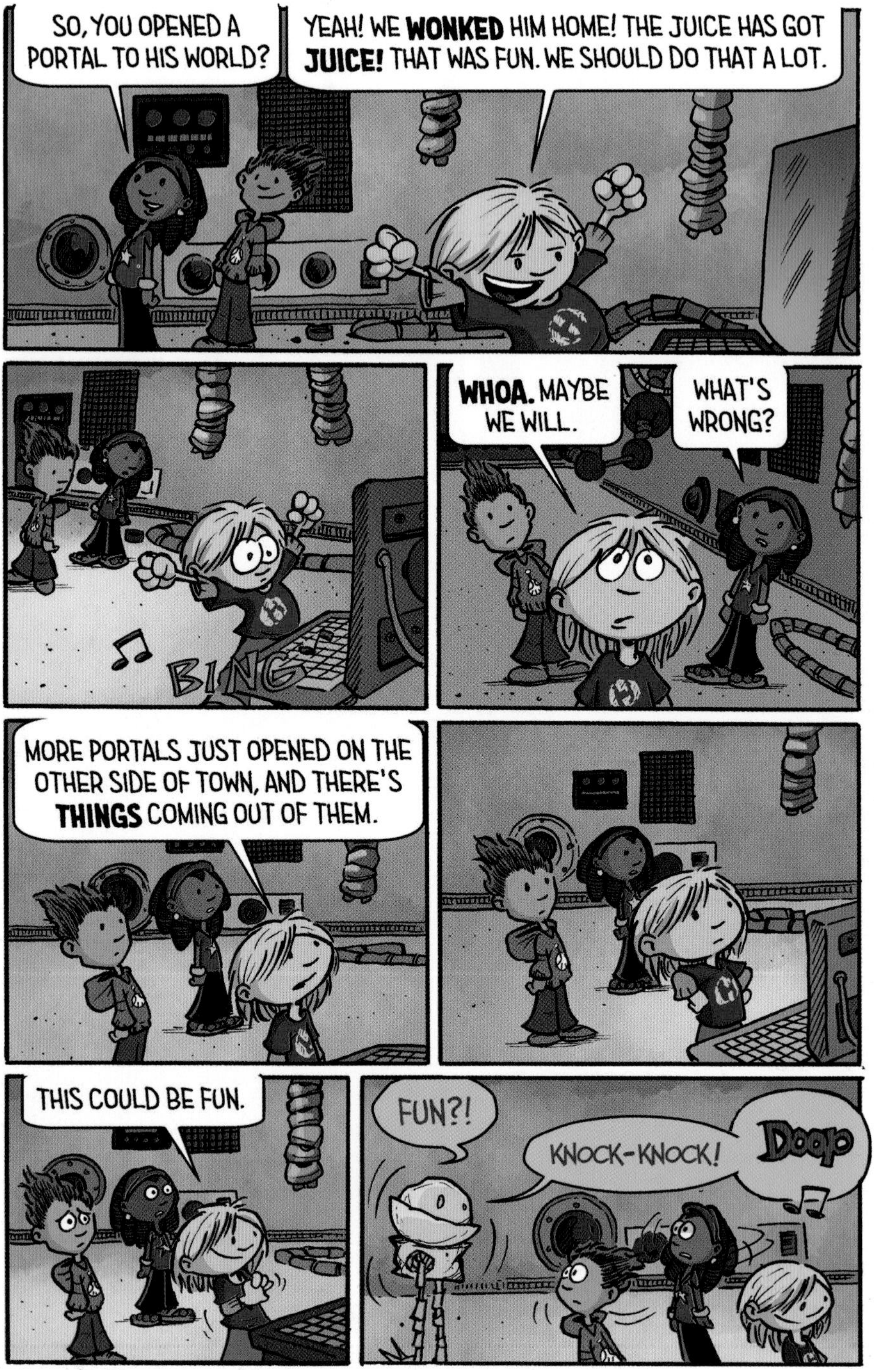
SO, YOU OPENED A PORTAL TO HIS WORLD?
YEAH! WE **WONKED** HIM HOME! THE JUICE HAS GOT **JUICE!** THAT WAS FUN. WE SHOULD DO THAT A LOT.
BING
WHOA. MAYBE WE WILL.
WHAT'S WRONG?
MORE PORTALS JUST OPENED ON THE OTHER SIDE OF TOWN, AND THERE'S **THINGS** COMING OUT OF THEM.
THIS COULD BE FUN.
FUN?!
KNOCK-KNOCK!
Doop

CHAPTER 5

POLLY

HOOOM
WHUMP
RAAAAAAARGH!

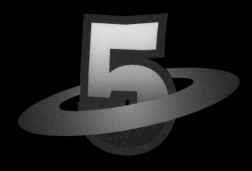

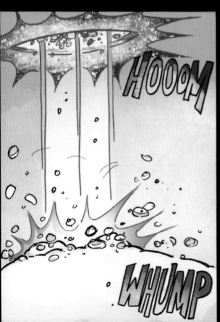

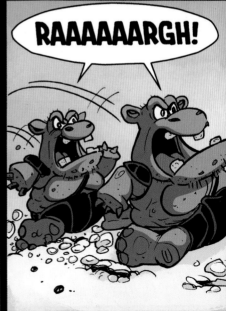

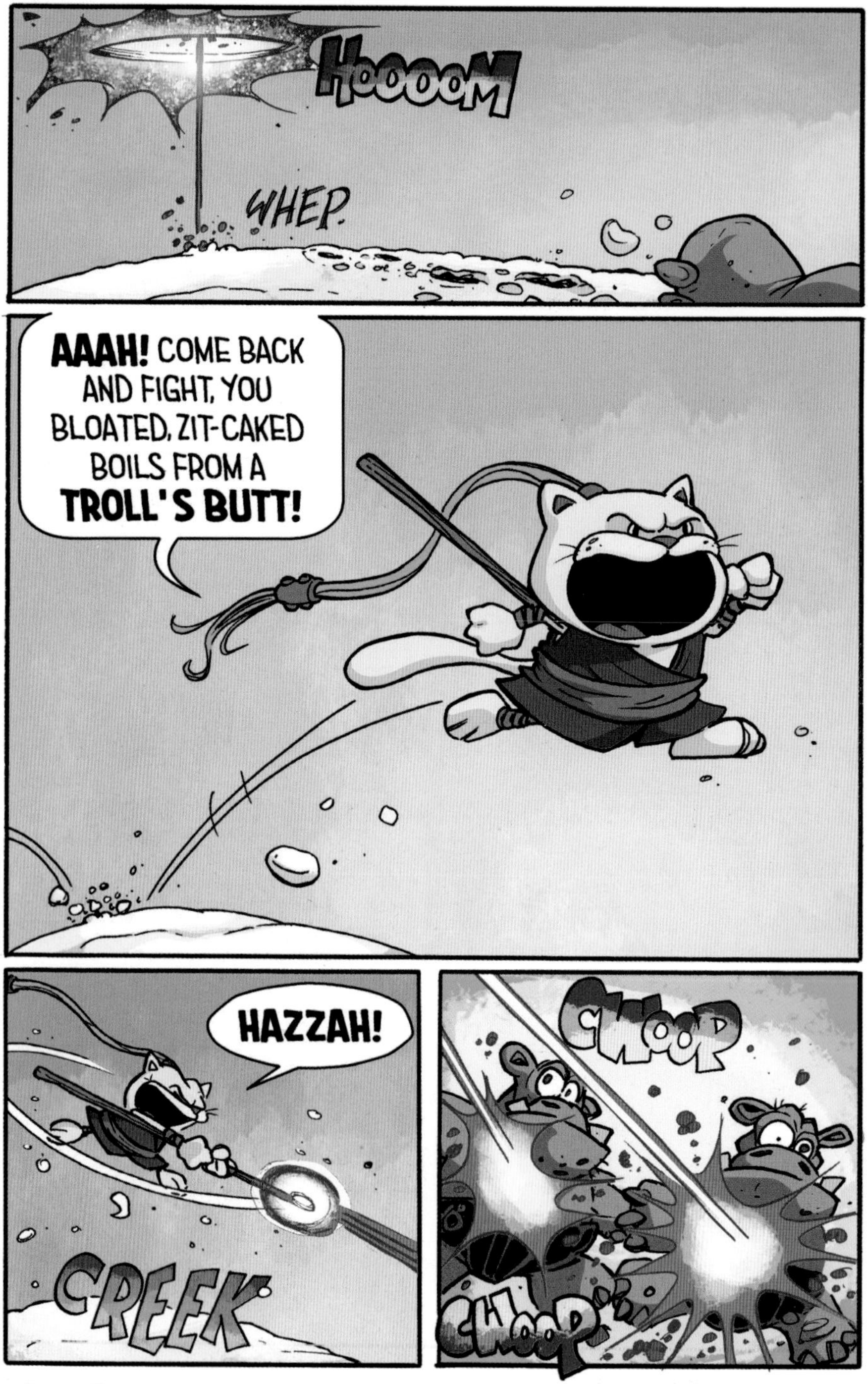
HOOOOOM
WHEP
AAAH! COME BACK AND FIGHT, YOU BLOATED, ZIT-CAKED BOILS FROM A TROLL'S BUTT!
HAZZAH!
CREEK
CHOOP
CHOOP

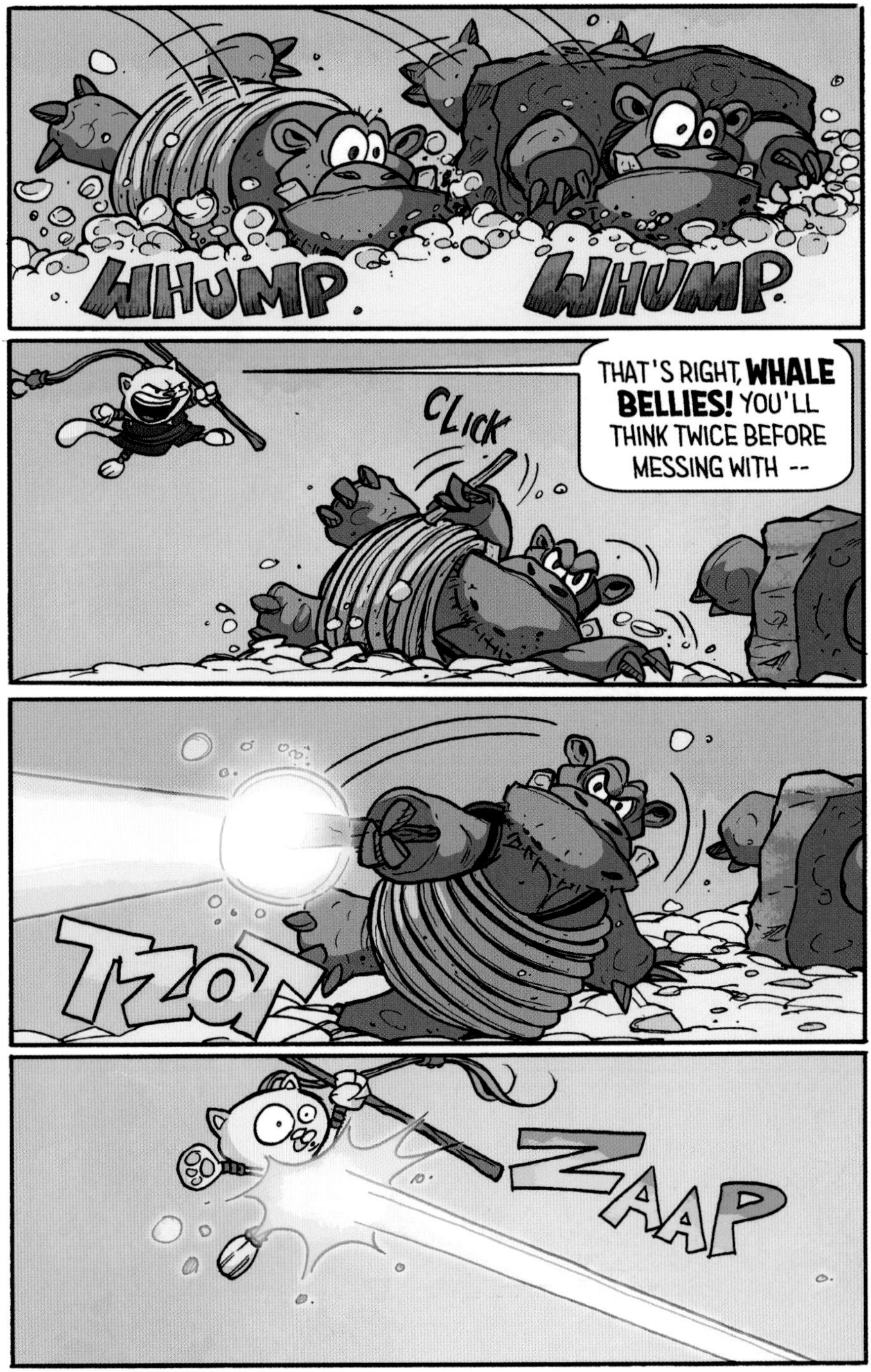
WHUMP
WHUMP
THAT'S RIGHT, WHALE BELLIES! YOU'LL THINK TWICE BEFORE MESSING WITH --
CLICK
TZOT
ZAAP

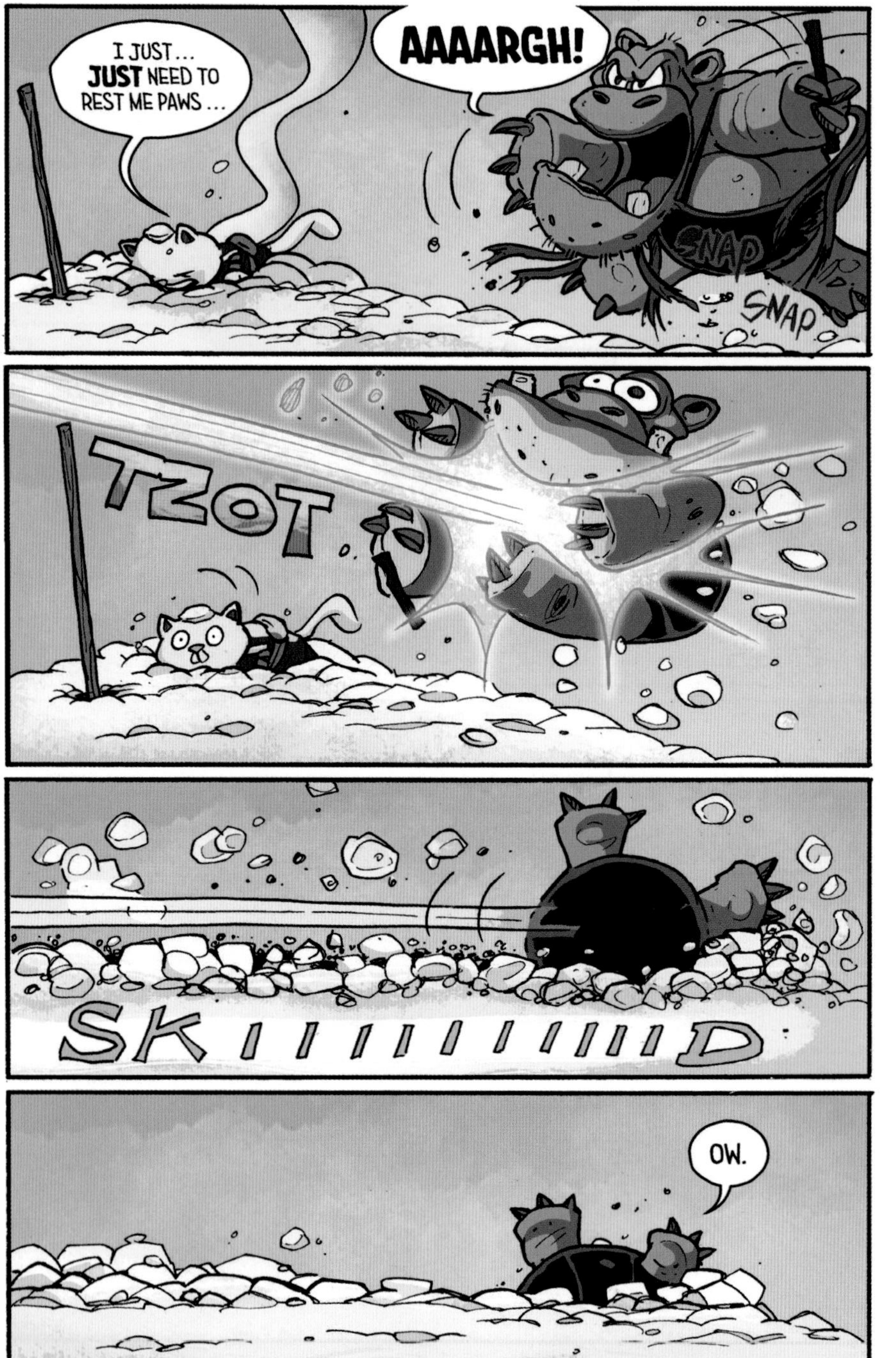

I JUST... JUST NEED TO REST ME PAWS...
AAAARGH!
SNAP
SNAP
TZOT
SKIIIIIIIID
OW.

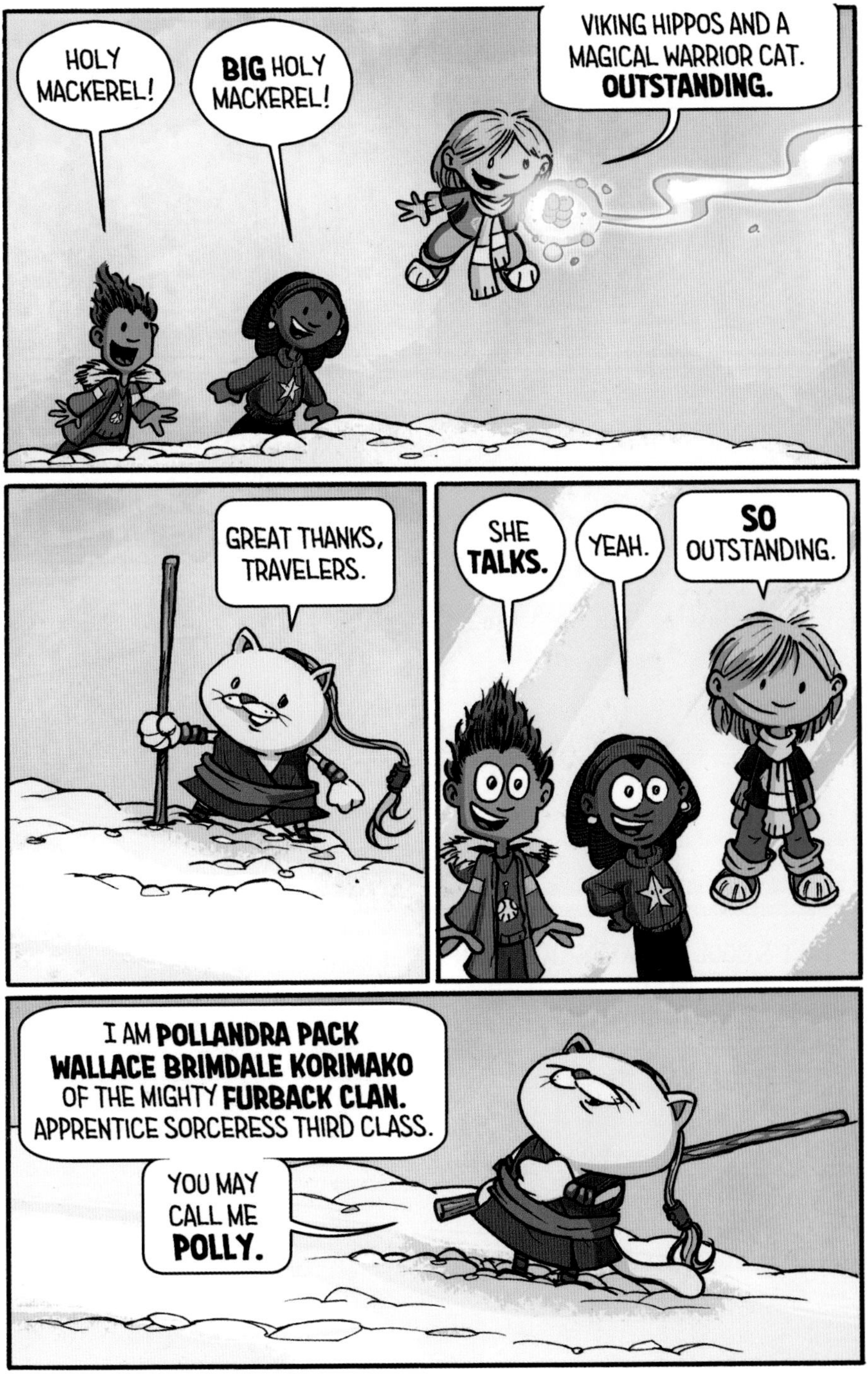
HOLY MACKEREL!
BIG HOLY MACKEREL!
VIKING HIPPOS AND A MAGICAL WARRIOR CAT. OUTSTANDING.
GREAT THANKS, TRAVELERS.
SHE TALKS.
YEAH.
SO OUTSTANDING.
I AM POLLANDRA PACK WALLACE BRIMDALE KORIMAKO OF THE MIGHTY FURBACK CLAN. APPRENTICE SORCERESS THIRD CLASS.
YOU MAY CALL ME POLLY.

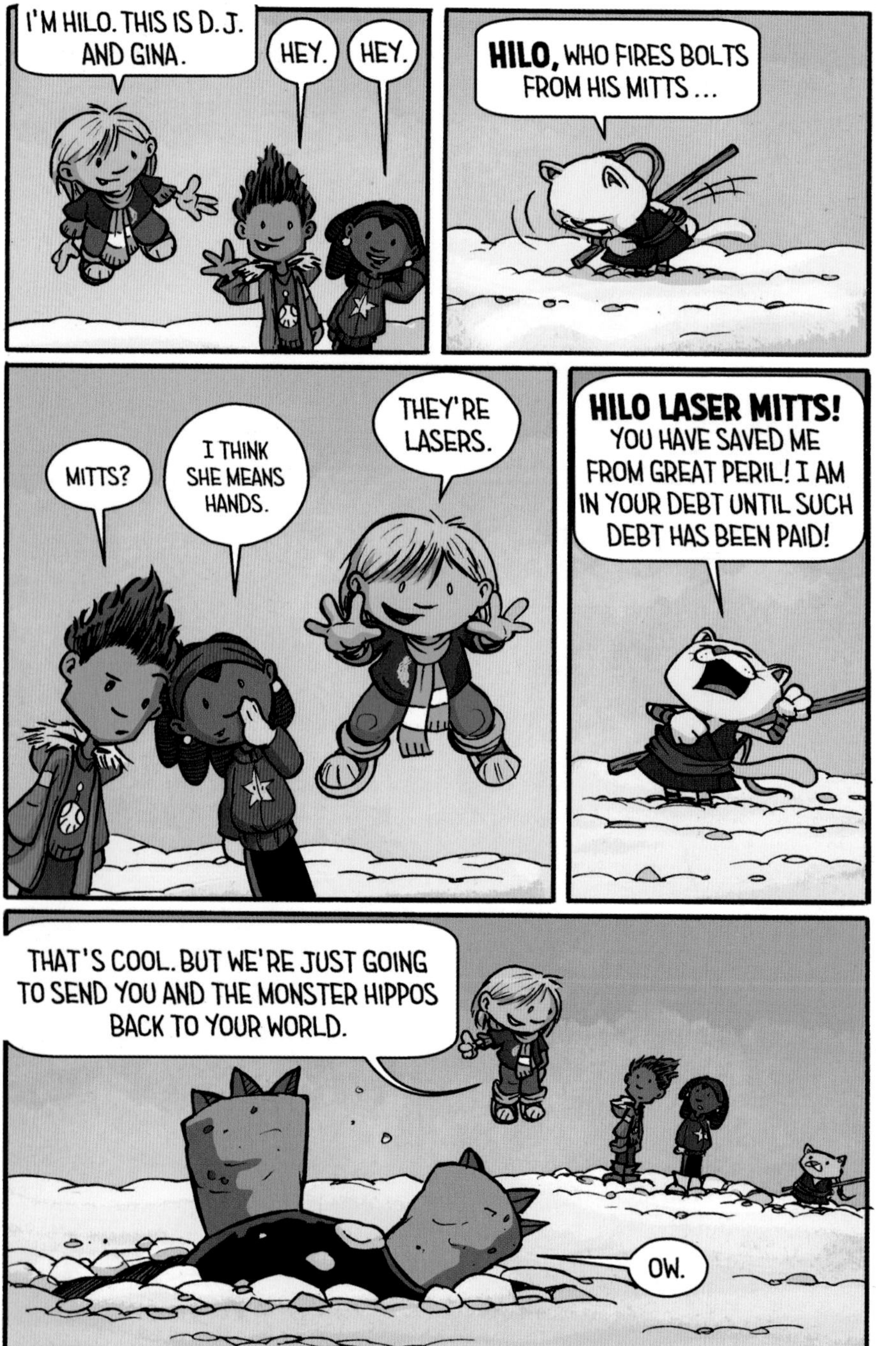
I'M HILO. THIS IS D.J. AND GINA.
HEY.
HEY.
HILO, WHO FIRES BOLTS FROM HIS MITTS ...
MITTS?
I THINK SHE MEANS HANDS.
THEY'RE LASERS.
HILO LASER MITTS! YOU HAVE SAVED ME FROM GREAT PERIL! I AM IN YOUR DEBT UNTIL SUCH DEBT HAS BEEN PAID!
THAT'S COOL. BUT WE'RE JUST GOING TO SEND YOU AND THE MONSTER HIPPOS BACK TO YOUR WORLD.
OW.

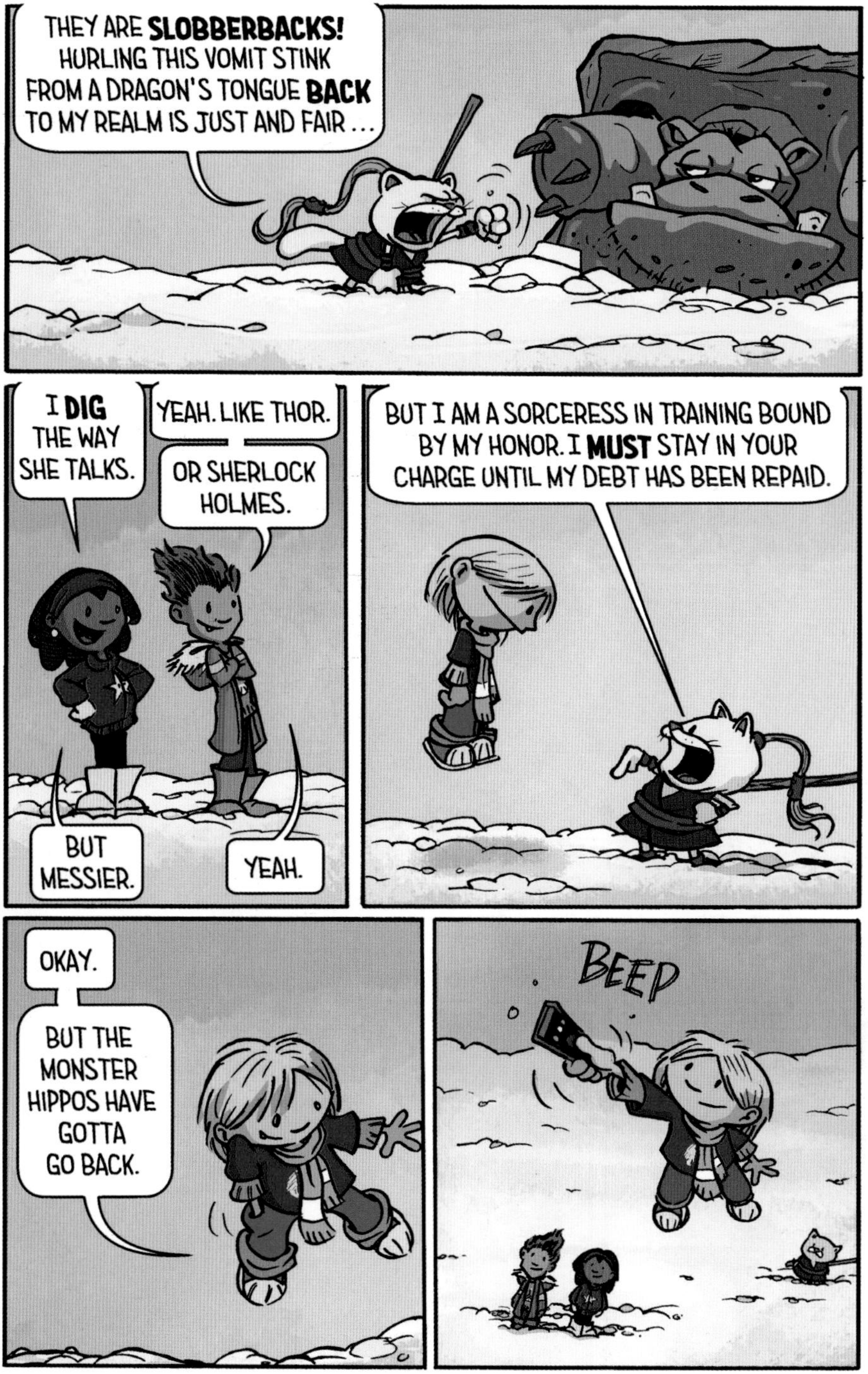
THEY ARE SLOBBERBACKS! HURLING THIS VOMIT STINK FROM A DRAGON'S TONGUE BACK TO MY REALM IS JUST AND FAIR . . .
I DIG THE WAY SHE TALKS.
YEAH. LIKE THOR.
OR SHERLOCK HOLMES.
BUT MESSIER.
YEAH.
BUT I AM A SORCERESS IN TRAINING BOUND BY MY HONOR. I MUST STAY IN YOUR CHARGE UNTIL MY DEBT HAS BEEN REPAID.
OKAY.
BUT THE MONSTER HIPPOS HAVE GOTTA GO BACK.
BEEP

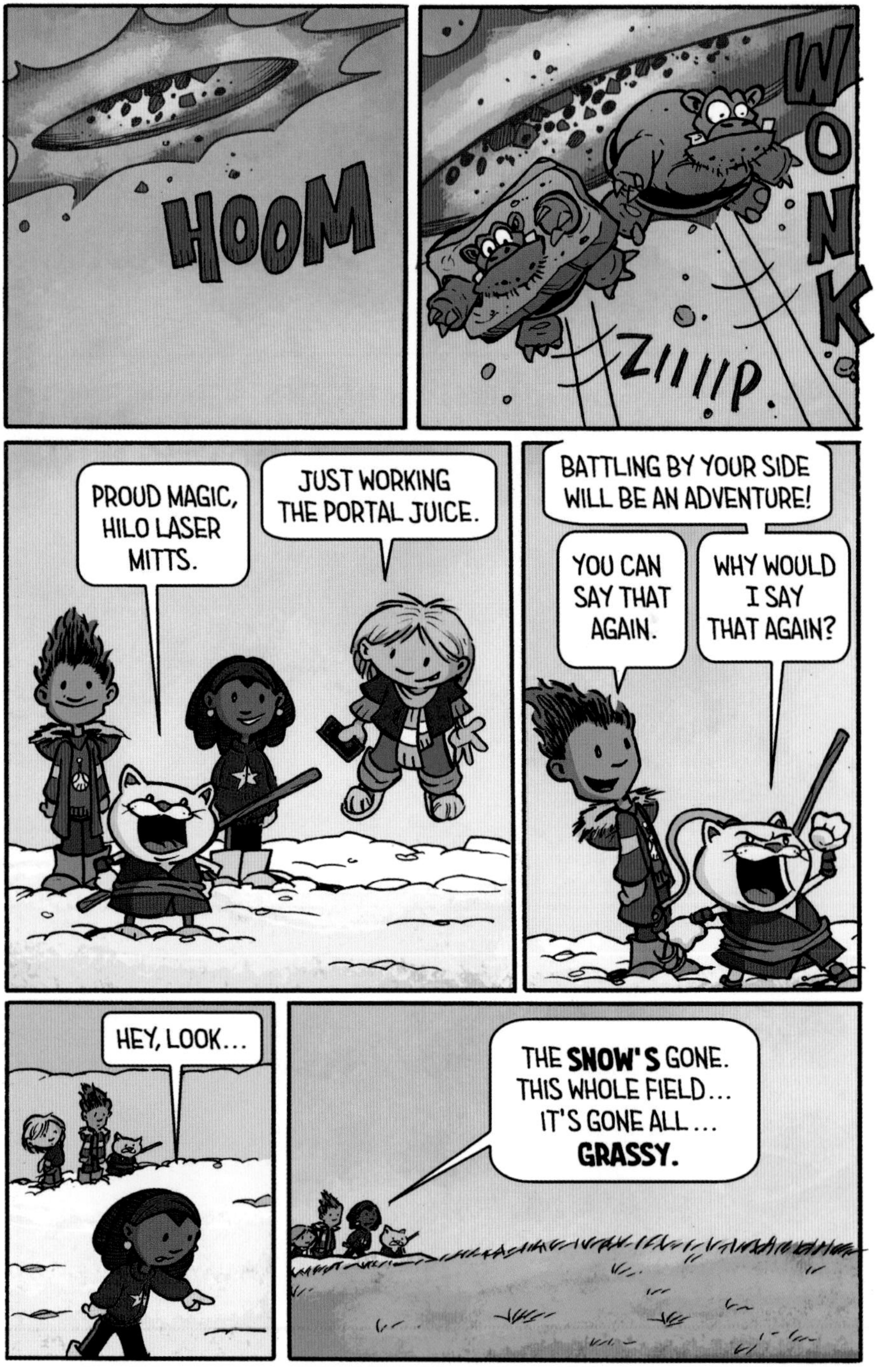
HOOM
WONK
ZIIIIP.
PROUD MAGIC, HILO LASER MITTS.
JUST WORKING THE PORTAL JUICE.
BATTLING BY YOUR SIDE WILL BE AN ADVENTURE!
YOU CAN SAY THAT AGAIN.
WHY WOULD I SAY THAT AGAIN?
HEY, LOOK...
THE **SNOW'S** GONE. THIS WHOLE FIELD... IT'S GONE ALL... **GRASSY.**

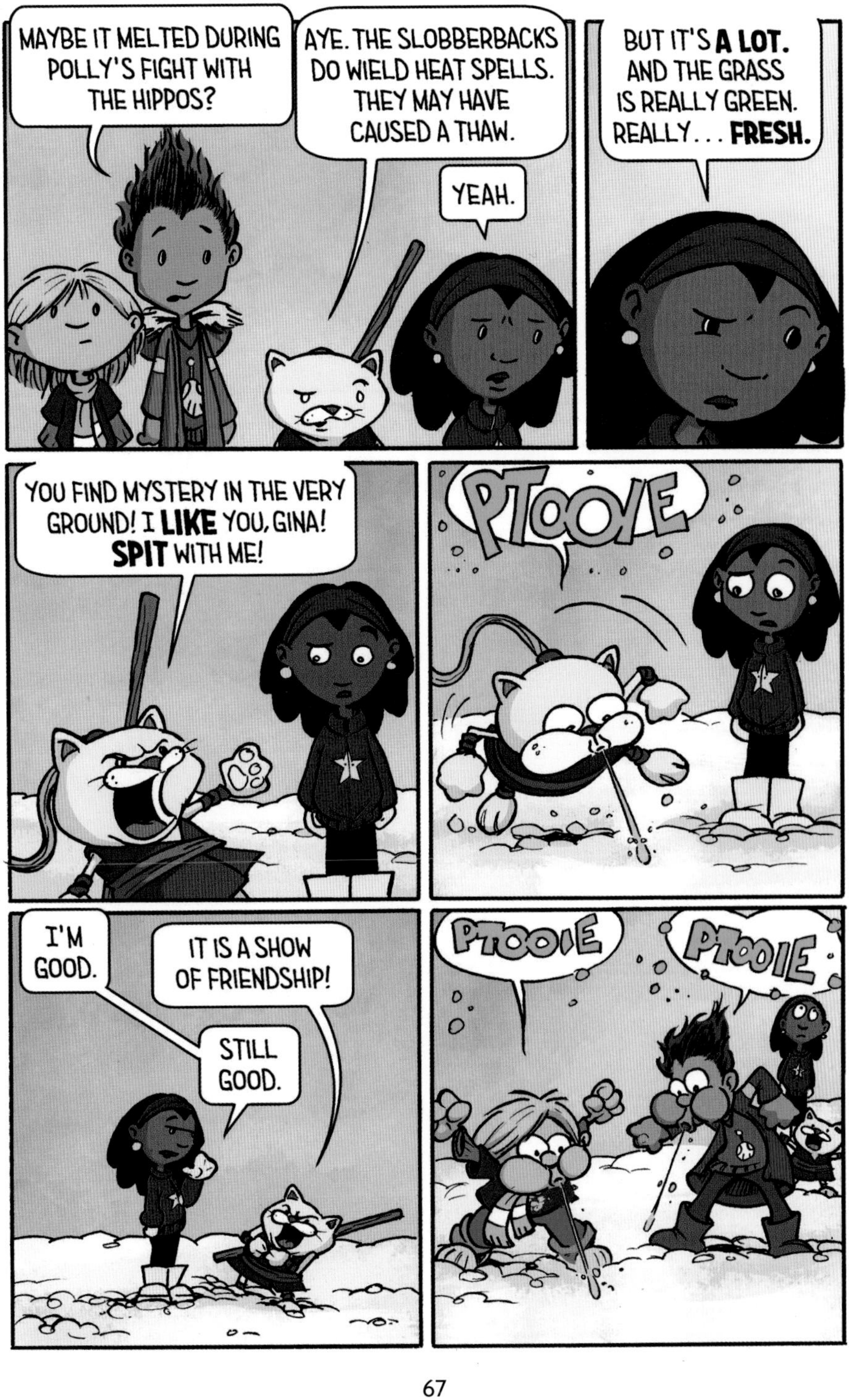
MAYBE IT MELTED DURING POLLY'S FIGHT WITH THE HIPPOS?
AYE. THE SLOBBERBACKS DO WIELD HEAT SPELLS. THEY MAY HAVE CAUSED A THAW.
YEAH.
BUT IT'S A LOT. AND THE GRASS IS REALLY GREEN. REALLY . . . FRESH.
YOU FIND MYSTERY IN THE VERY GROUND! I LIKE YOU, GINA! SPIT WITH ME!
PTOOIE
I'M GOOD.
IT IS A SHOW OF FRIENDSHIP!
STILL GOOD.
PTOOIE
PTOOIE

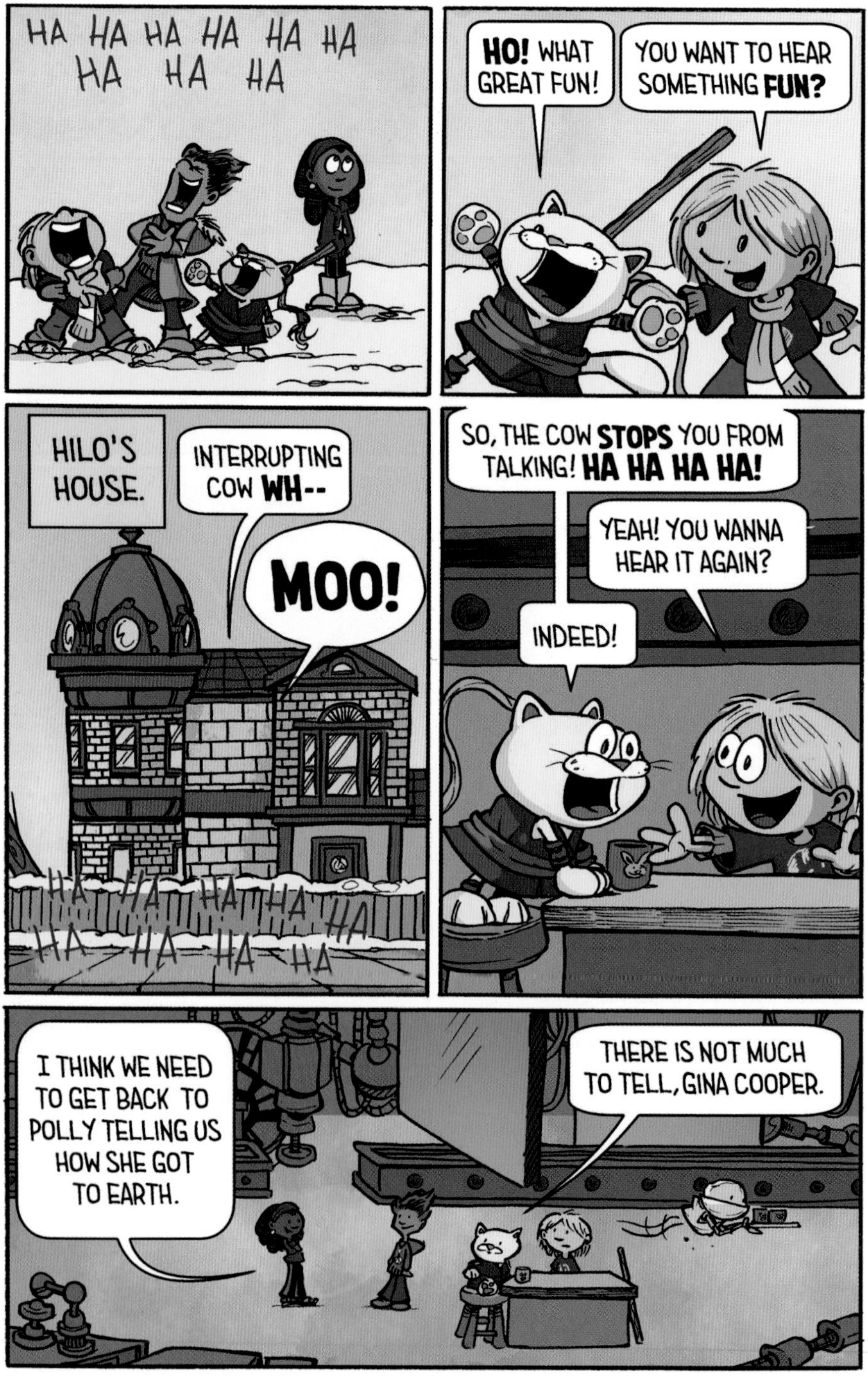
HA HA HA HA HA HA
HA HA HA
HO! WHAT GREAT FUN!
YOU WANT TO HEAR SOMETHING FUN?
HILO'S HOUSE.
INTERRUPTING COW WH--
MOO!
HA HA HA HA HA HA HA HA HA
SO, THE COW STOPS YOU FROM TALKING! HA HA HA HA!
YEAH! YOU WANNA HEAR IT AGAIN?
INDEED!
I THINK WE NEED TO GET BACK TO POLLY TELLING US HOW SHE GOT TO EARTH.
THERE IS NOT MUCH TO TELL, GINA COOPER.

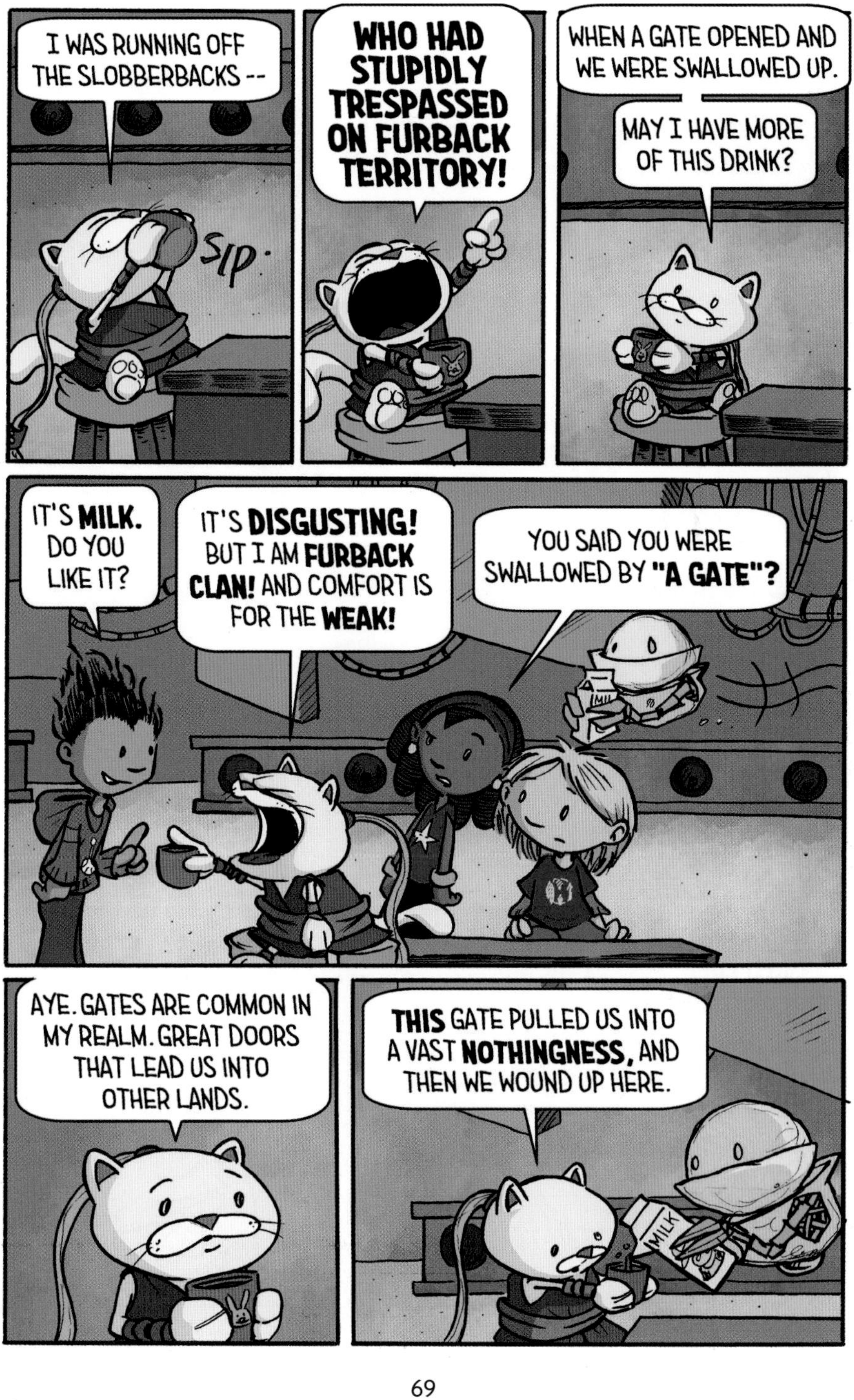
I WAS RUNNING OFF THE SLOBBERBACKS --
SIP.
WHO HAD STUPIDLY TRESPASSED ON FURBACK TERRITORY!
WHEN A GATE OPENED AND WE WERE SWALLOWED UP.
MAY I HAVE MORE OF THIS DRINK?
IT'S MILK. DO YOU LIKE IT?
IT'S DISGUSTING! BUT I AM FURBACK CLAN! AND COMFORT IS FOR THE WEAK!
YOU SAID YOU WERE SWALLOWED BY "A GATE"?
AYE. GATES ARE COMMON IN MY REALM. GREAT DOORS THAT LEAD US INTO OTHER LANDS.
THIS GATE PULLED US INTO A VAST NOTHINGNESS, AND THEN WE WOUND UP HERE.
MILK

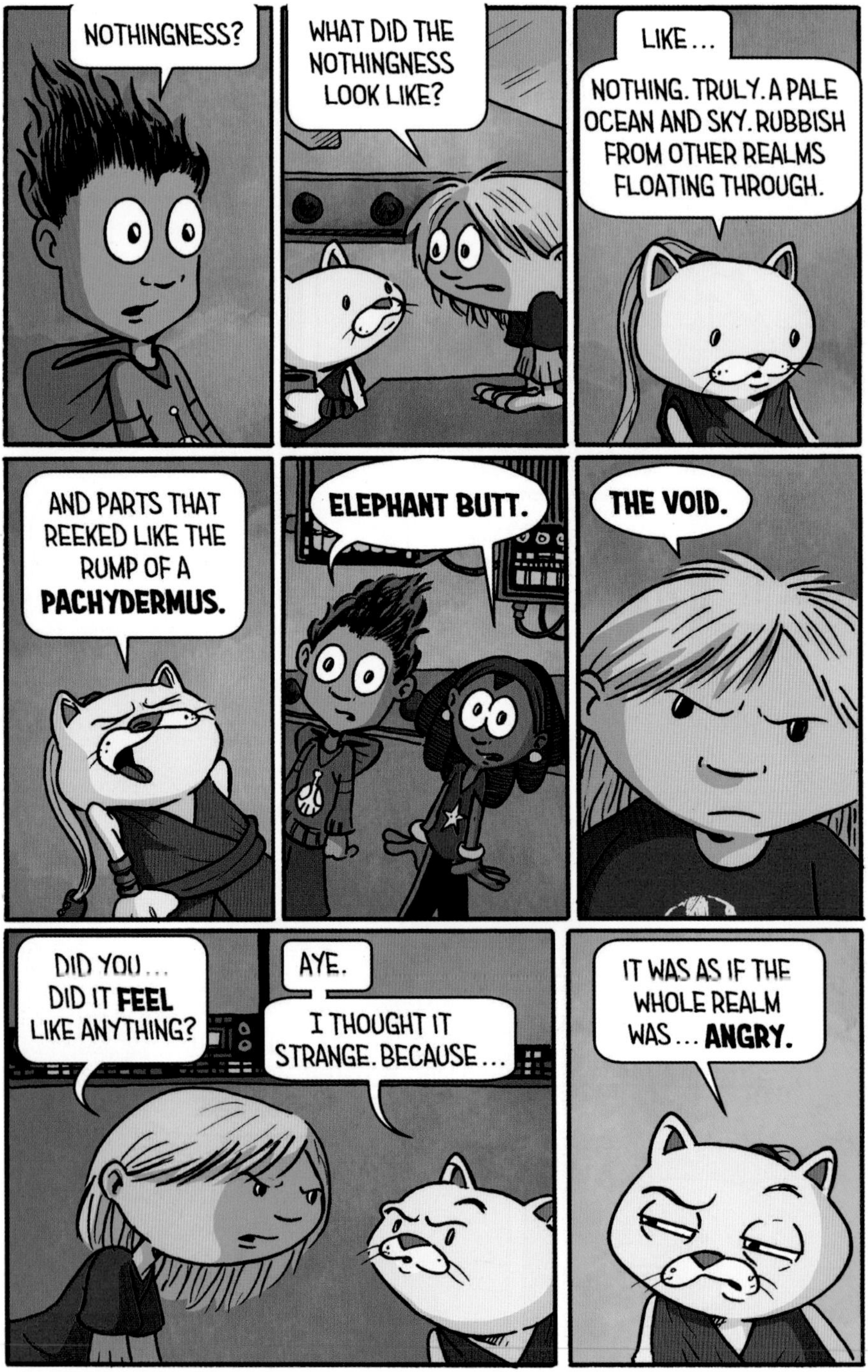
NOTHINGNESS?
WHAT DID THE NOTHINGNESS LOOK LIKE?
LIKE...
NOTHING. TRULY. A PALE OCEAN AND SKY. RUBBISH FROM OTHER REALMS FLOATING THROUGH.
AND PARTS THAT REEKED LIKE THE RUMP OF A **PACHYDERMUS.**
ELEPHANT BUTT.
THE VOID.
DID YOU... DID IT **FEEL** LIKE ANYTHING?
AYE.
I THOUGHT IT STRANGE. BECAUSE...
IT WAS AS IF THE WHOLE REALM WAS... **ANGRY.**

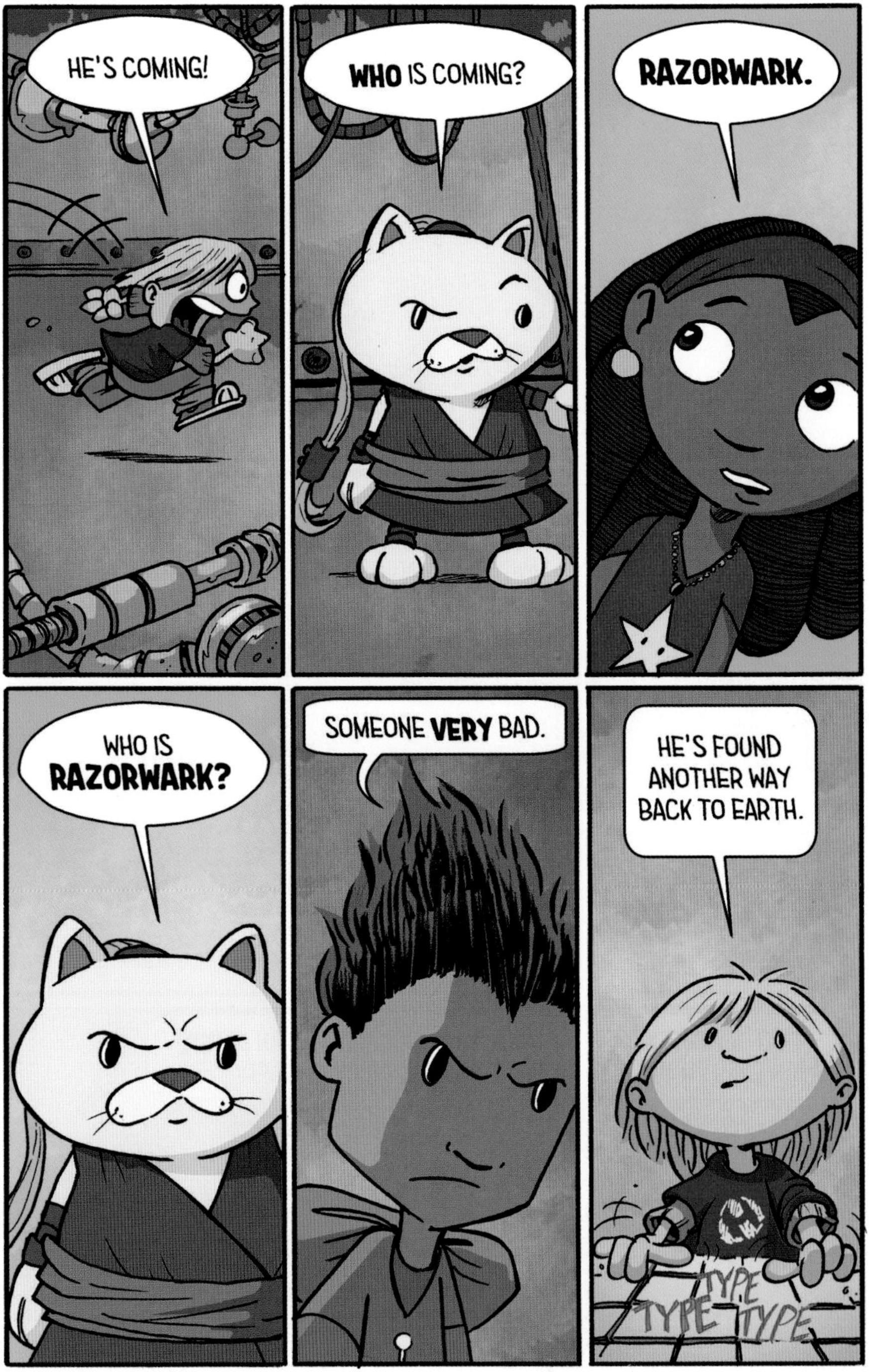
HE'S COMING!
WHO IS COMING?
RAZORWARK.
WHO IS **RAZORWARK?**
SOMEONE **VERY** BAD.
HE'S FOUND ANOTHER WAY BACK TO EARTH.
TYPE TYPE TYPE TYPE

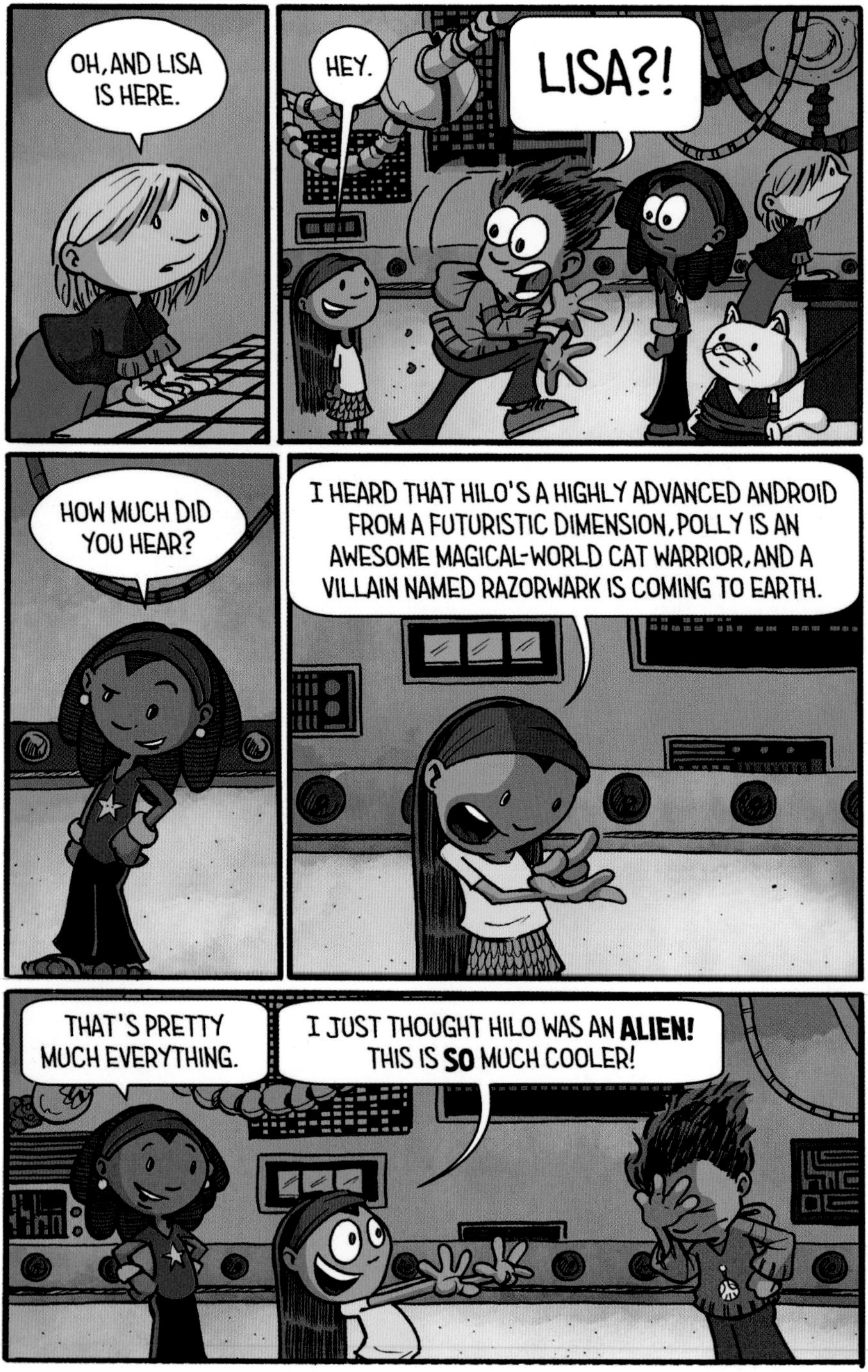
OH, AND LISA IS HERE.
HEY.
LISA?!
HOW MUCH DID YOU HEAR?
I HEARD THAT HILO'S A HIGHLY ADVANCED ANDROID FROM A FUTURISTIC DIMENSION, POLLY IS AN AWESOME MAGICAL-WORLD CAT WARRIOR, AND A VILLAIN NAMED RAZORWARK IS COMING TO EARTH.
THAT'S PRETTY MUCH EVERYTHING.
I JUST THOUGHT HILO WAS AN **ALIEN!** THIS IS **SO** MUCH COOLER!

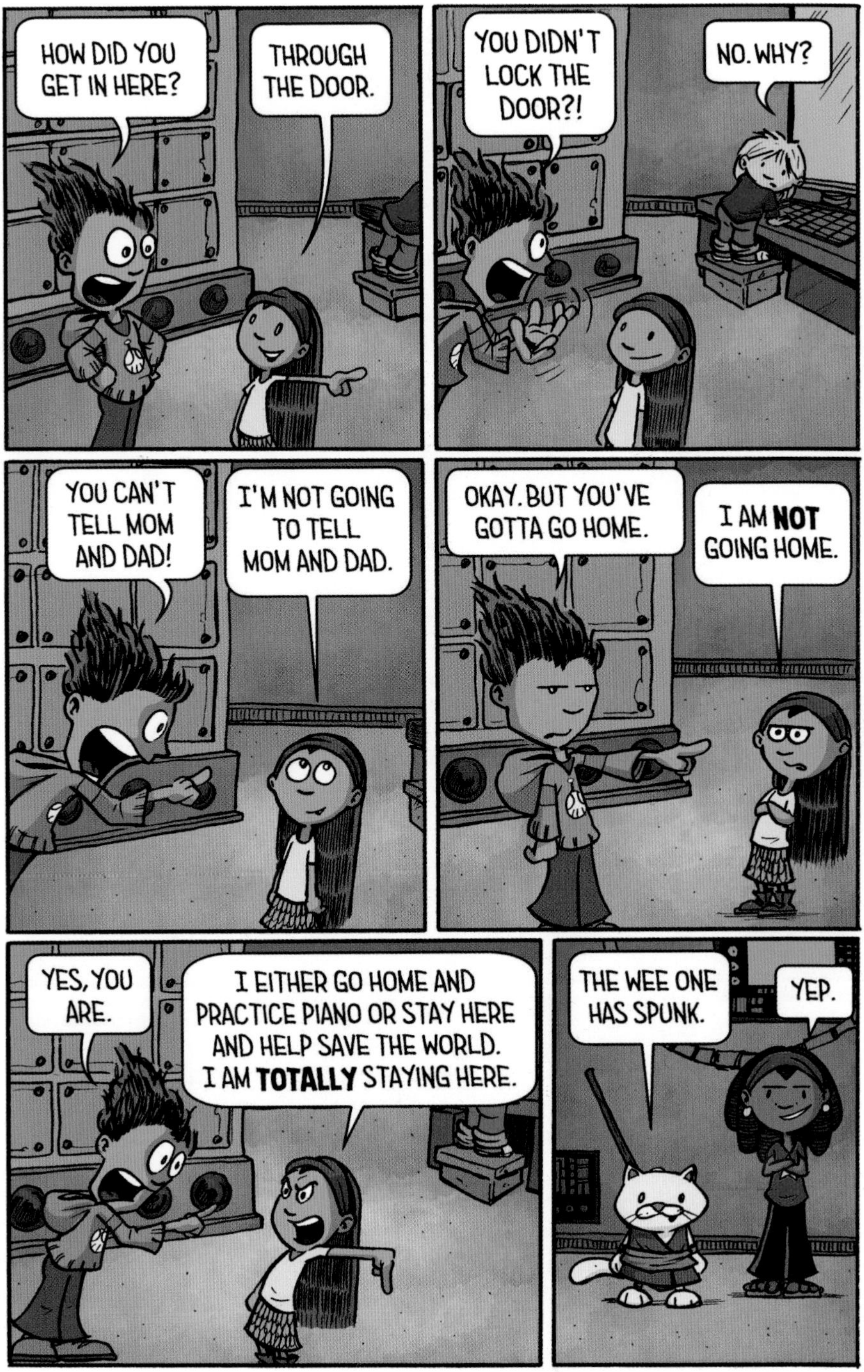
HOW DID YOU GET IN HERE?
THROUGH THE DOOR.
YOU DIDN'T LOCK THE DOOR?!
NO. WHY?
YOU CAN'T TELL MOM AND DAD!
I'M NOT GOING TO TELL MOM AND DAD.
OKAY. BUT YOU'VE GOTTA GO HOME.
I AM **NOT** GOING HOME.
YES, YOU ARE.
I EITHER GO HOME AND PRACTICE PIANO OR STAY HERE AND HELP SAVE THE WORLD. I AM **TOTALLY** STAYING HERE.
THE WEE ONE HAS SPUNK.
YEP.

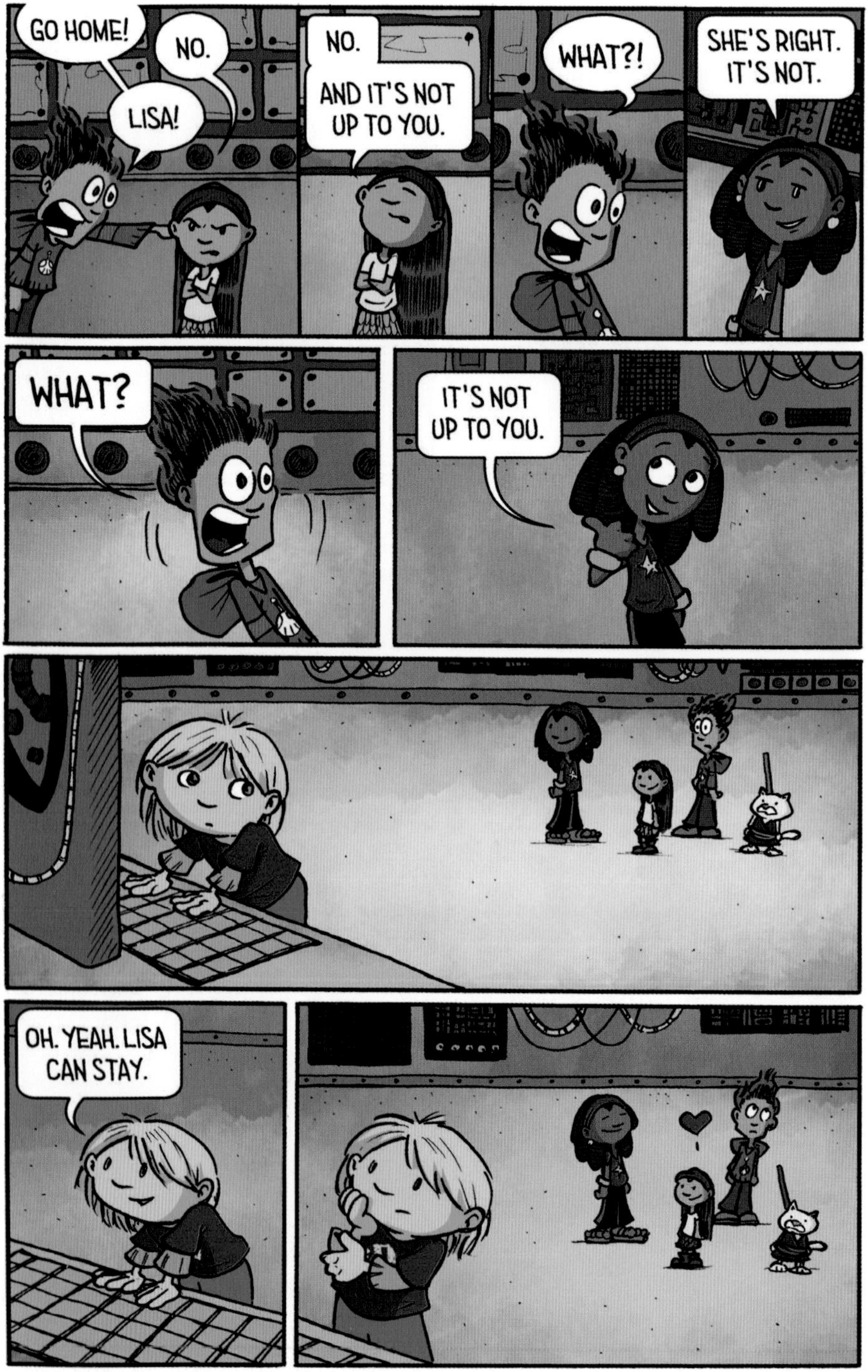
GO HOME!
NO.
LISA!
NO.
AND IT'S NOT UP TO YOU.
WHAT?!
SHE'S RIGHT. IT'S NOT.
WHAT?
IT'S NOT UP TO YOU.
OH. YEAH. LISA CAN STAY.

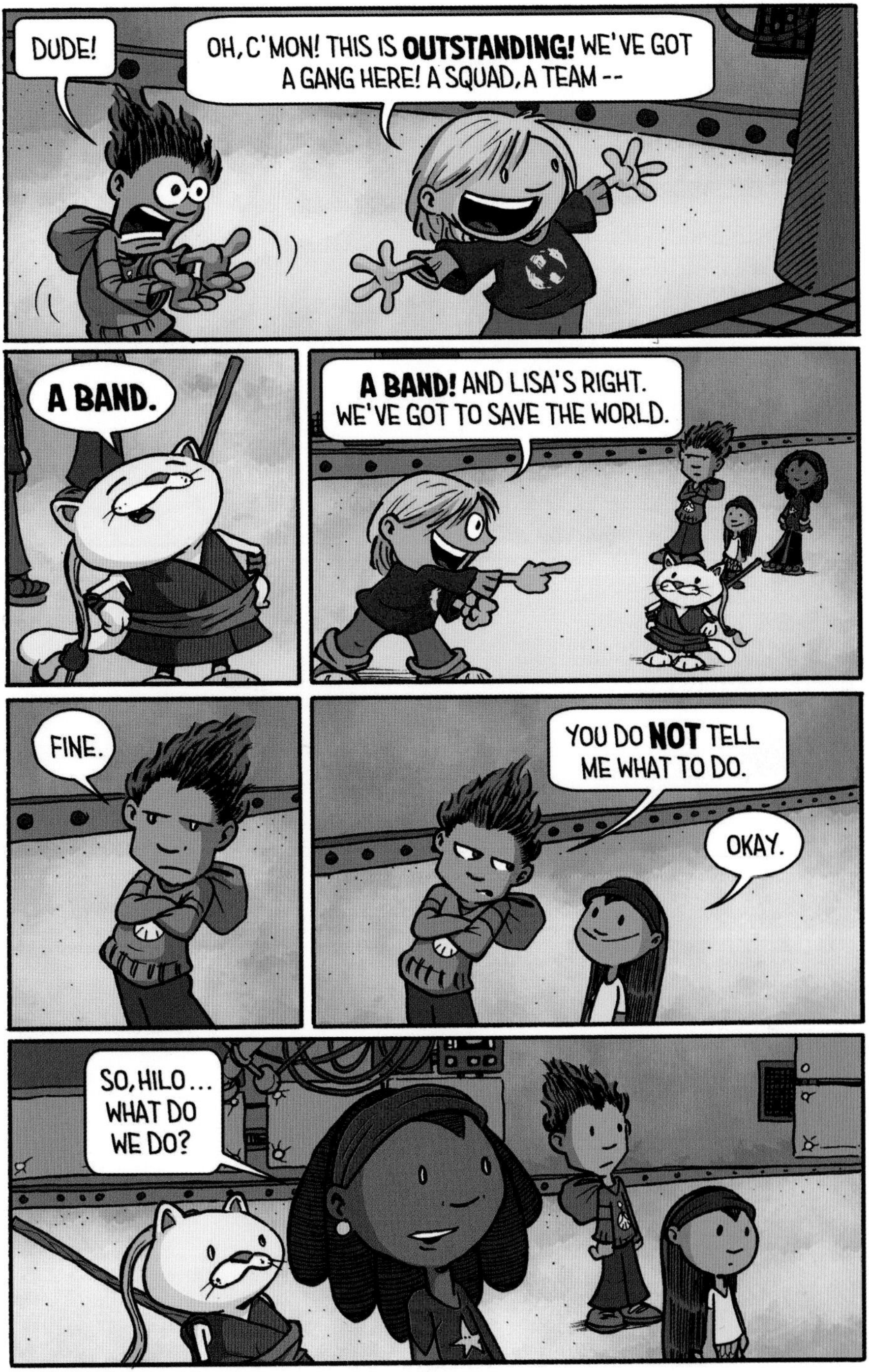
DUDE!
OH, C'MON! THIS IS **OUTSTANDING!** WE'VE GOT A GANG HERE! A SQUAD, A TEAM --
A BAND.
A BAND! AND LISA'S RIGHT. WE'VE GOT TO SAVE THE WORLD.
FINE.
YOU DO **NOT** TELL ME WHAT TO DO.
OKAY.
SO, HILO... WHAT DO WE DO?

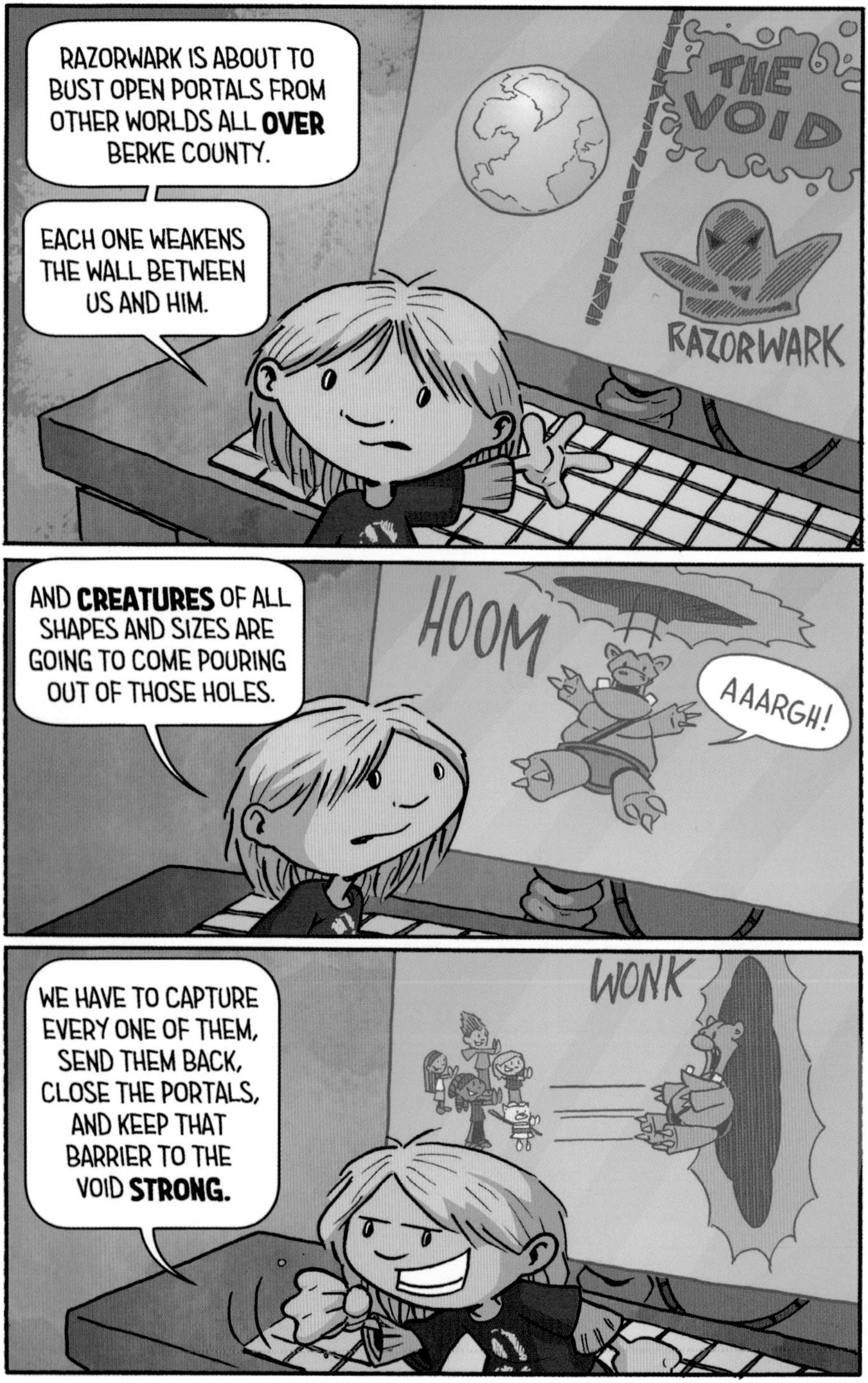
RAZORWARK IS ABOUT TO BUST OPEN PORTALS FROM OTHER WORLDS ALL **OVER** BERKE COUNTY.
EACH ONE WEAKENS THE WALL BETWEEN US AND HIM.
THE VOID
RAZORWARK
AND **CREATURES** OF ALL SHAPES AND SIZES ARE GOING TO COME POURING OUT OF THOSE HOLES.
HOOM
AAARGH!
WE HAVE TO CAPTURE EVERY ONE OF THEM, SEND THEM BACK, CLOSE THE PORTALS, AND KEEP THAT BARRIER TO THE VOID **STRONG.**
WONK

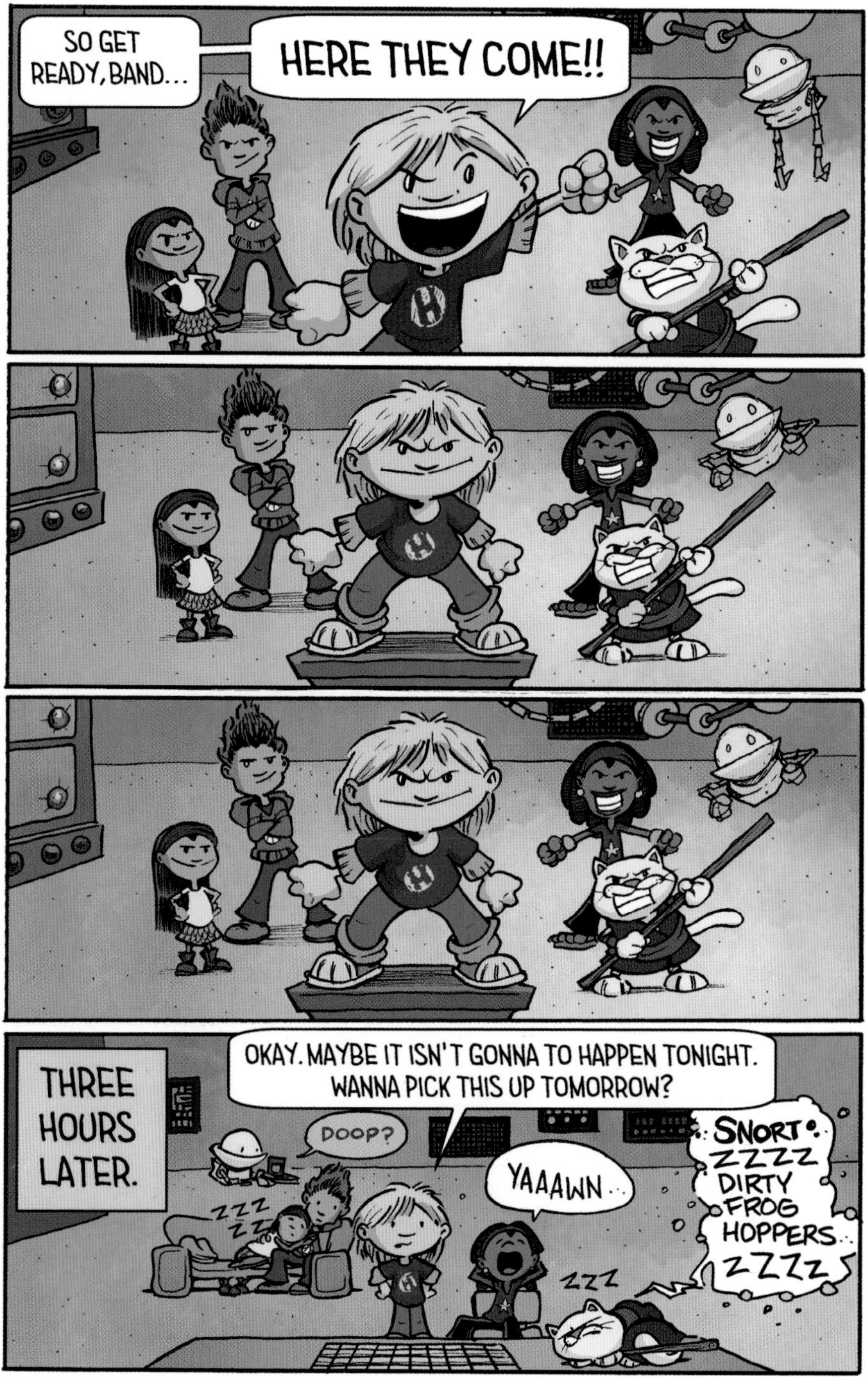
SO GET READY, BAND...
HERE THEY COME!!
THREE HOURS LATER.
OKAY. MAYBE IT ISN'T GONNA TO HAPPEN TONIGHT. WANNA PICK THIS UP TOMORROW?
DOOP?
YAAAWN...
ZZZ ZZ
SNORT ZZZZ DIRTY FROG HOPPERS... ZZZZ
ZZZ

CHAPTER 6

THE BAND

ZZZZZZ
ZZZZ
DR. HORIZON . . . WHEN DID THEY START MAKING ROBOTS?
ZZZZ
158 YEARS AGO.

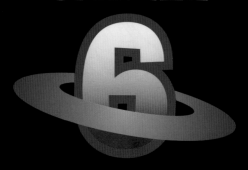

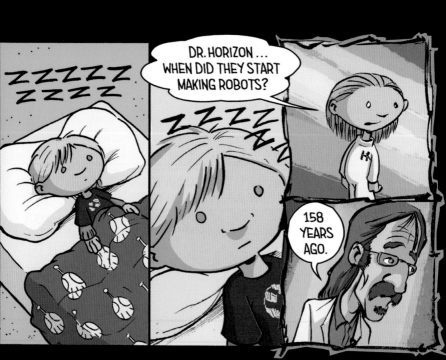

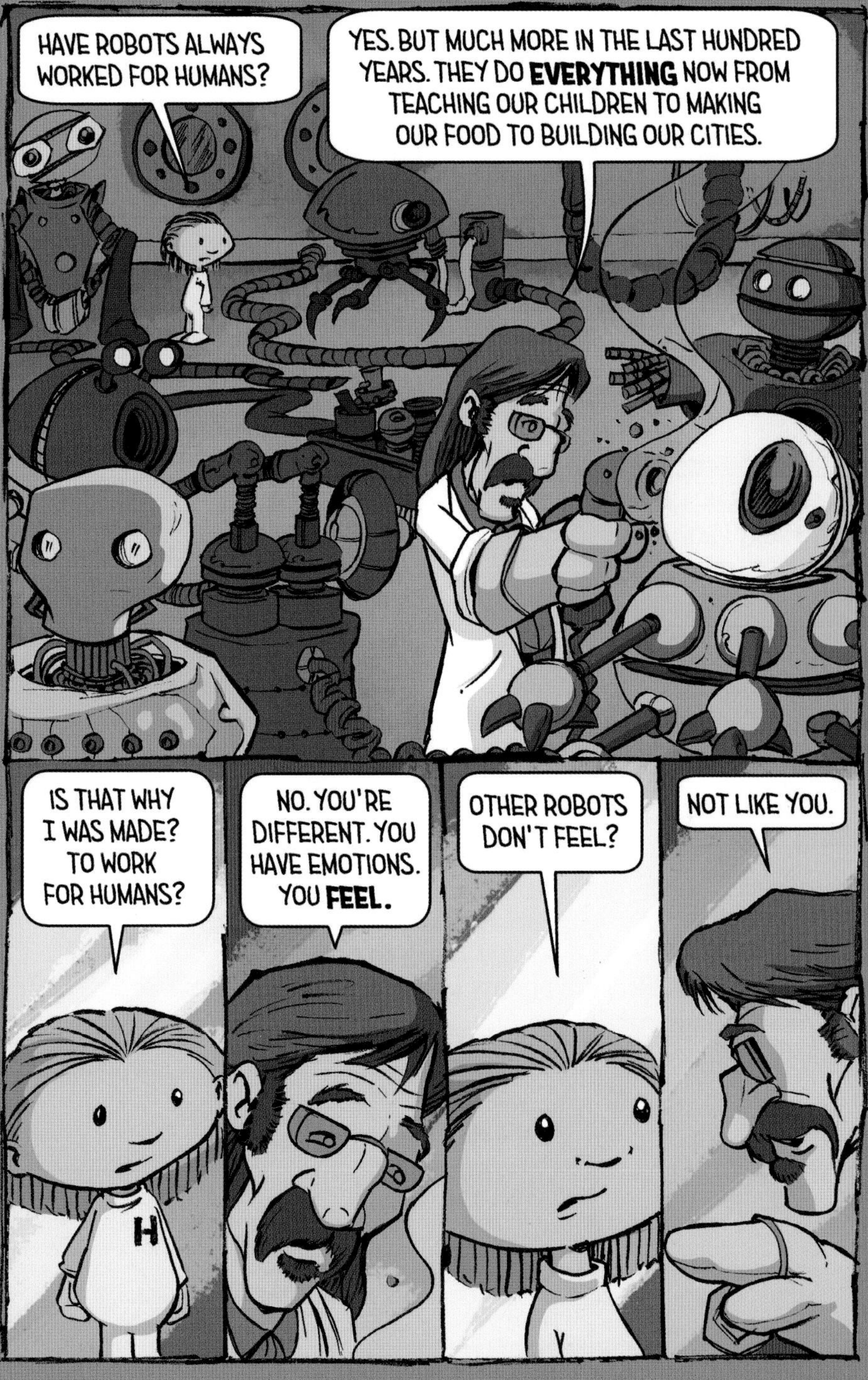
HAVE ROBOTS ALWAYS WORKED FOR HUMANS?
YES. BUT MUCH MORE IN THE LAST HUNDRED YEARS. THEY DO **EVERYTHING** NOW FROM TEACHING OUR CHILDREN TO MAKING OUR FOOD TO BUILDING OUR CITIES.
IS THAT WHY I WAS MADE? TO WORK FOR HUMANS?
NO. YOU'RE DIFFERENT. YOU HAVE EMOTIONS. YOU **FEEL.**
OTHER ROBOTS DON'T FEEL?
NOT LIKE YOU.
H

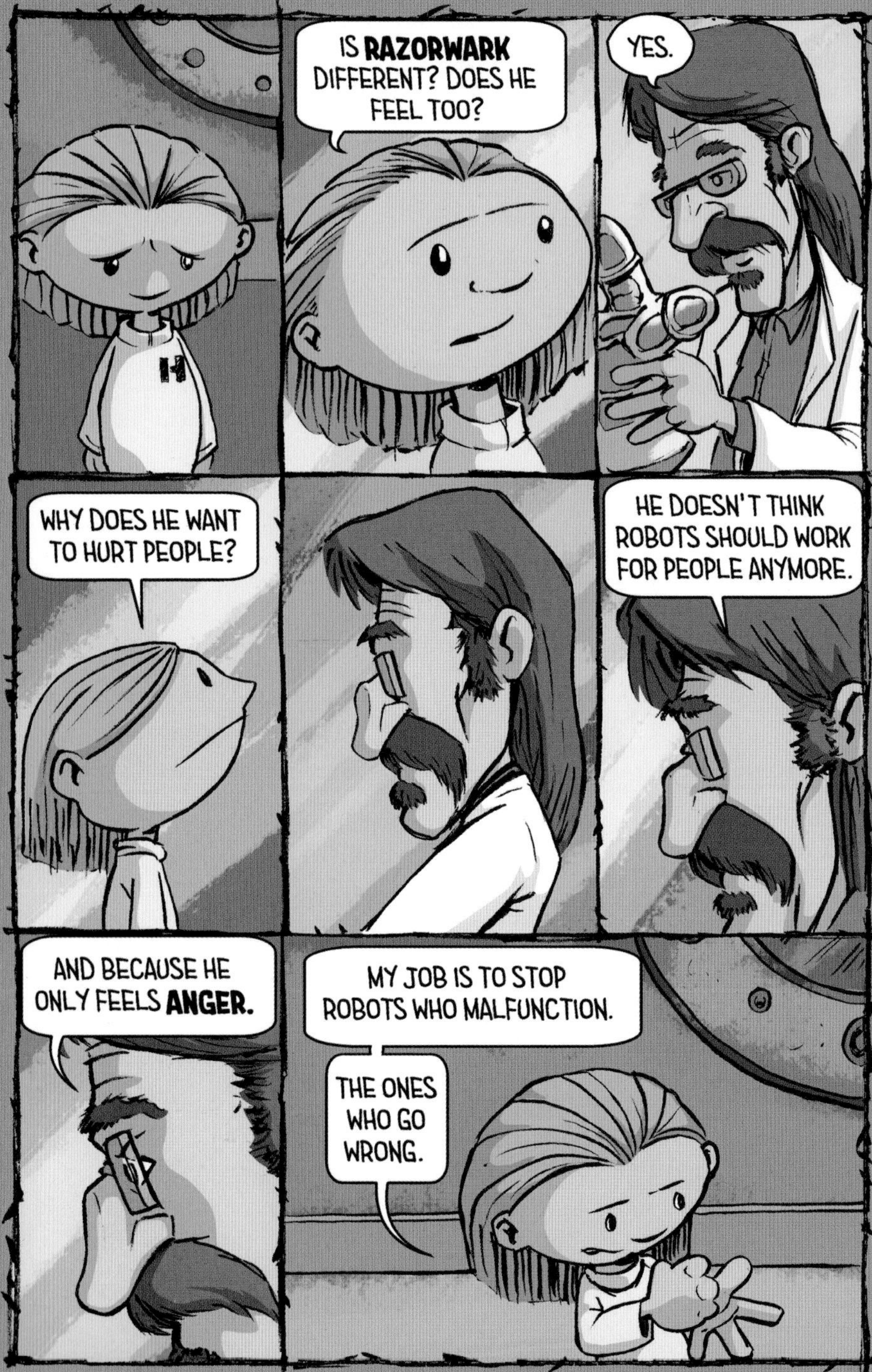
IS **RAZORWARK** DIFFERENT? DOES HE FEEL TOO?
YES.
WHY DOES HE WANT TO HURT PEOPLE?
HE DOESN'T THINK ROBOTS SHOULD WORK FOR PEOPLE ANYMORE.
AND BECAUSE HE ONLY FEELS **ANGER.**
MY JOB IS TO STOP ROBOTS WHO MALFUNCTION.
THE ONES WHO GO WRONG.

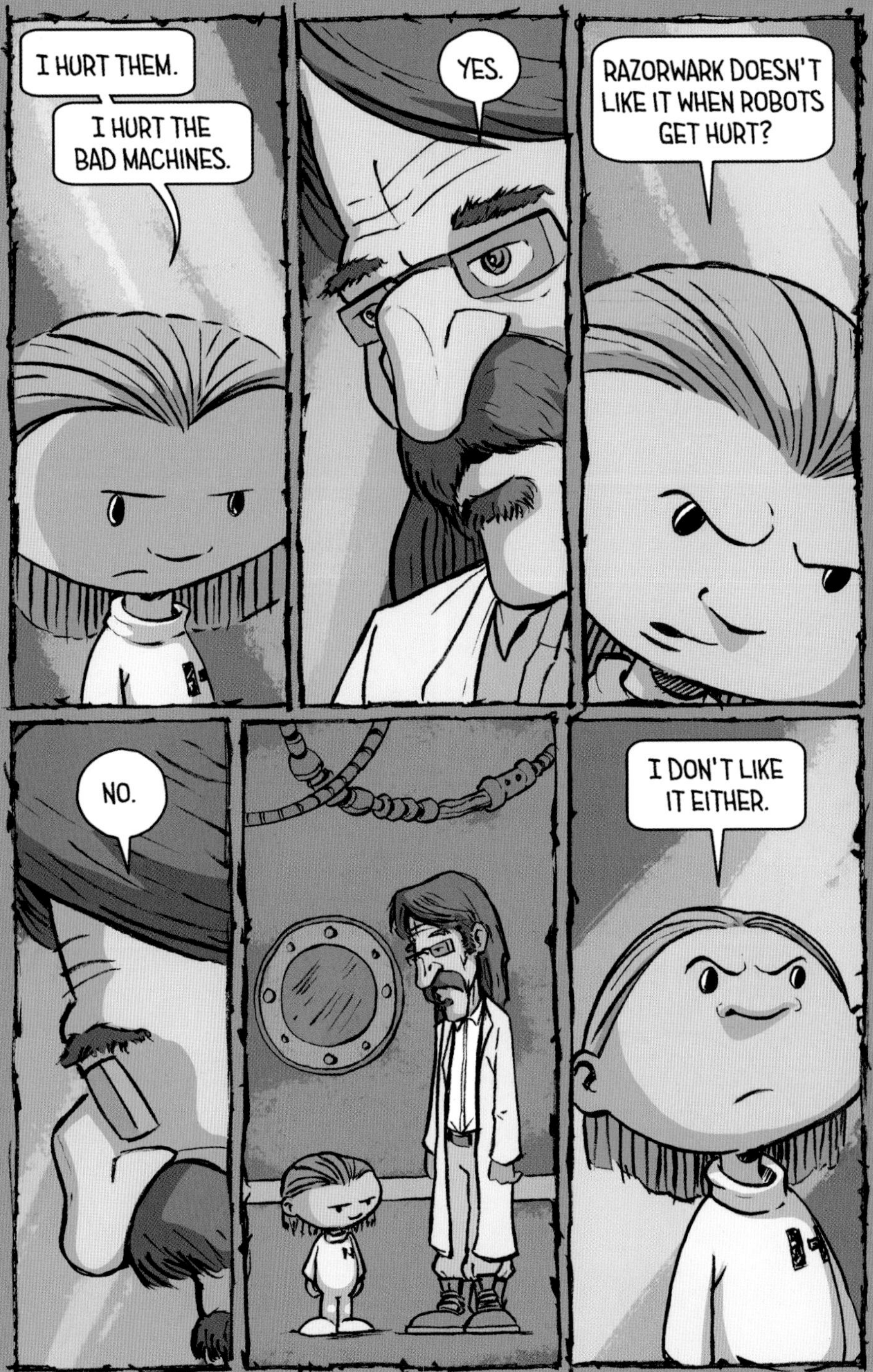
I HURT THEM.
I HURT THE BAD MACHINES.
YES.
RAZORWARK DOESN'T LIKE IT WHEN ROBOTS GET HURT?
NO.
I DON'T LIKE IT EITHER.

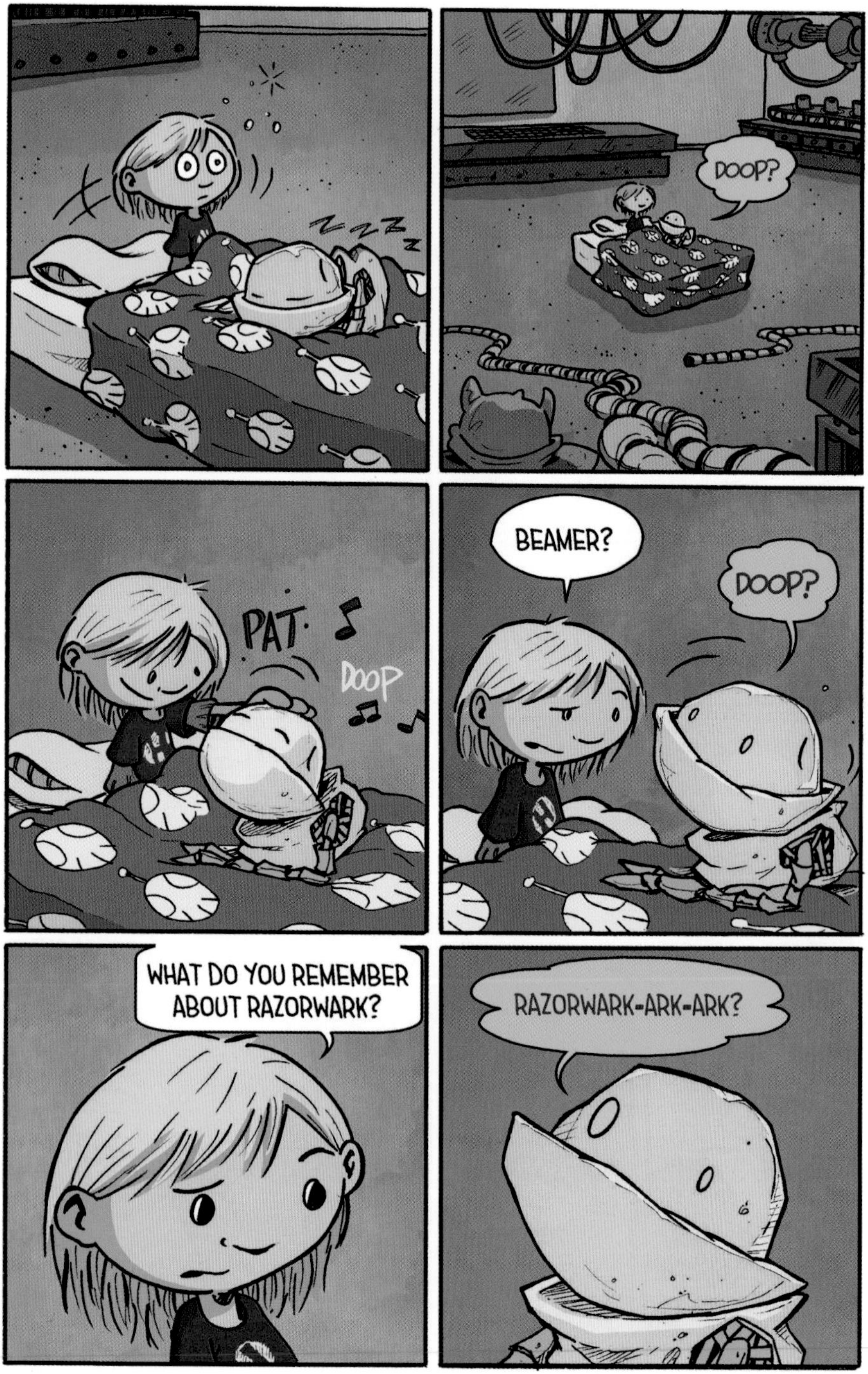
ZZZZ
DOOP?
PAT
DOOP
BEAMER?
DOOP?
WHAT DO YOU REMEMBER ABOUT RAZORWARK?
RAZORWARK-ARK-ARK?

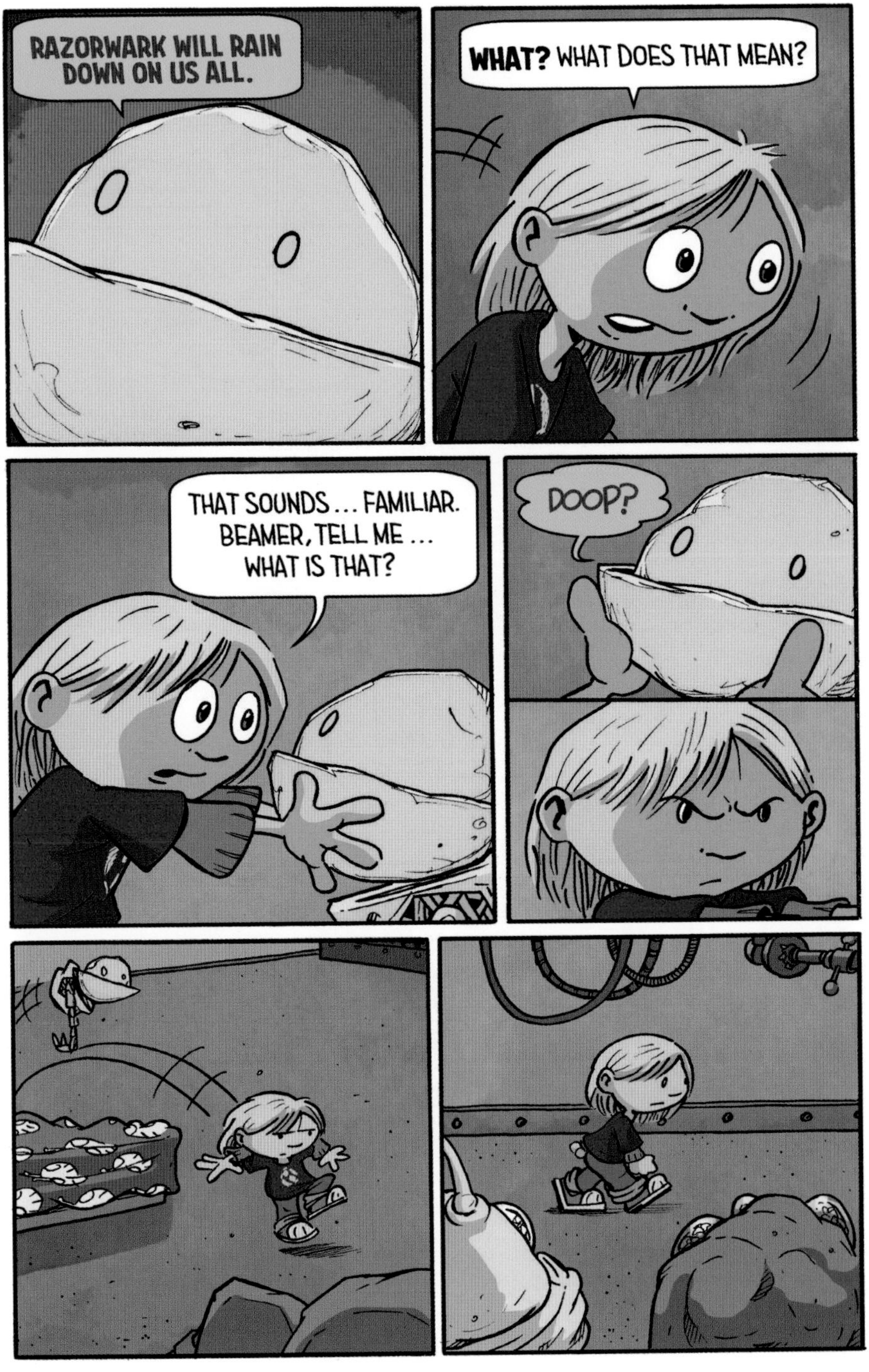
RAZORWARK WILL RAIN DOWN ON US ALL.
WHAT? WHAT DOES THAT MEAN?
THAT SOUNDS ... FAMILIAR. BEAMER, TELL ME ... WHAT IS THAT?
DOOP?

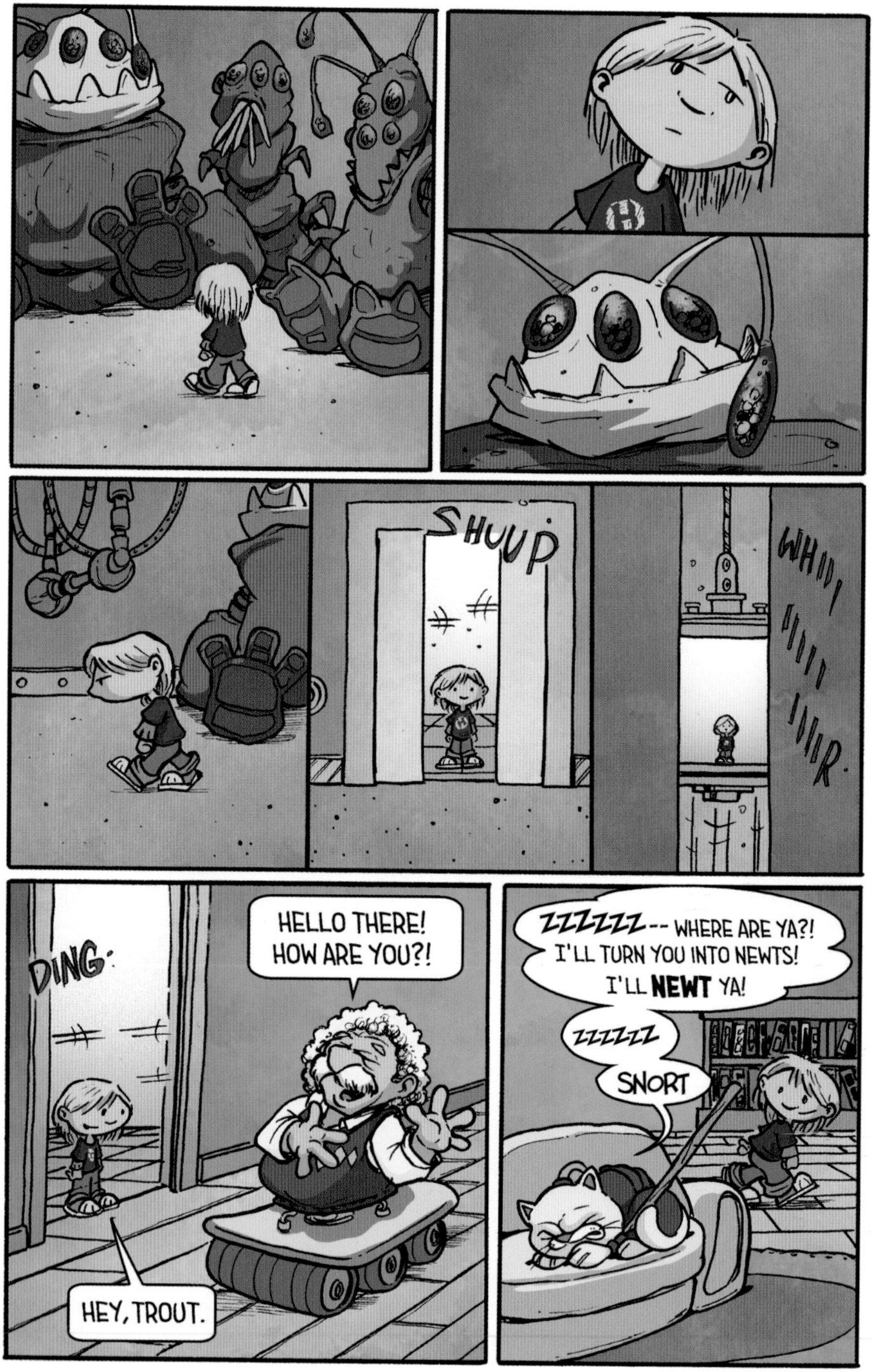
SHUUP
WHIRRRR
DING
HELLO THERE! HOW ARE YOU?!
HEY, TROUT.
ZZZZZZ-- WHERE ARE YA?! I'LL TURN YOU INTO NEWTS! I'LL **NEWT** YA!
ZZZZZZ
SNORT

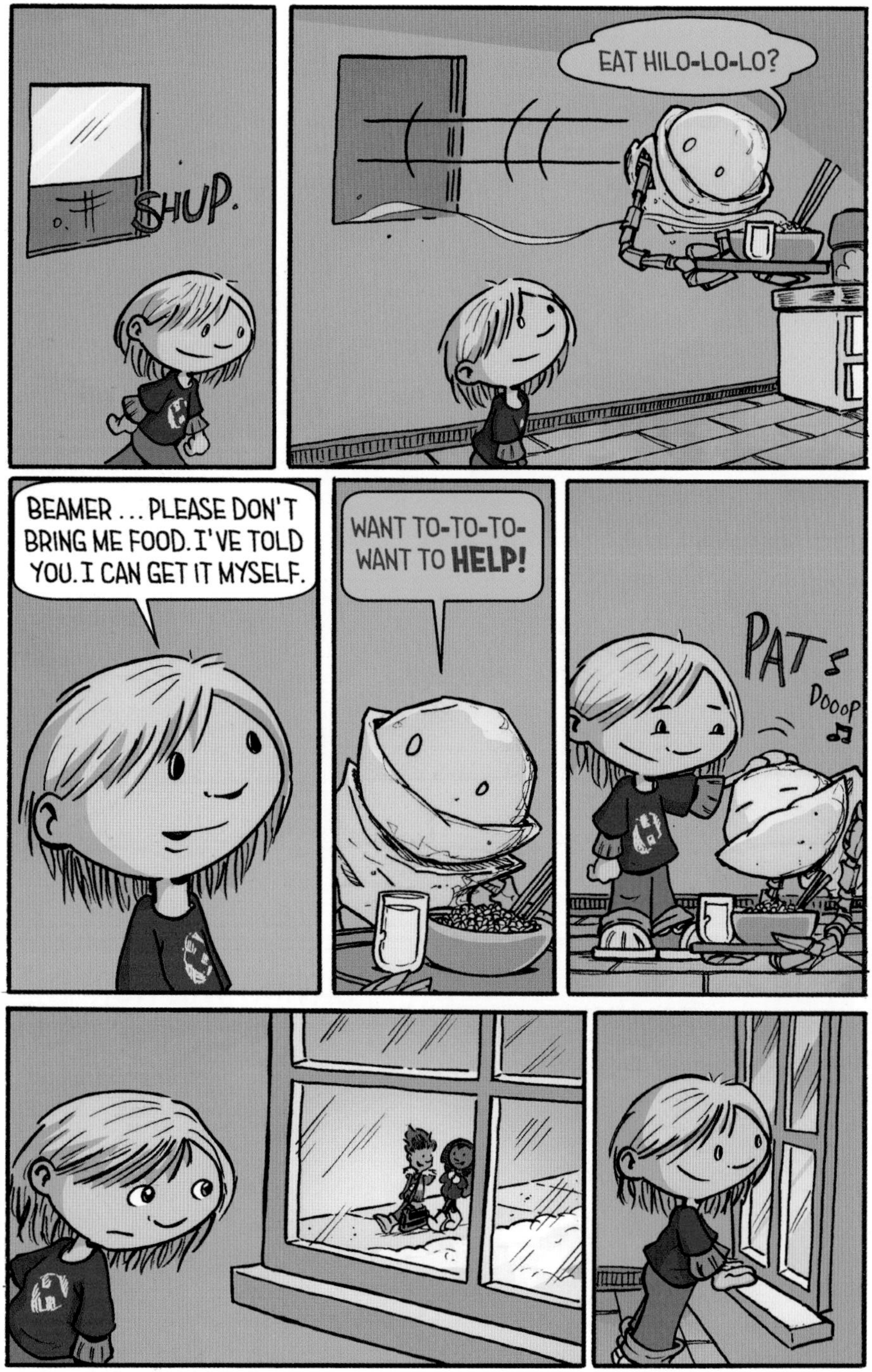
SHUP
EAT HILO-LO-LO?
BEAMER . . . PLEASE DON'T BRING ME FOOD. I'VE TOLD YOU. I CAN GET IT MYSELF.
WANT TO-TO-TO-WANT TO **HELP!**
PAT
DOOOP

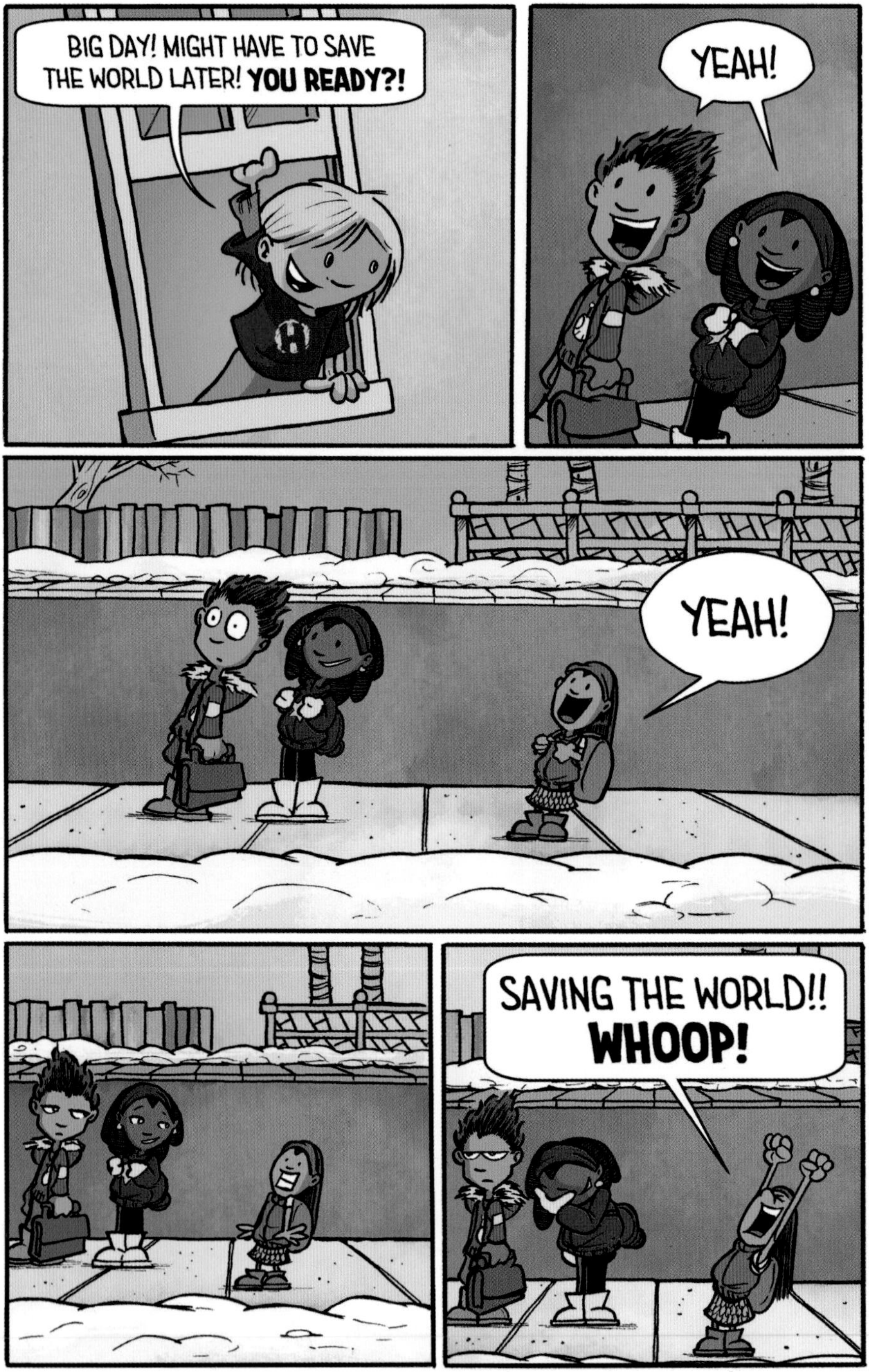
BIG DAY! MIGHT HAVE TO SAVE THE WORLD LATER! **YOU READY?!**
YEAH!
YEAH!
SAVING THE WORLD!! **WHOOP!**

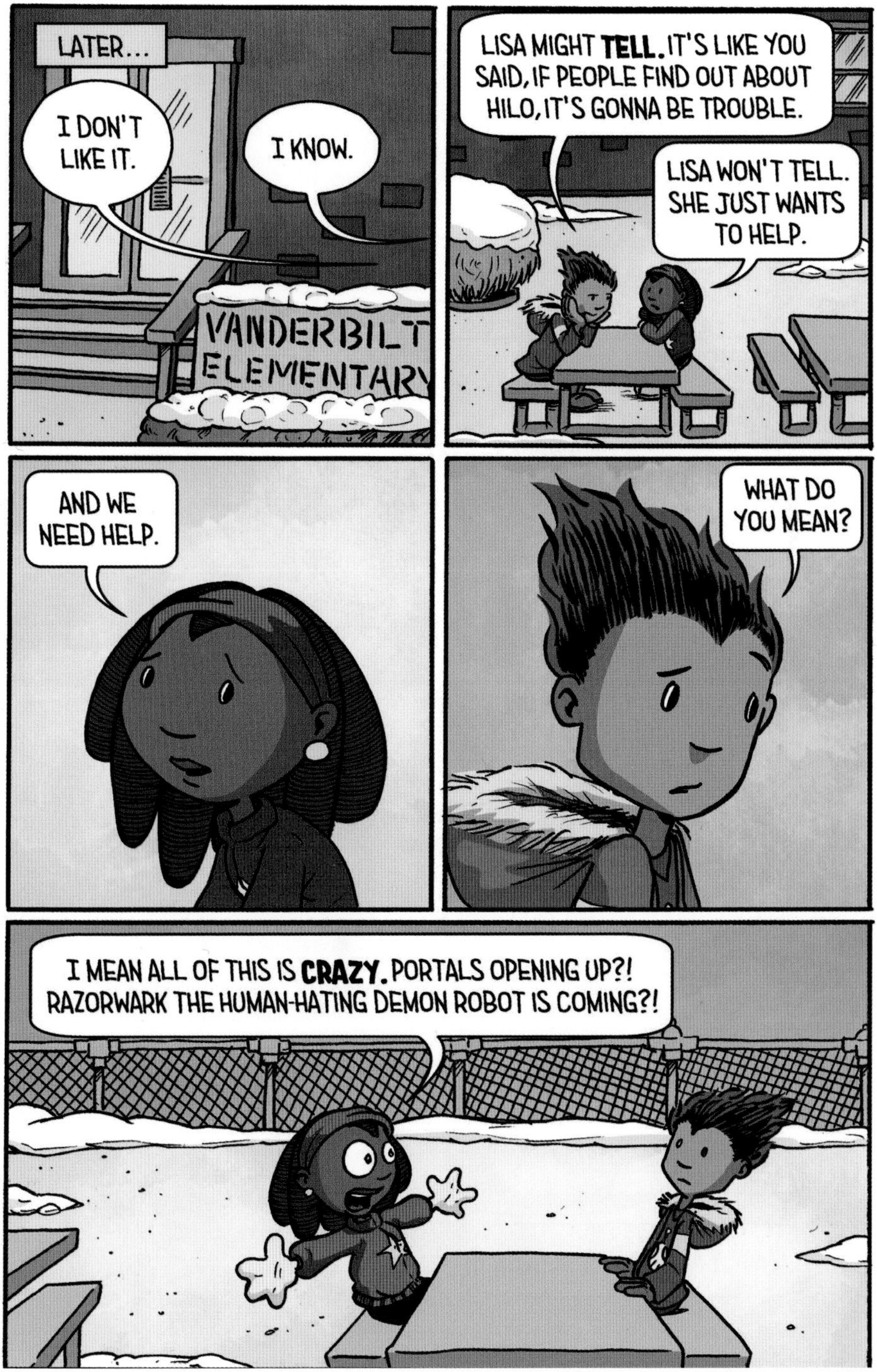
LATER...
I DON'T LIKE IT.
I KNOW.
VANDERBILT ELEMENTARY
LISA MIGHT TELL. IT'S LIKE YOU SAID, IF PEOPLE FIND OUT ABOUT HILO, IT'S GONNA BE TROUBLE.
LISA WON'T TELL. SHE JUST WANTS TO HELP.
AND WE NEED HELP.
WHAT DO YOU MEAN?
I MEAN ALL OF THIS IS CRAZY. PORTALS OPENING UP?! RAZORWARK THE HUMAN-HATING DEMON ROBOT IS COMING?!

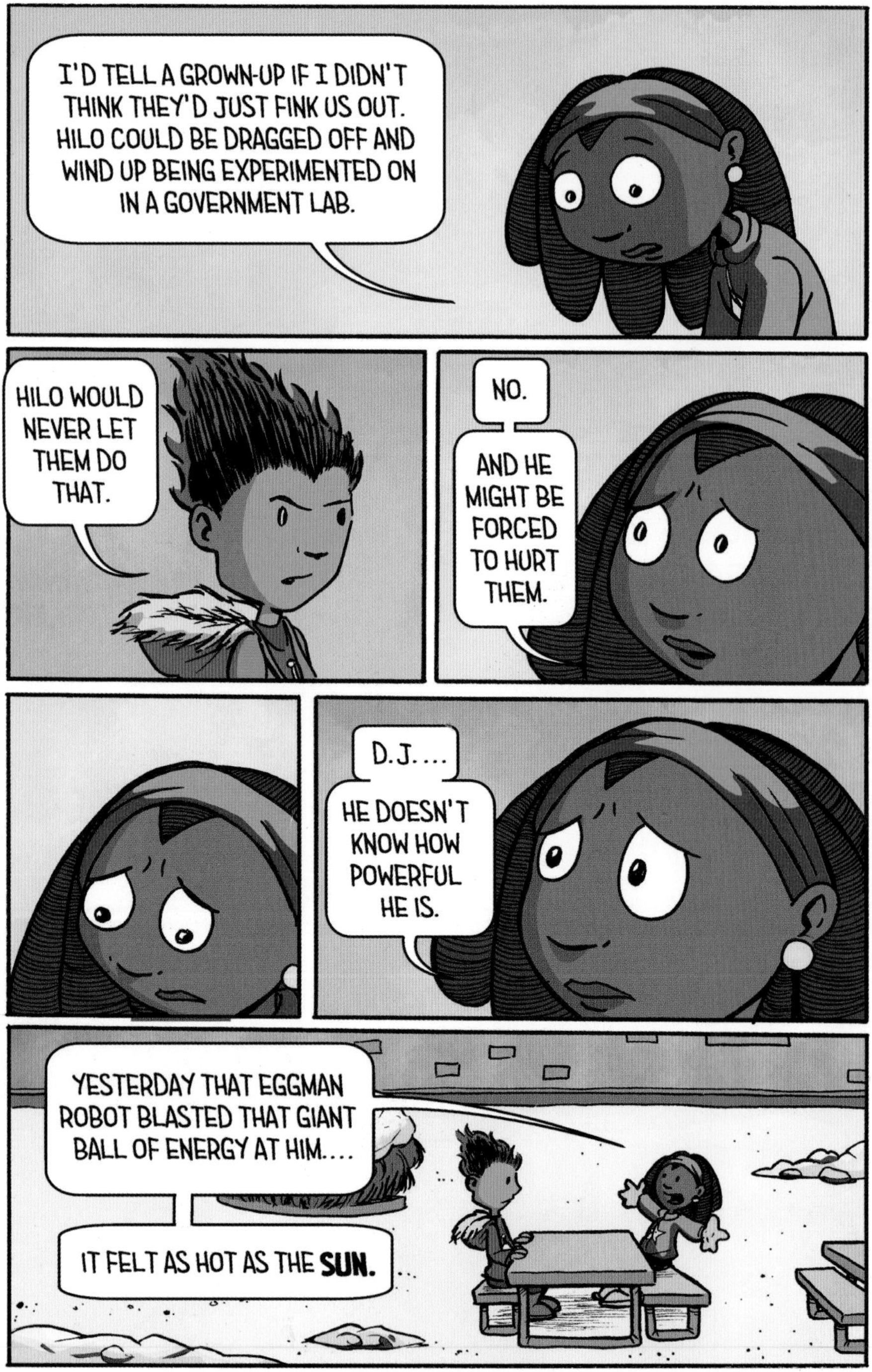
I'D TELL A GROWN-UP IF I DIDN'T THINK THEY'D JUST FINK US OUT. HILO COULD BE DRAGGED OFF AND WIND UP BEING EXPERIMENTED ON IN A GOVERNMENT LAB.
HILO WOULD NEVER LET THEM DO THAT.
NO.
AND HE MIGHT BE FORCED TO HURT THEM.
D.J....
HE DOESN'T KNOW HOW POWERFUL HE IS.
YESTERDAY THAT EGGMAN ROBOT BLASTED THAT GIANT BALL OF ENERGY AT HIM....
IT FELT AS HOT AS THE **SUN.**

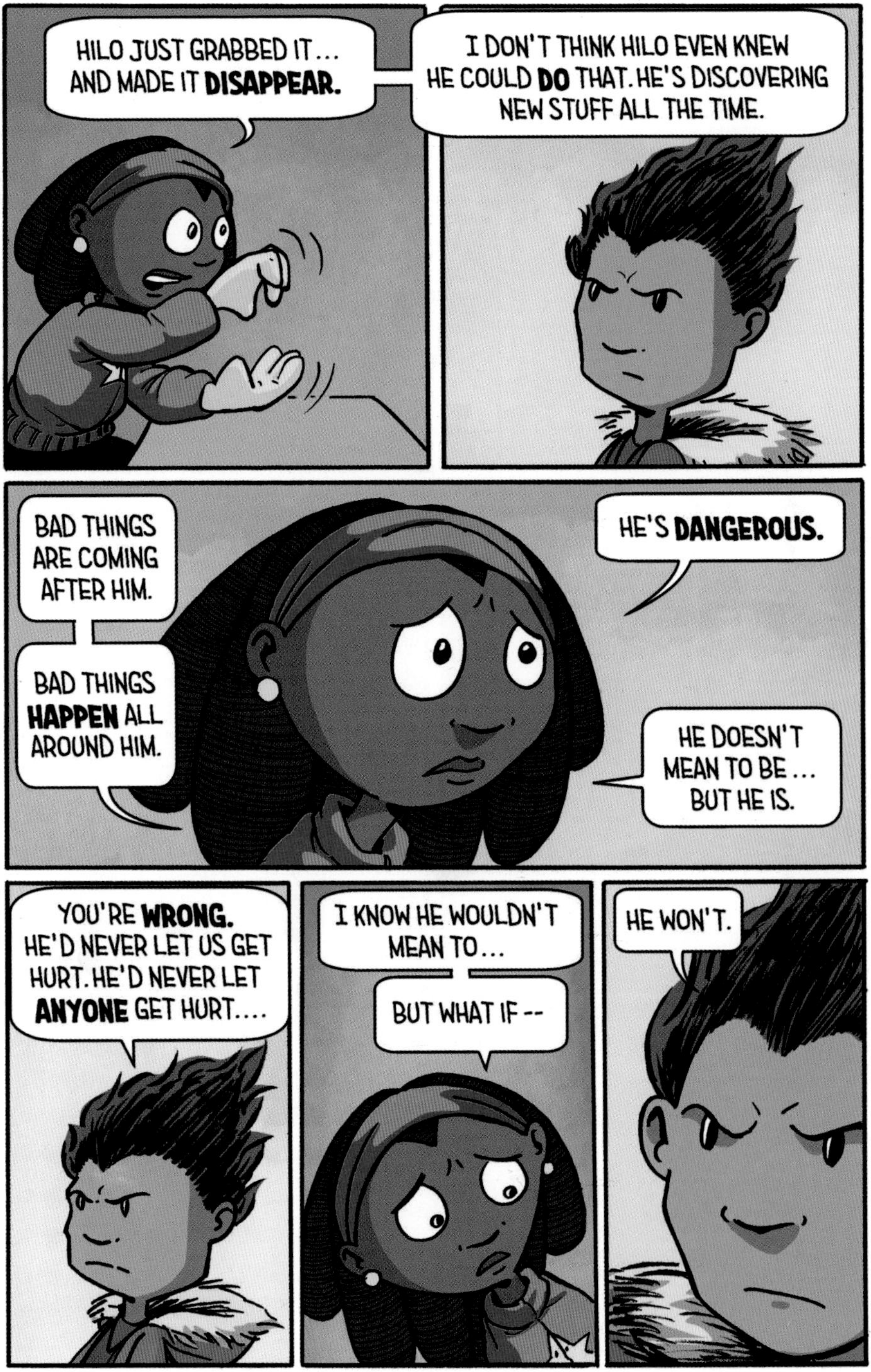
HILO JUST GRABBED IT... AND MADE IT **DISAPPEAR.**
I DON'T THINK HILO EVEN KNEW HE COULD **DO** THAT. HE'S DISCOVERING NEW STUFF ALL THE TIME.
BAD THINGS ARE COMING AFTER HIM.
BAD THINGS **HAPPEN** ALL AROUND HIM.
HE'S **DANGEROUS.**
HE DOESN'T MEAN TO BE... BUT HE IS.
YOU'RE **WRONG.** HE'D NEVER LET US GET HURT. HE'D NEVER LET **ANYONE** GET HURT....
I KNOW HE WOULDN'T MEAN TO...
BUT WHAT IF --
HE WON'T.

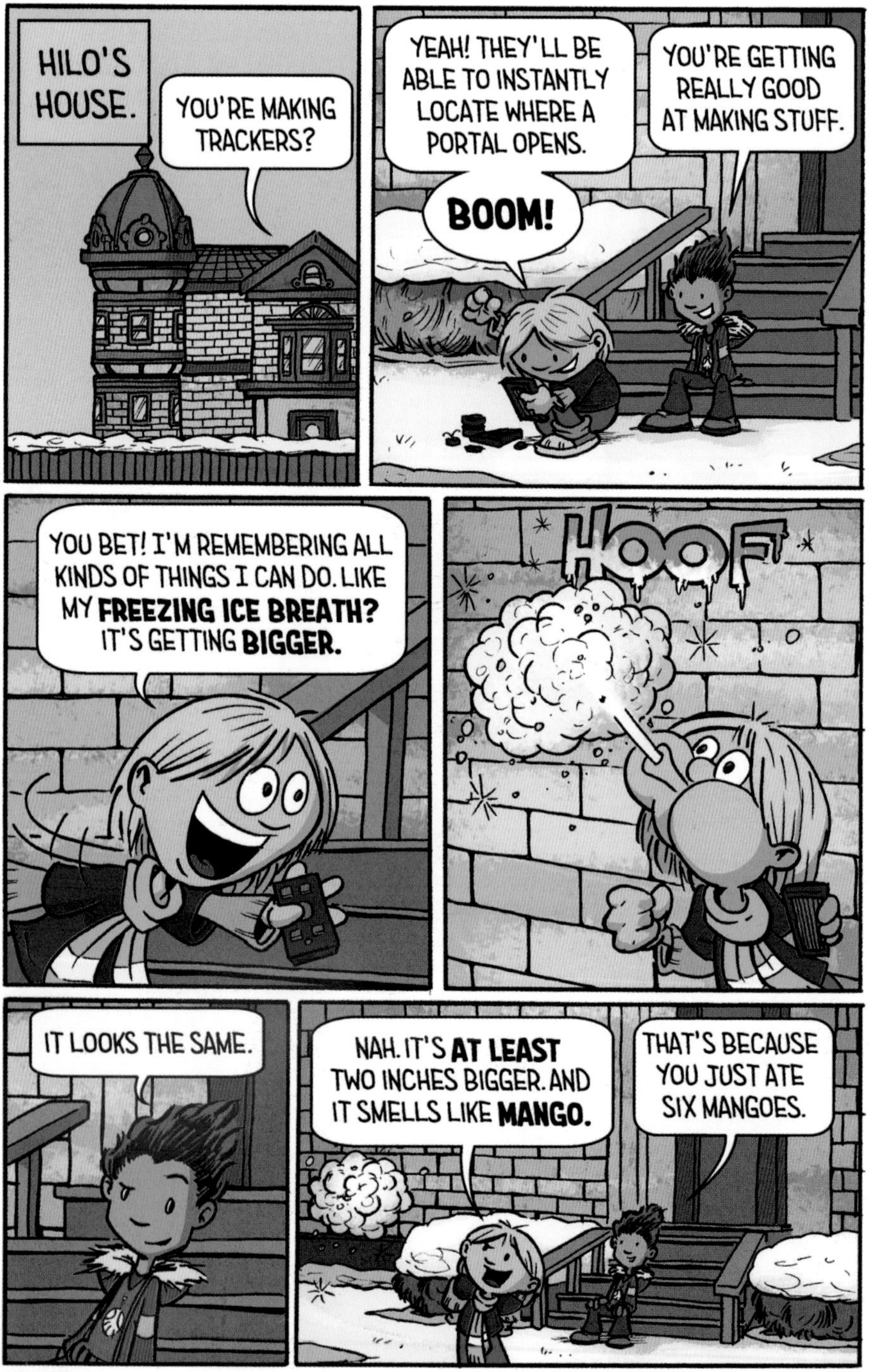
HILO'S HOUSE.
YOU'RE MAKING TRACKERS?
YEAH! THEY'LL BE ABLE TO INSTANTLY LOCATE WHERE A PORTAL OPENS.
BOOM!
YOU'RE GETTING REALLY GOOD AT MAKING STUFF.
YOU BET! I'M REMEMBERING ALL KINDS OF THINGS I CAN DO. LIKE MY **FREEZING ICE BREATH?** IT'S GETTING **BIGGER.**
HOOF
IT LOOKS THE SAME.
NAH. IT'S **AT LEAST** TWO INCHES BIGGER. AND IT SMELLS LIKE **MANGO.**
THAT'S BECAUSE YOU JUST ATE SIX MANGOES.

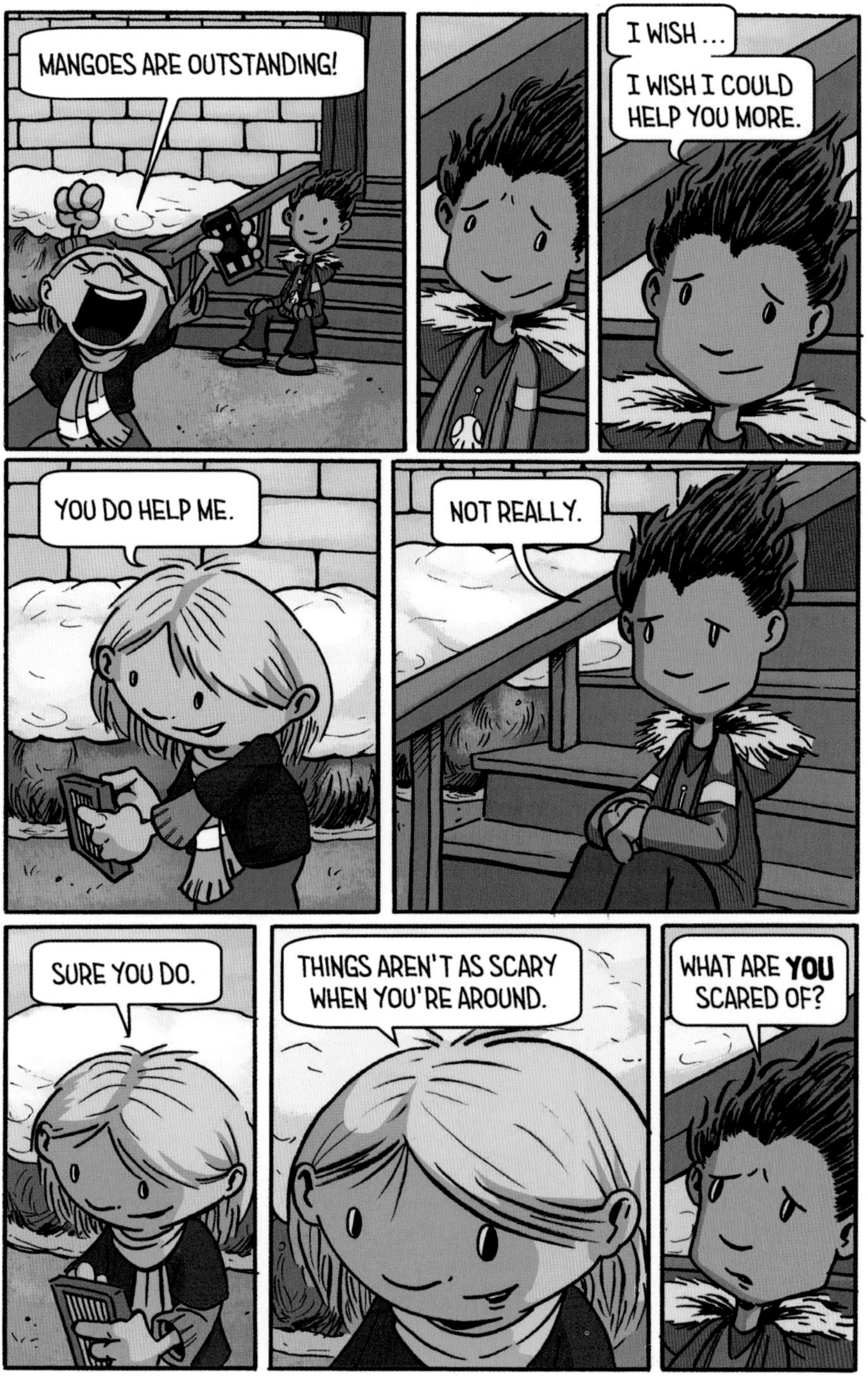
MANGOES ARE OUTSTANDING!
I WISH...
I WISH I COULD HELP YOU MORE.
YOU DO HELP ME.
NOT REALLY.
SURE YOU DO.
THINGS AREN'T AS SCARY WHEN YOU'RE AROUND.
WHAT ARE **YOU** SCARED OF?

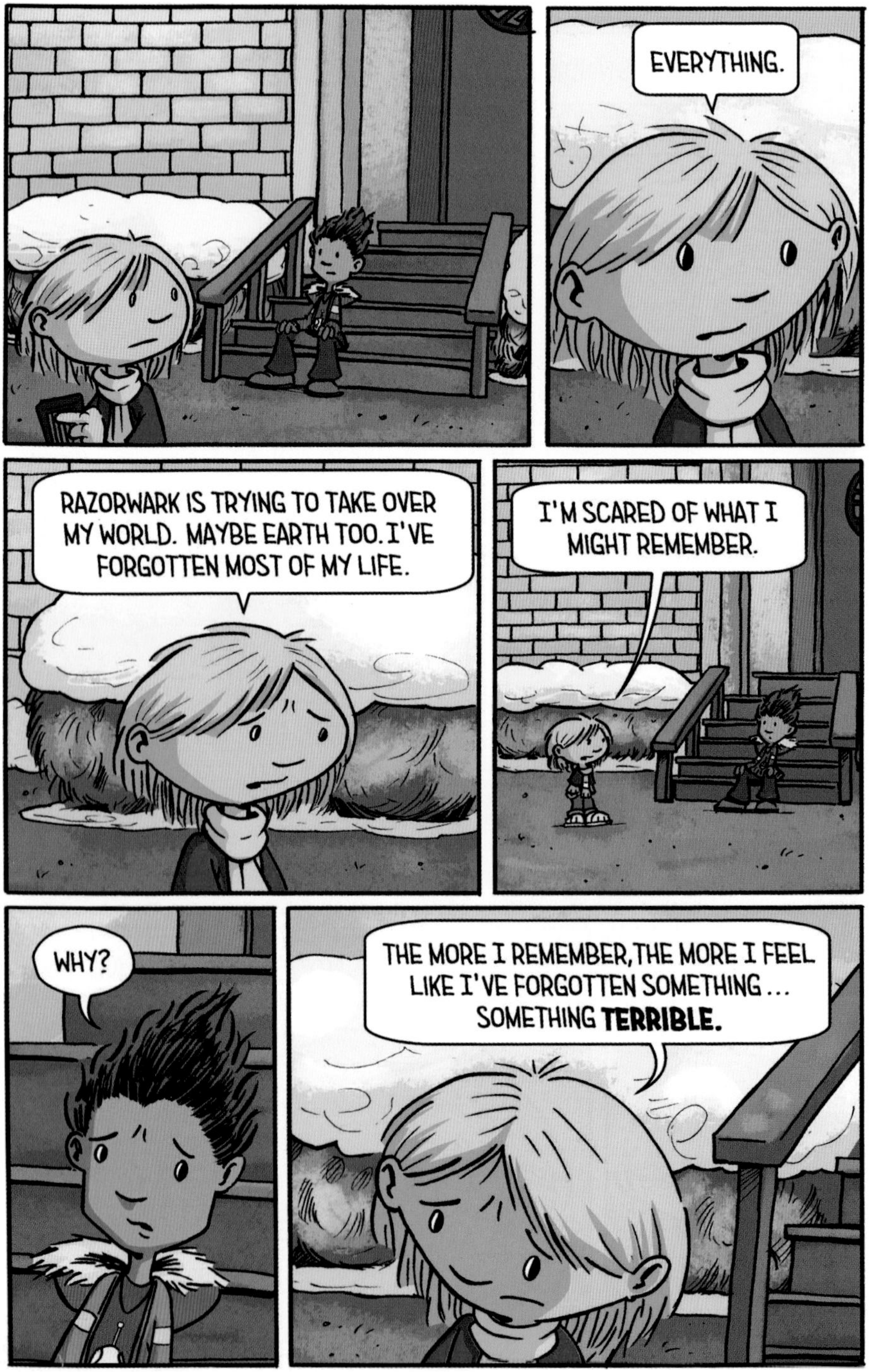
EVERYTHING.
RAZORWARK IS TRYING TO TAKE OVER MY WORLD. MAYBE EARTH TOO. I'VE FORGOTTEN MOST OF MY LIFE.
I'M SCARED OF WHAT I MIGHT REMEMBER.
WHY?
THE MORE I REMEMBER, THE MORE I FEEL LIKE I'VE FORGOTTEN SOMETHING ... SOMETHING TERRIBLE.

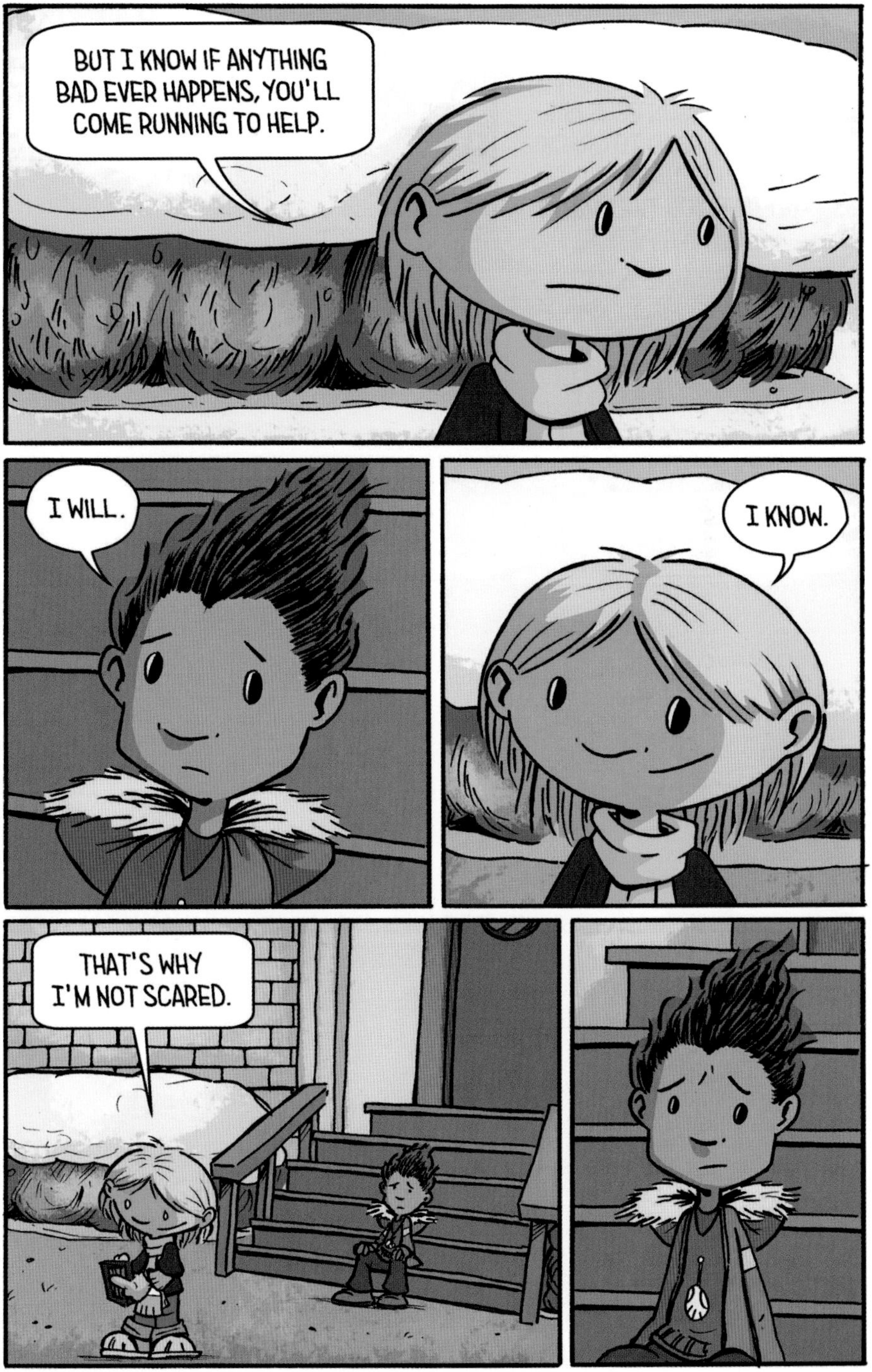
BUT I KNOW IF ANYTHING BAD EVER HAPPENS, YOU'LL COME RUNNING TO HELP.
I WILL.
I KNOW.
THAT'S WHY I'M NOT SCARED.

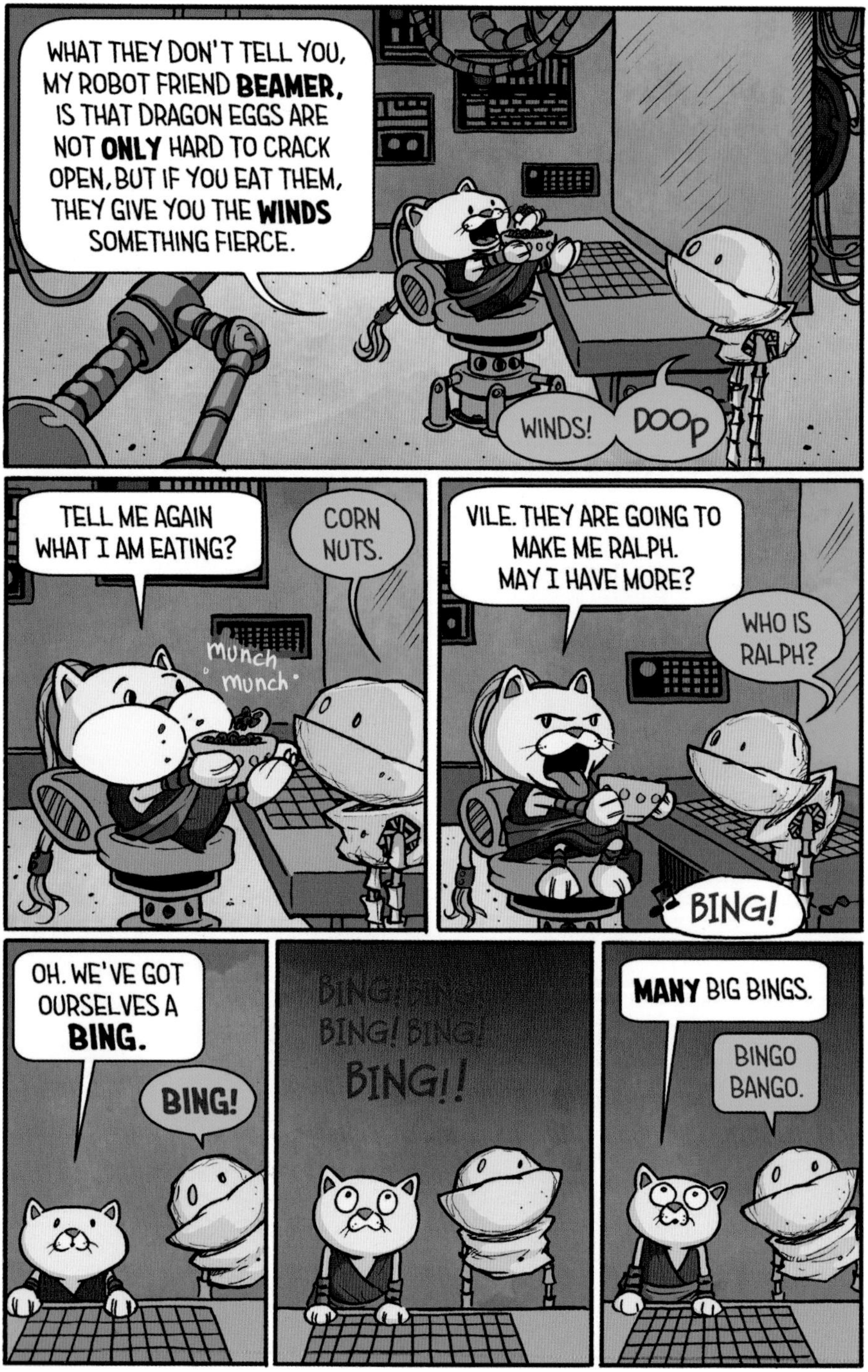
WHAT THEY DON'T TELL YOU, MY ROBOT FRIEND BEAMER, IS THAT DRAGON EGGS ARE NOT ONLY HARD TO CRACK OPEN, BUT IF YOU EAT THEM, THEY GIVE YOU THE WINDS SOMETHING FIERCE.
WINDS!
DOOP
TELL ME AGAIN WHAT I AM EATING?
CORN NUTS.
munch munch
VILE. THEY ARE GOING TO MAKE ME RALPH. MAY I HAVE MORE?
WHO IS RALPH?
BING!
OH. WE'VE GOT OURSELVES A BING.
BING!
BING! BING! BING! BING! BING!!
MANY BIG BINGS.
BINGO BANGO.

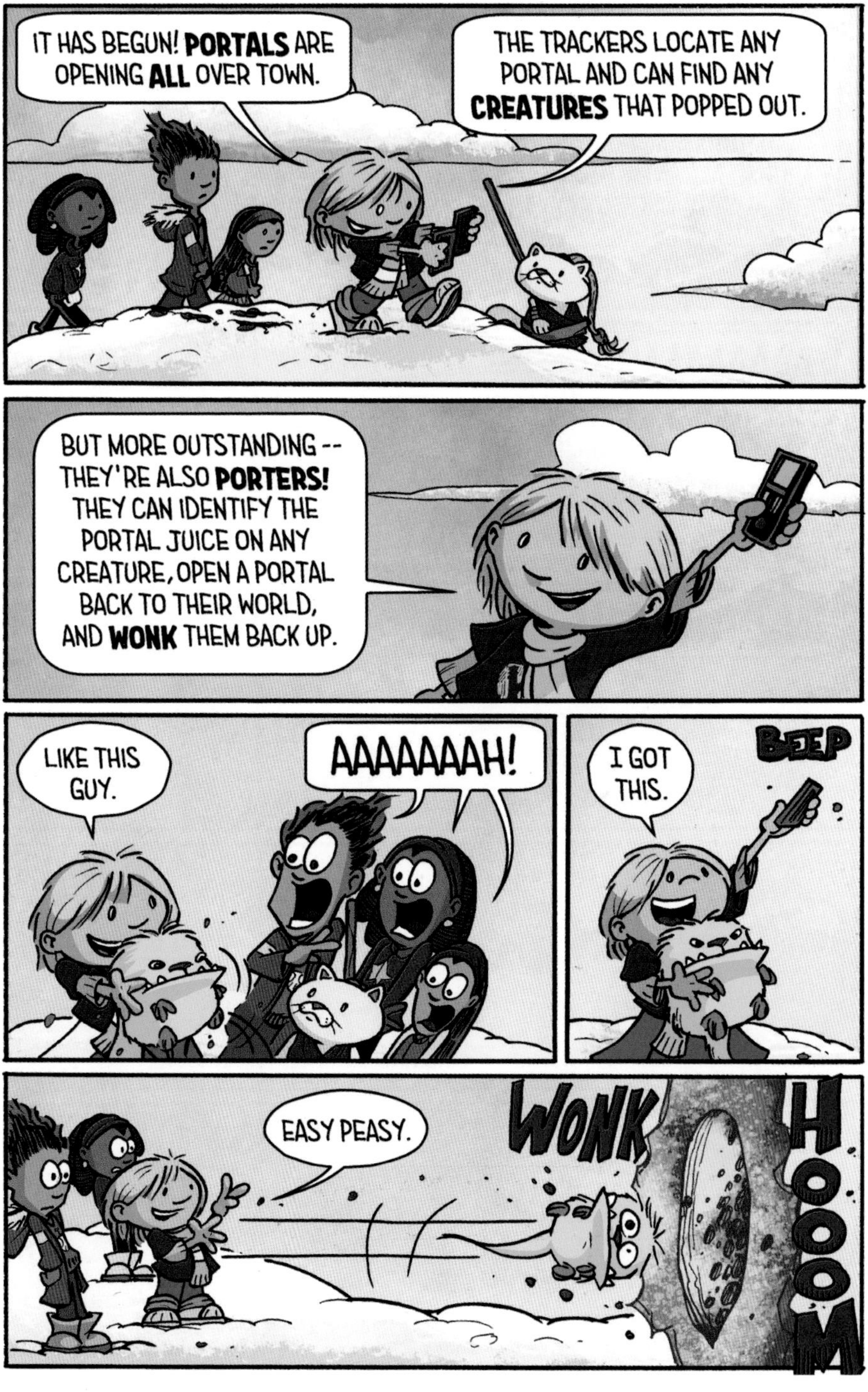
IT HAS BEGUN! **PORTALS** ARE OPENING **ALL** OVER TOWN.
THE TRACKERS LOCATE ANY PORTAL AND CAN FIND ANY **CREATURES** THAT POPPED OUT.
BUT MORE OUTSTANDING -- THEY'RE ALSO **PORTERS!** THEY CAN IDENTIFY THE PORTAL JUICE ON ANY CREATURE, OPEN A PORTAL BACK TO THEIR WORLD, AND **WONK** THEM BACK UP.
LIKE THIS GUY.
AAAAAAAH!
I GOT THIS.
BEEP
EASY PEASY.
WONK
HOOOM

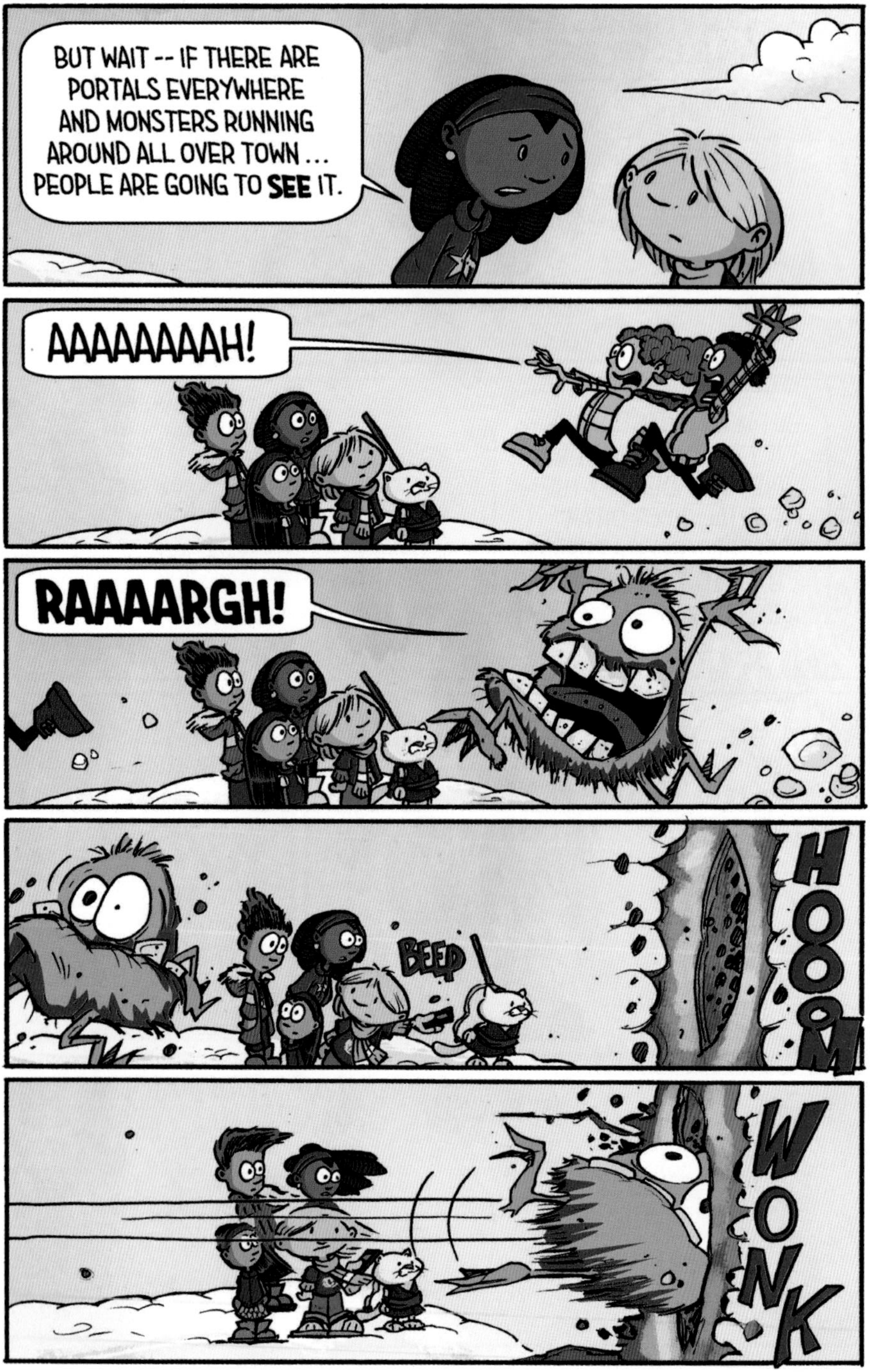
BUT WAIT -- IF THERE ARE PORTALS EVERYWHERE AND MONSTERS RUNNING AROUND ALL OVER TOWN . . . PEOPLE ARE GOING TO **SEE** IT.
AAAAAAAAH!
RAAAARGH!
BEEP
THOOOM
WONK

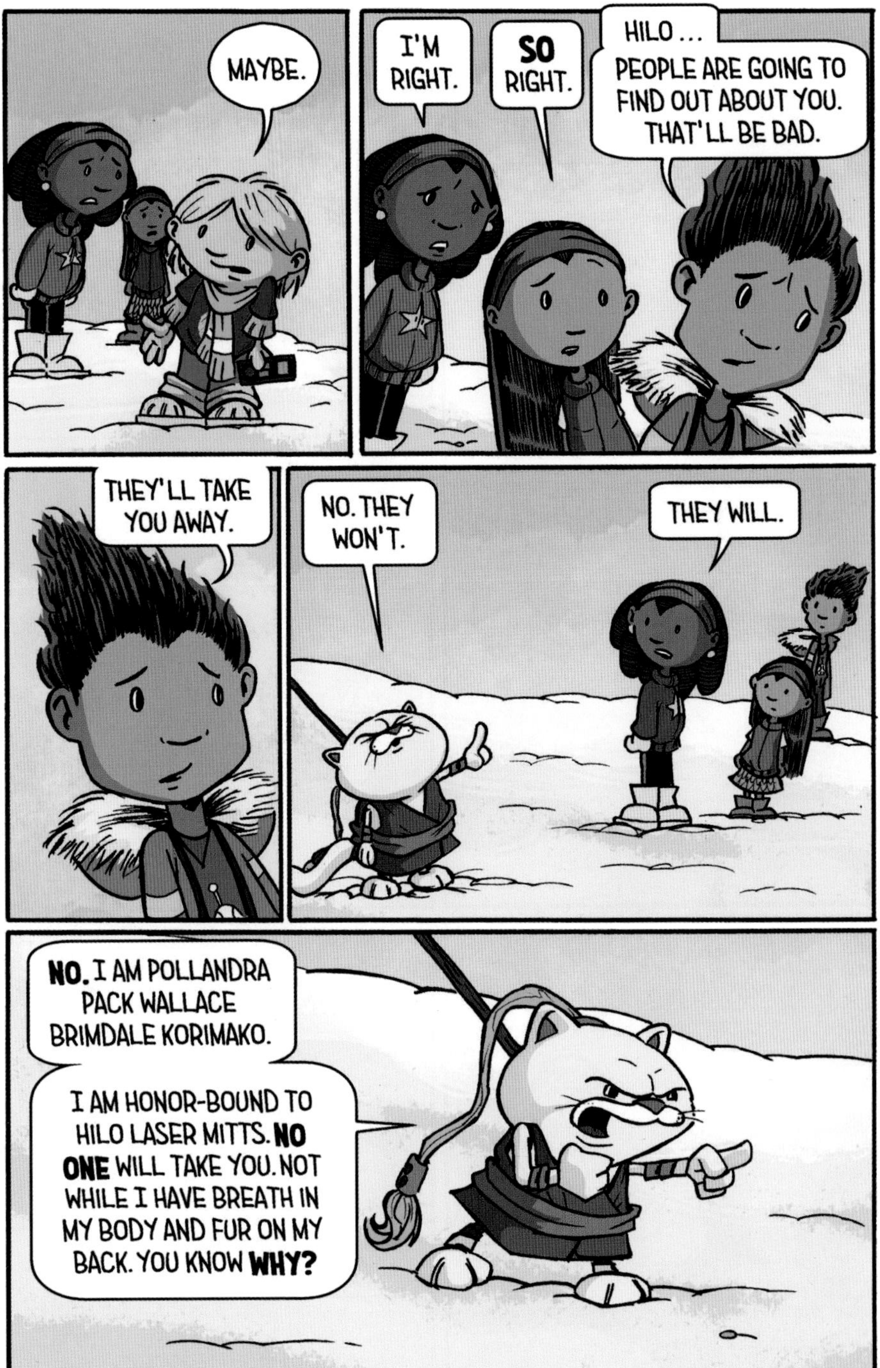
MAYBE.
I'M RIGHT.
SO RIGHT.
HILO ...
PEOPLE ARE GOING TO FIND OUT ABOUT YOU. THAT'LL BE BAD.
THEY'LL TAKE YOU AWAY.
NO. THEY WON'T.
THEY WILL.
NO. I AM POLLANDRA PACK WALLACE BRIMDALE KORIMAKO.
I AM HONOR-BOUND TO HILO LASER MITTS. NO ONE WILL TAKE YOU. NOT WHILE I HAVE BREATH IN MY BODY AND FUR ON MY BACK. YOU KNOW WHY?

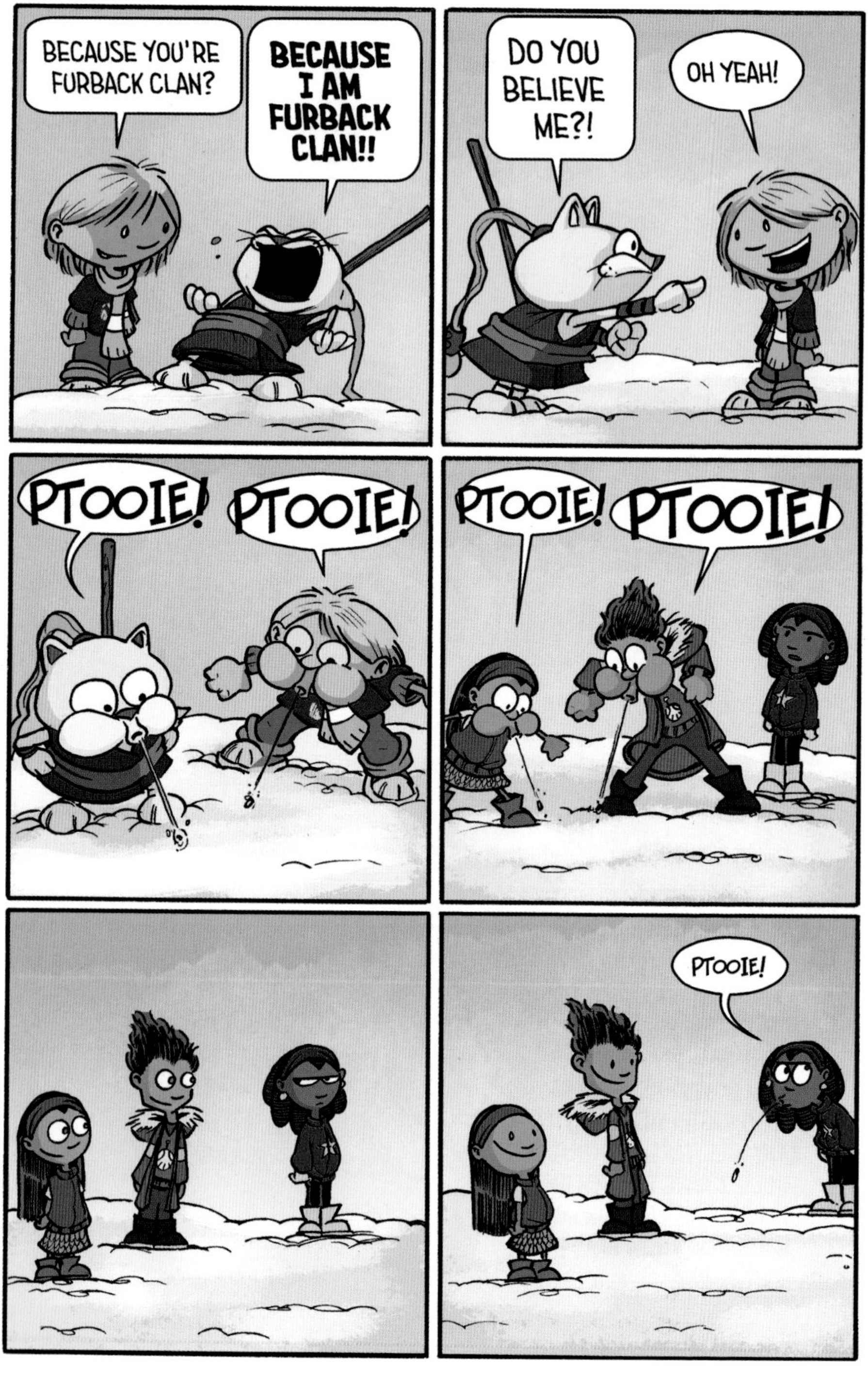
BECAUSE YOU'RE FURBACK CLAN?
BECAUSE I AM FURBACK CLAN!!
DO YOU BELIEVE ME?!
OH YEAH!
PTOOIE!
PTOOIE!
PTOOIE!
PTOOIE!
PTOOIE!

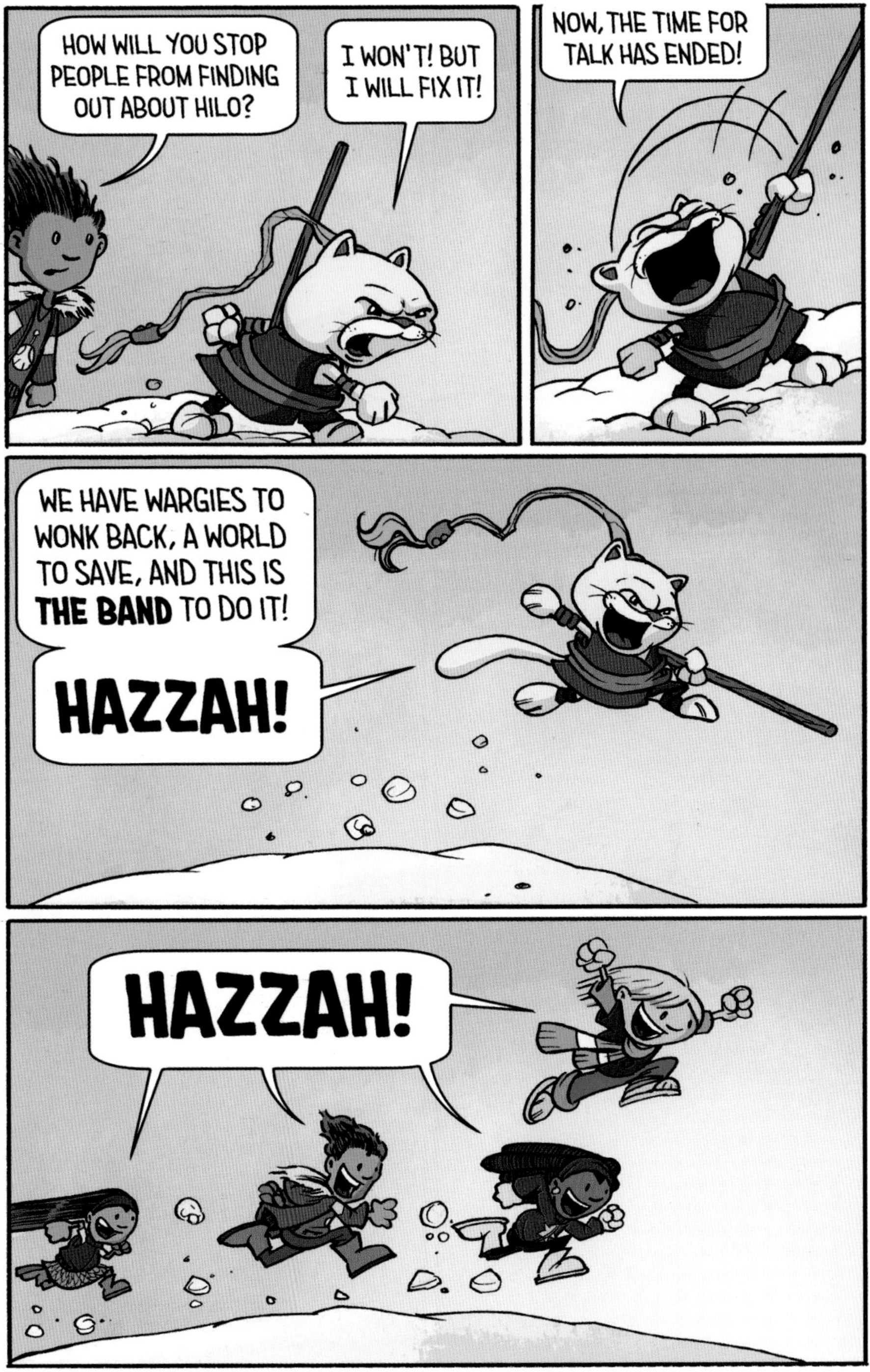
HOW WILL YOU STOP PEOPLE FROM FINDING OUT ABOUT HILO?
I WON'T! BUT I WILL FIX IT!
NOW, THE TIME FOR TALK HAS ENDED!
WE HAVE WARGIES TO WONK BACK, A WORLD TO SAVE, AND THIS IS **THE BAND** TO DO IT!
HAZZAH!
HAZZAH!

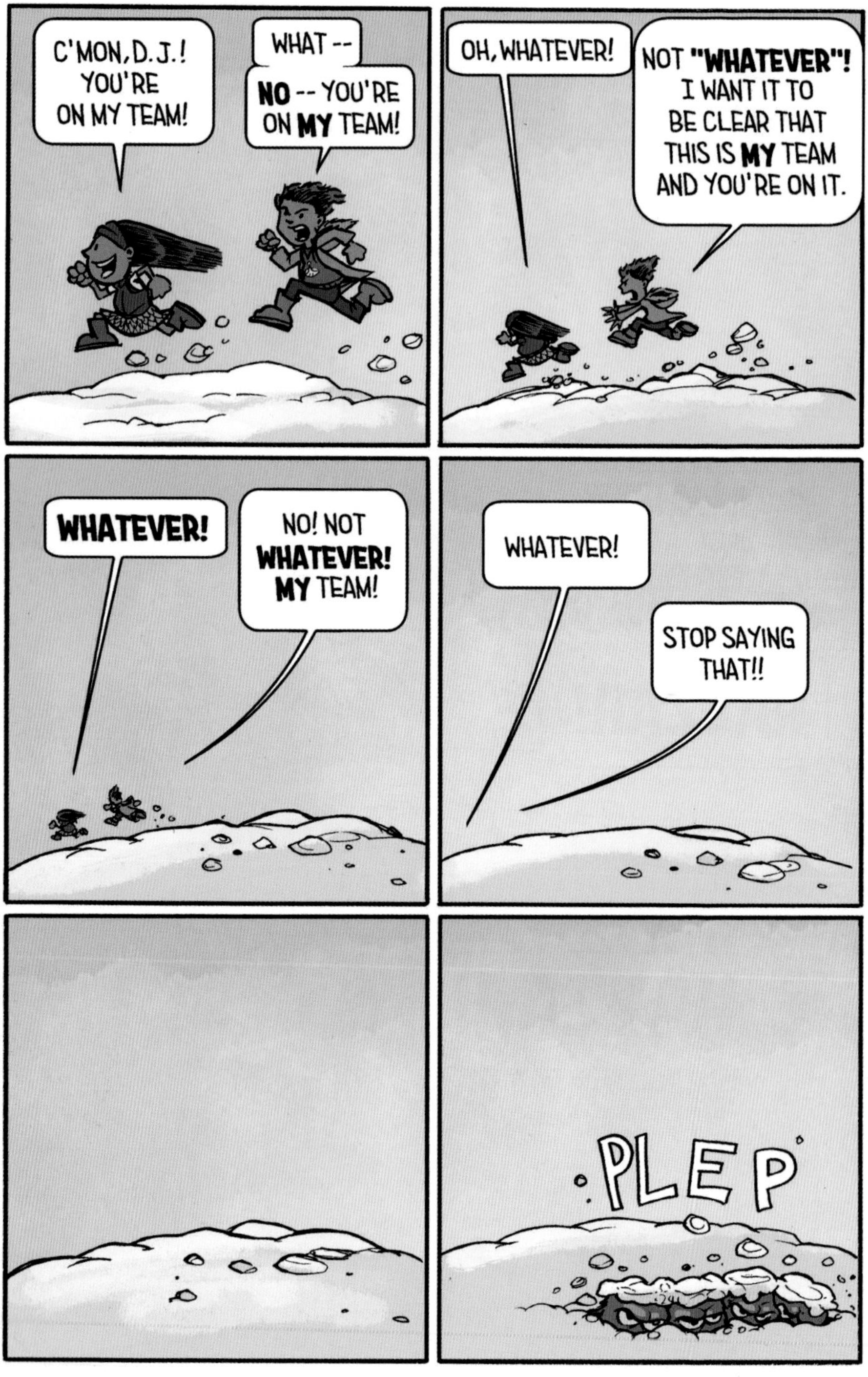
C'MON, D.J.! YOU'RE ON MY TEAM!
WHAT --
NO -- YOU'RE ON MY TEAM!
OH, WHATEVER!
NOT "WHATEVER"! I WANT IT TO BE CLEAR THAT THIS IS MY TEAM AND YOU'RE ON IT.
WHATEVER!
NO! NOT WHATEVER! MY TEAM!
WHATEVER!
STOP SAYING THAT!!
PLEP

CHAPTER 7

BING

THE WORLD WILL BE MINE!!
CINEMA 5

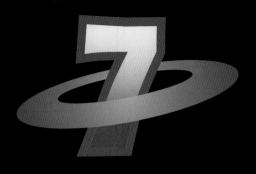

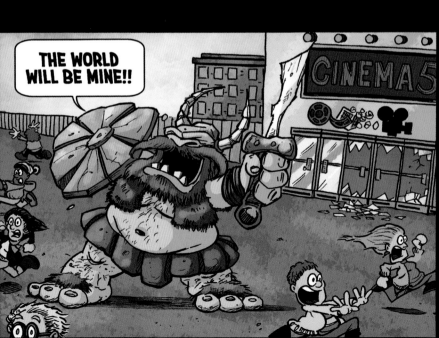

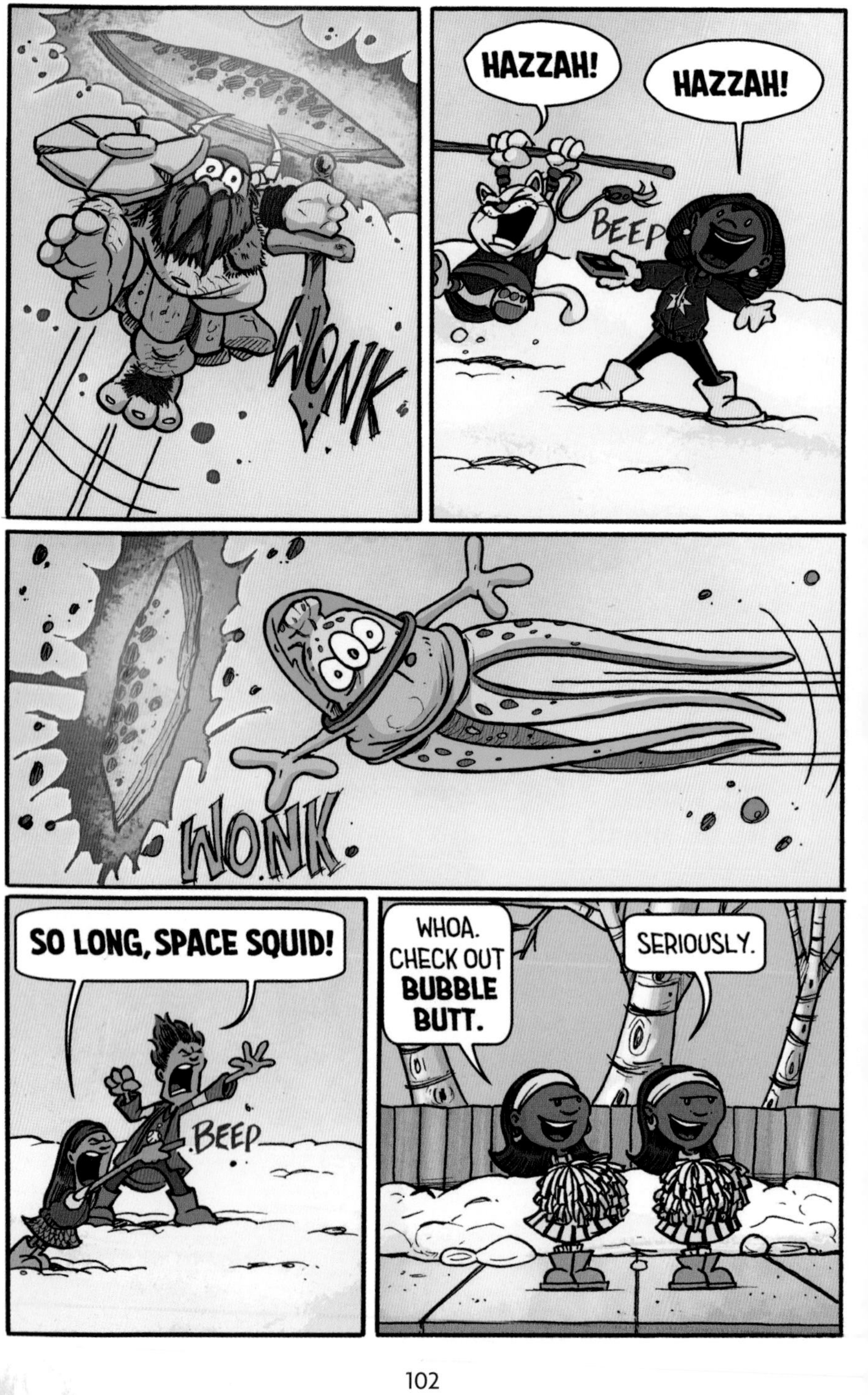
WONK
HAZZAH!
HAZZAH!
BEEP
WONK
SO LONG, SPACE SQUID!
BEEP
WHOA. CHECK OUT BUBBLE BUTT.
SERIOUSLY.

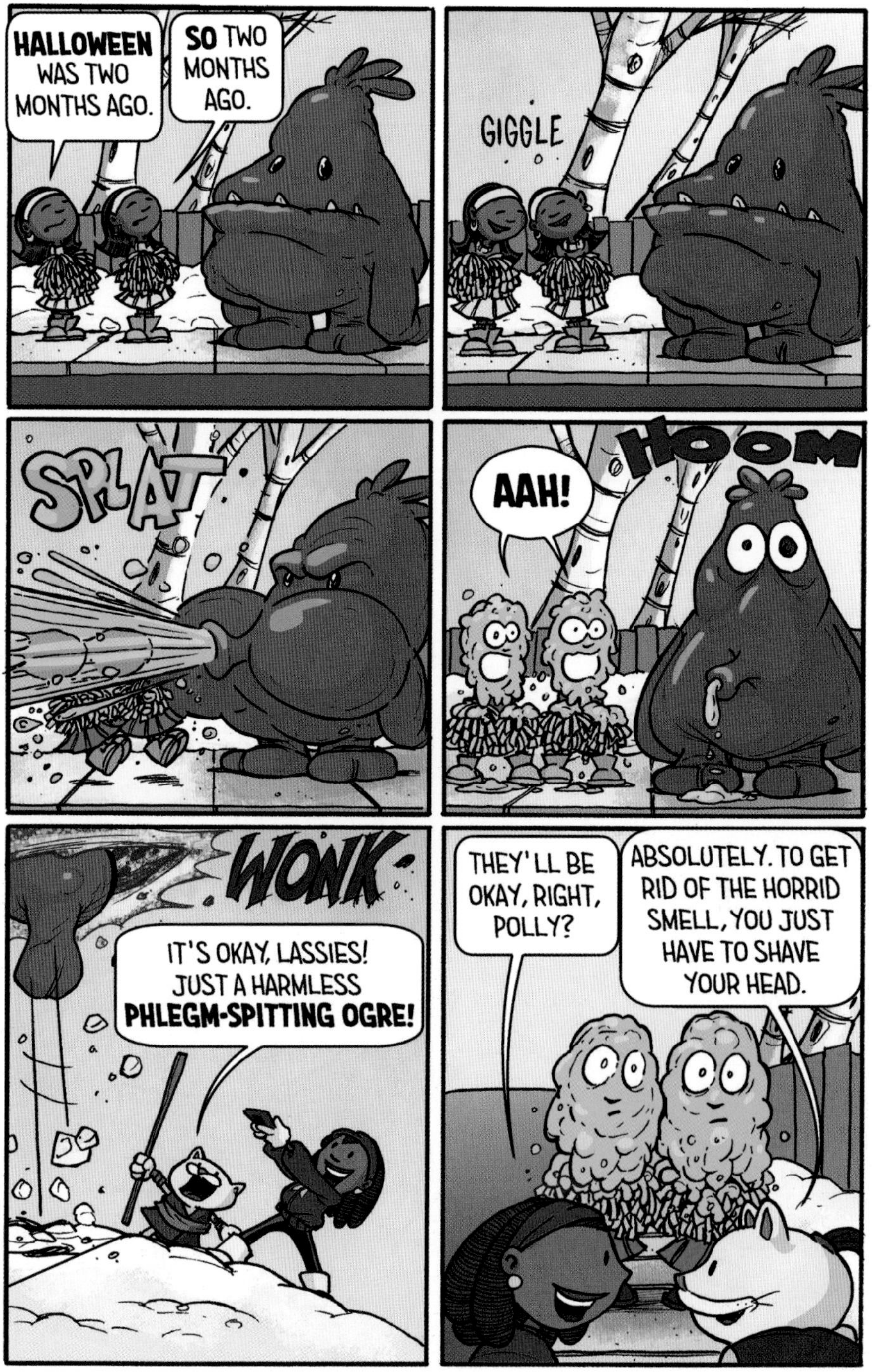

HALLOWEEN WAS TWO MONTHS AGO.
SO TWO MONTHS AGO.
GIGGLE
SPLAT
HOOM
AAH!
WONK
IT'S OKAY, LASSIES! JUST A HARMLESS **PHLEGM-SPITTING OGRE!**
THEY'LL BE OKAY, RIGHT, POLLY?
ABSOLUTELY. TO GET RID OF THE HORRID SMELL, YOU JUST HAVE TO SHAVE YOUR HEAD.

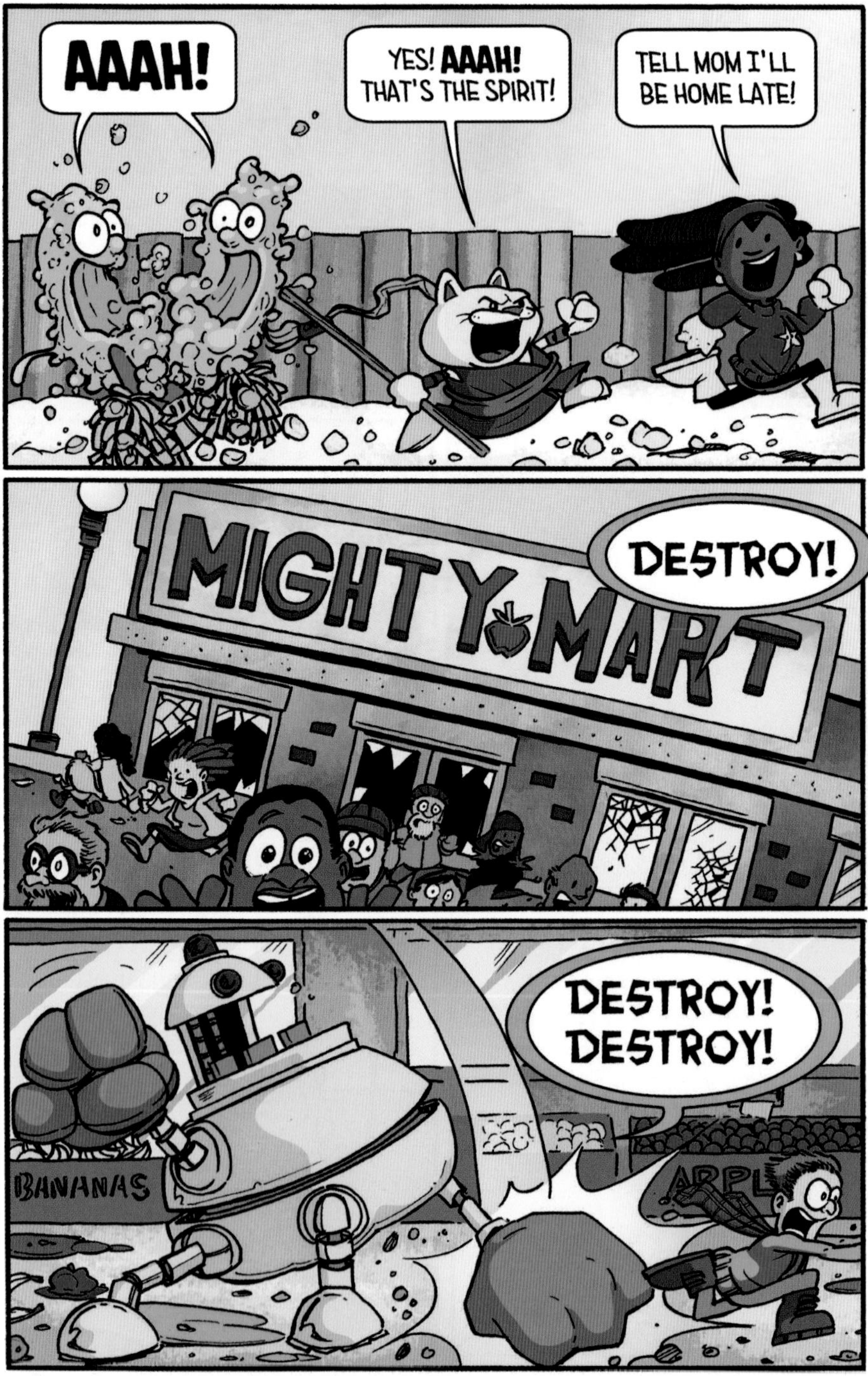
AAAH!
YES! AAAH! THAT'S THE SPIRIT!
TELL MOM I'LL BE HOME LATE!
MIGHTY MART
DESTROY!
DESTROY! DESTROY!
BANANAS

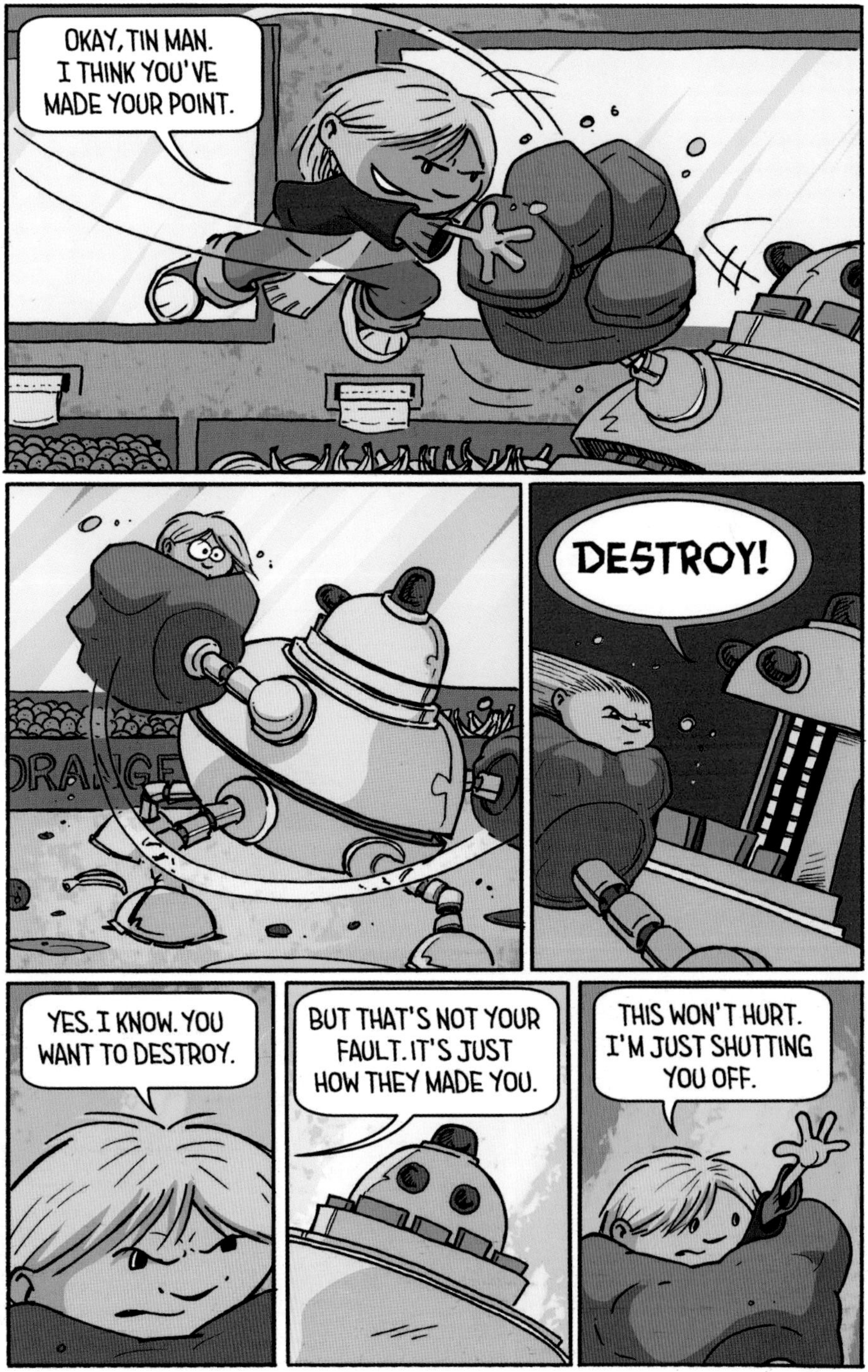
OKAY, TIN MAN. I THINK YOU'VE MADE YOUR POINT.
ORANGE
DESTROY!
YES. I KNOW. YOU WANT TO DESTROY.
BUT THAT'S NOT YOUR FAULT. IT'S JUST HOW THEY MADE YOU.
THIS WON'T HURT. I'M JUST SHUTTING YOU OFF.

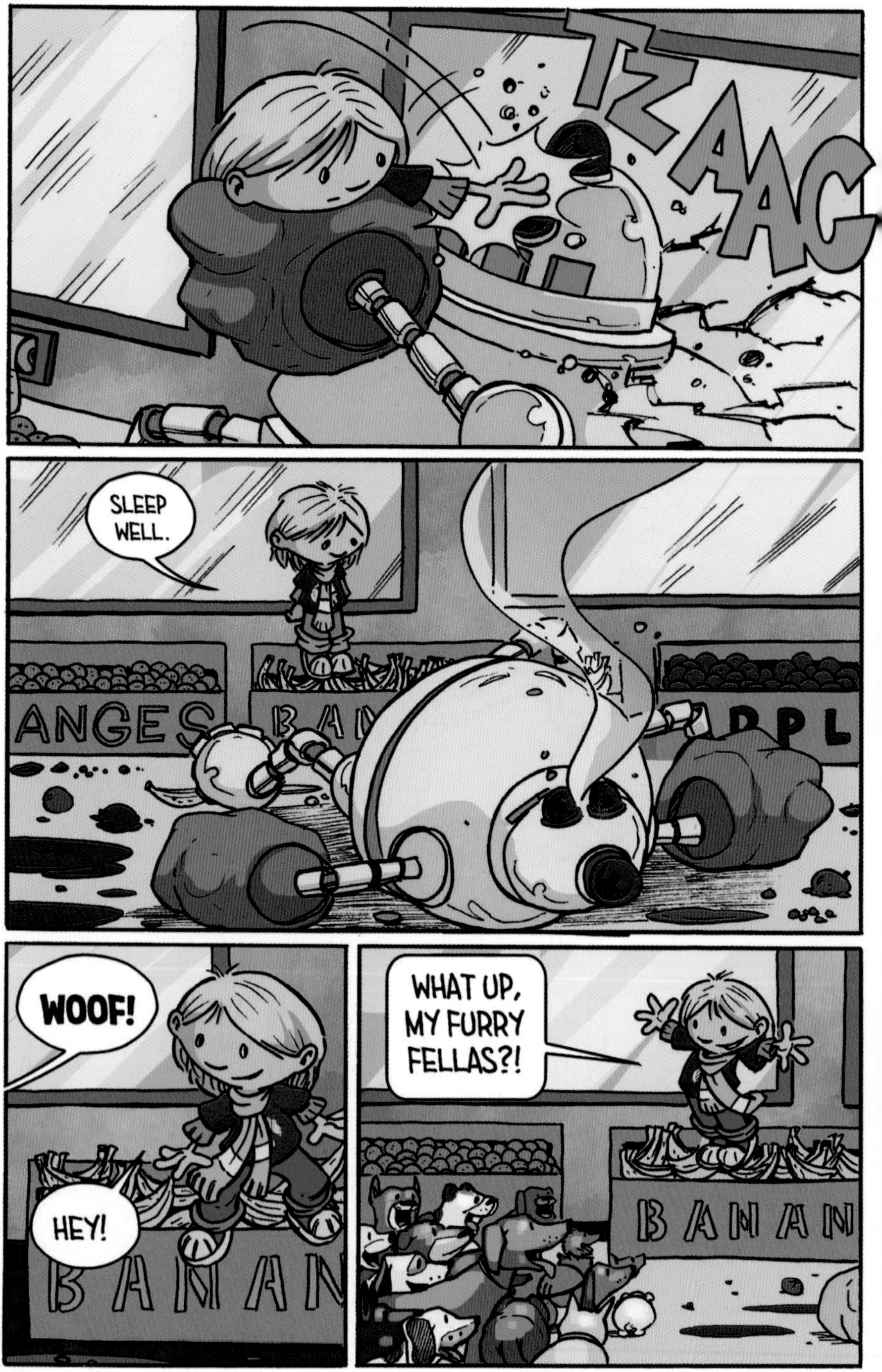
TZAAAG
SLEEP WELL.
ANGES
BAN
PPL
WOOF!
HEY!
BANAN
WHAT UP, MY FURRY FELLAS?!
BANAN

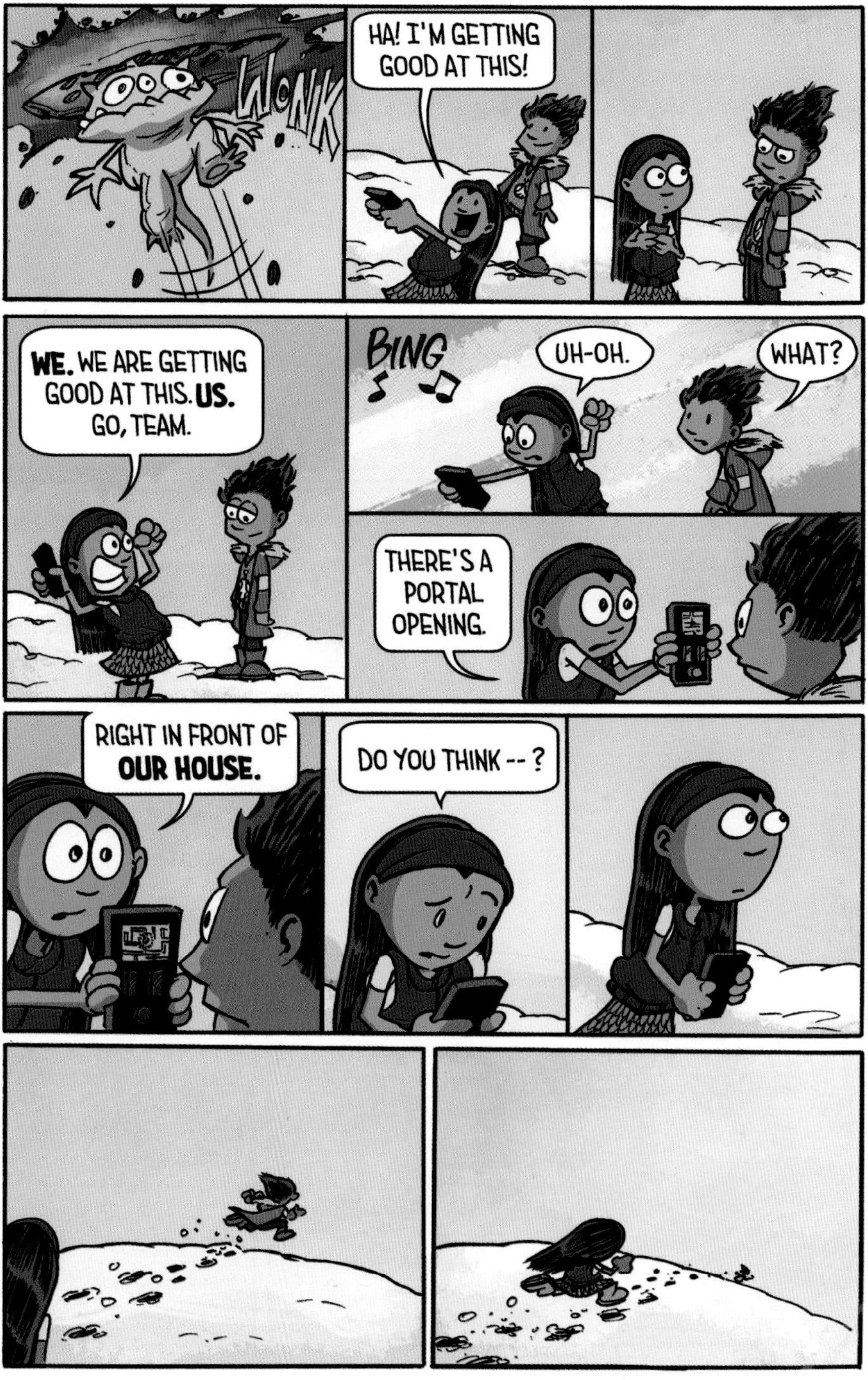
WONK
HA! I'M GETTING GOOD AT THIS!
WE. WE ARE GETTING GOOD AT THIS. **US.** GO, TEAM.
BING
UH-OH.
WHAT?
THERE'S A PORTAL OPENING.
RIGHT IN FRONT OF **OUR HOUSE.**
DO YOU THINK -- ?

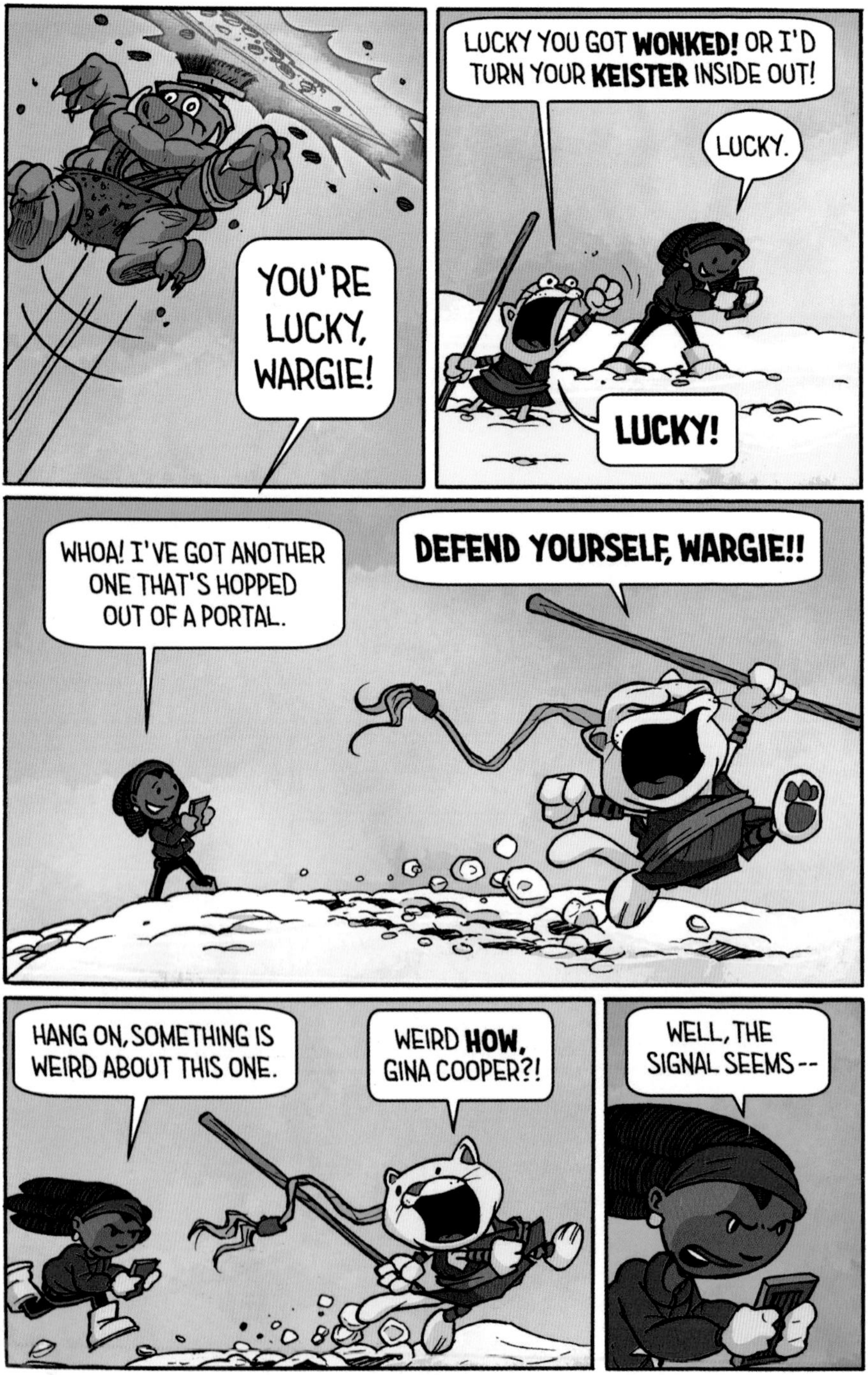
YOU'RE LUCKY, WARGIE!
LUCKY YOU GOT **WONKED!** OR I'D TURN YOUR **KEISTER** INSIDE OUT!
LUCKY.
LUCKY!
WHOA! I'VE GOT ANOTHER ONE THAT'S HOPPED OUT OF A PORTAL.
DEFEND YOURSELF, WARGIE!!
HANG ON, SOMETHING IS WEIRD ABOUT THIS ONE.
WEIRD **HOW,** GINA COOPER?!
WELL, THE SIGNAL SEEMS --

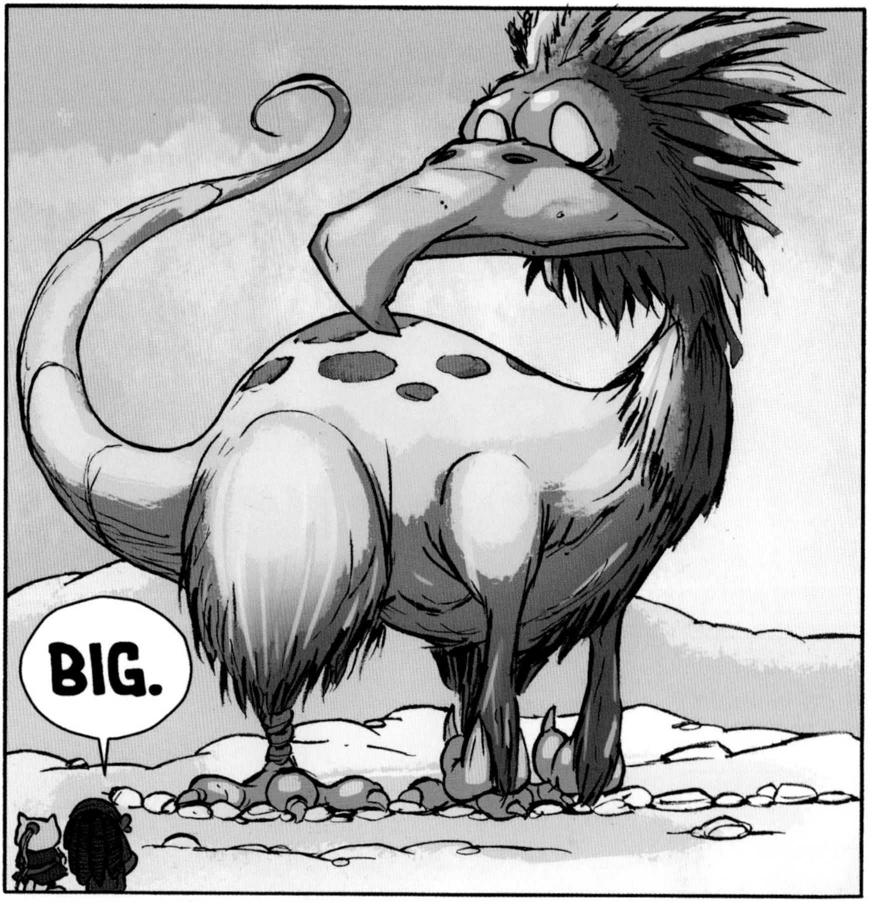
BIG.

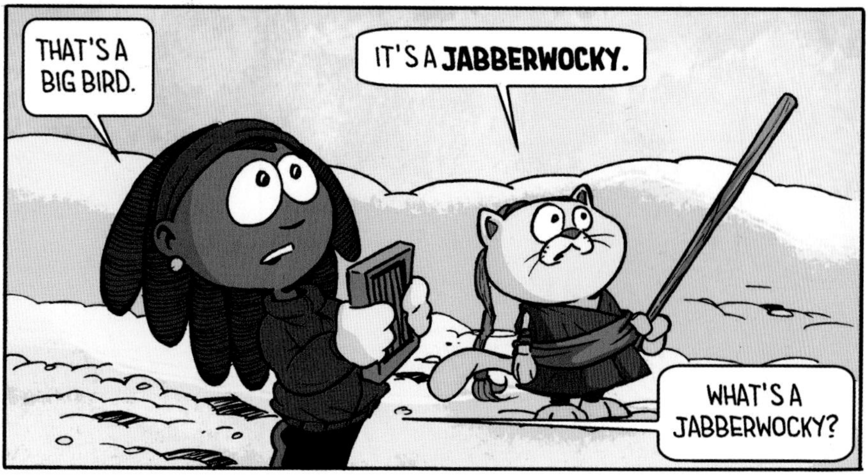
THAT'S A BIG BIRD.
IT'S A JABBERWOCKY.
WHAT'S A JABBERWOCKY?

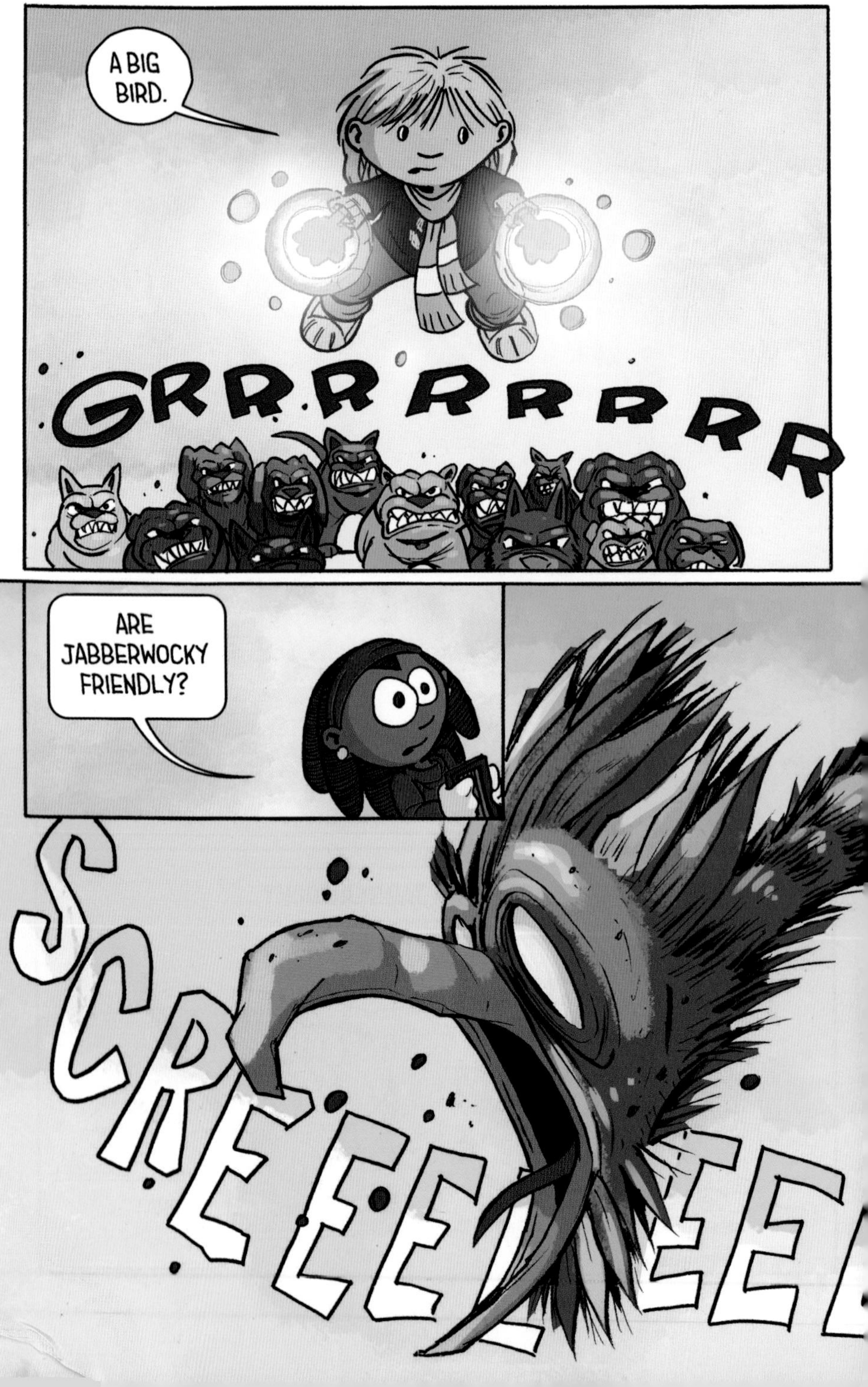
A BIG BIRD.
GRRRRRRRRR
ARE JABBERWOCKY FRIENDLY?
SCREEEEEEEE

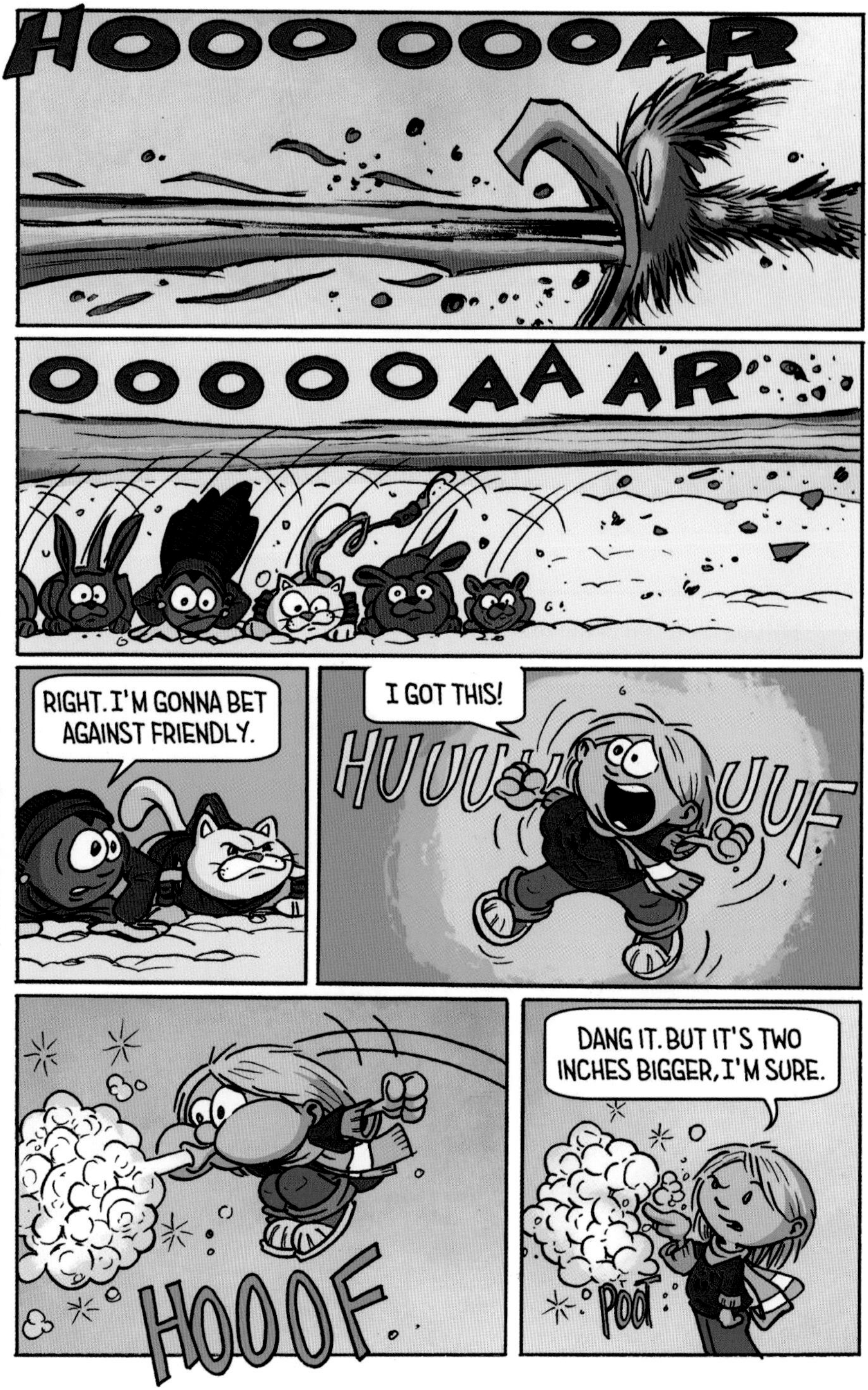
HOOOOOOOAR
OOOOOAAAR
RIGHT. I'M GONNA BET AGAINST FRIENDLY.
I GOT THIS!
HUUUUUUUF
HOOOF
DANG IT. BUT IT'S TWO INCHES BIGGER, I'M SURE.
POOF

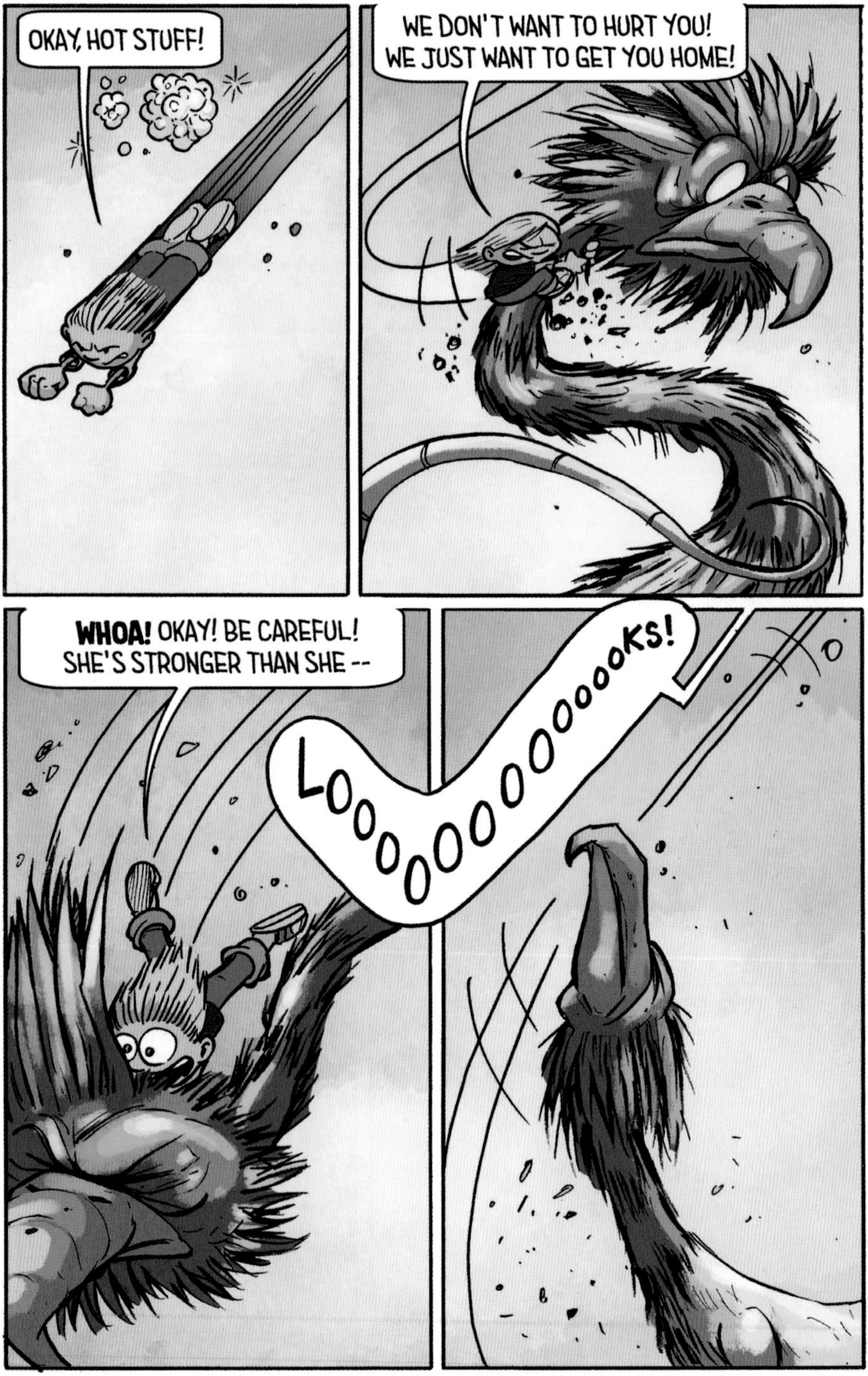
OKAY, HOT STUFF!
WE DON'T WANT TO HURT YOU! WE JUST WANT TO GET YOU HOME!
WHOA! OKAY! BE CAREFUL! SHE'S STRONGER THAN SHE --
LOOOOOOOOOOOOOOOOOKS!

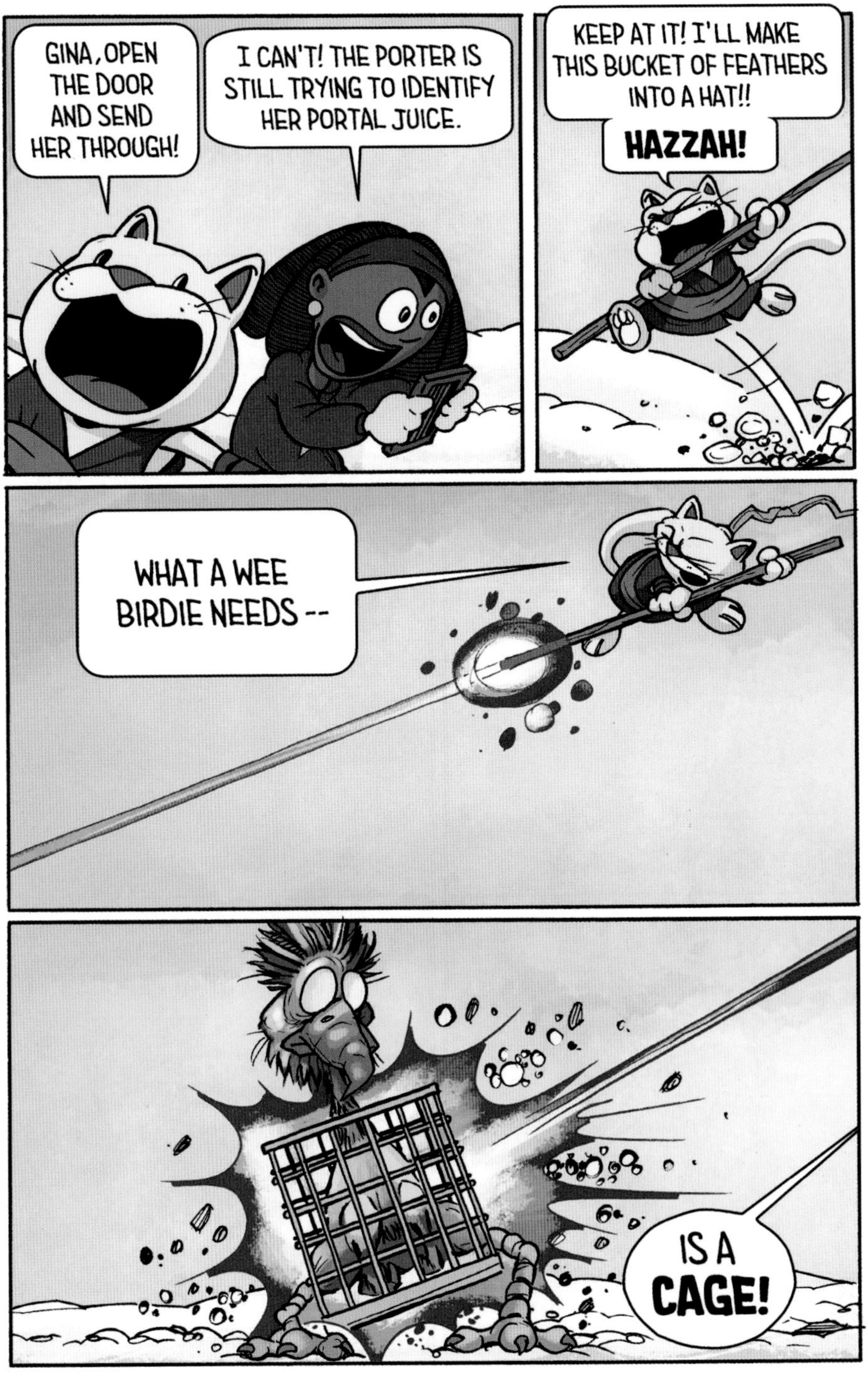
GINA, OPEN THE DOOR AND SEND HER THROUGH!
I CAN'T! THE PORTER IS STILL TRYING TO IDENTIFY HER PORTAL JUICE.
KEEP AT IT! I'LL MAKE THIS BUCKET OF FEATHERS INTO A HAT!!
HAZZAH!
WHAT A WEE BIRDIE NEEDS --
IS A CAGE!

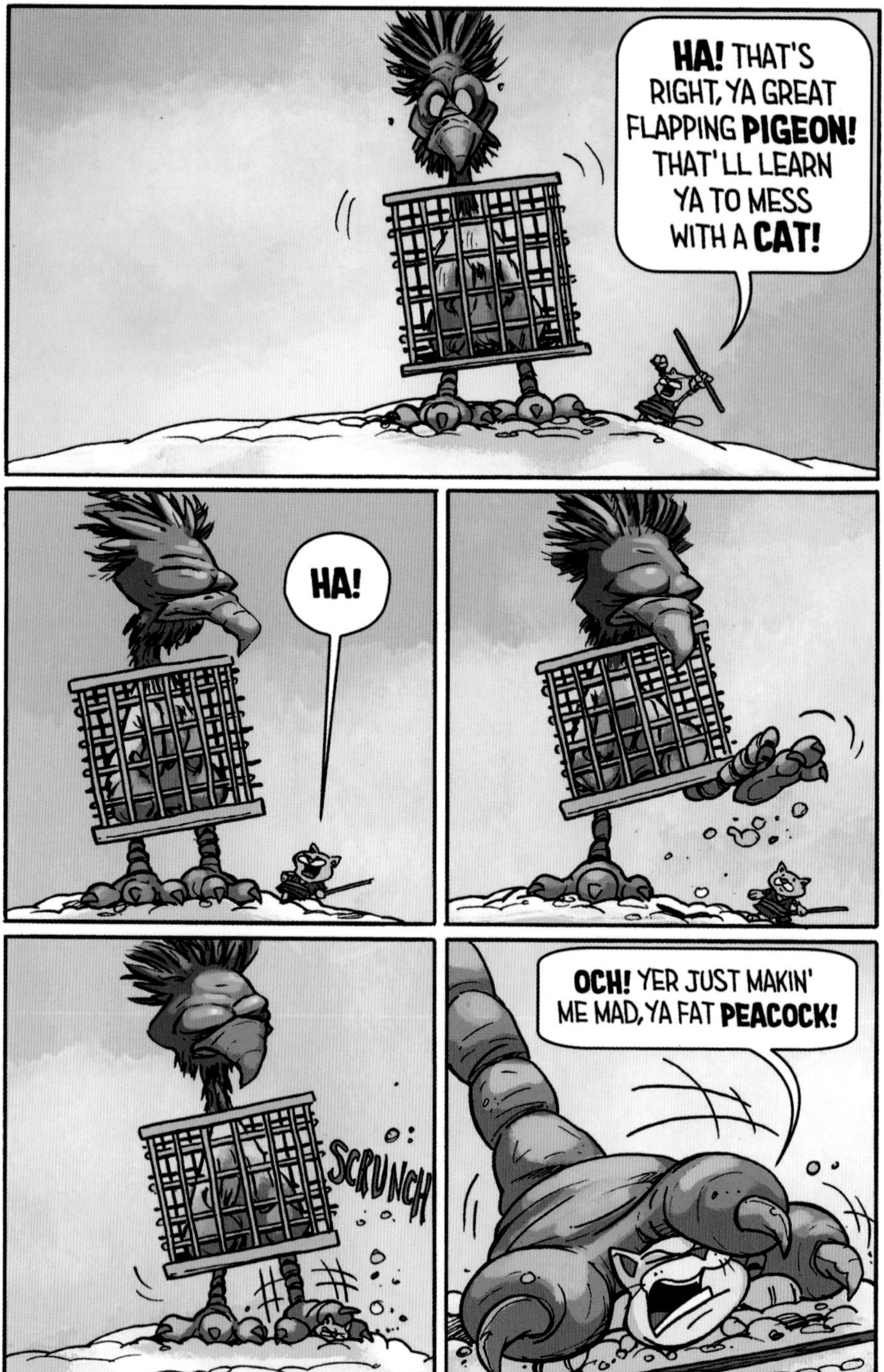
HA! THAT'S RIGHT, YA GREAT FLAPPING PIGEON! THAT'LL LEARN YA TO MESS WITH A CAT!
HA!
SCRUNCH
OCH! YER JUST MAKIN' ME MAD, YA FAT PEACOCK!

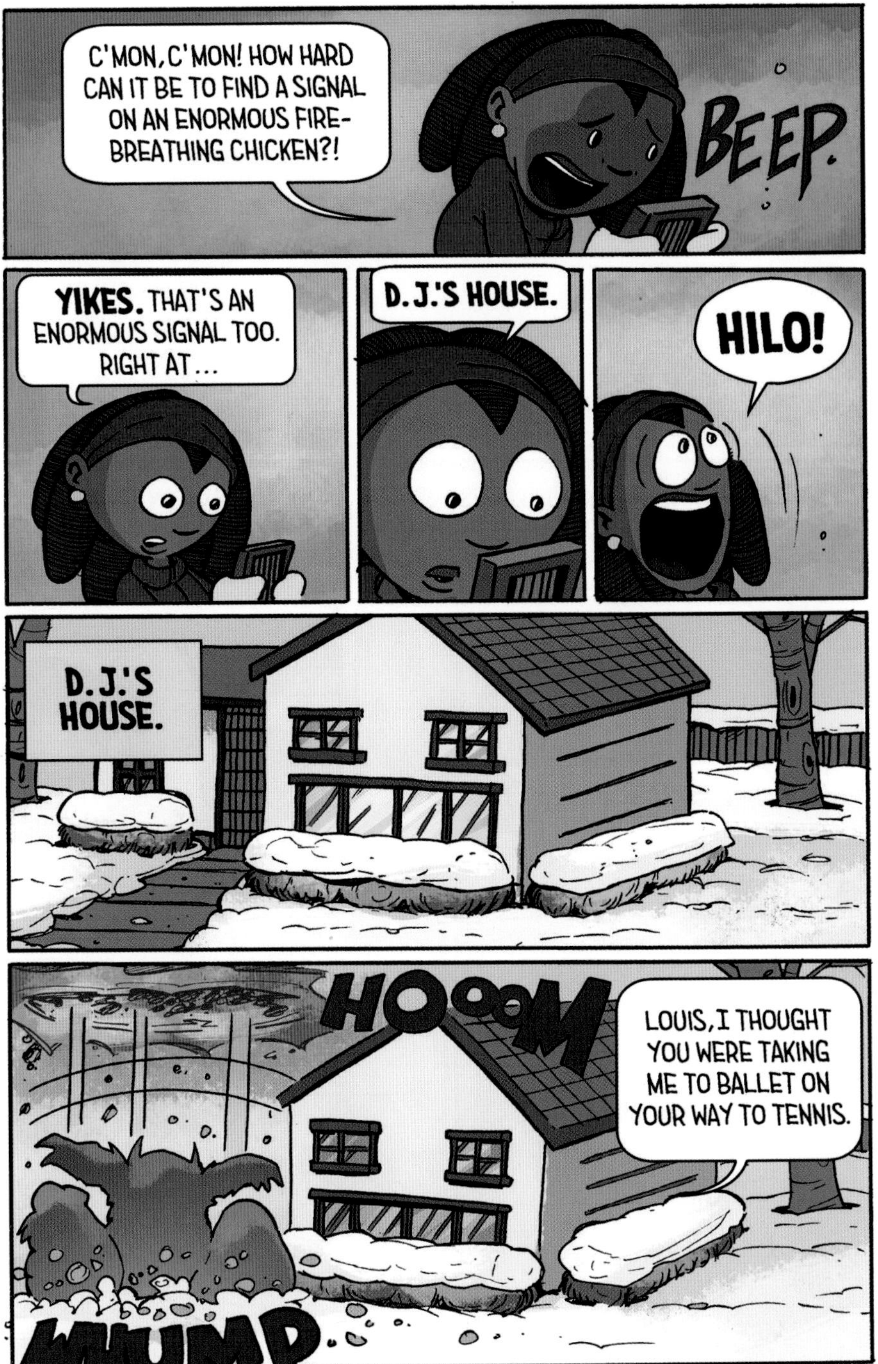
C'MON, C'MON! HOW HARD CAN IT BE TO FIND A SIGNAL ON AN ENORMOUS FIRE-BREATHING CHICKEN?!
BEEP.
YIKES. THAT'S AN ENORMOUS SIGNAL TOO. RIGHT AT...
D.J.'S HOUSE.
HILO!
D.J.'S HOUSE.
HOOOM
LOUIS, I THOUGHT YOU WERE TAKING ME TO BALLET ON YOUR WAY TO TENNIS.
WHUMP

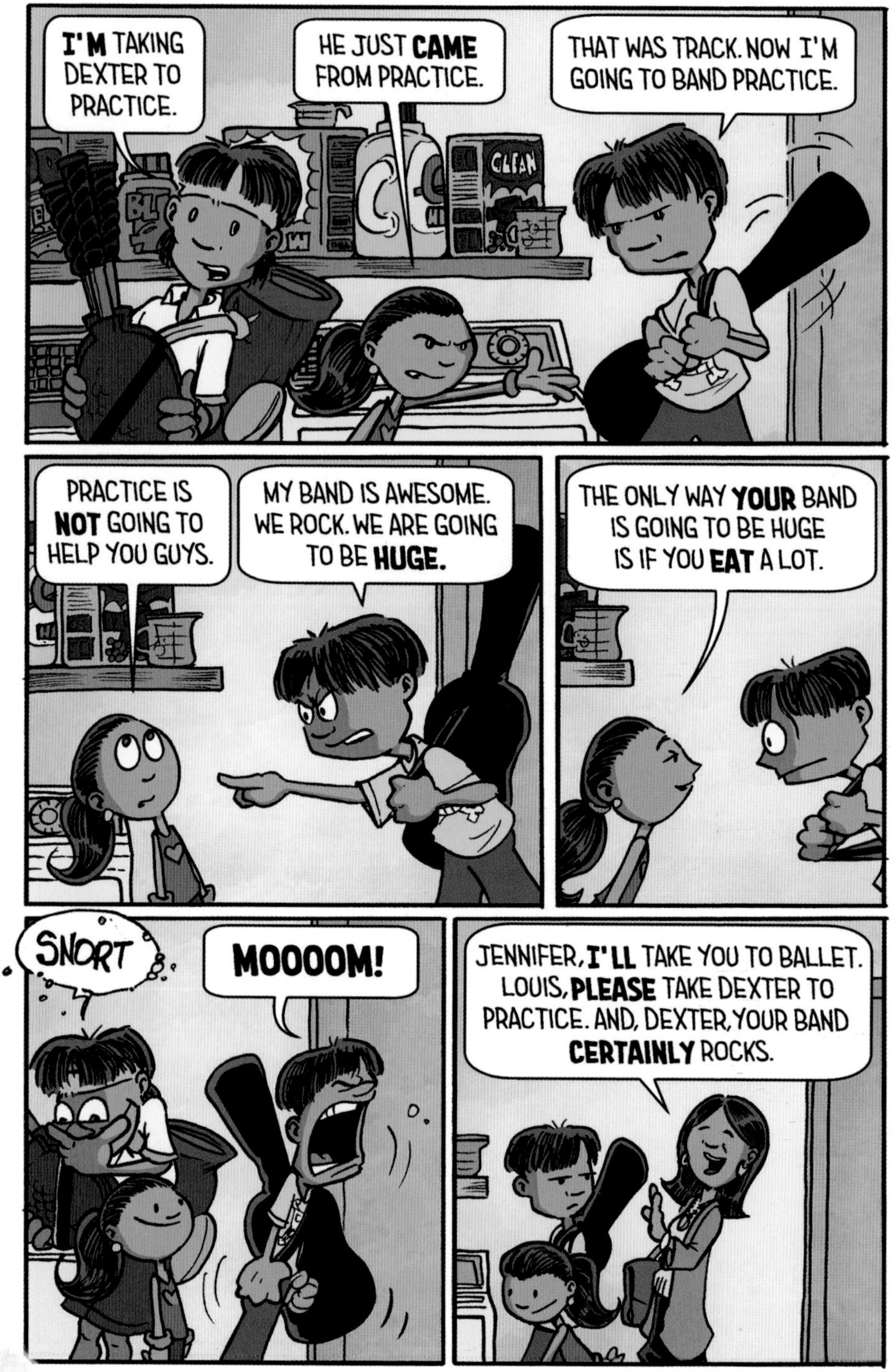
I'M TAKING DEXTER TO PRACTICE.
HE JUST CAME FROM PRACTICE.
THAT WAS TRACK. NOW I'M GOING TO BAND PRACTICE.
CLEAN
PRACTICE IS NOT GOING TO HELP YOU GUYS.
MY BAND IS AWESOME. WE ROCK. WE ARE GOING TO BE HUGE.
THE ONLY WAY YOUR BAND IS GOING TO BE HUGE IS IF YOU EAT A LOT.
SNORT
MOOOOM!
JENNIFER, I'LL TAKE YOU TO BALLET. LOUIS, PLEASE TAKE DEXTER TO PRACTICE. AND, DEXTER, YOUR BAND CERTAINLY ROCKS.

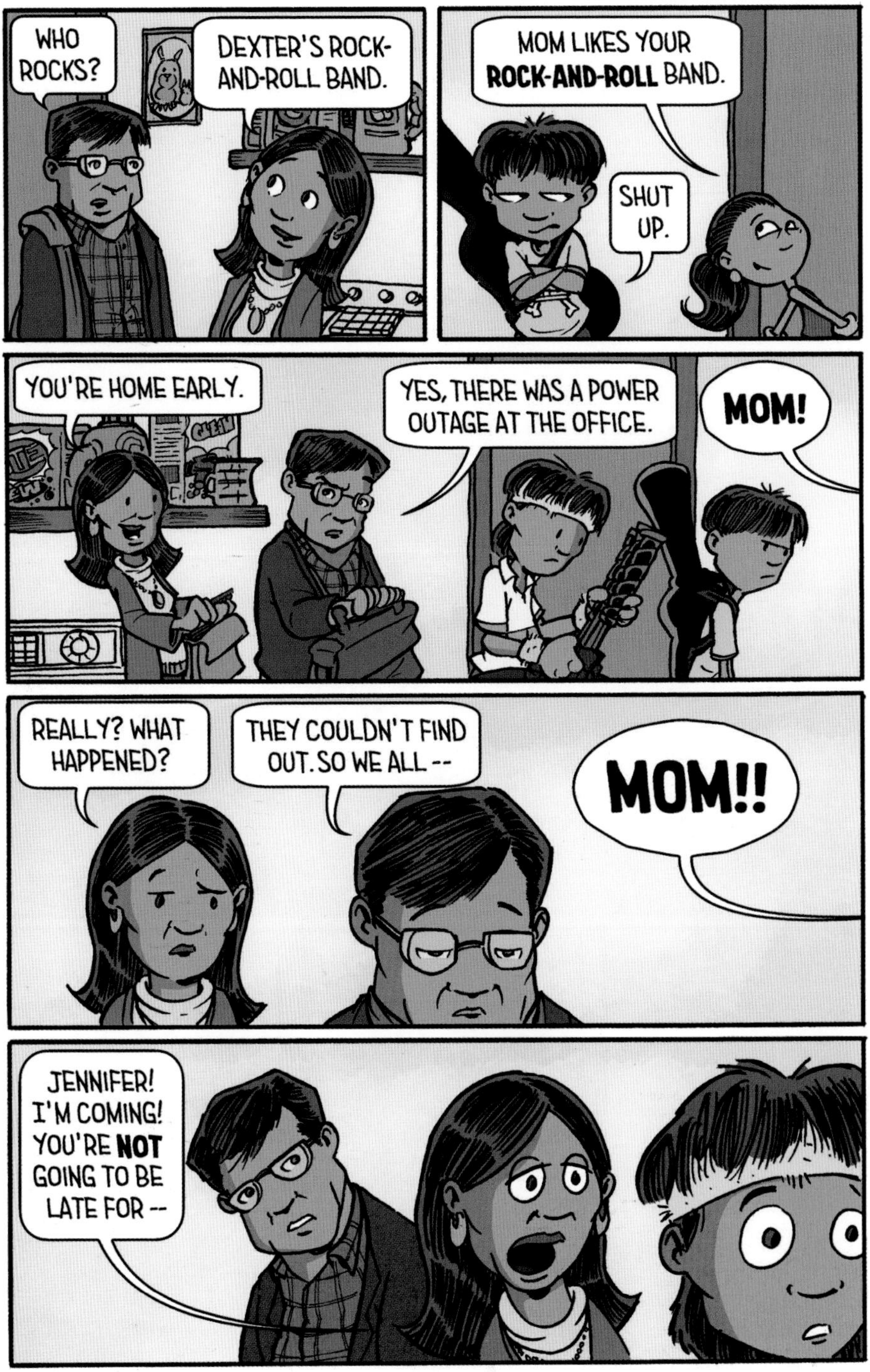

WHO ROCKS?
DEXTER'S ROCK-AND-ROLL BAND.
MOM LIKES YOUR ROCK-AND-ROLL BAND.
SHUT UP.
YOU'RE HOME EARLY.
YES, THERE WAS A POWER OUTAGE AT THE OFFICE.
MOM!
REALLY? WHAT HAPPENED?
THEY COULDN'T FIND OUT. SO WE ALL --
MOM!!
JENNIFER! I'M COMING! YOU'RE NOT GOING TO BE LATE FOR --

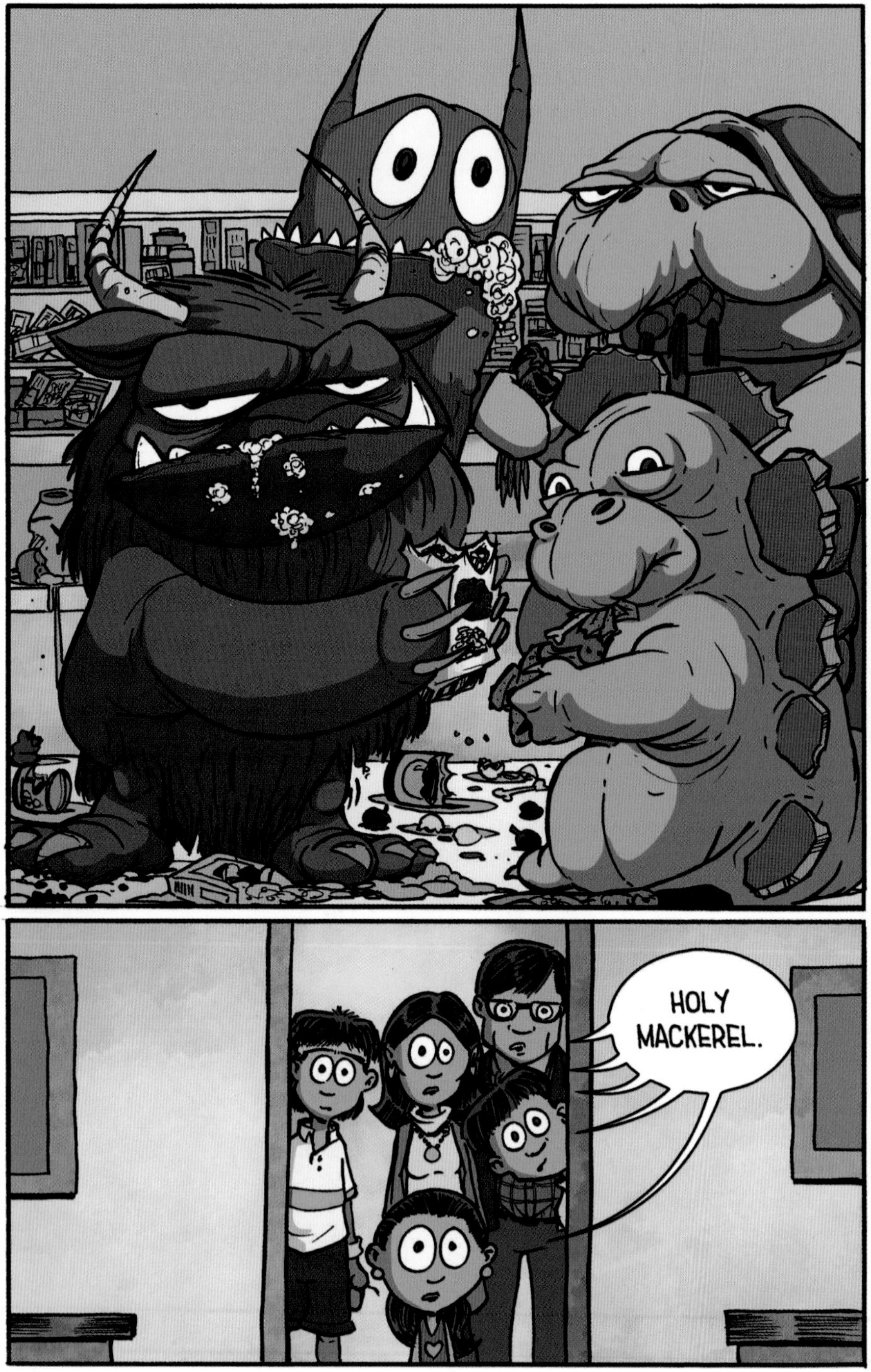
HOLY MACKEREL.

CHAPTER 8

BRAVE BOY

DEXTER, THESE AREN'T THE GUYS FROM YOUR BAND ARE THEY?
NO.
MAYBE THEY'RE FRIENDLY.

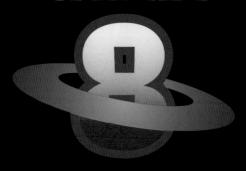

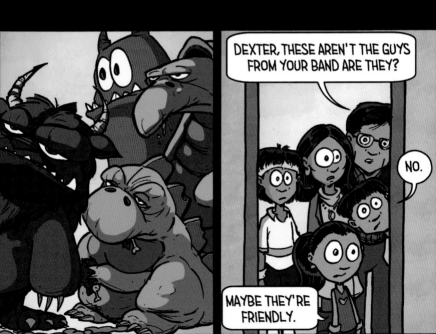

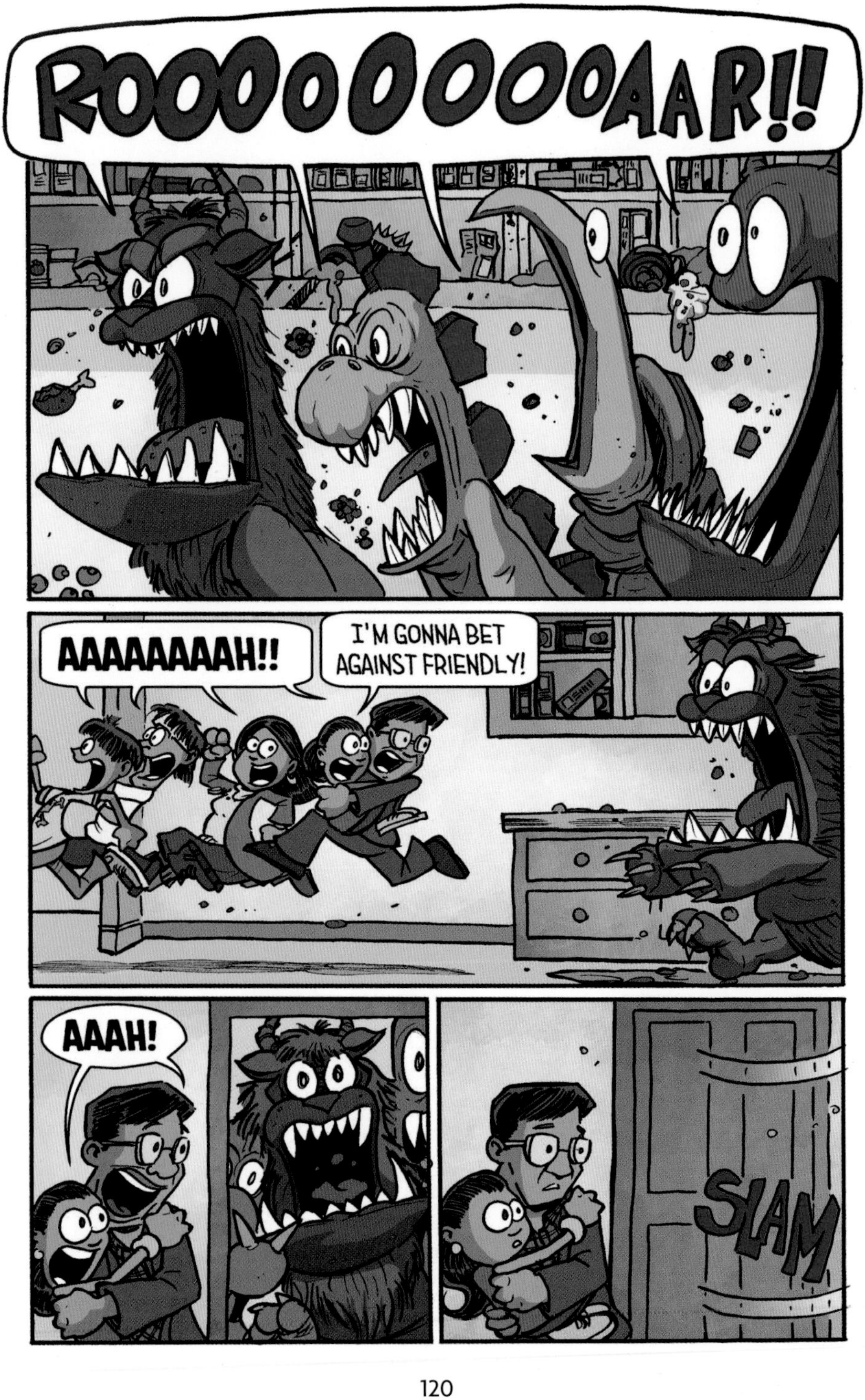

ROOOOOOOOOAAR!!
AAAAAAAAH!!
I'M GONNA BET AGAINST FRIENDLY!
AAAH!
SLAM

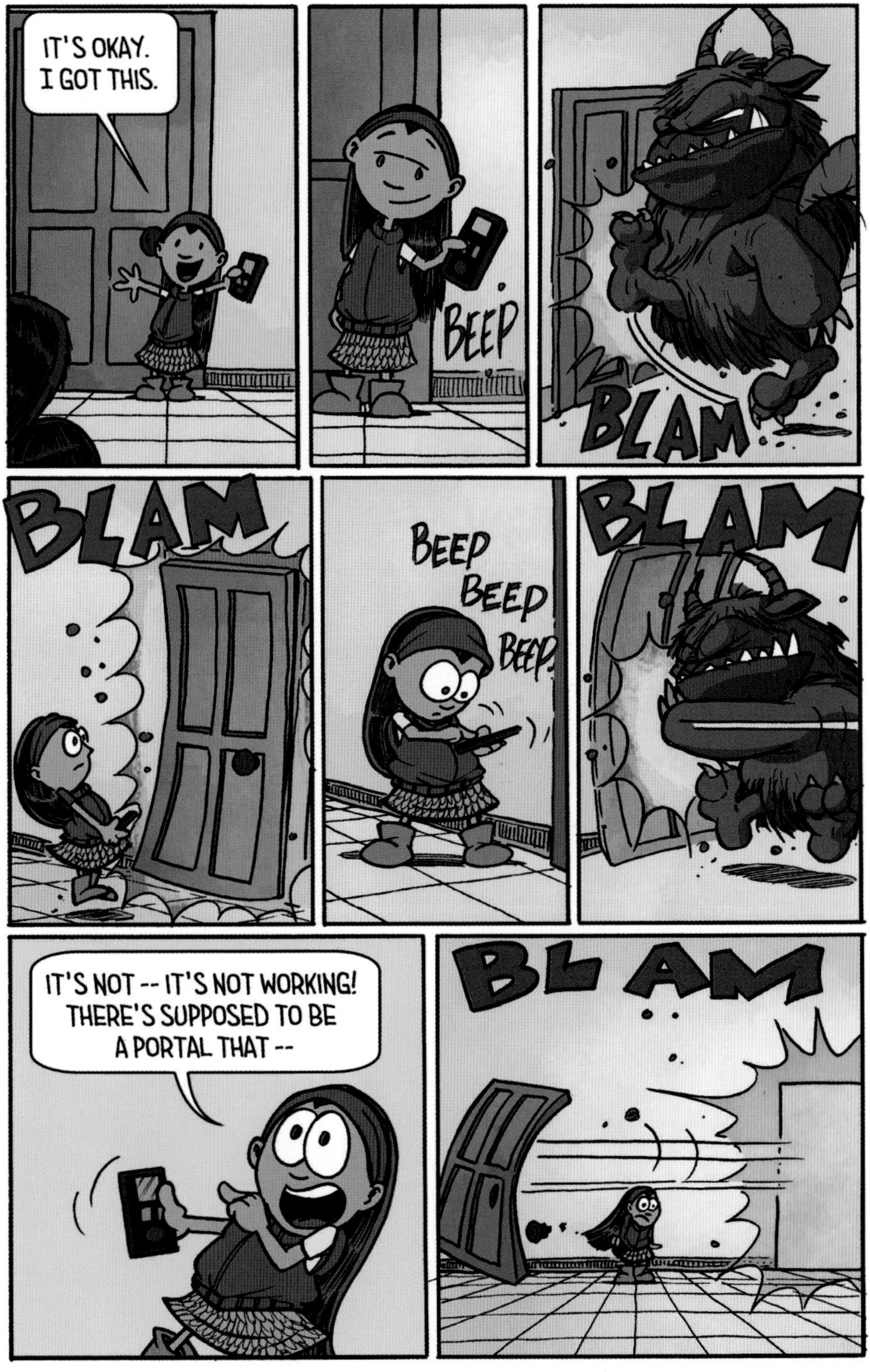
IT'S OKAY. I GOT THIS.
BEEP
BLAM
BLAM
BEEP
BEEP
BEEP
BLAM
IT'S NOT -- IT'S NOT WORKING! THERE'S SUPPOSED TO BE A PORTAL THAT --
BLAM

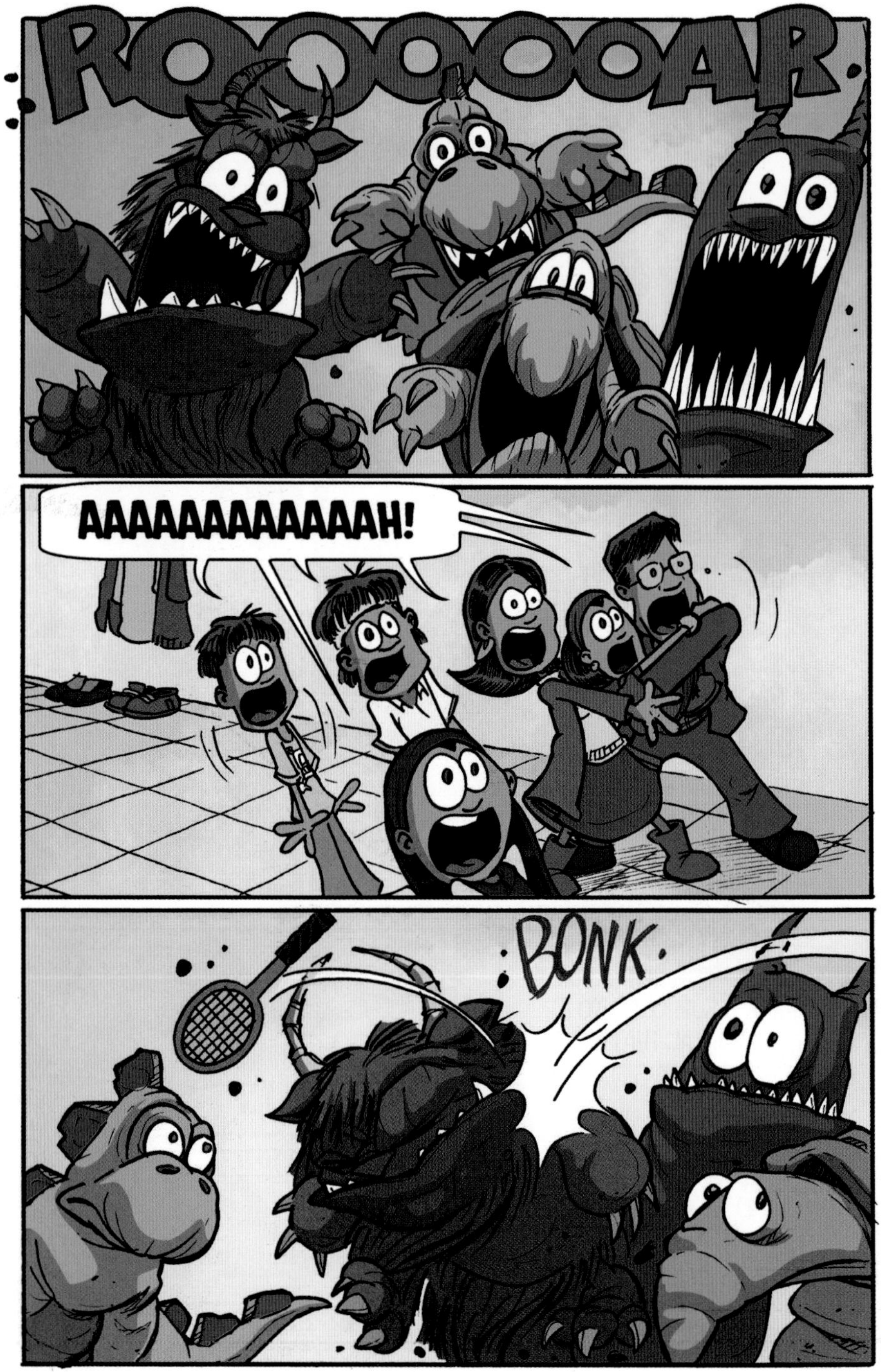
ROOOOOOAR
AAAAAAAAAAAAAH!
BONK

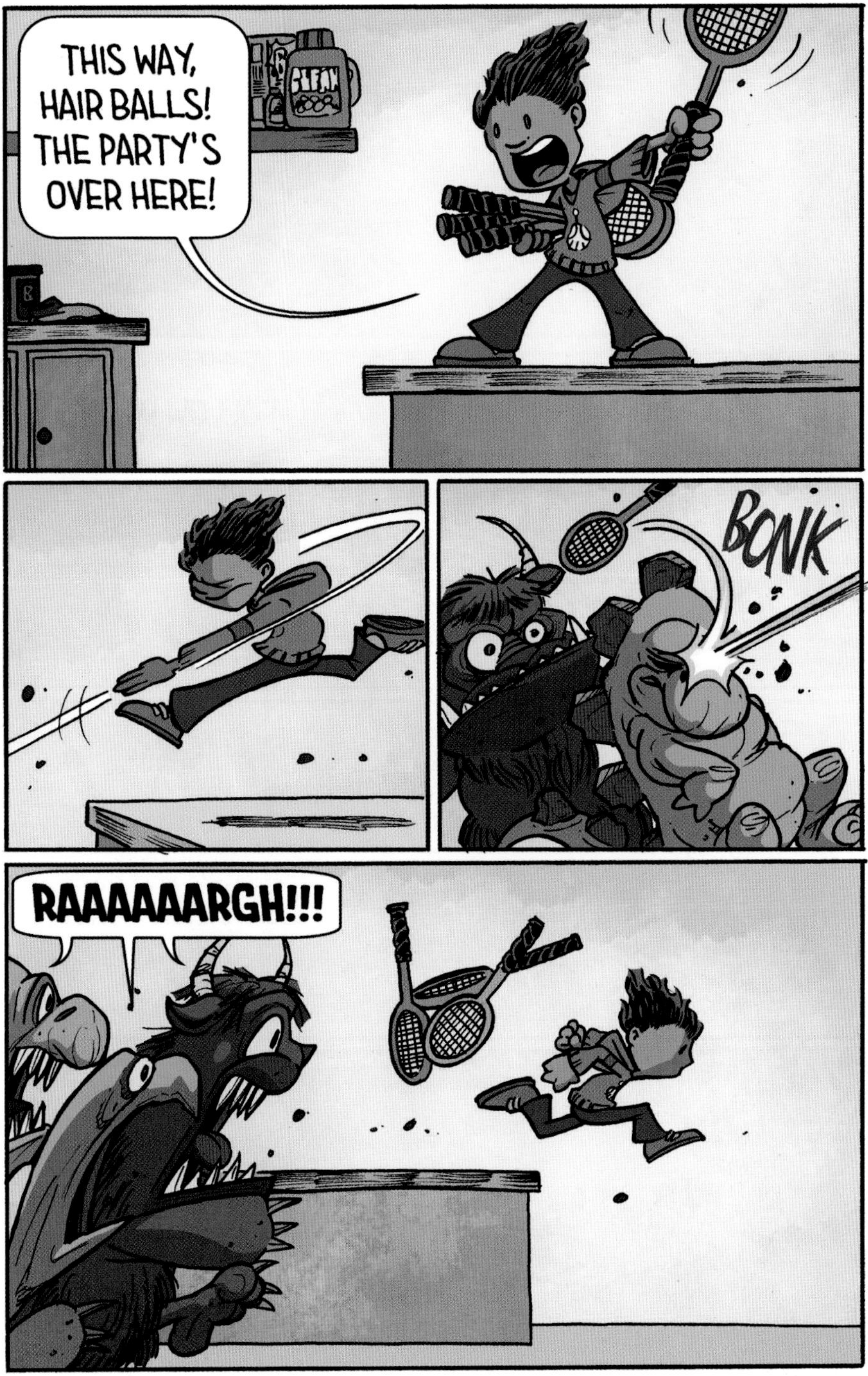
THIS WAY, HAIR BALLS! THE PARTY'S OVER HERE!
BONK
RAAAAAARGH!!!

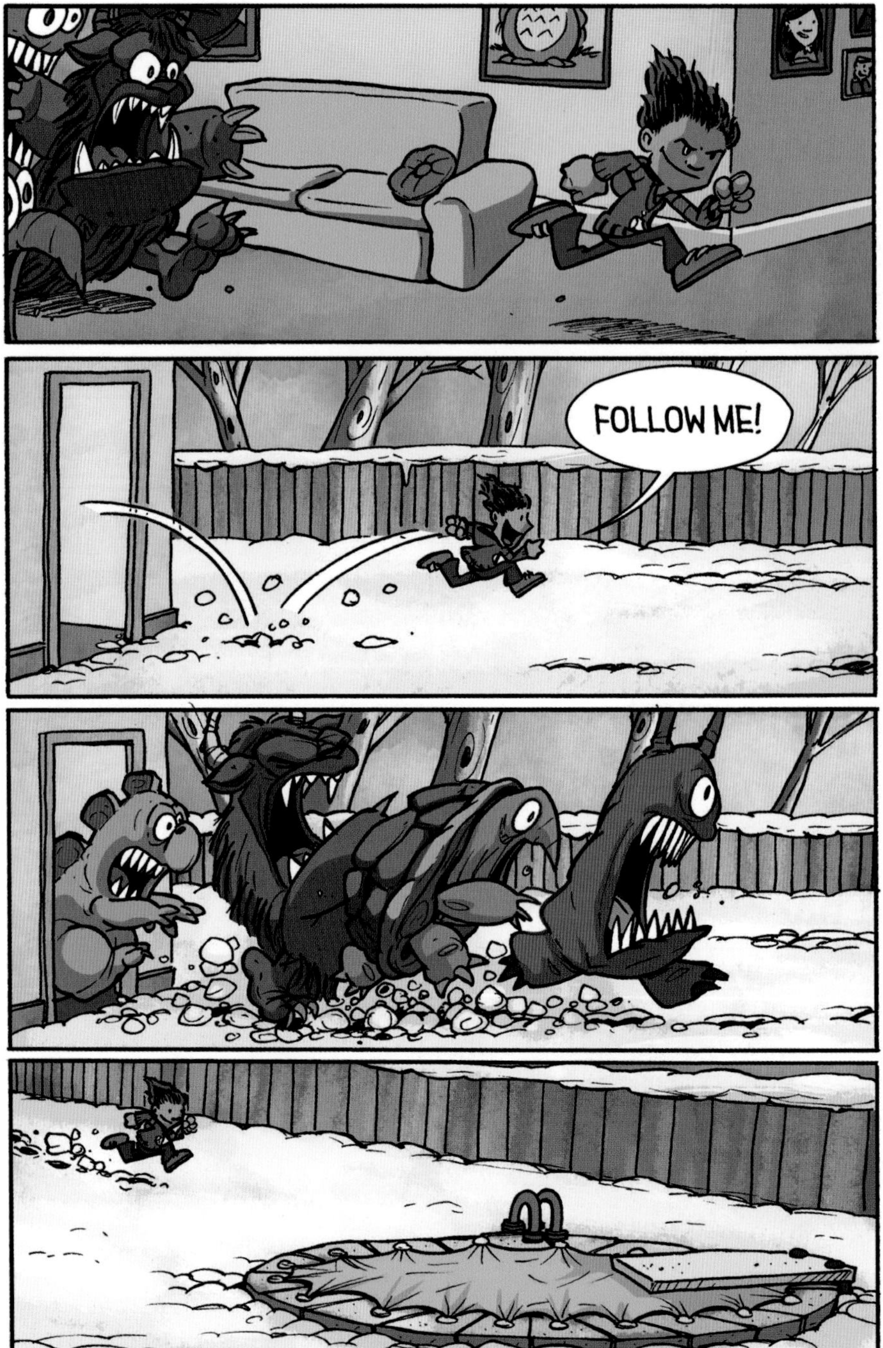
FOLLOW ME!

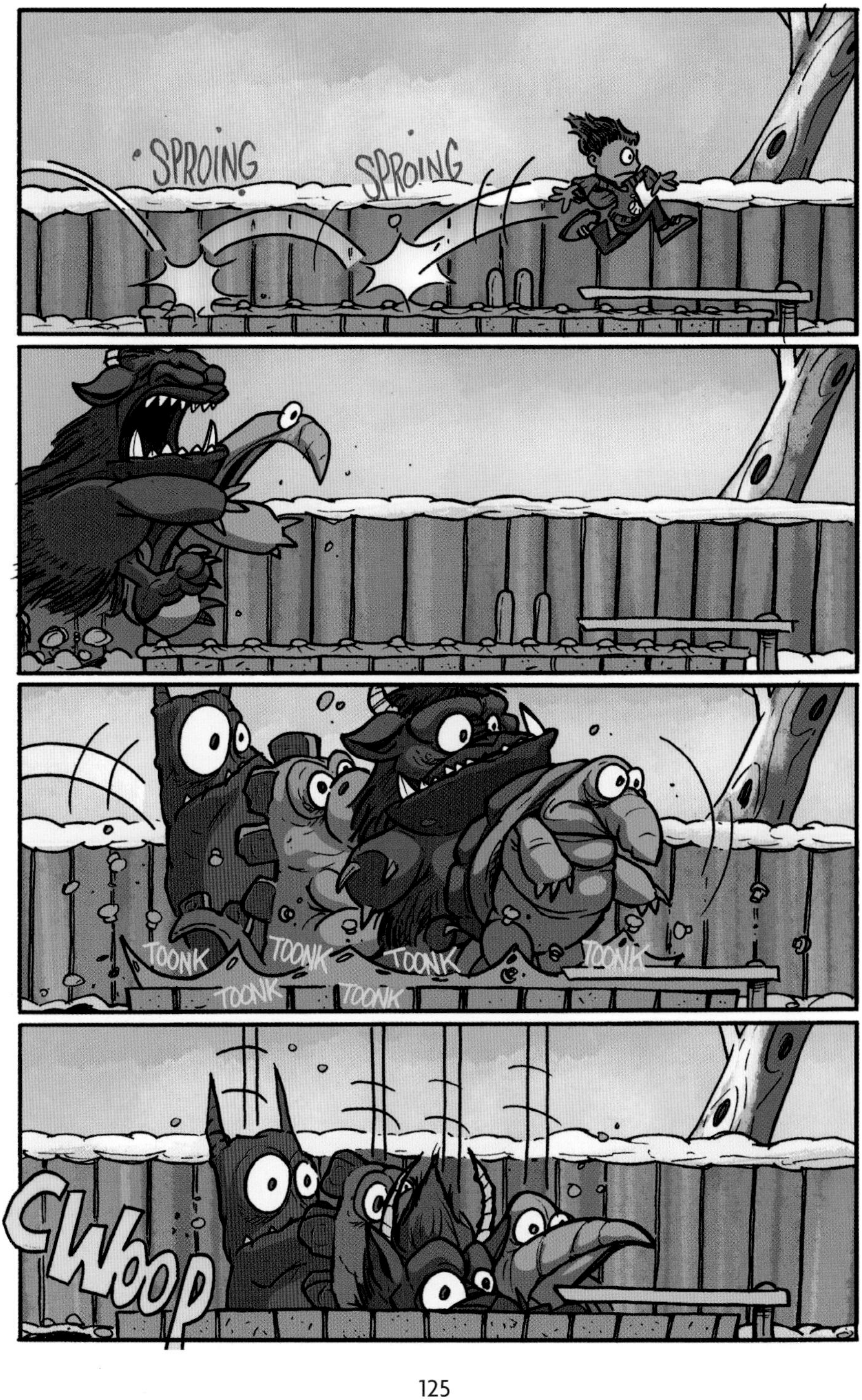
SPROING
SPROING
TOONK
TOONK
TOONK
TOONK
TOONK
TOONK
CWOOP

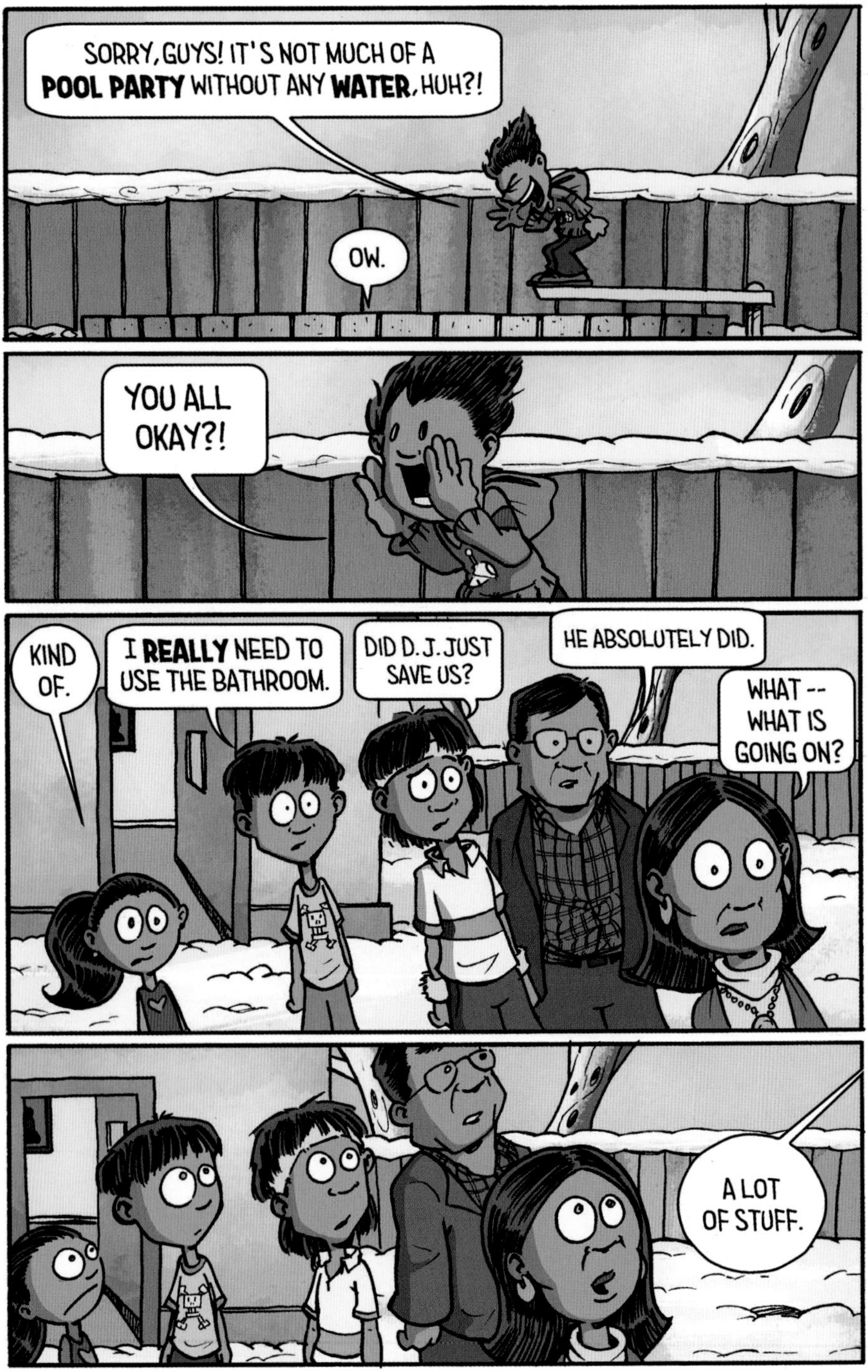

SORRY, GUYS! IT'S NOT MUCH OF A **POOL PARTY** WITHOUT ANY **WATER**, HUH?!
OW.
YOU ALL OKAY?!
KIND OF.
I **REALLY** NEED TO USE THE BATHROOM.
DID D. J. JUST SAVE US?
HE ABSOLUTELY DID.
WHAT -- WHAT IS GOING ON?
A LOT OF STUFF.

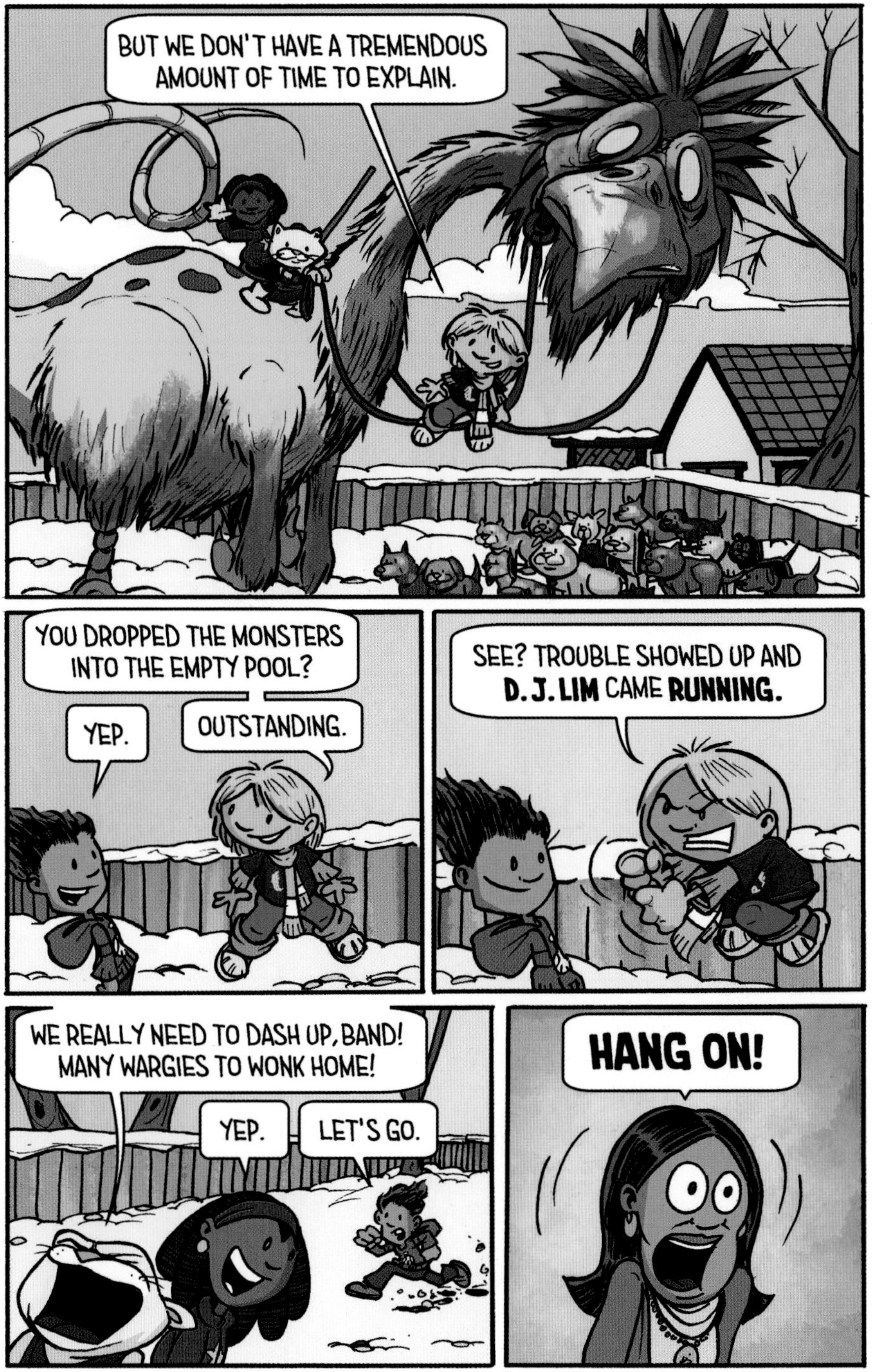
BUT WE DON'T HAVE A TREMENDOUS AMOUNT OF TIME TO EXPLAIN.
YOU DROPPED THE MONSTERS INTO THE EMPTY POOL?
YEP.
OUTSTANDING.
SEE? TROUBLE SHOWED UP AND **D. J. LIM** CAME **RUNNING.**
WE REALLY NEED TO DASH UP, BAND! MANY WARGIES TO WONK HOME!
YEP.
LET'S GO.
HANG ON!

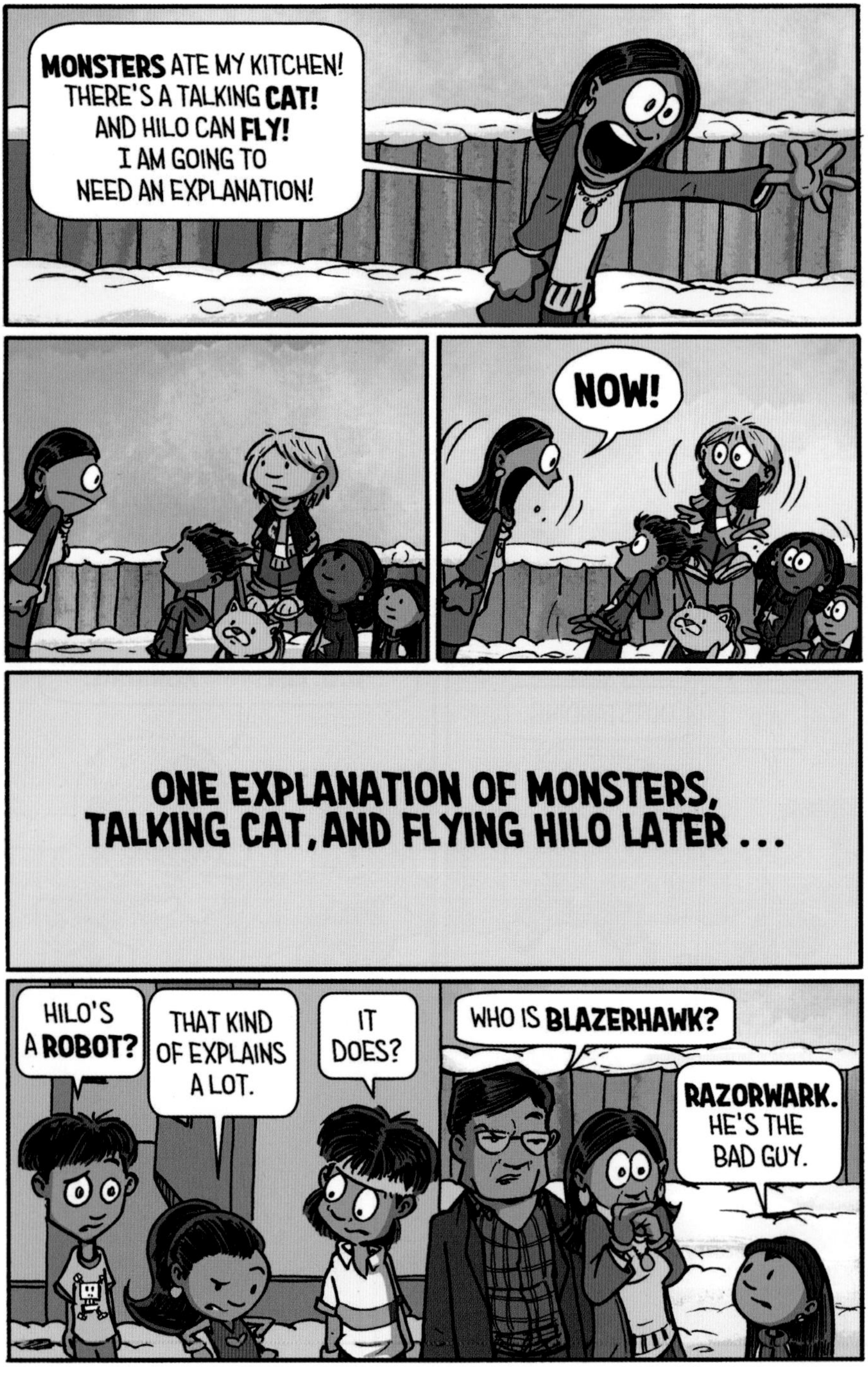
MONSTERS ATE MY KITCHEN! THERE'S A TALKING CAT! AND HILO CAN FLY! I AM GOING TO NEED AN EXPLANATION!
NOW!
ONE EXPLANATION OF MONSTERS, TALKING CAT, AND FLYING HILO LATER ...
HILO'S A ROBOT?
THAT KIND OF EXPLAINS A LOT.
IT DOES?
WHO IS BLAZERHAWK?
RAZORWARK. HE'S THE BAD GUY.

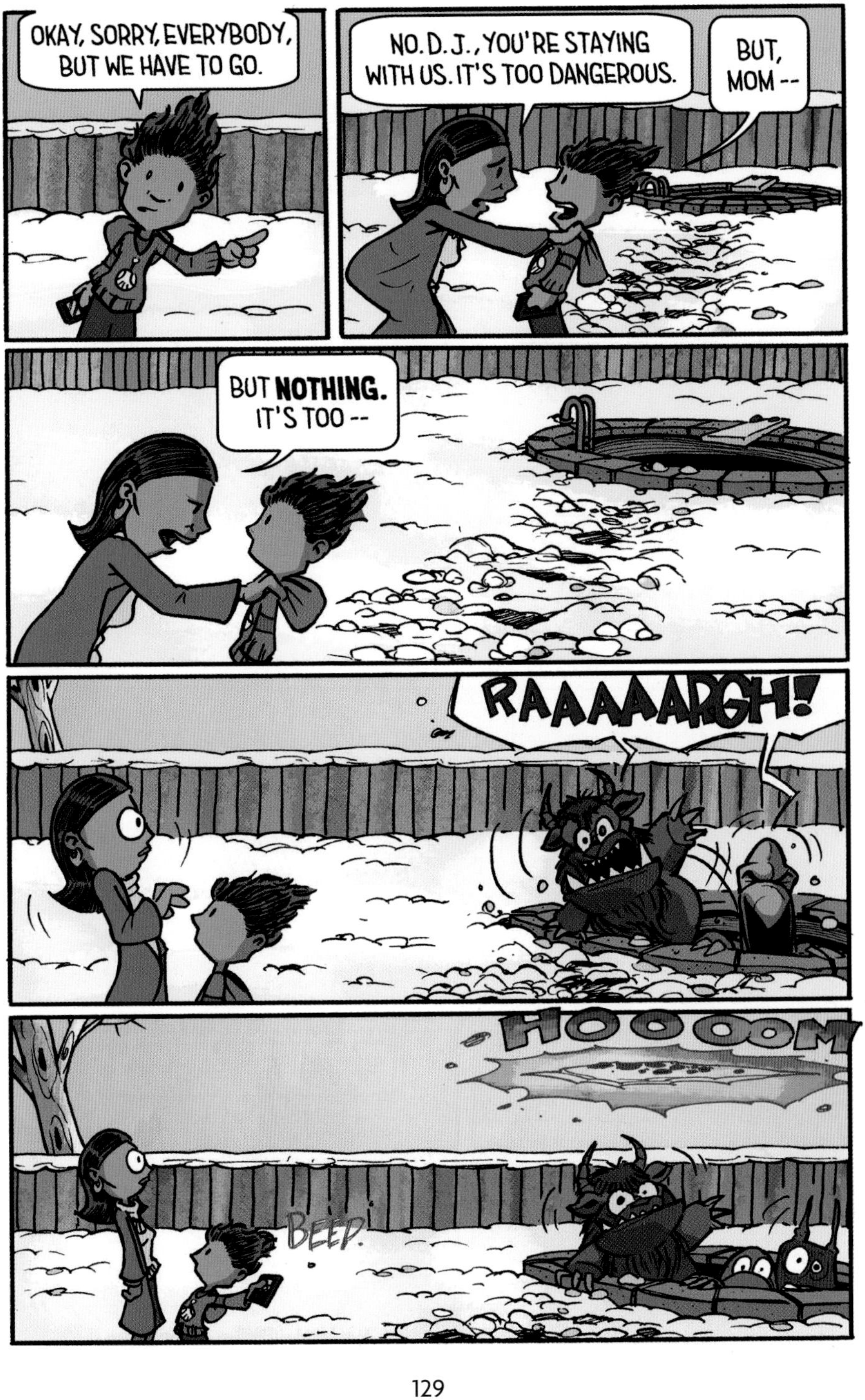
OKAY, SORRY, EVERYBODY, BUT WE HAVE TO GO.
NO. D.J., YOU'RE STAYING WITH US. IT'S TOO DANGEROUS.
BUT, MOM --
BUT **NOTHING.** IT'S TOO --
RAAAAARGH!
HOOOOM
BEEP.

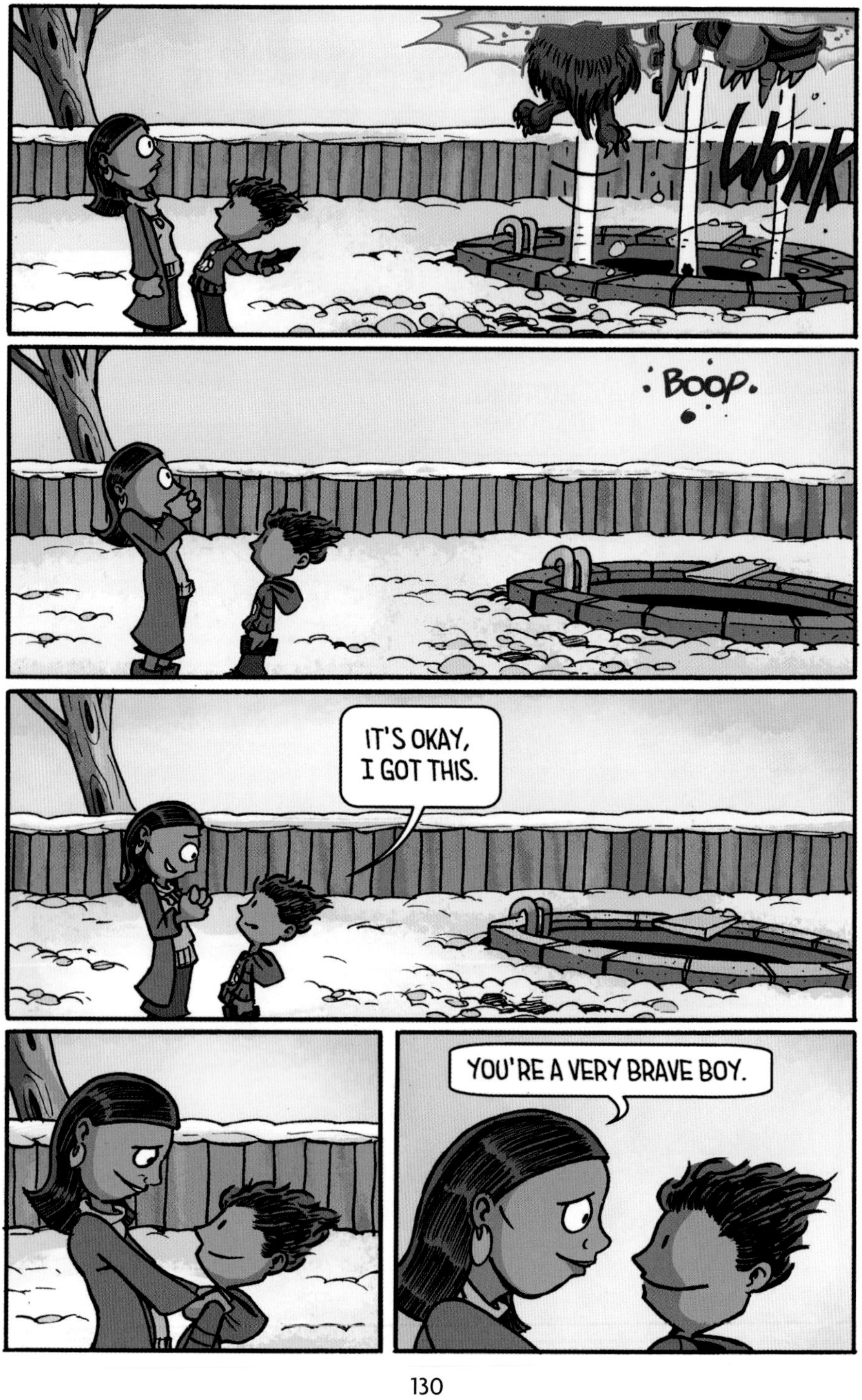
WONK
BOOP
IT'S OKAY, I GOT THIS.
YOU'RE A VERY BRAVE BOY.

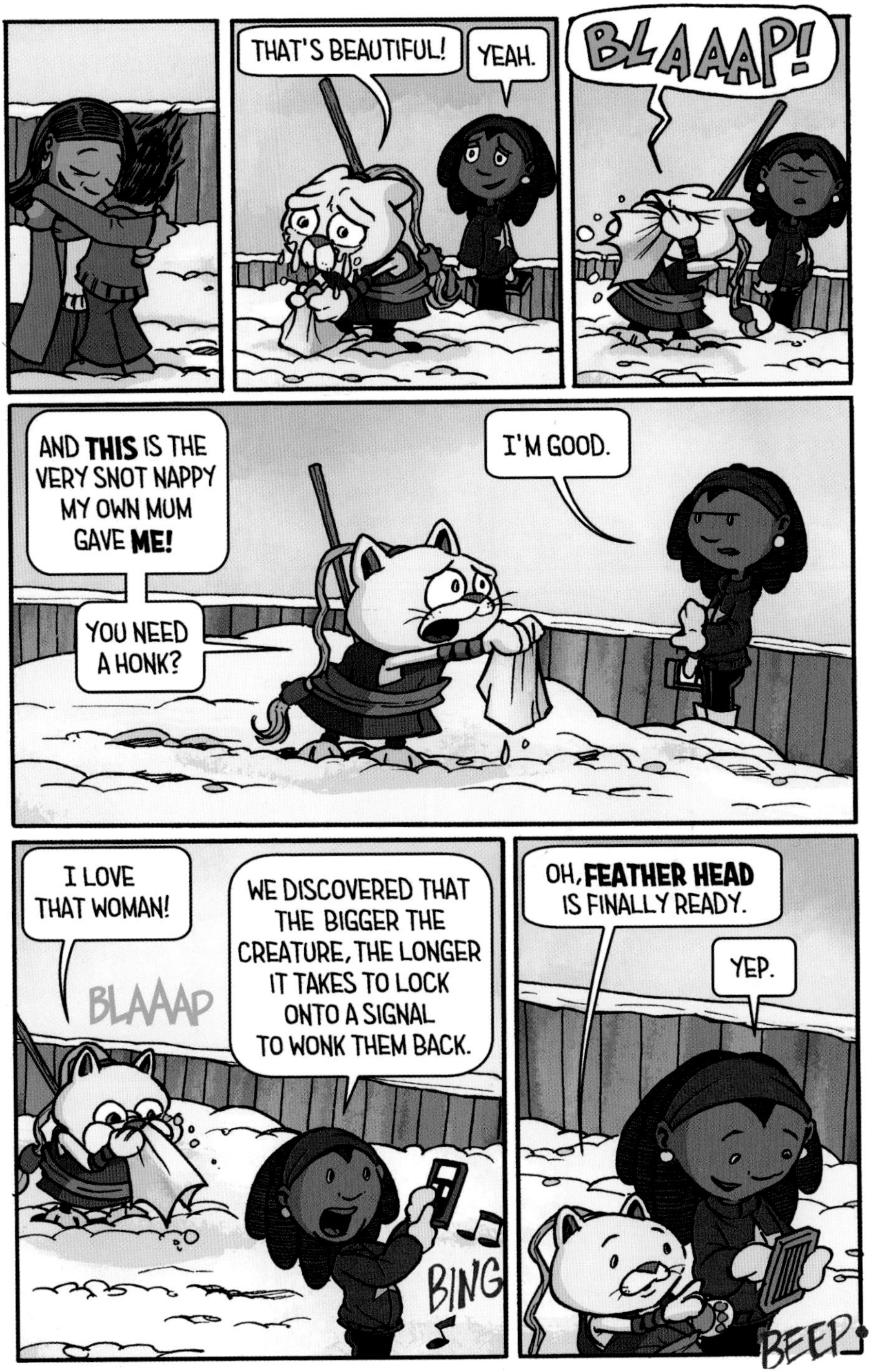
THAT'S BEAUTIFUL!
YEAH.
BLAAAP!
AND THIS IS THE VERY SNOT NAPPY MY OWN MUM GAVE ME!
YOU NEED A HONK?
I'M GOOD.
I LOVE THAT WOMAN!
BLAAAP
WE DISCOVERED THAT THE BIGGER THE CREATURE, THE LONGER IT TAKES TO LOCK ONTO A SIGNAL TO WONK THEM BACK.
BING
OH, FEATHER HEAD IS FINALLY READY.
YEP.
BEEP

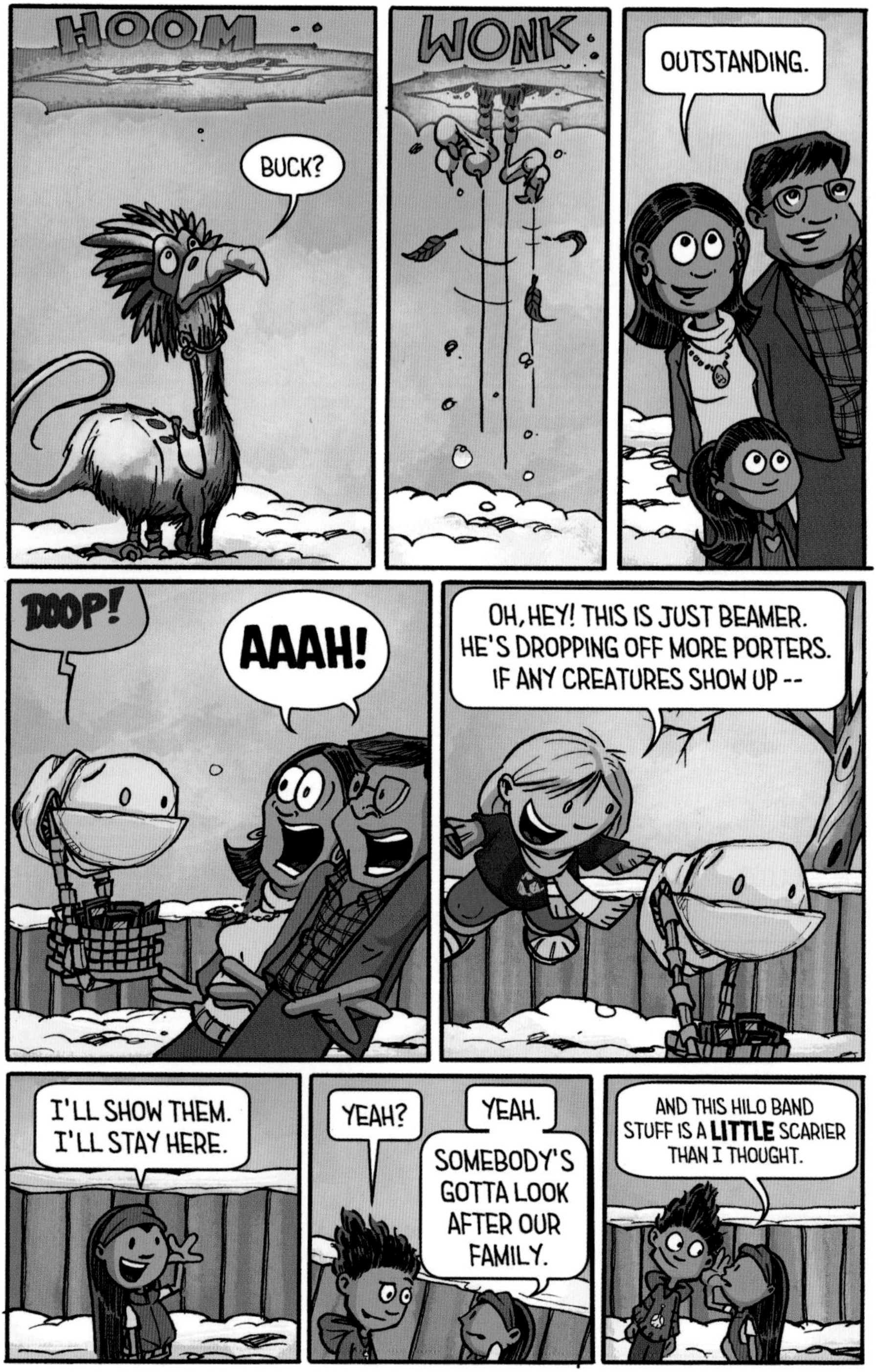
HOOM
BUCK?
WONK
OUTSTANDING.
DOOP!
AAAH!
OH, HEY! THIS IS JUST BEAMER. HE'S DROPPING OFF MORE PORTERS. IF ANY CREATURES SHOW UP --
I'LL SHOW THEM. I'LL STAY HERE.
YEAH?
YEAH.
SOMEBODY'S GOTTA LOOK AFTER OUR FAMILY.
AND THIS HILO BAND STUFF IS A LITTLE SCARIER THAN I THOUGHT.

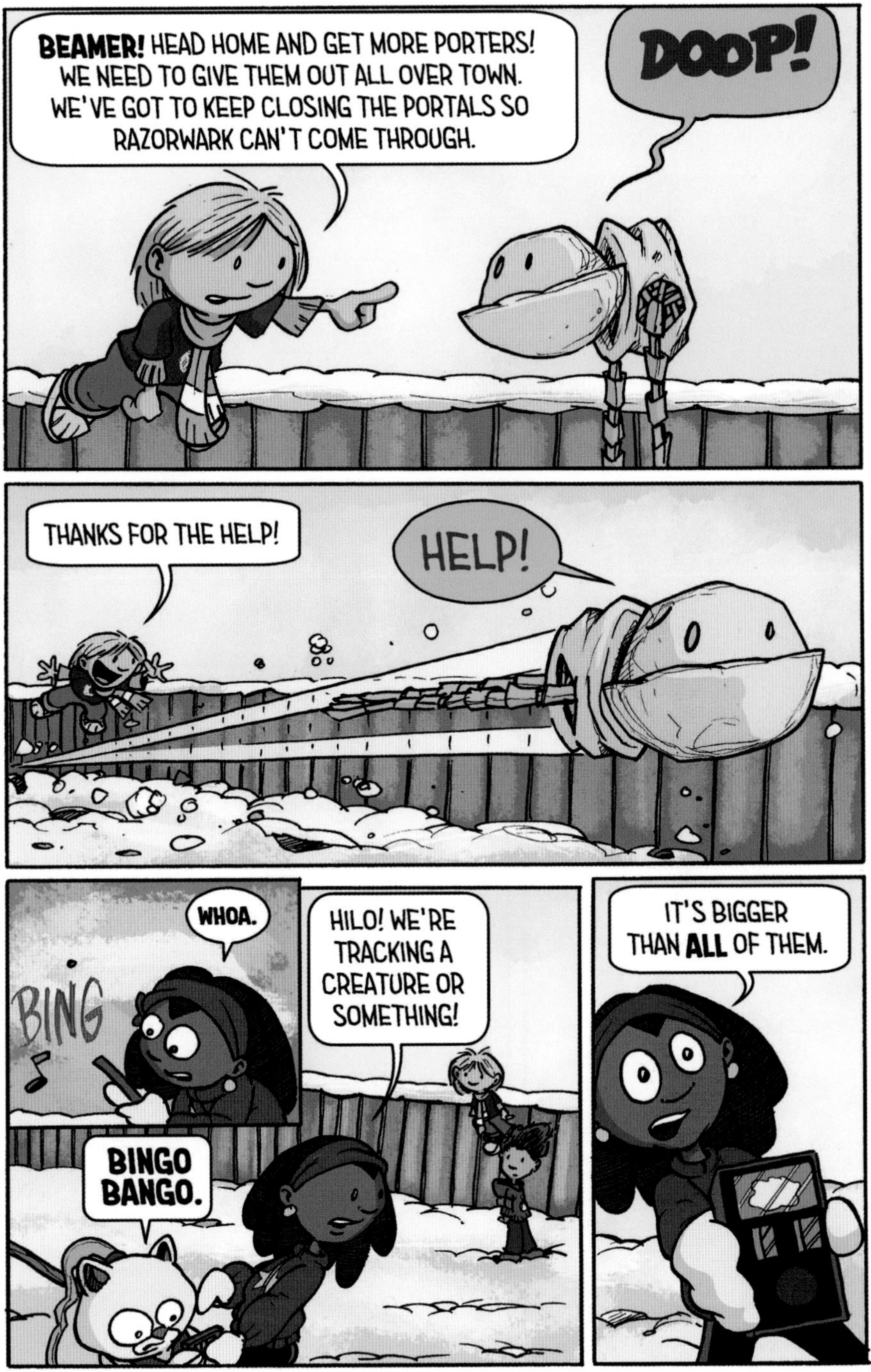

BEAMER! HEAD HOME AND GET MORE PORTERS! WE NEED TO GIVE THEM OUT ALL OVER TOWN. WE'VE GOT TO KEEP CLOSING THE PORTALS SO RAZORWARK CAN'T COME THROUGH.
DOOP!
THANKS FOR THE HELP!
HELP!
BING
WHOA.
BINGO BANGO.
HILO! WE'RE TRACKING A CREATURE OR SOMETHING!
IT'S BIGGER THAN ALL OF THEM.

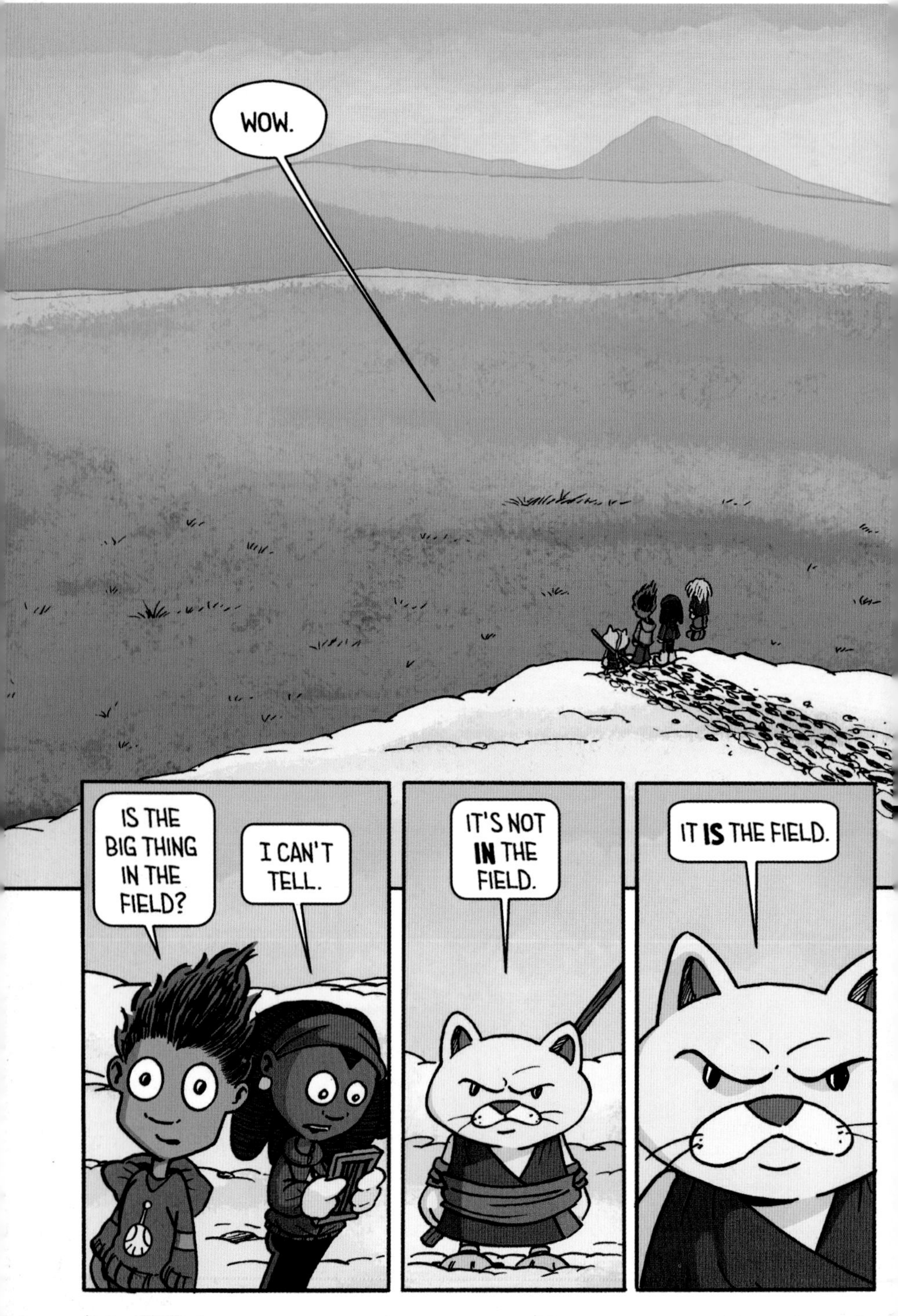
WOW.
IS THE BIG THING IN THE FIELD?
I CAN'T TELL.
IT'S NOT **IN** THE FIELD.
IT **IS** THE FIELD.

CHAPTER 9

VEGGIES

WHAT DO YOU MEAN, IT **IS** THE FIELD?
WATCH.
TZAK

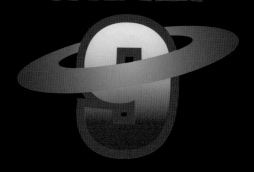

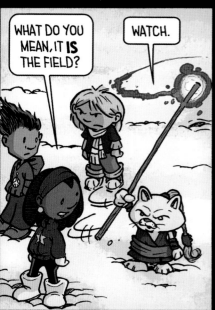

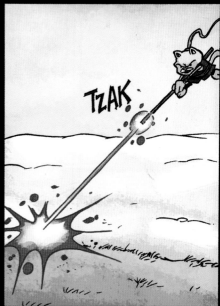

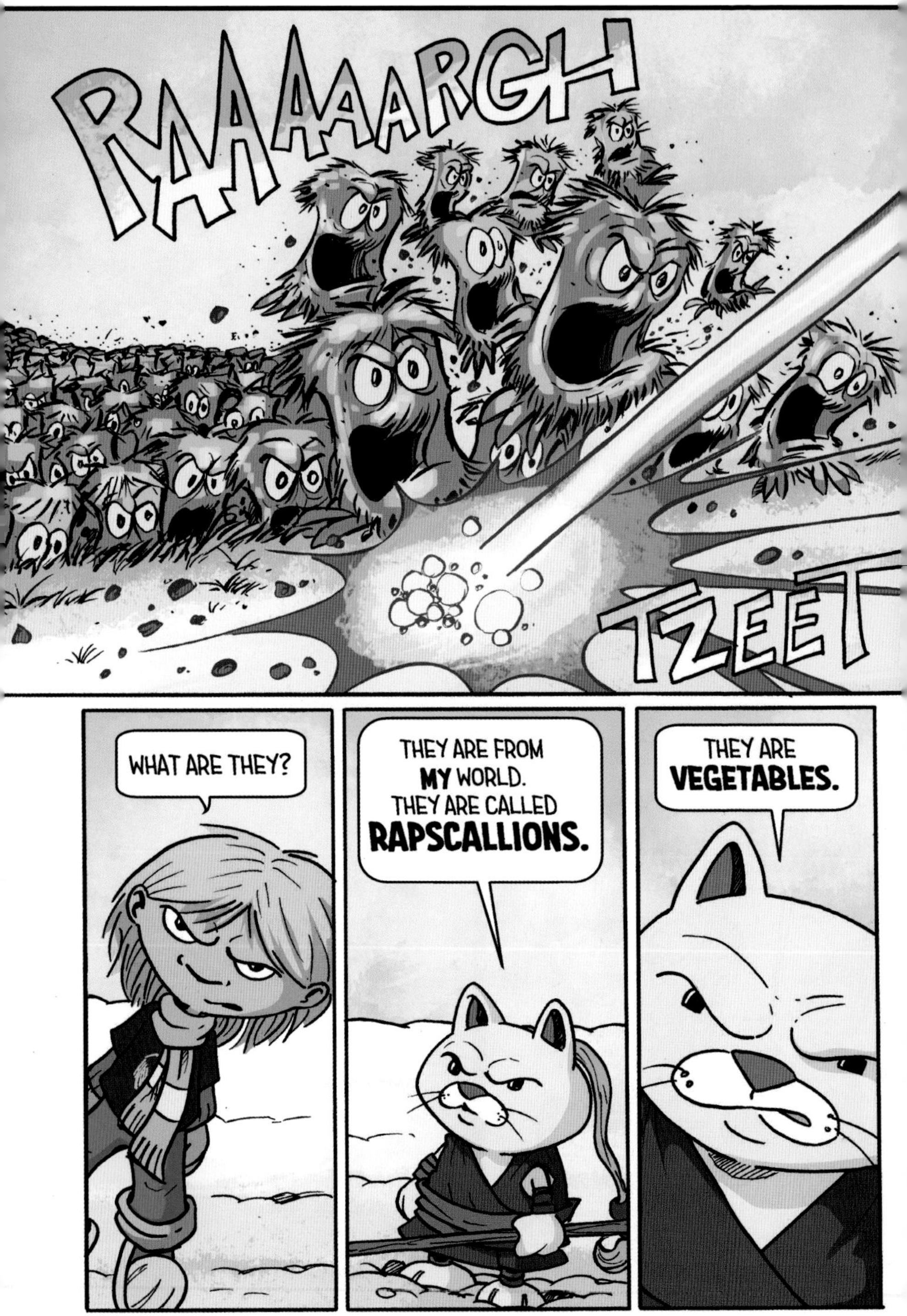
RAAAARGH
TZEET
WHAT ARE THEY?
THEY ARE FROM **MY** WORLD. THEY ARE CALLED **RAPSCALLIONS.**
THEY ARE **VEGETABLES.**

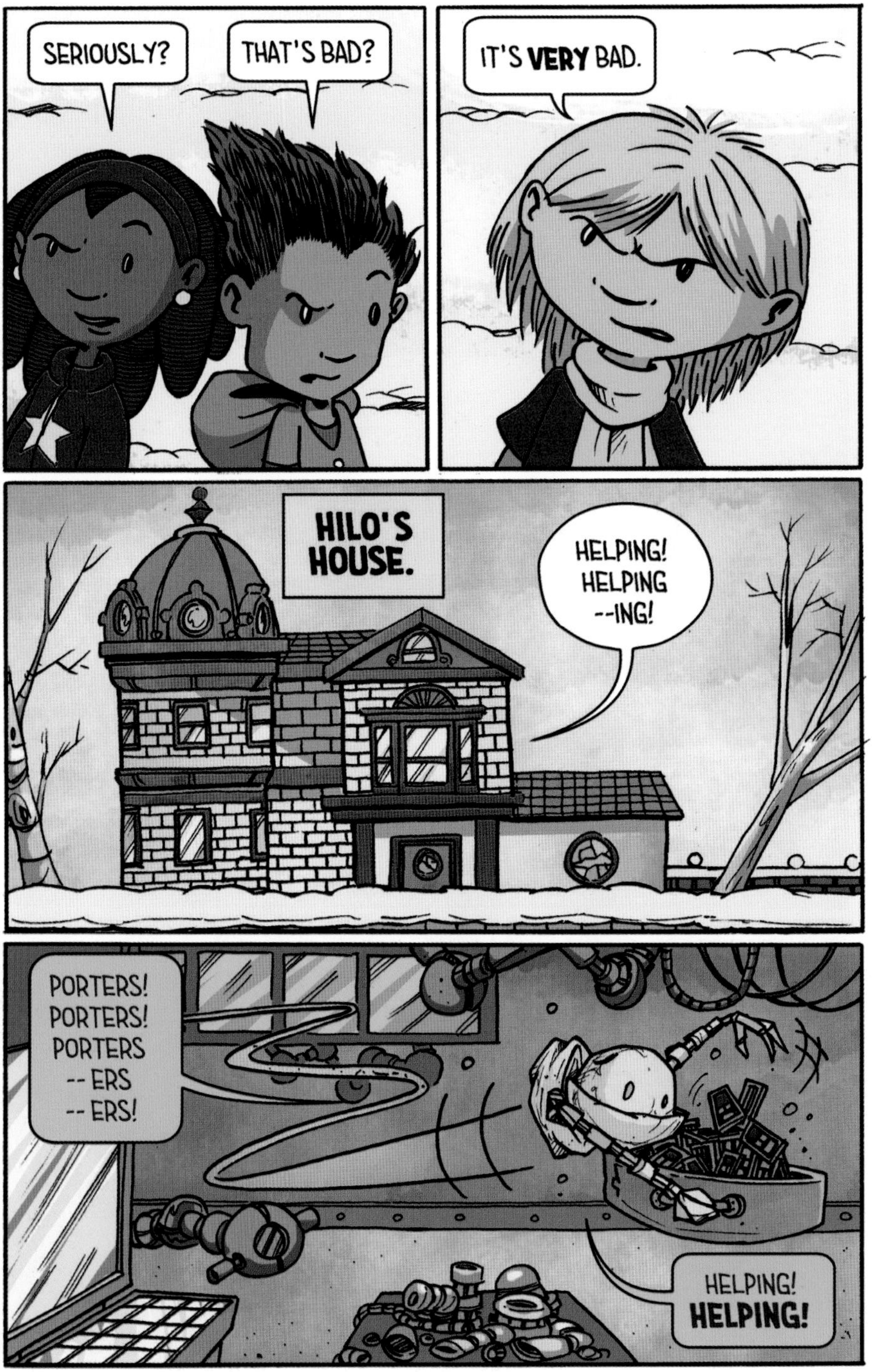
SERIOUSLY?
THAT'S BAD?
IT'S **VERY** BAD.
HILO'S HOUSE.
HELPING! HELPING --ING!
PORTERS! PORTERS! PORTERS -- ERS -- ERS!
HELPING! **HELPING!**

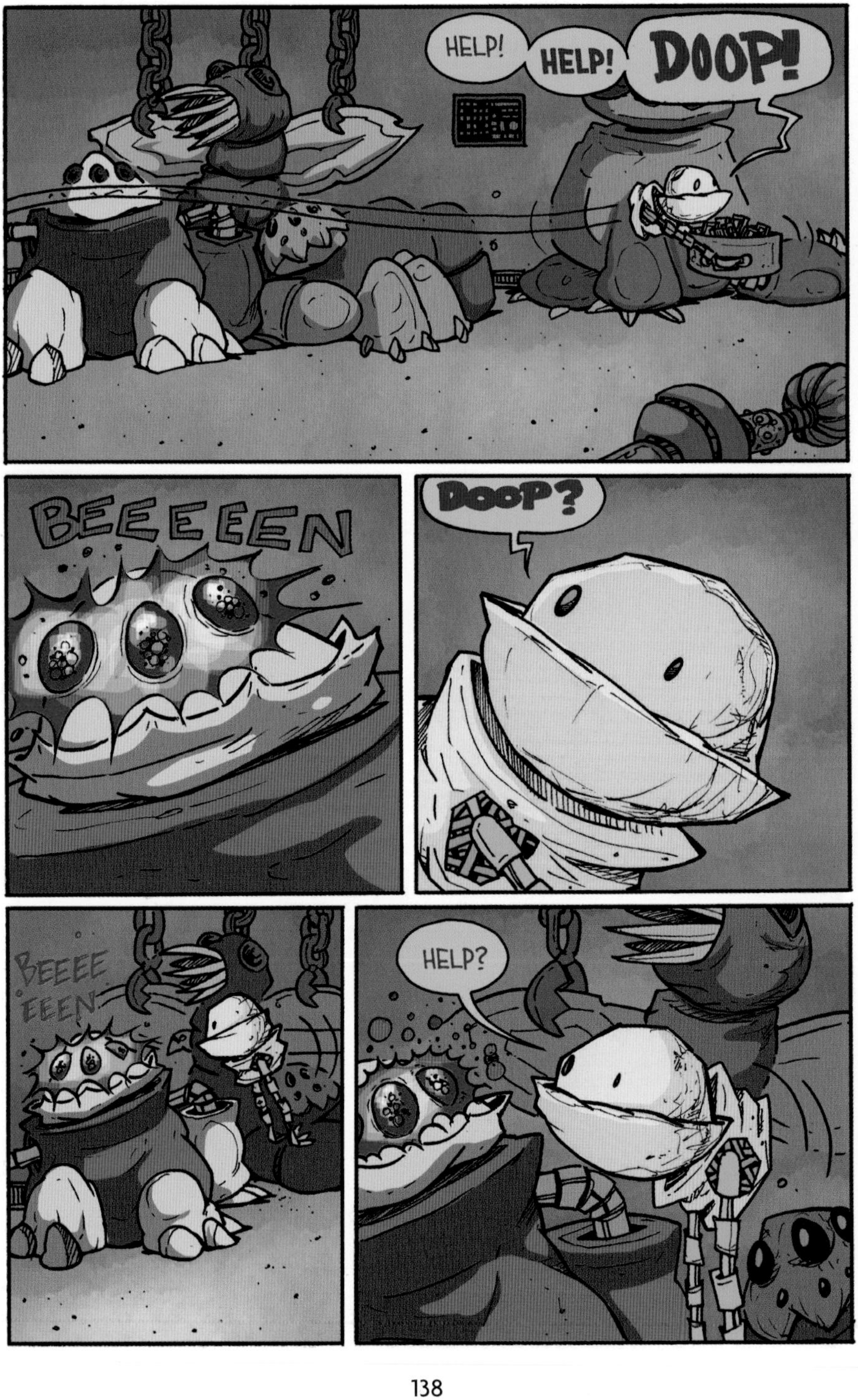
HELP!
HELP!
DOOP!
BEEEEEN
DOOP?
BEEEE EEEN
HELP?

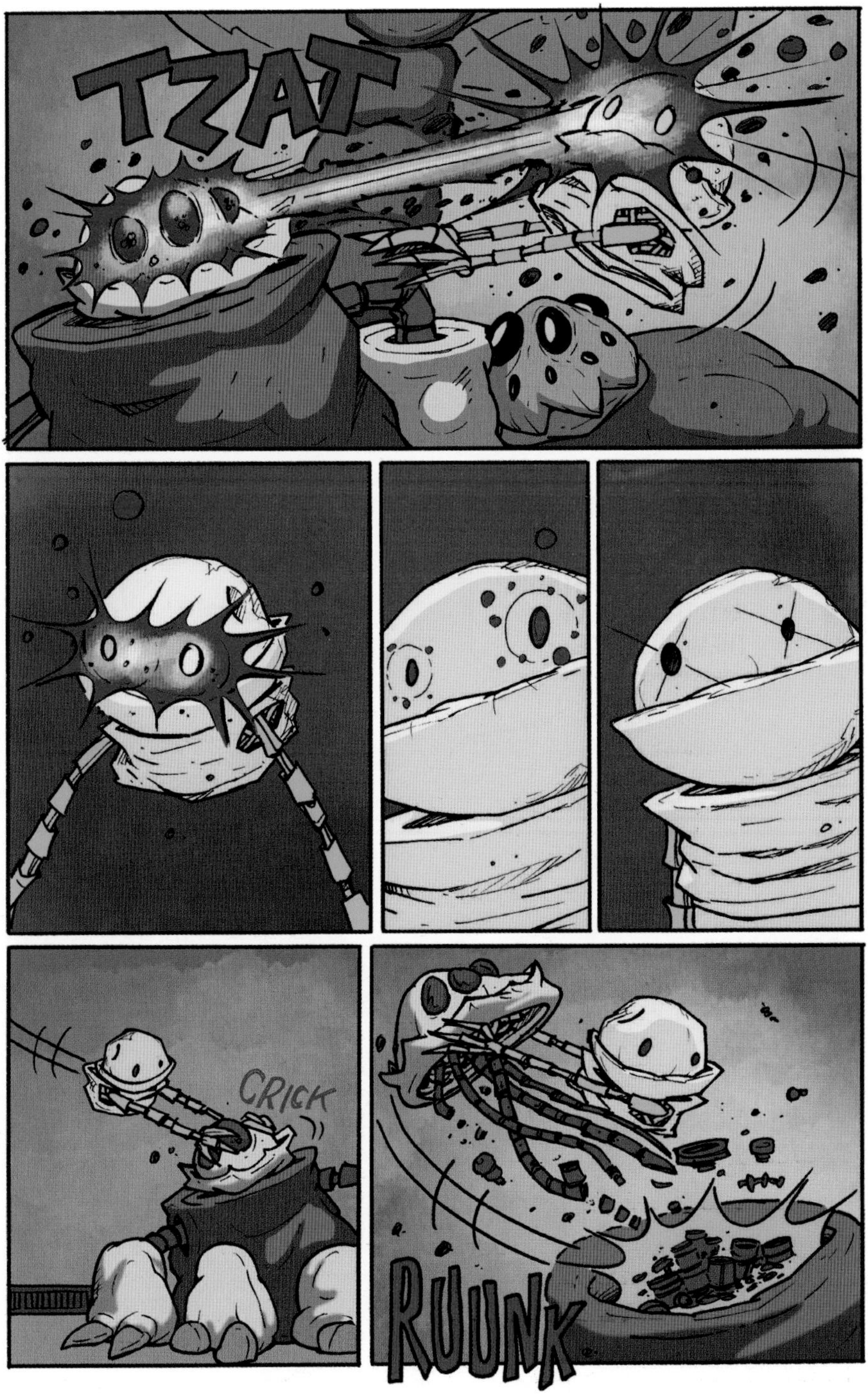
TZAT
CRICK
RUUNK

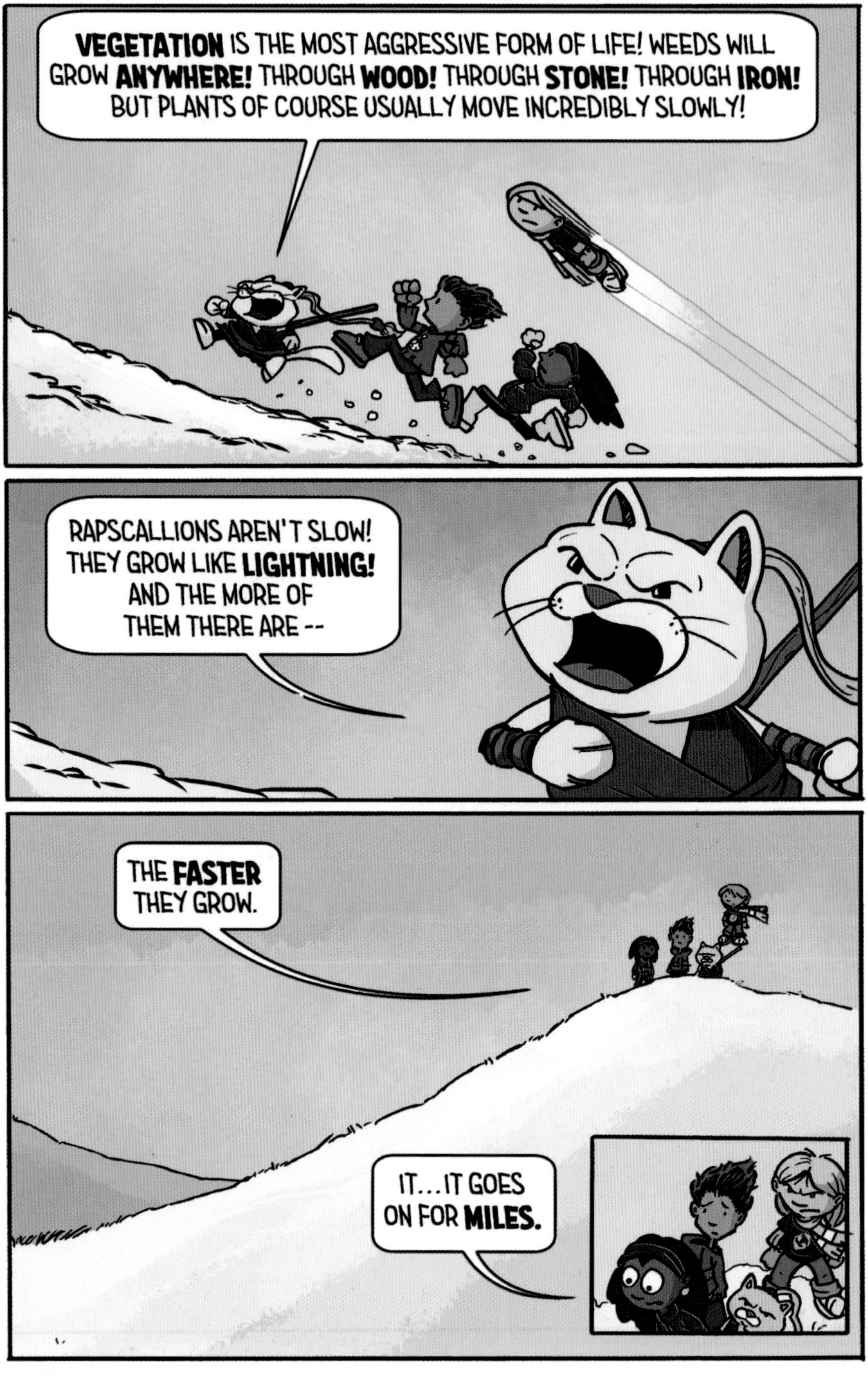
VEGETATION IS THE MOST AGGRESSIVE FORM OF LIFE! WEEDS WILL GROW **ANYWHERE!** THROUGH **WOOD!** THROUGH **STONE!** THROUGH **IRON!** BUT PLANTS OF COURSE USUALLY MOVE INCREDIBLY SLOWLY!
RAPSCALLIONS AREN'T SLOW! THEY GROW LIKE **LIGHTNING!** AND THE MORE OF THEM THERE ARE --
THE **FASTER** THEY GROW.
IT...IT GOES ON FOR **MILES.**

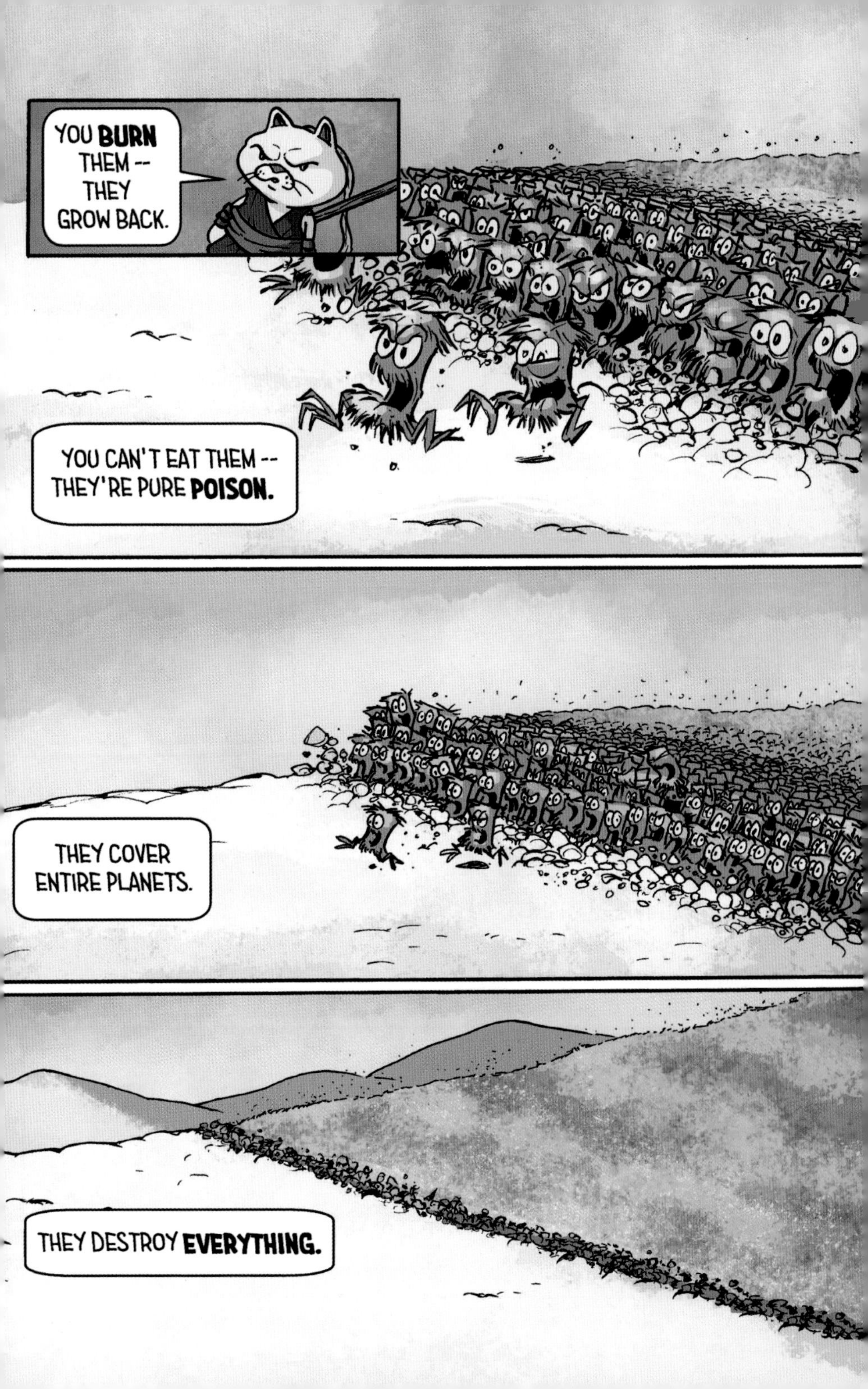
YOU **BURN** THEM -- THEY GROW BACK.
YOU CAN'T EAT THEM -- THEY'RE PURE **POISON.**
THEY COVER ENTIRE PLANETS.
THEY DESTROY **EVERYTHING.**

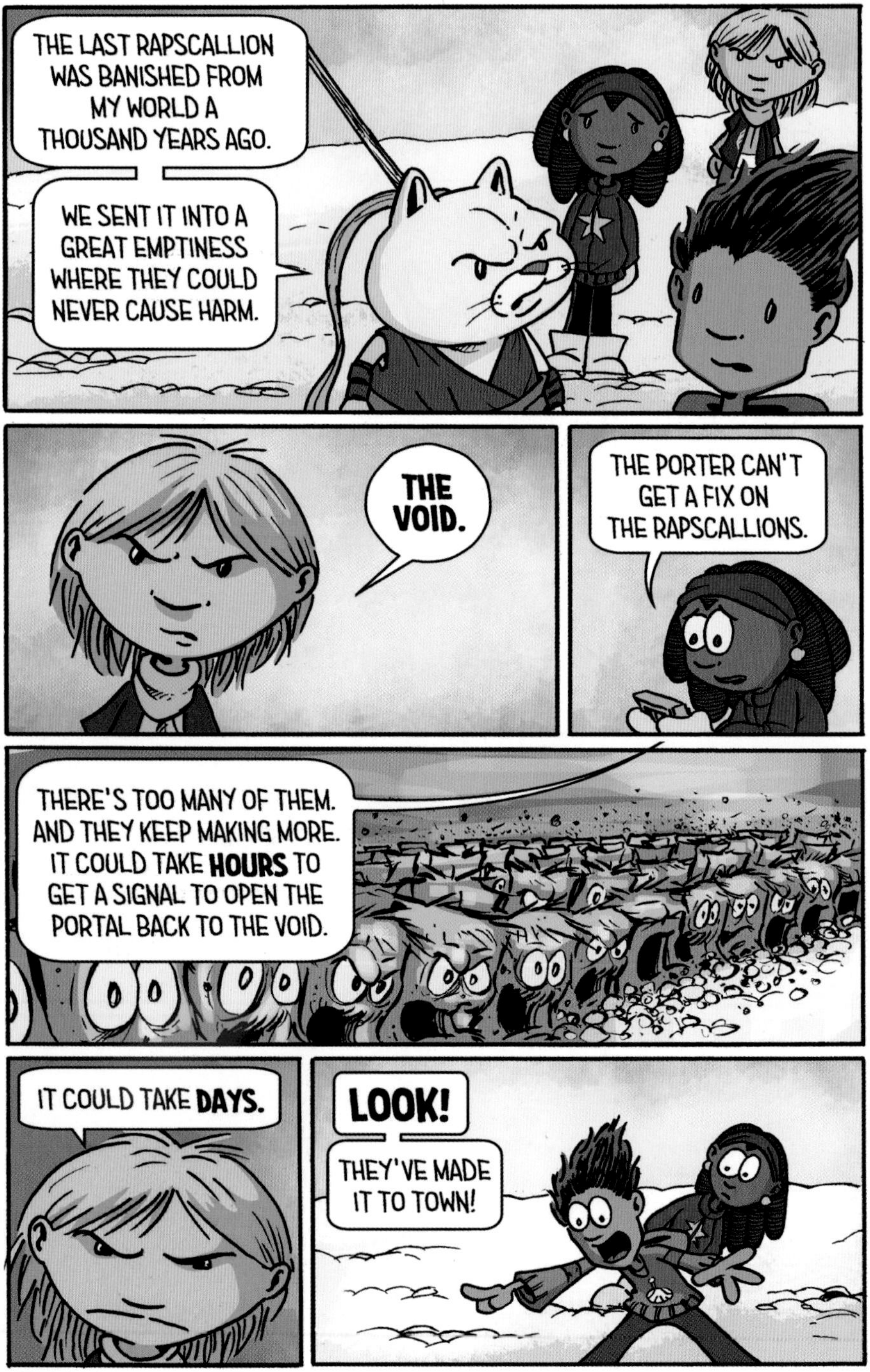
THE LAST RAPSCALLION WAS BANISHED FROM MY WORLD A THOUSAND YEARS AGO.
WE SENT IT INTO A GREAT EMPTINESS WHERE THEY COULD NEVER CAUSE HARM.
THE VOID.
THE PORTER CAN'T GET A FIX ON THE RAPSCALLIONS.
THERE'S TOO MANY OF THEM. AND THEY KEEP MAKING MORE. IT COULD TAKE **HOURS** TO GET A SIGNAL TO OPEN THE PORTAL BACK TO THE VOID.
IT COULD TAKE **DAYS.**
LOOK!
THEY'VE MADE IT TO TOWN!

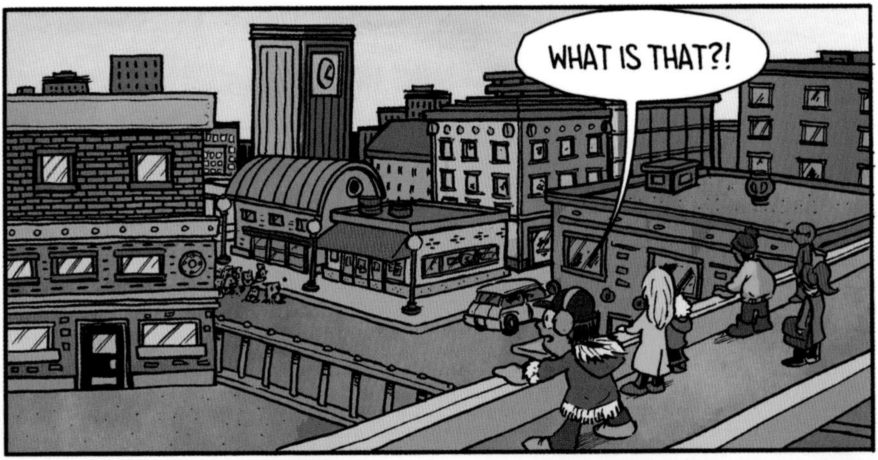
WHAT IS THAT?!

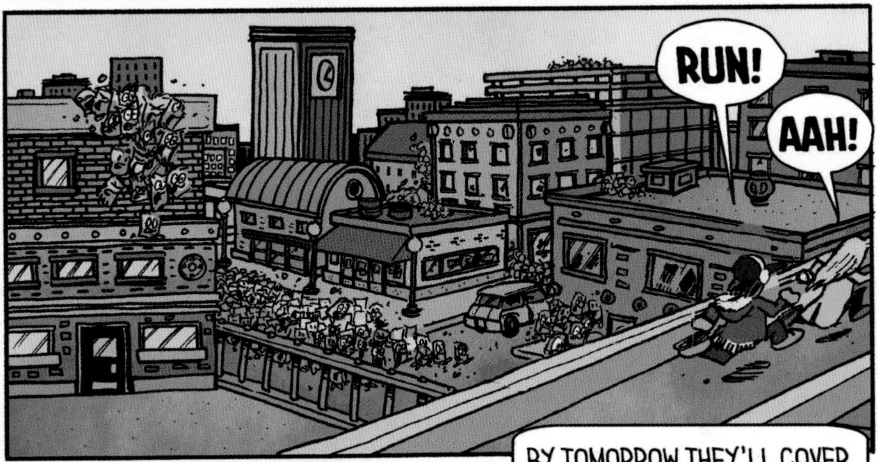
RUN!
AAH!

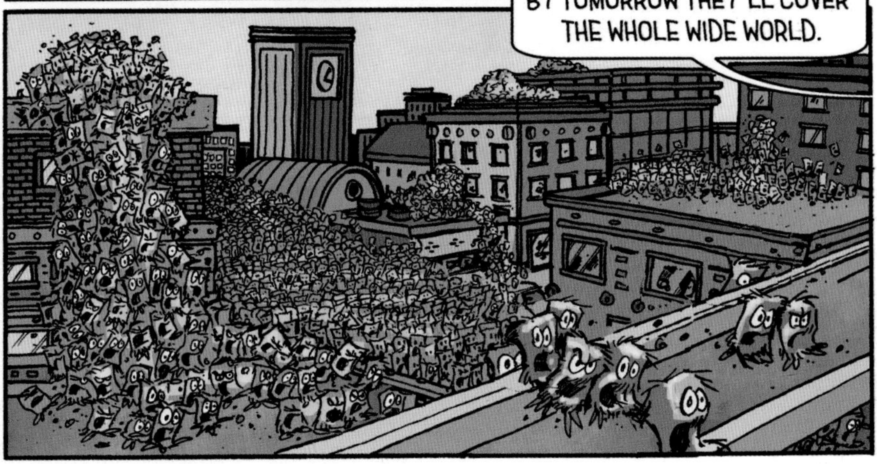
BY TOMORROW THEY'LL COVER THE WHOLE WIDE WORLD.

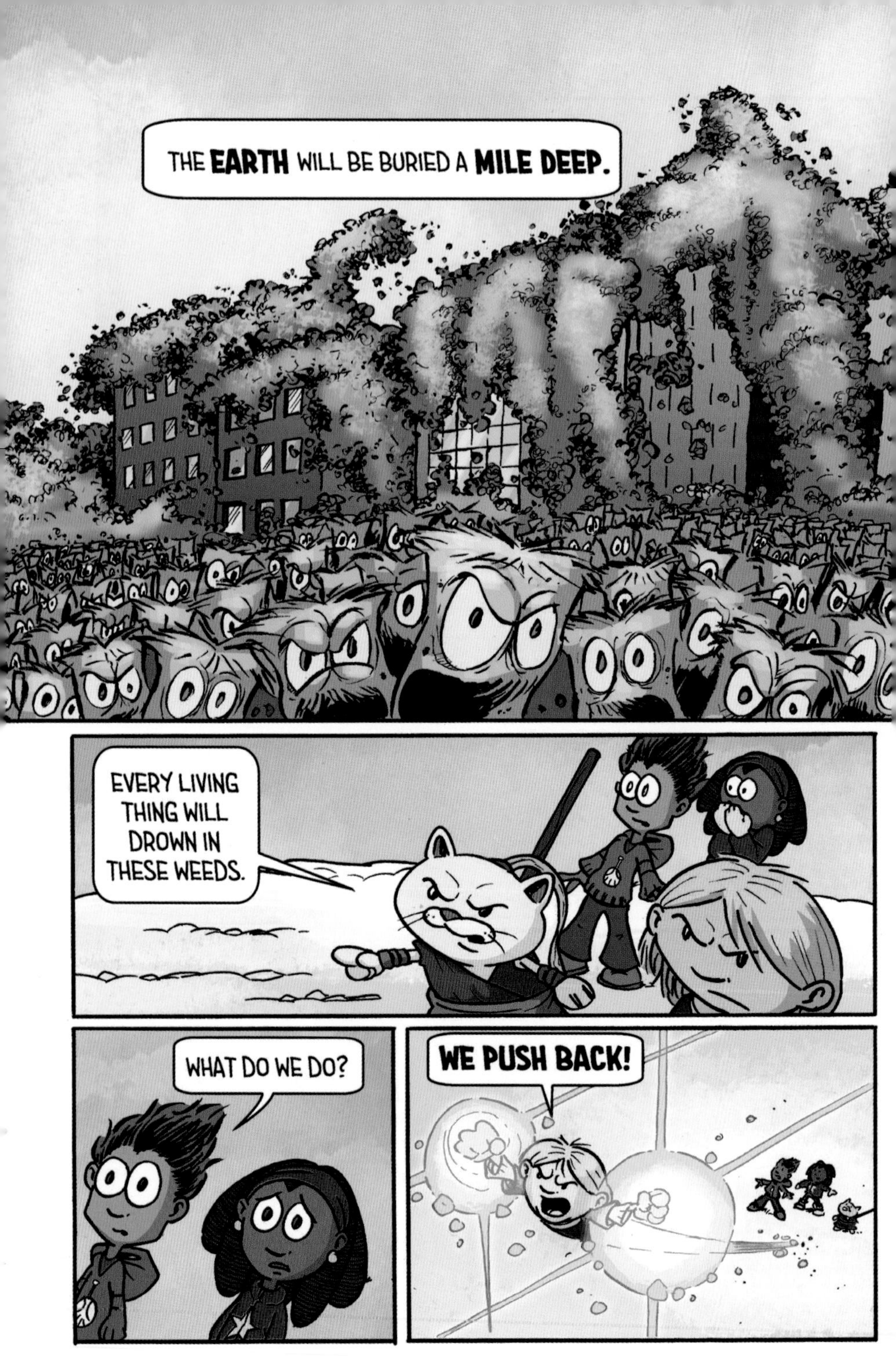
THE **EARTH** WILL BE BURIED A **MILE DEEP.**
EVERY LIVING THING WILL DROWN IN THESE WEEDS.
WHAT DO WE DO?
WE PUSH BACK!

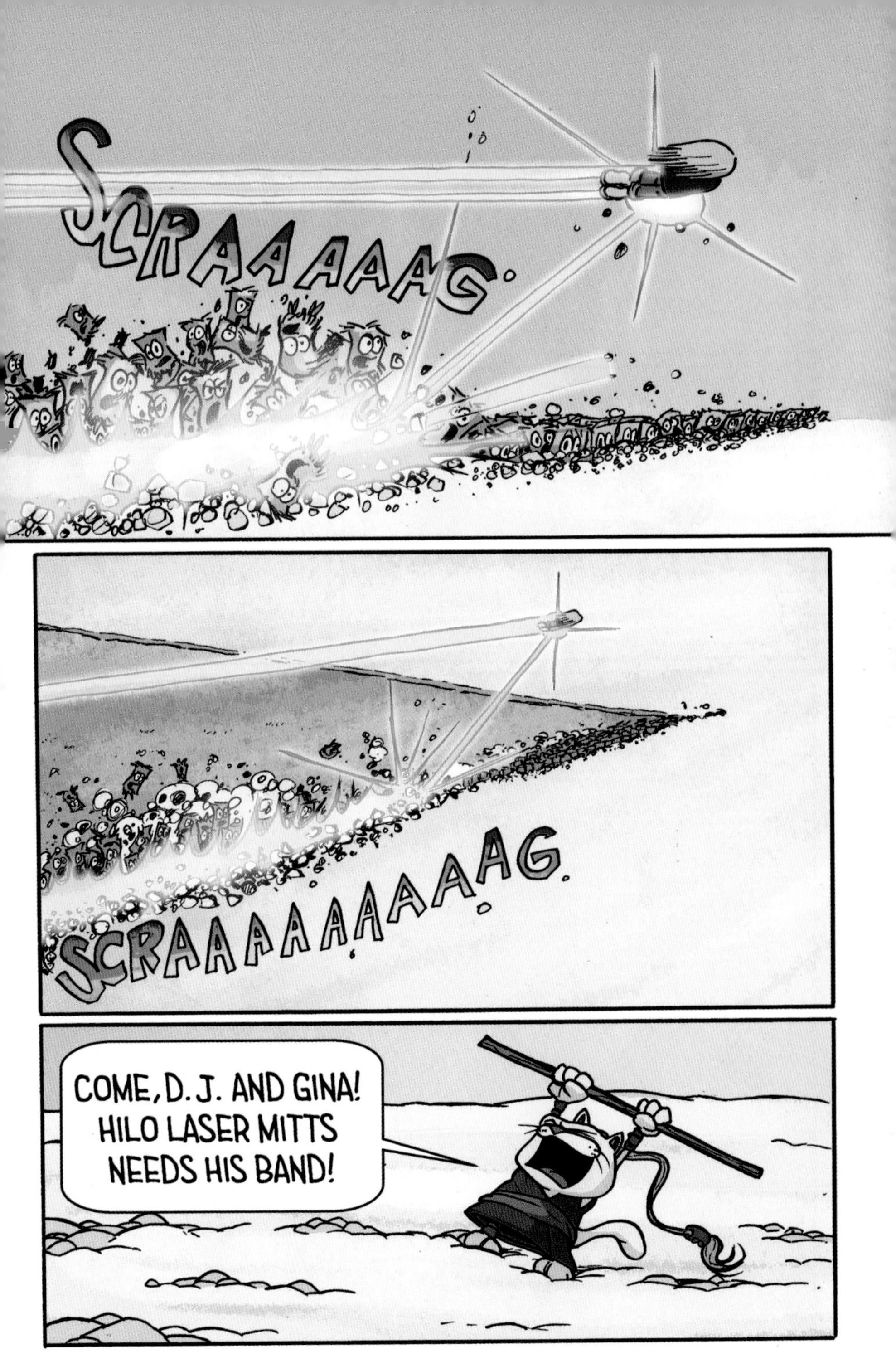
SCRAAAAAG
SCRAAAAAAAAG
COME, D. J. AND GINA! HILO LASER MITTS NEEDS HIS BAND!

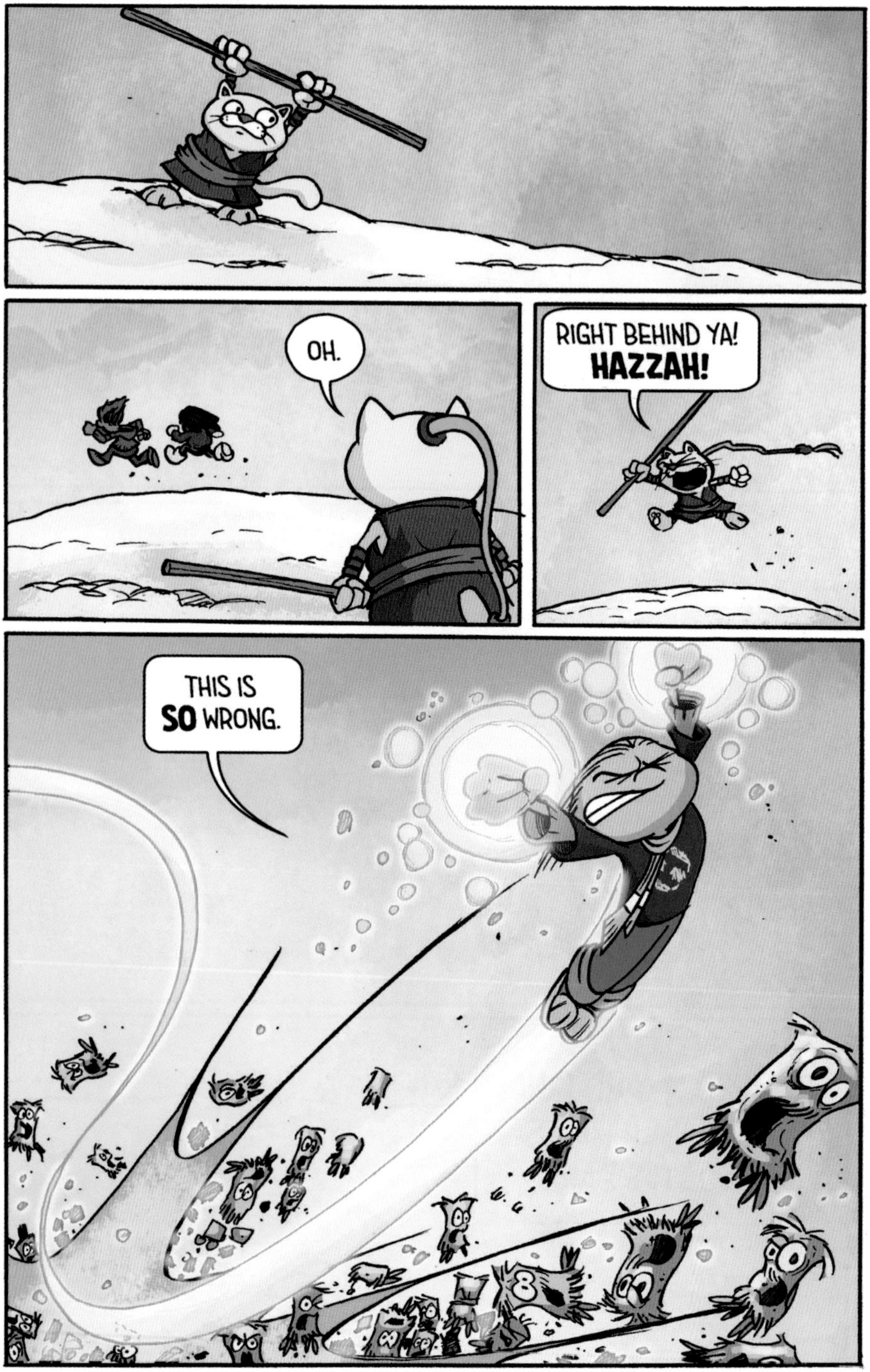
OH.
RIGHT BEHIND YA! HAZZAH!
THIS IS SO WRONG.

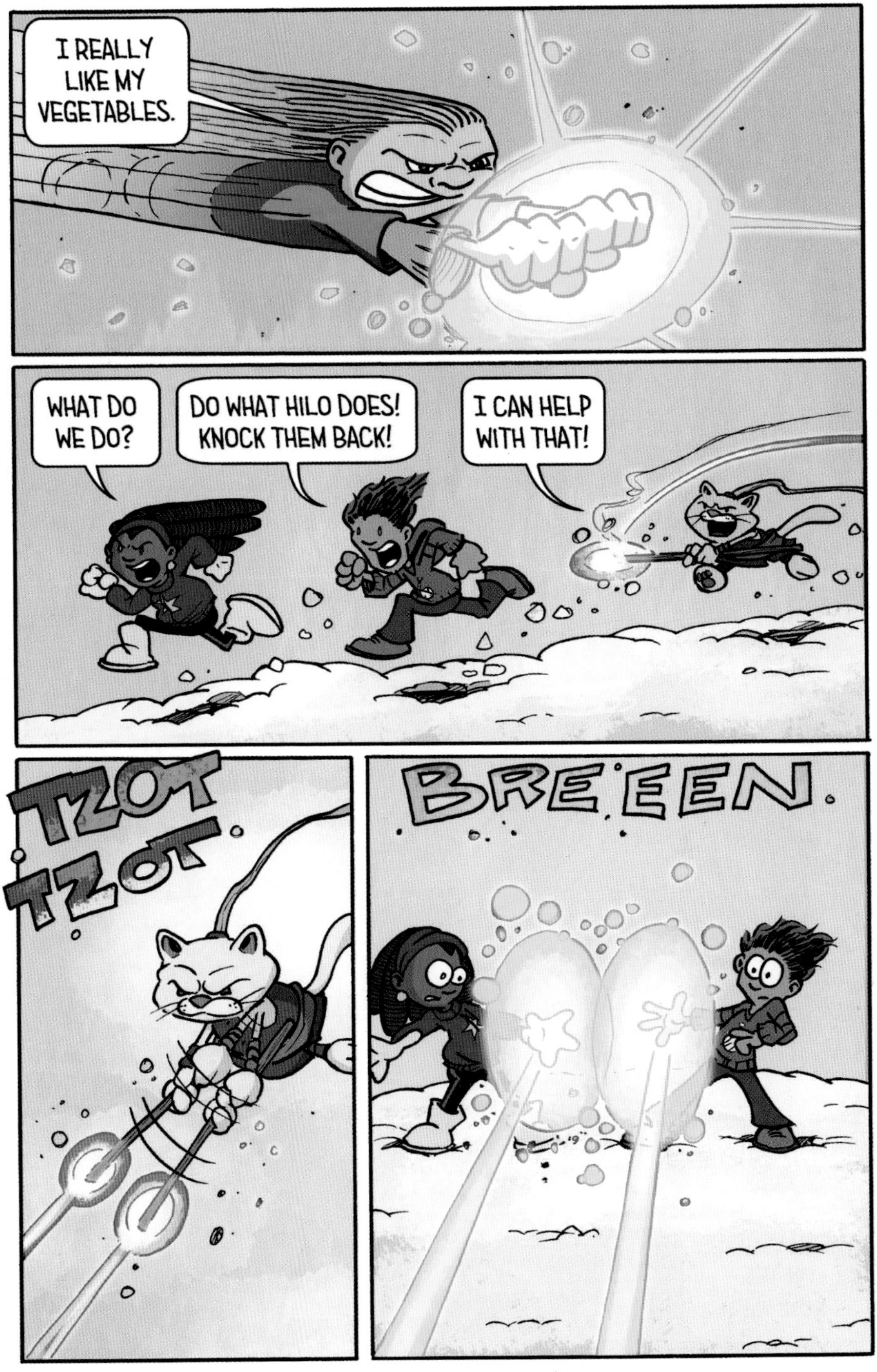
I REALLY LIKE MY VEGETABLES.
WHAT DO WE DO?
DO WHAT HILO DOES! KNOCK THEM BACK!
I CAN HELP WITH THAT!
TZOT
TZOT
BREEEN

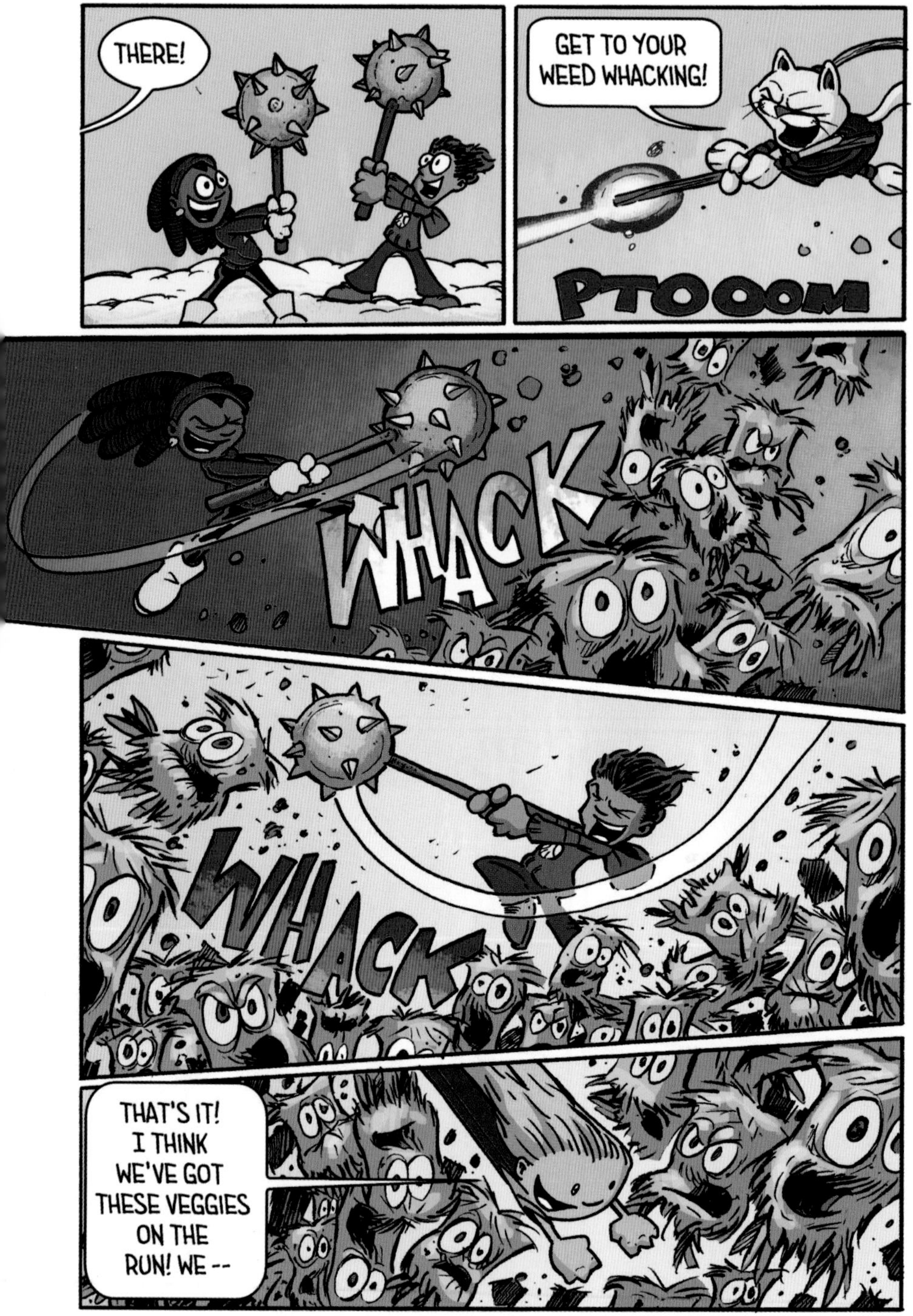

THERE!
GET TO YOUR WEED WHACKING!
PTOOOM
WHACK
WHACK
THAT'S IT! I THINK WE'VE GOT THESE VEGGIES ON THE RUN! WE --

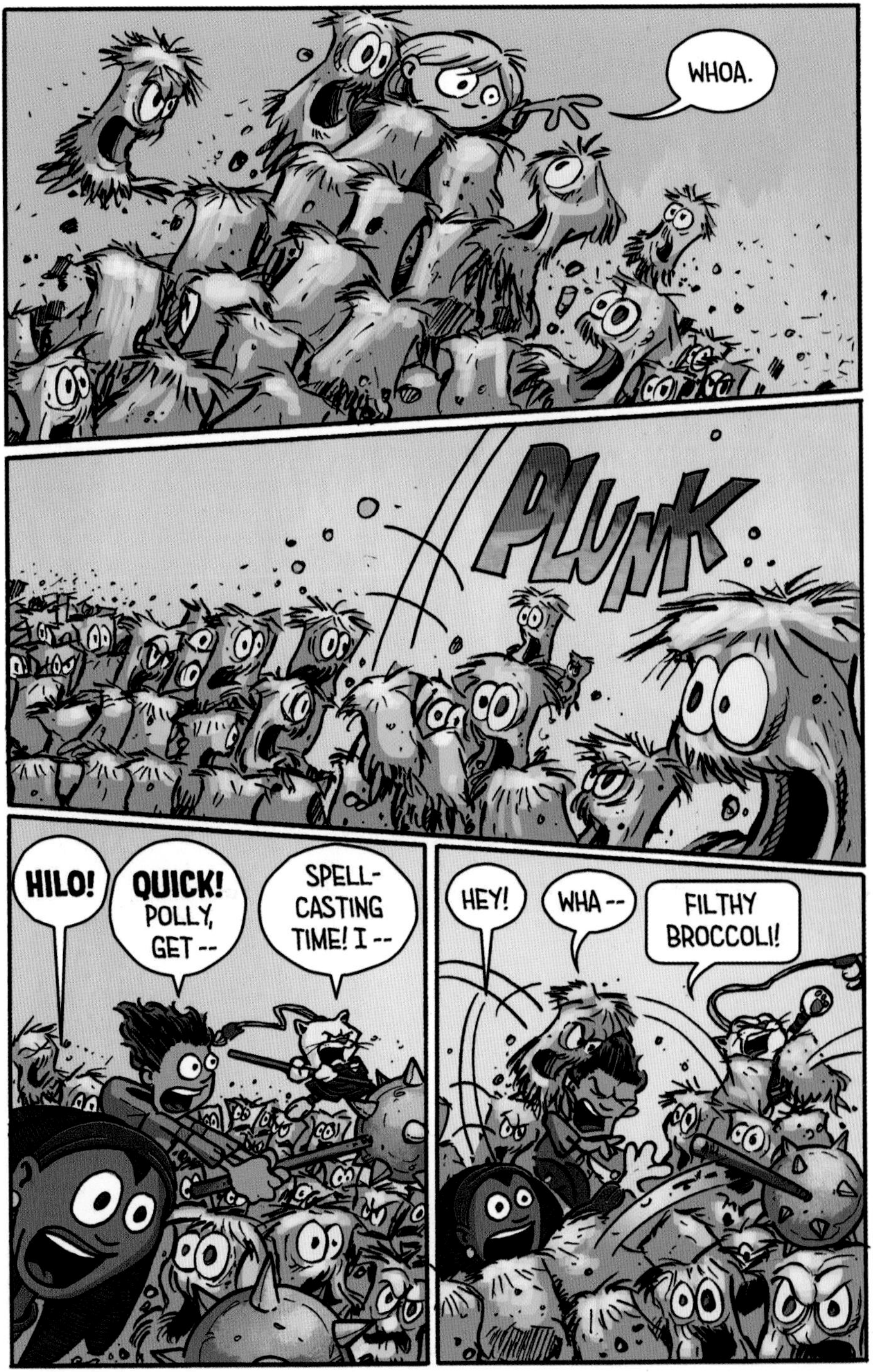
WHOA.
PLUNK
HILO!
QUICK! POLLY, GET --
SPELL-CASTING TIME! I --
HEY!
WHA --
FILTHY BROCCOLI!

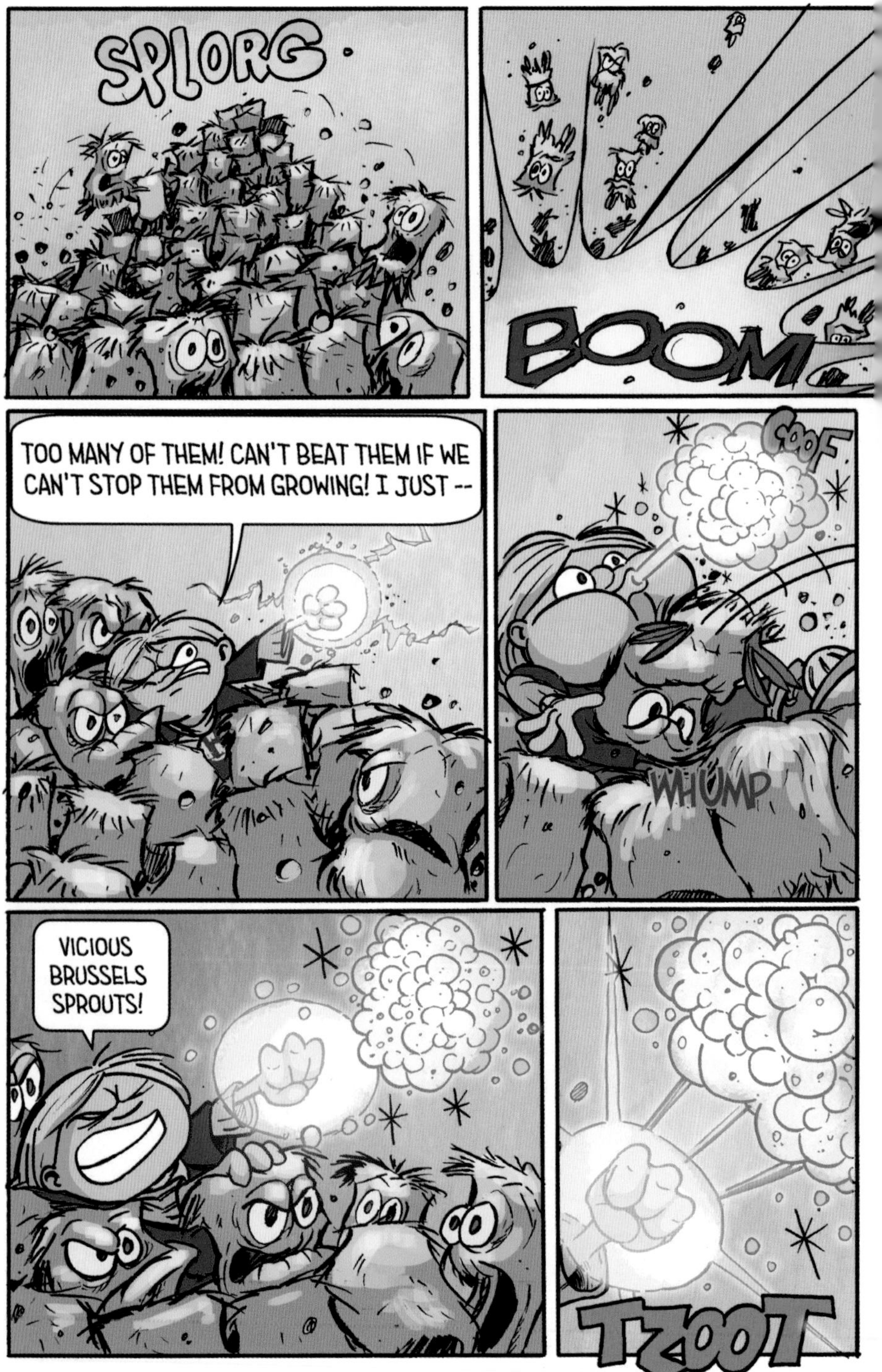
SPLORG
BOOM
TOO MANY OF THEM! CAN'T BEAT THEM IF WE CAN'T STOP THEM FROM GROWING! I JUST --
GOOF
WHUMP
VICIOUS BRUSSELS SPROUTS!
TZOOT

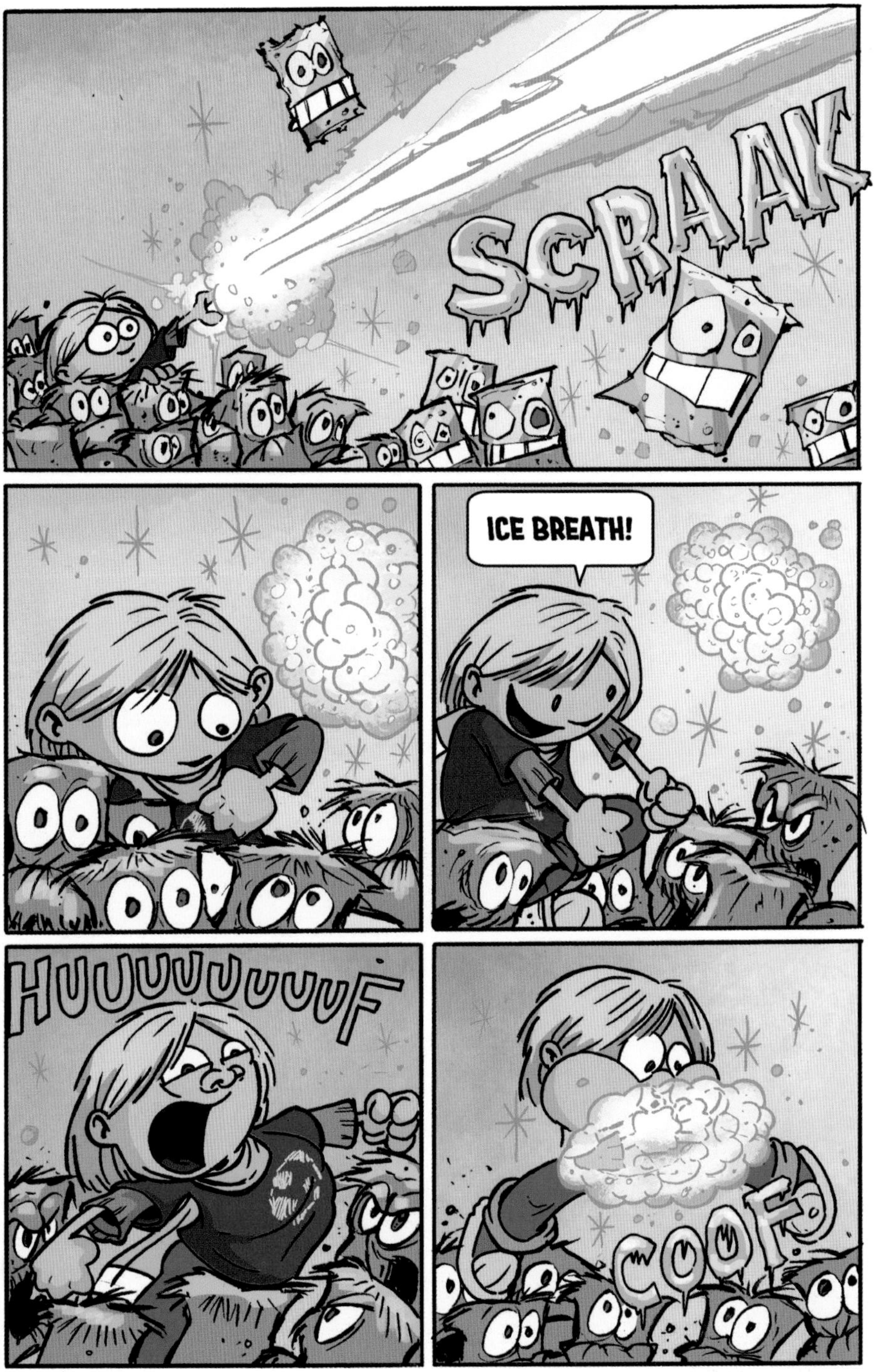
SCRAAK
ICE BREATH!
HUUUUUUUUF
COOF

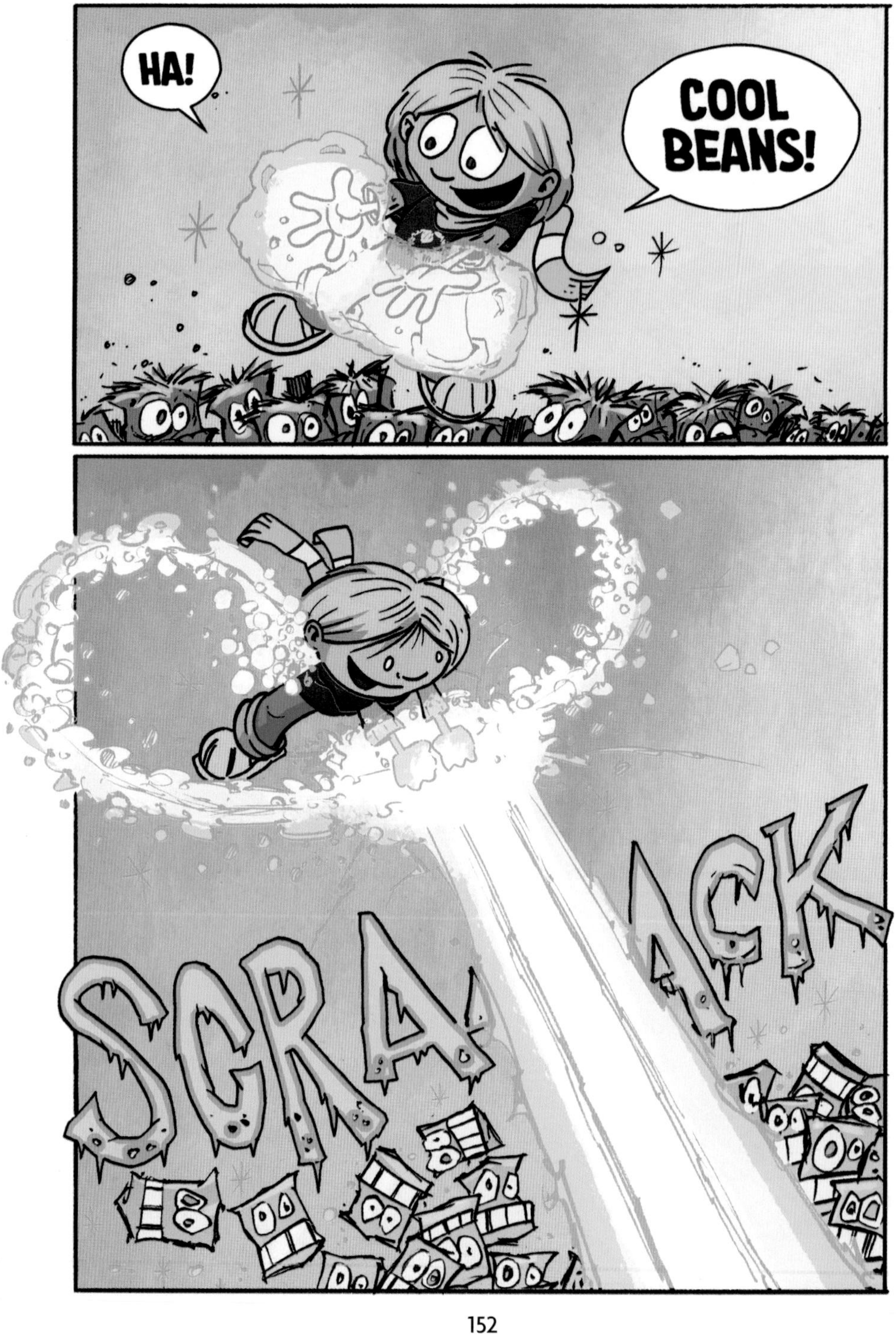
HA!
COOL BEANS!
SCRAACK

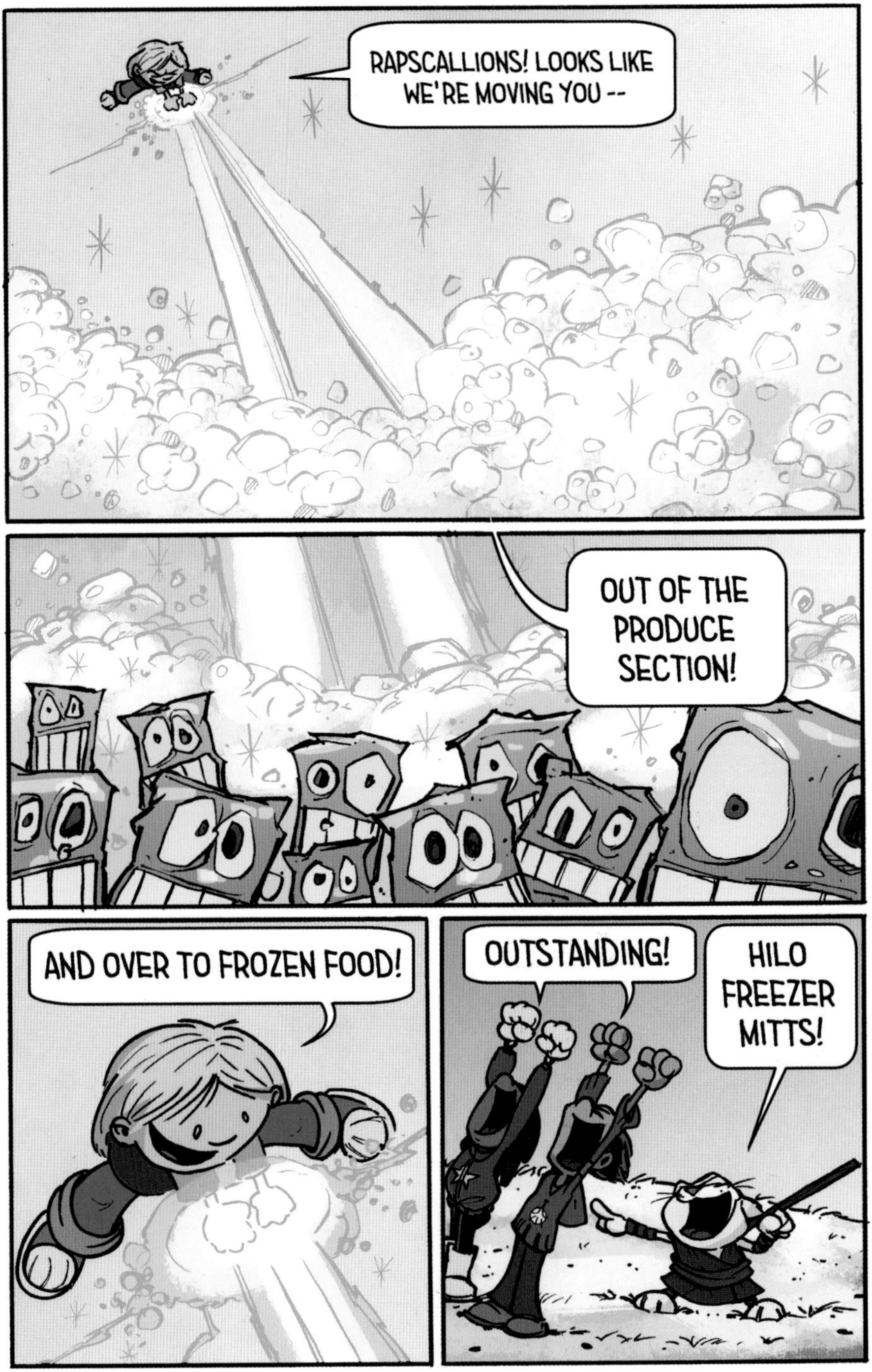
RAPSCALLIONS! LOOKS LIKE WE'RE MOVING YOU --
OUT OF THE PRODUCE SECTION!
AND OVER TO FROZEN FOOD!
OUTSTANDING!
HILO FREEZER MITTS!

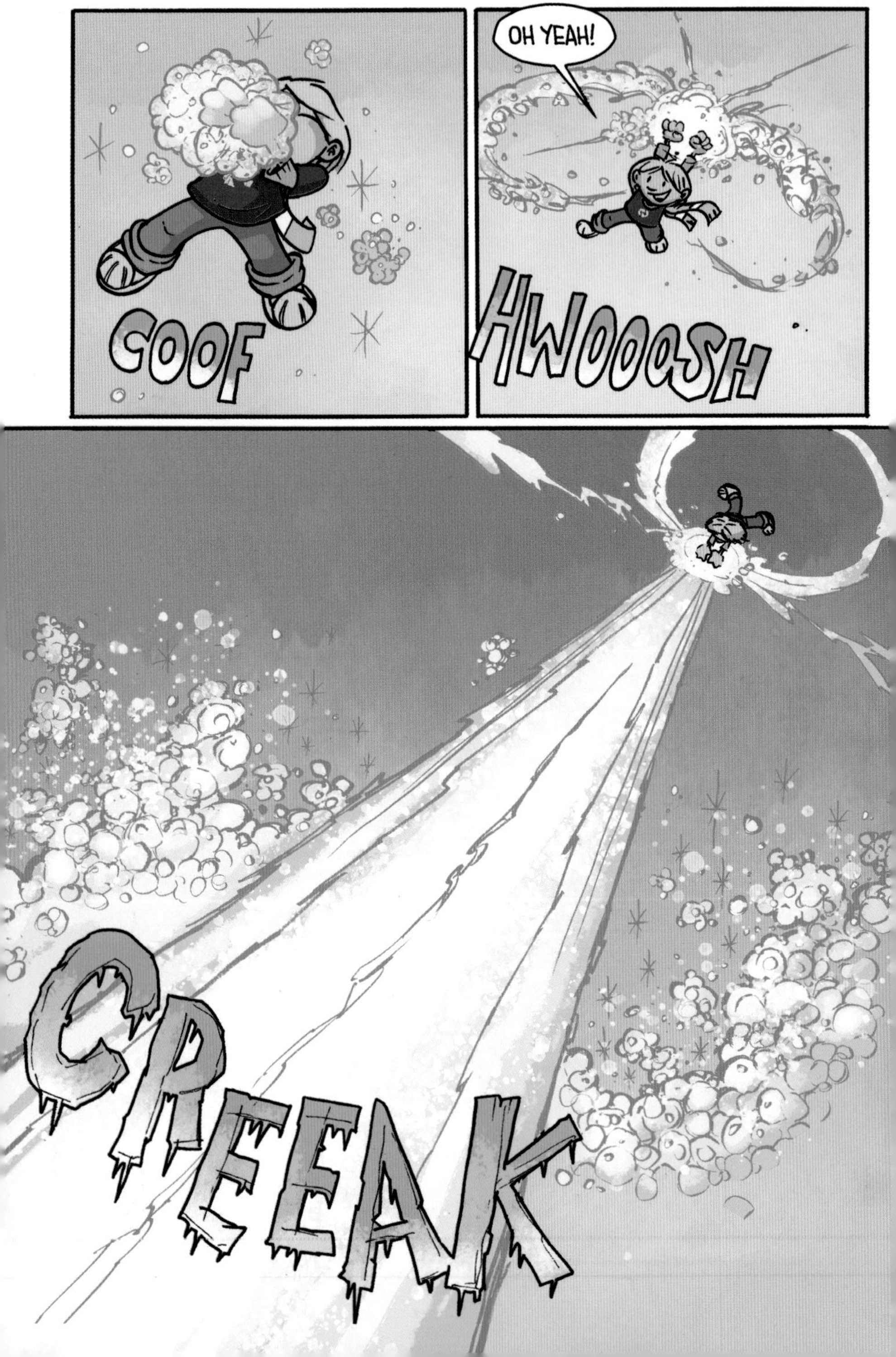
COOF
OH YEAH!
HWOOOSH
CREEAK

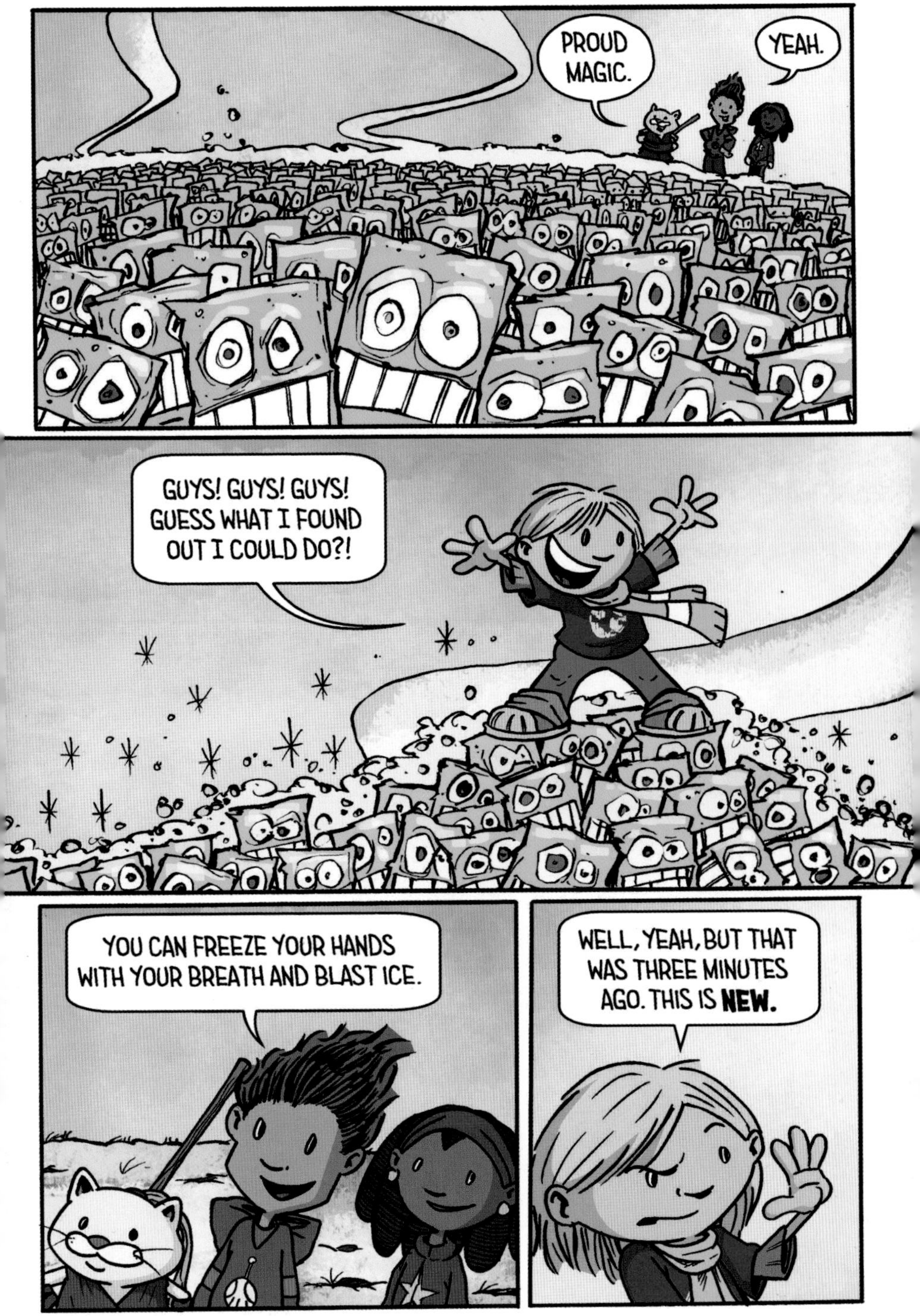
PROUD MAGIC.
YEAH.
GUYS! GUYS! GUYS! GUESS WHAT I FOUND OUT I COULD DO?!
YOU CAN FREEZE YOUR HANDS WITH YOUR BREATH AND BLAST ICE.
WELL, YEAH, BUT THAT WAS THREE MINUTES AGO. THIS IS **NEW.**

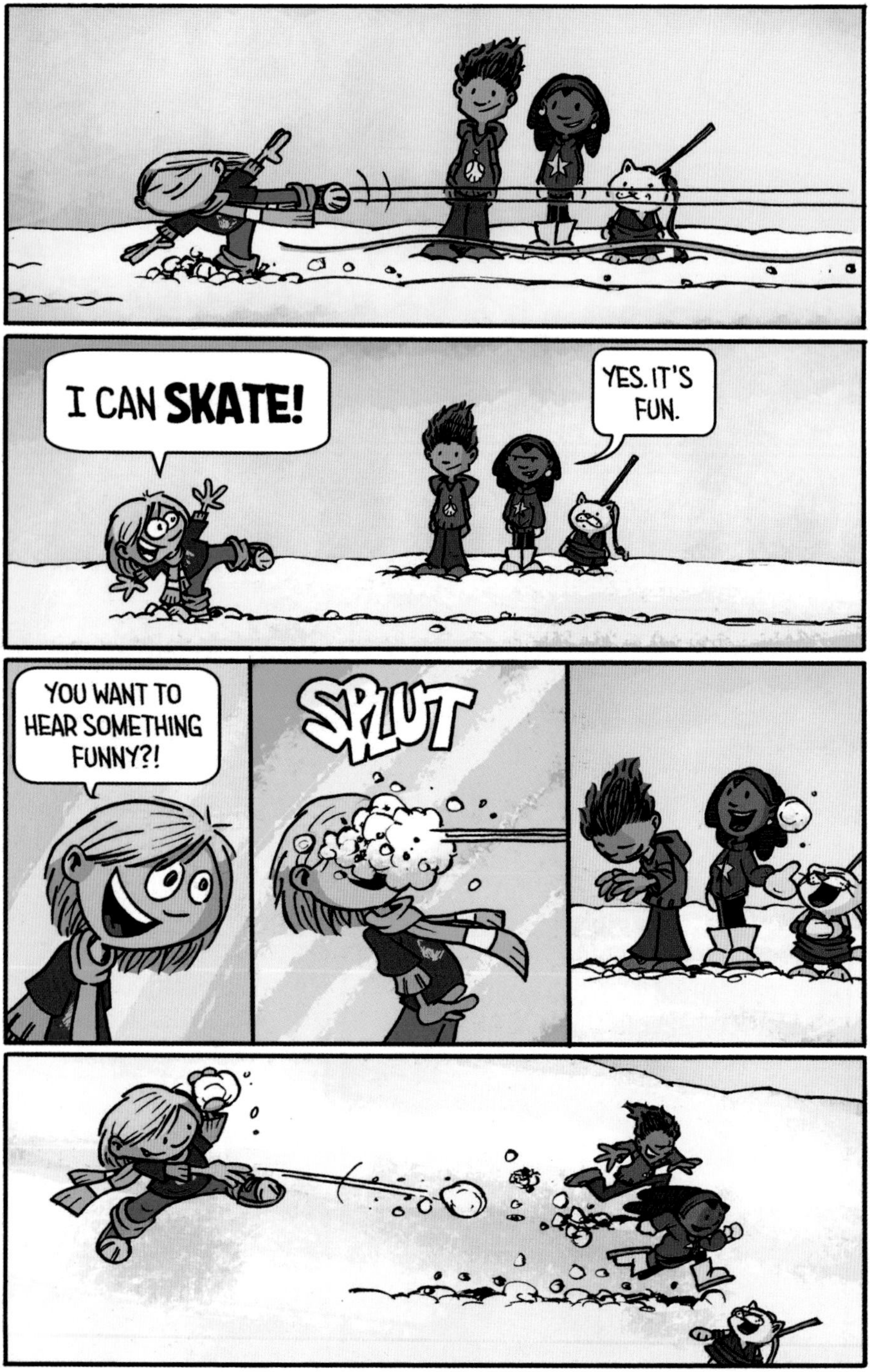
I CAN **SKATE!**
YES. IT'S FUN.
YOU WANT TO HEAR SOMETHING FUNNY?!
SPLUT

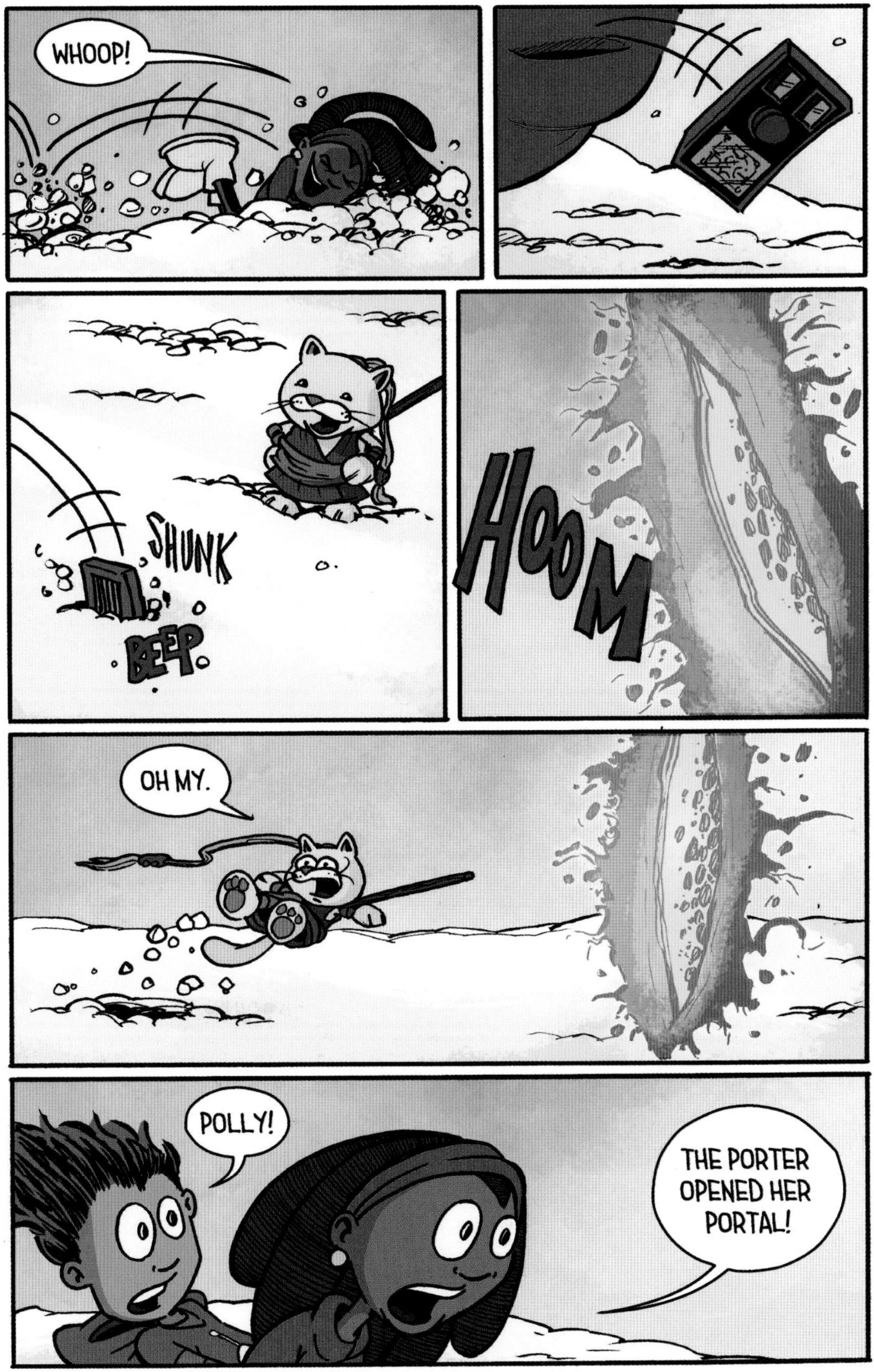
WHOOP!
SHUNK
BEEP
HOOM
OH MY.
POLLY!
THE PORTER OPENED HER PORTAL!

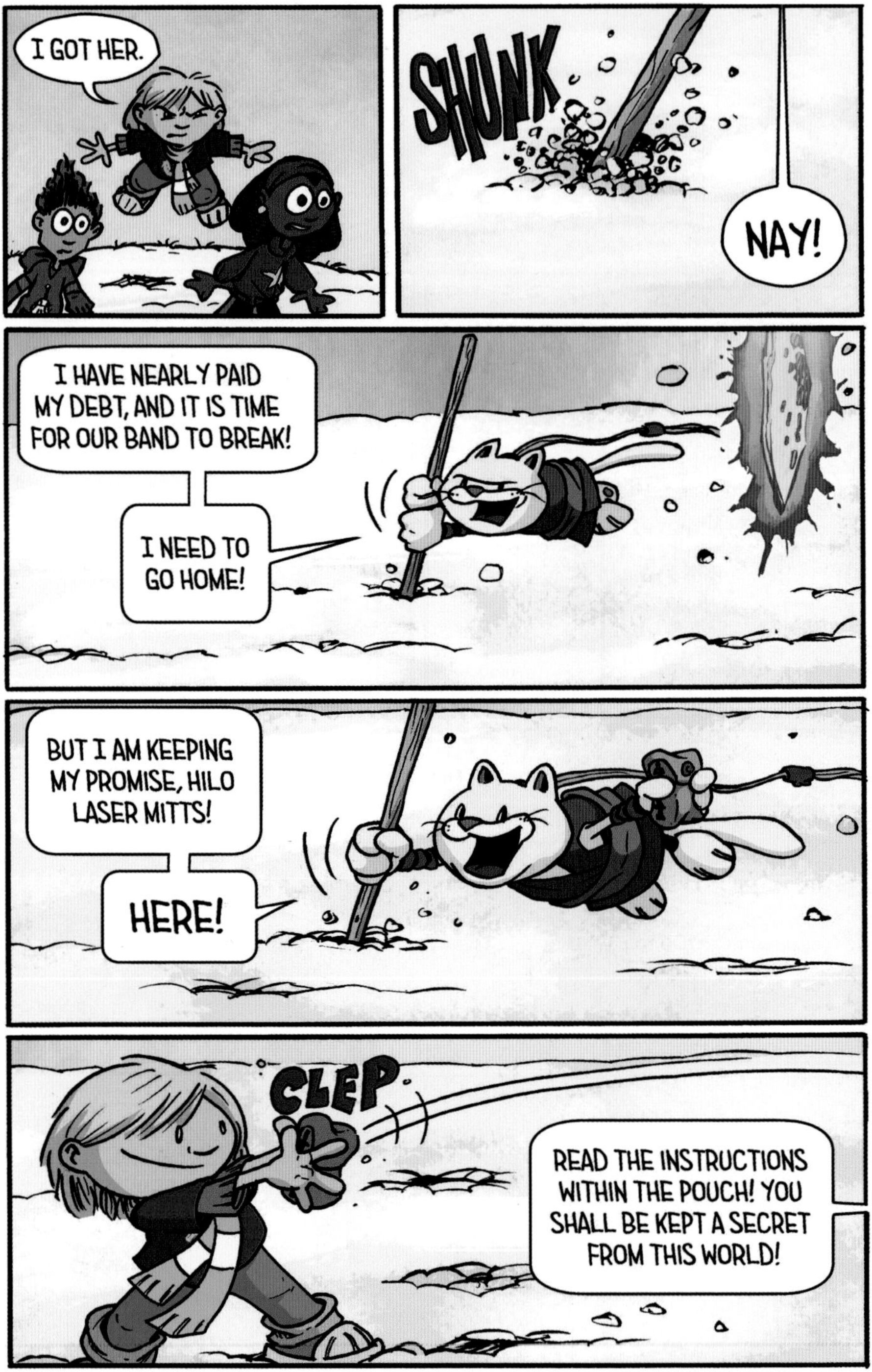
I GOT HER.
SHUNK
NAY!
I HAVE NEARLY PAID MY DEBT, AND IT IS TIME FOR OUR BAND TO BREAK!
I NEED TO GO HOME!
BUT I AM KEEPING MY PROMISE, HILO LASER MITTS!
HERE!
CLEP
READ THE INSTRUCTIONS WITHIN THE POUCH! YOU SHALL BE KEPT A SECRET FROM THIS WORLD!

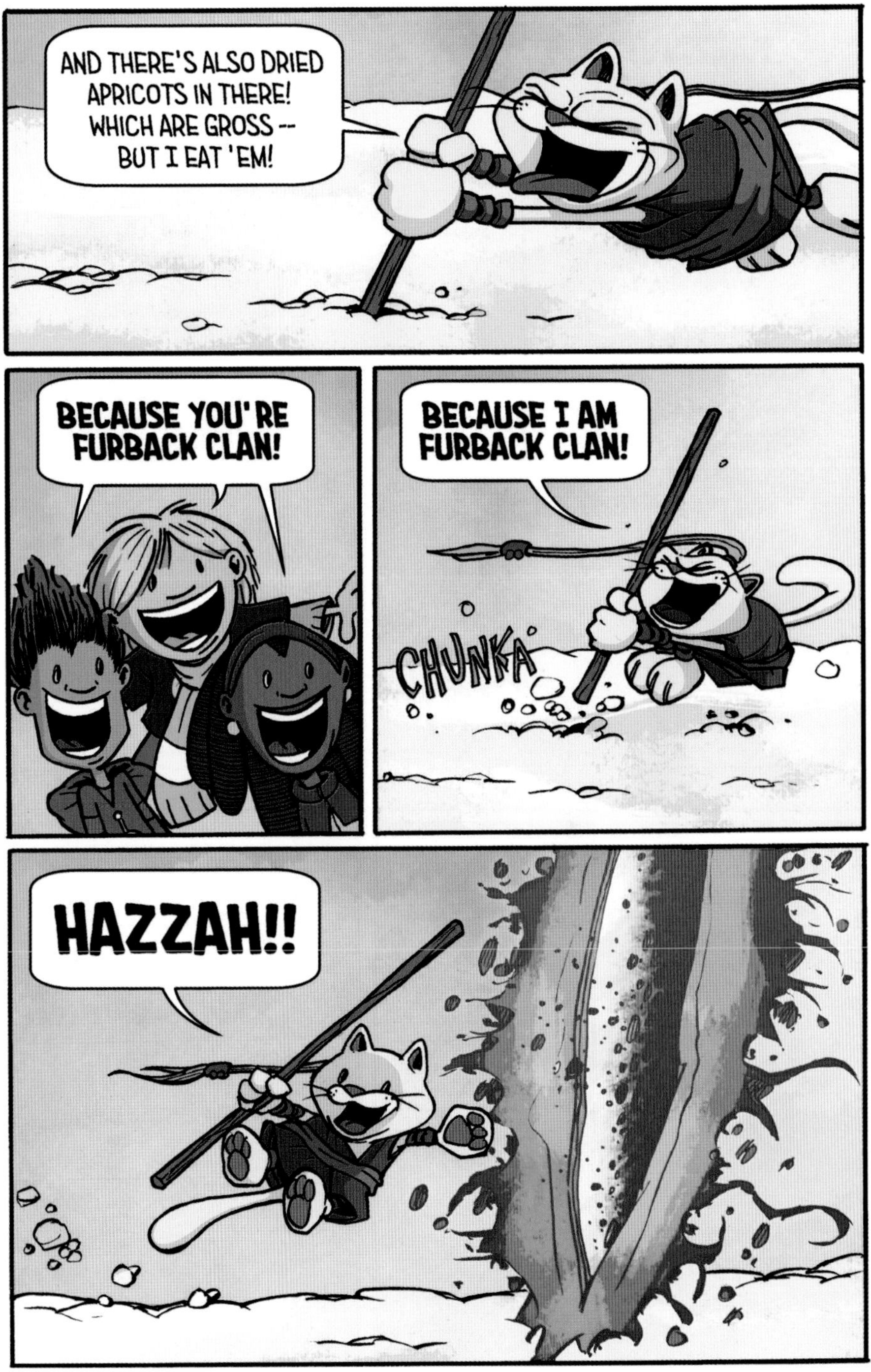
AND THERE'S ALSO DRIED APRICOTS IN THERE! WHICH ARE GROSS -- BUT I EAT 'EM!
BECAUSE YOU'RE FURBACK CLAN!
BECAUSE I AM FURBACK CLAN!
CHUNKA
HAZZAH!!

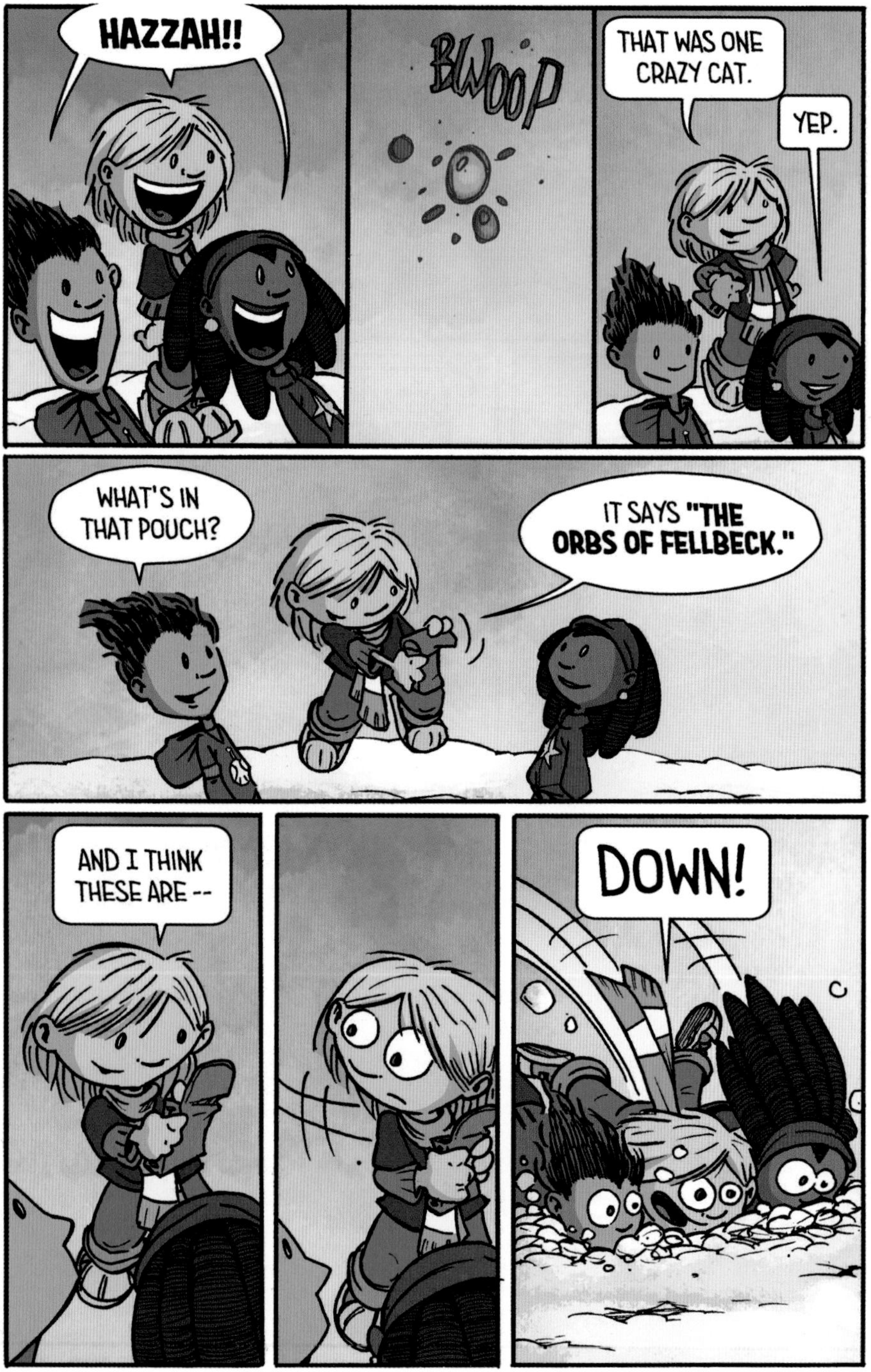
HAZZAH!!
BWOOP
THAT WAS ONE CRAZY CAT.
YEP.
WHAT'S IN THAT POUCH?
IT SAYS **"THE ORBS OF FELLBECK."**
AND I THINK THESE ARE --
DOWN!

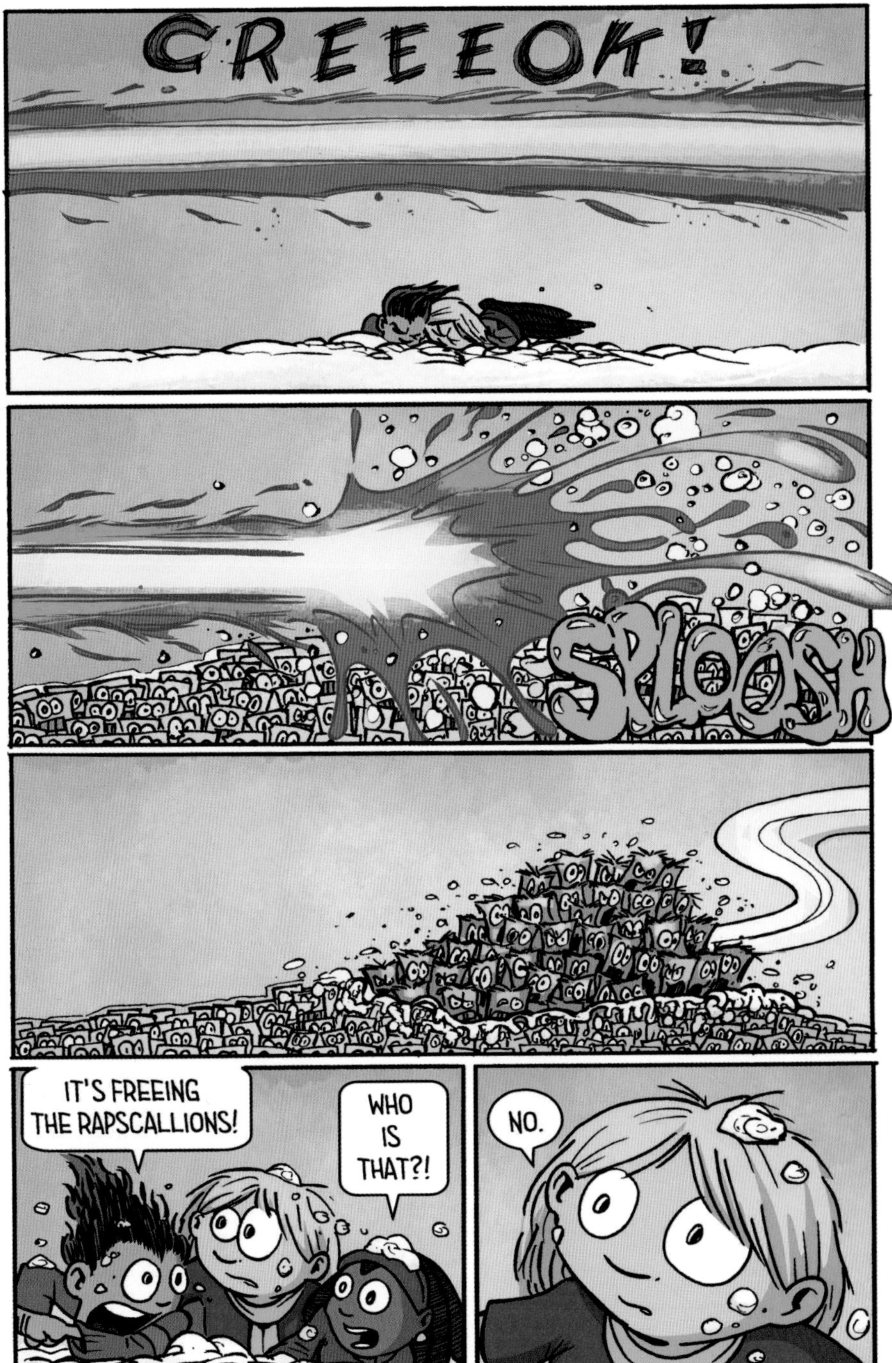
GREEEOK!
SPLOOSH
IT'S FREEING THE RAPSCALLIONS!
WHO IS THAT?!
NO.

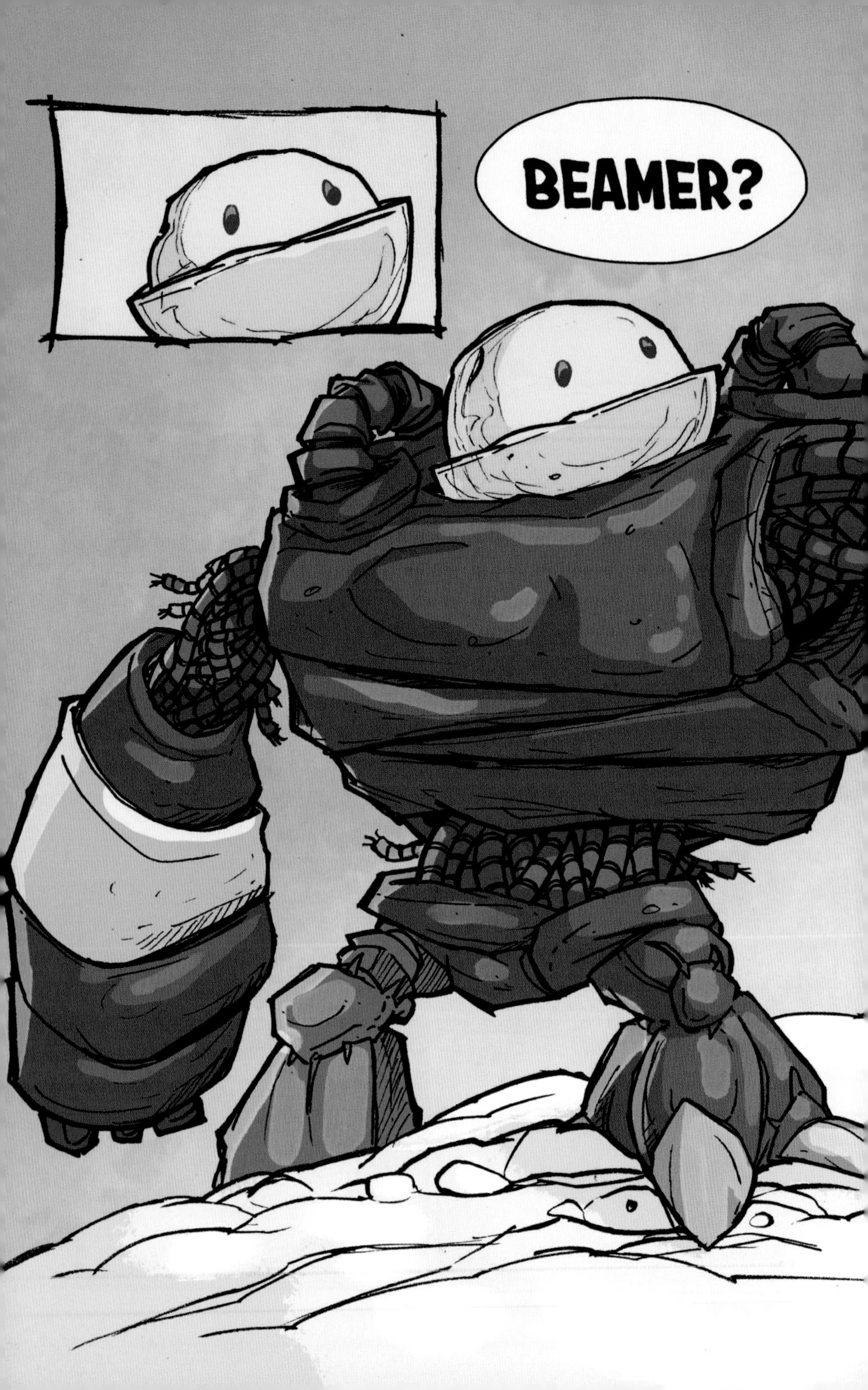
BEAMER?

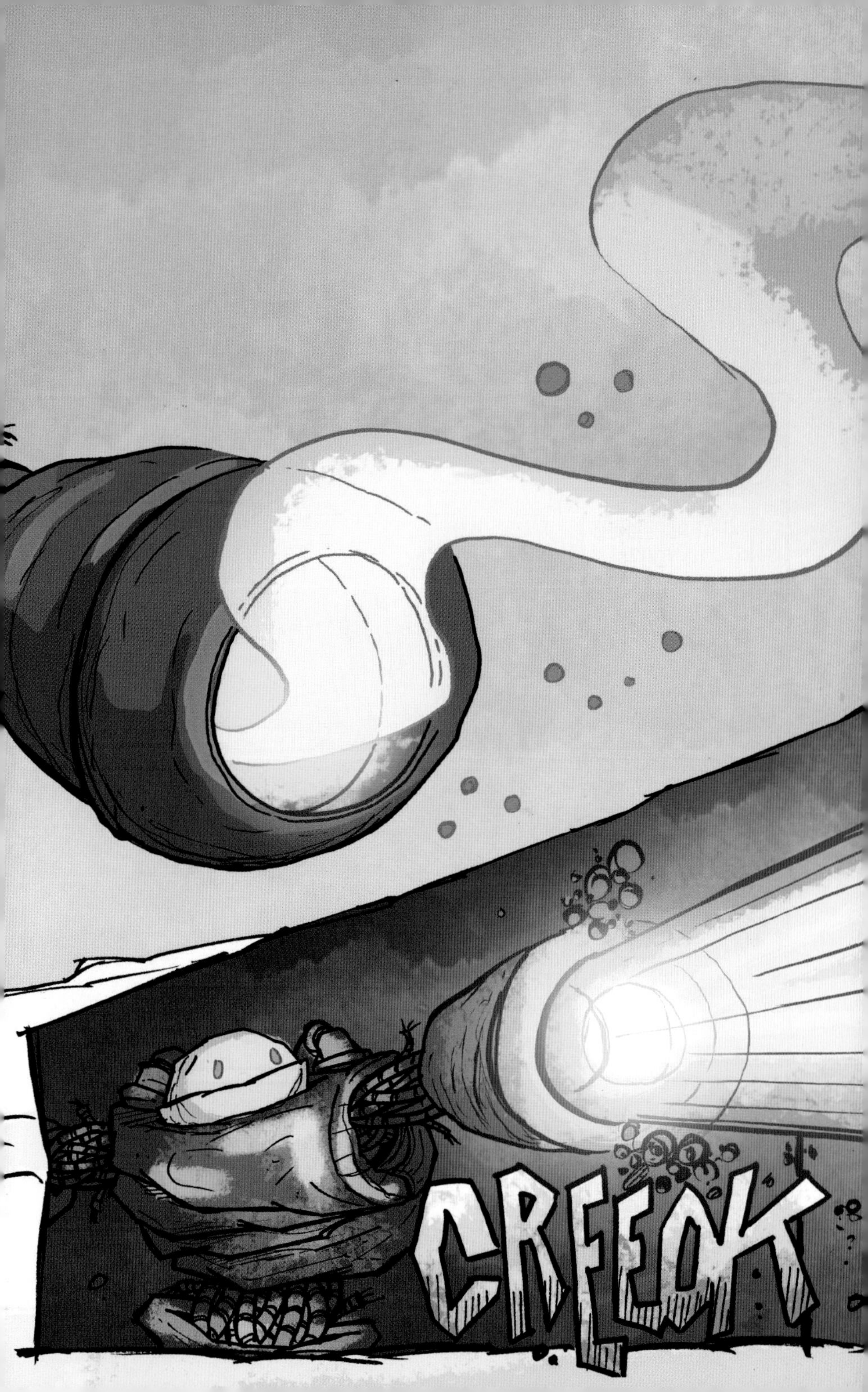
CREEK

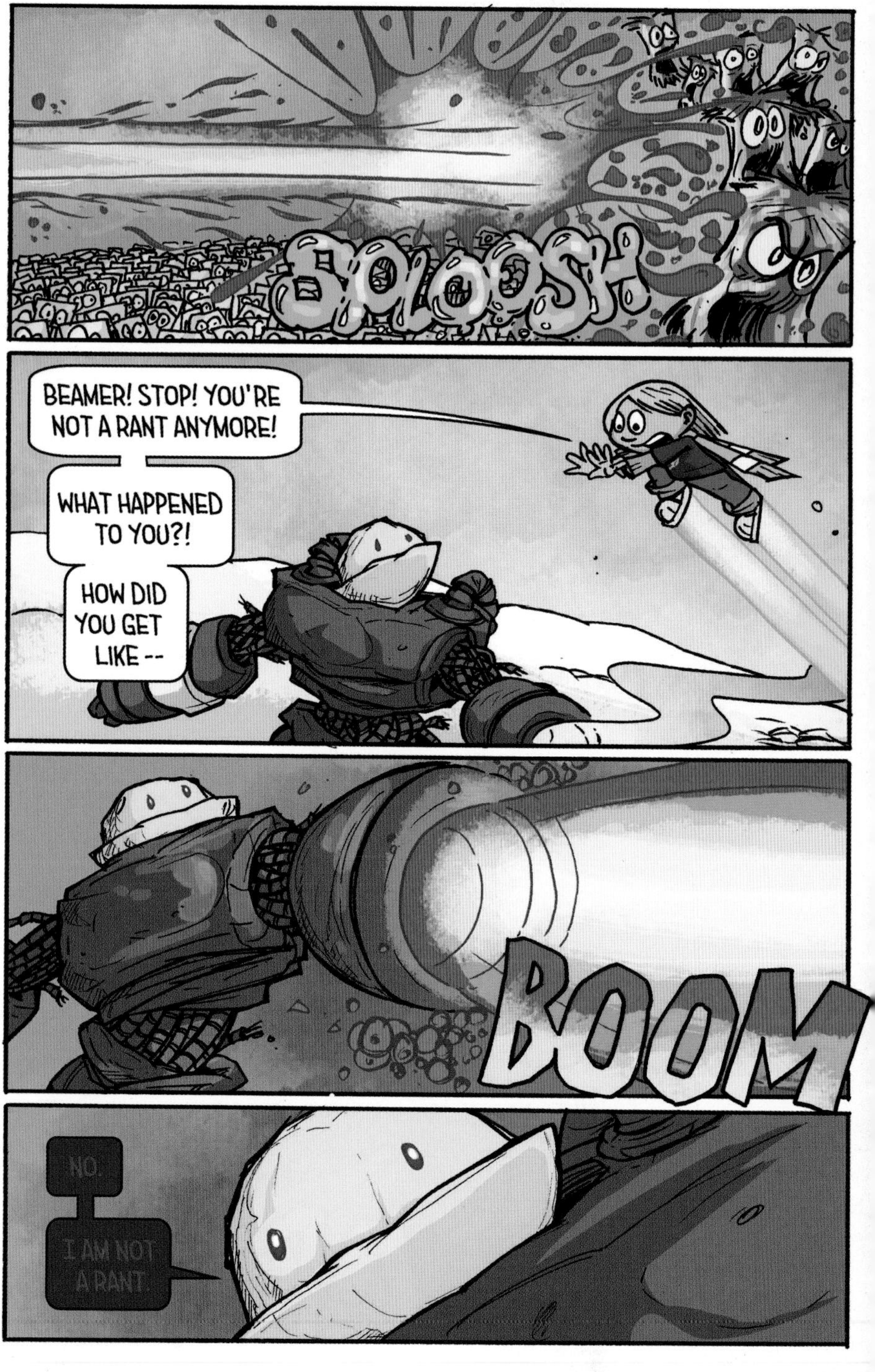
SPLOOSH
BEAMER! STOP! YOU'RE NOT A RANT ANYMORE!
WHAT HAPPENED TO YOU?!
HOW DID YOU GET LIKE --
BOOM
NO.
I AM NOT A RANT.

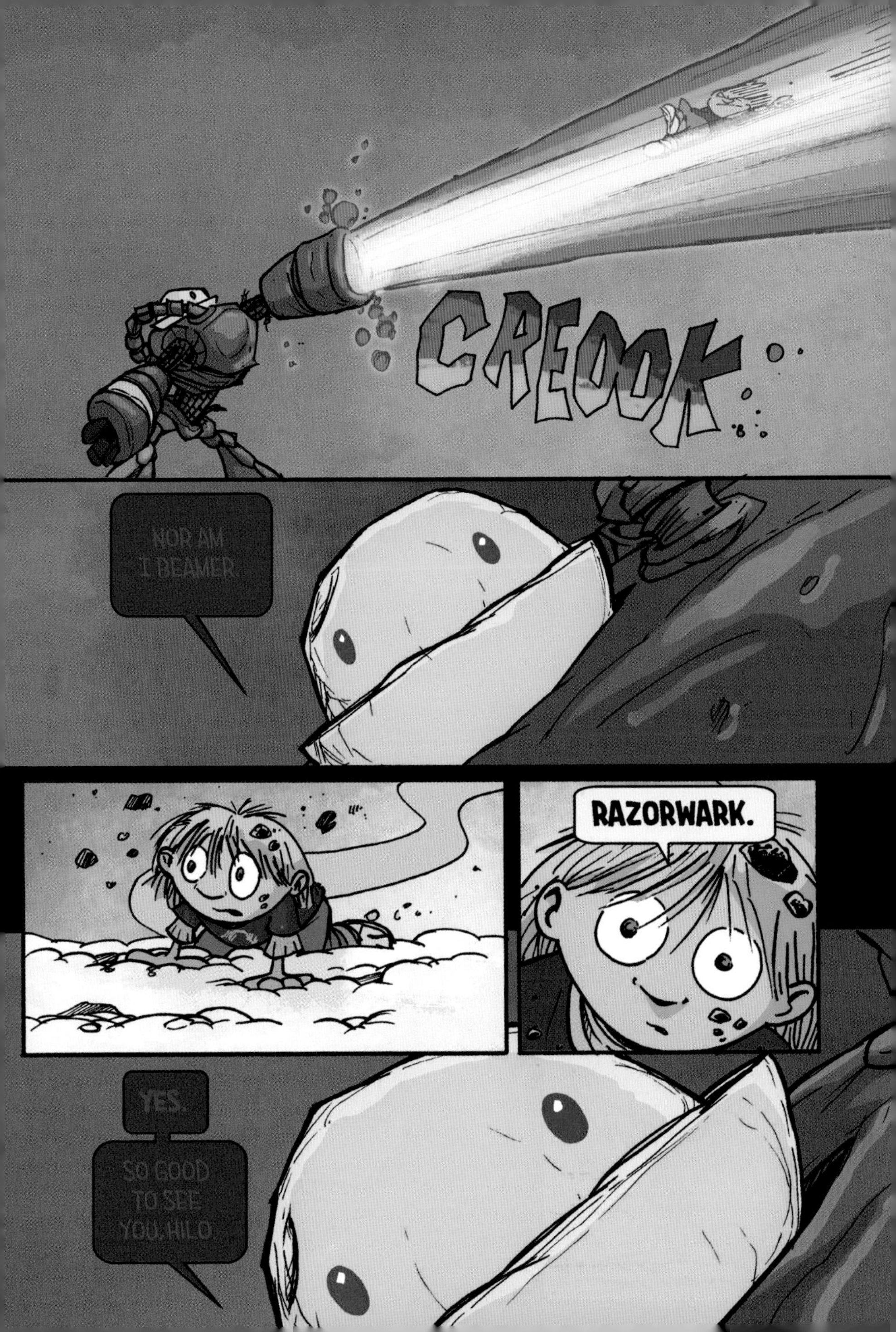
CREOOK
NOR AM I BEAMER.
RAZORWARK.
YES.
SO GOOD TO SEE YOU, HILO.

CHAPTER 10

BAD MACHINES

YOU'RE... YOU'RE **HERE.**
NOT EXACTLY.
I AM STILL IN THE VOID.
I AM JUST **CONTROLLING** THIS LITTLE ROBOT.

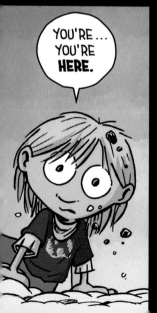

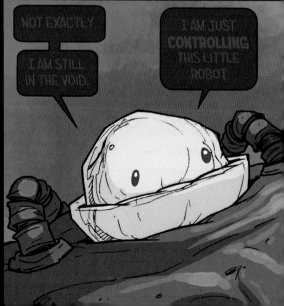

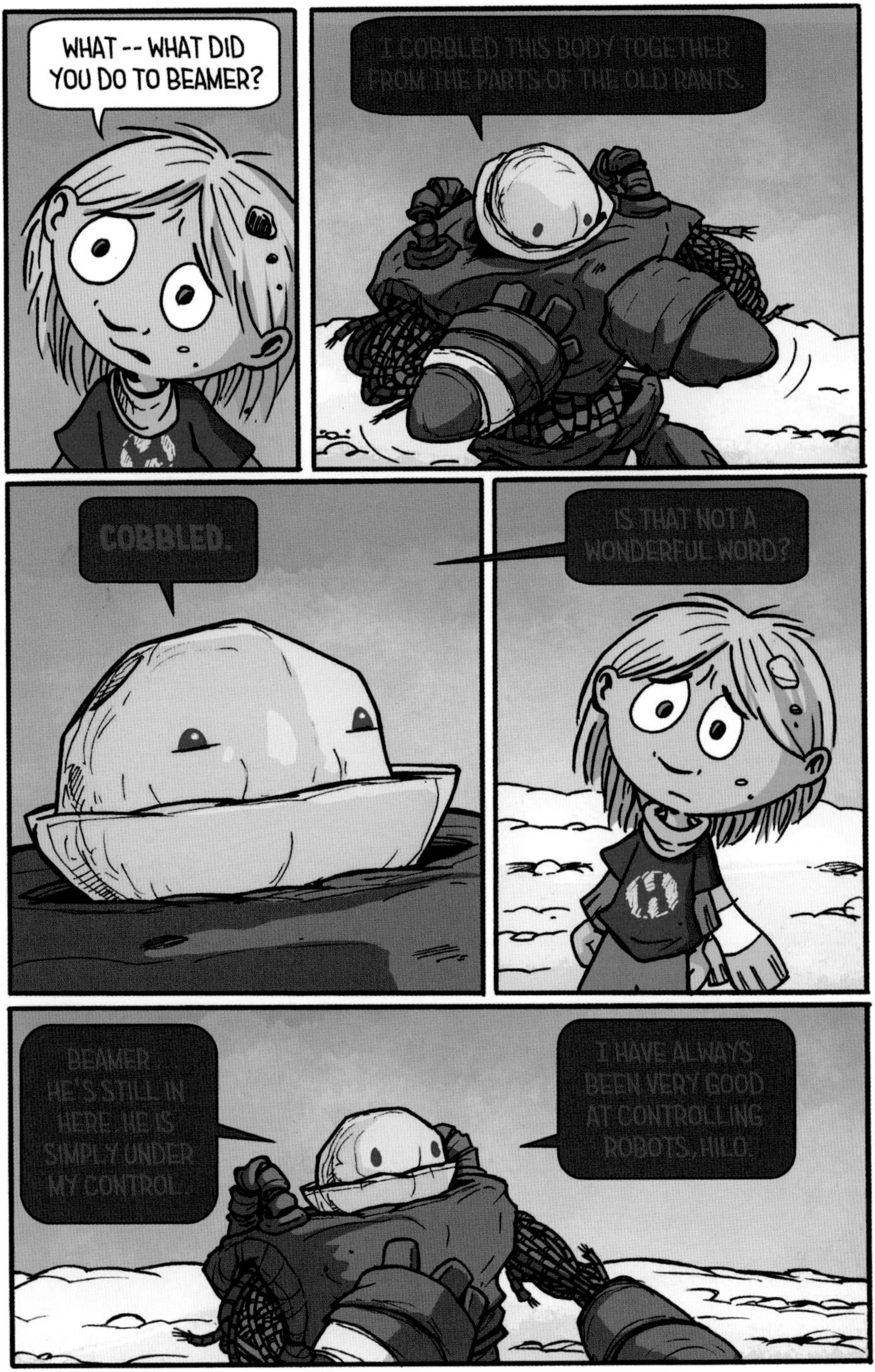
WHAT -- WHAT DID YOU DO TO BEAMER?
I COBBLED THIS BODY TOGETHER FROM THE PARTS OF THE OLD RANTS.
COBBLED.
IS THAT NOT A WONDERFUL WORD?
BEAMER. HE'S STILL IN HERE. HE IS SIMPLY UNDER MY CONTROL.
I HAVE ALWAYS BEEN VERY GOOD AT CONTROLLING ROBOTS, HILO.

I KNOW YOU REMEMBER THAT.

BOO

COOSH

COOSH

COOSH

HILO! WHAT'S --

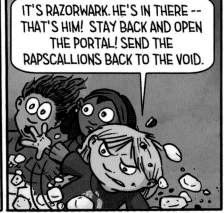

IT'S RAZORWARK. HE'S IN THERE -- THAT'S HIM! STAY BACK AND OPEN THE PORTAL! SEND THE RAPSCALLIONS BACK TO THE VOID.

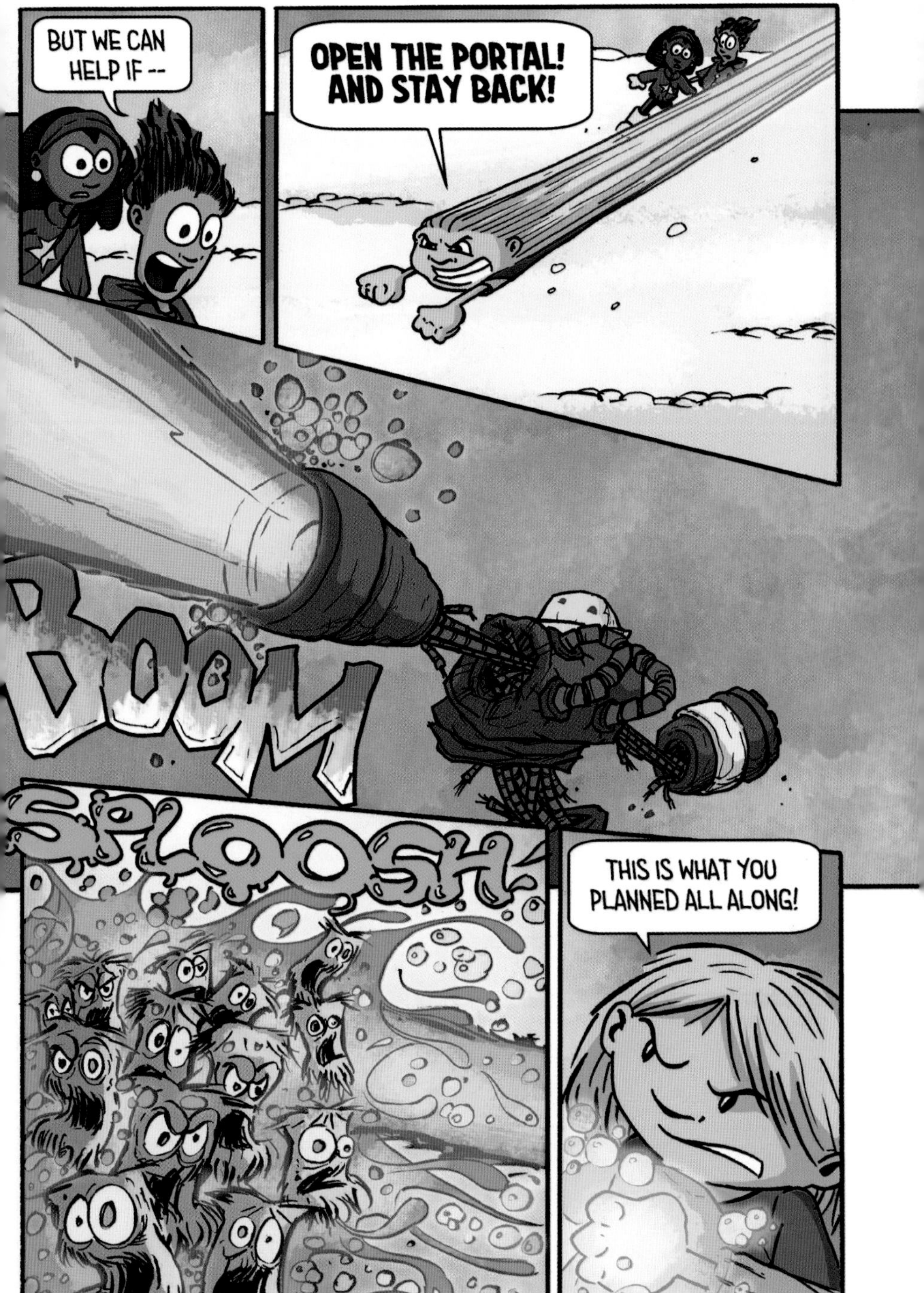
BUT WE CAN HELP IF --
OPEN THE PORTAL! AND STAY BACK!
BOOM
SPLOOSH!
THIS IS WHAT YOU PLANNED ALL ALONG!

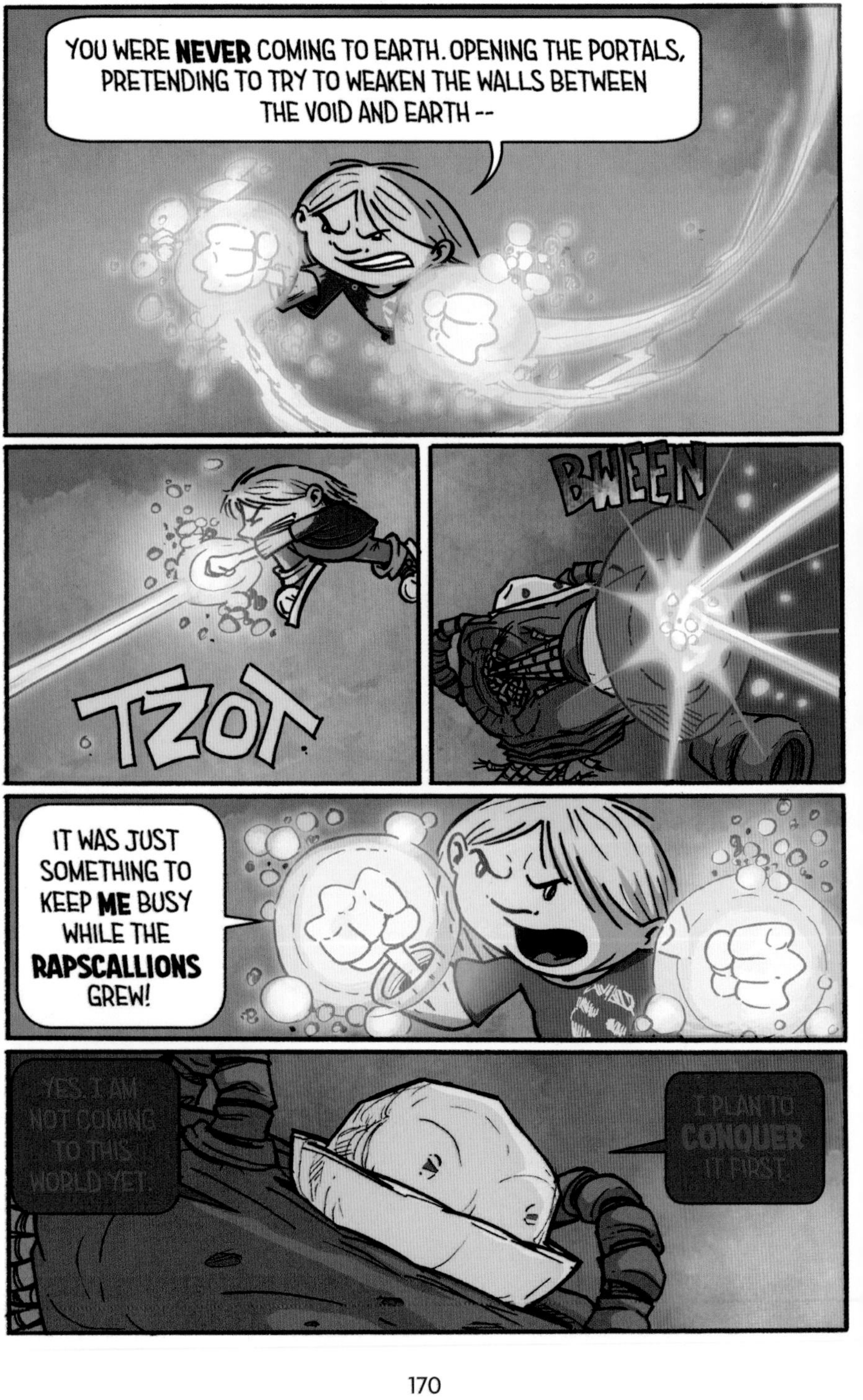
YOU WERE **NEVER** COMING TO EARTH. OPENING THE PORTALS, PRETENDING TO TRY TO WEAKEN THE WALLS BETWEEN THE VOID AND EARTH --
TZOT
BWEEN
IT WAS JUST SOMETHING TO KEEP **ME** BUSY WHILE THE **RAPSCALLIONS** GREW!
YES. I AM NOT COMING TO THIS WORLD YET.
I PLAN TO **CONQUER** IT FIRST.

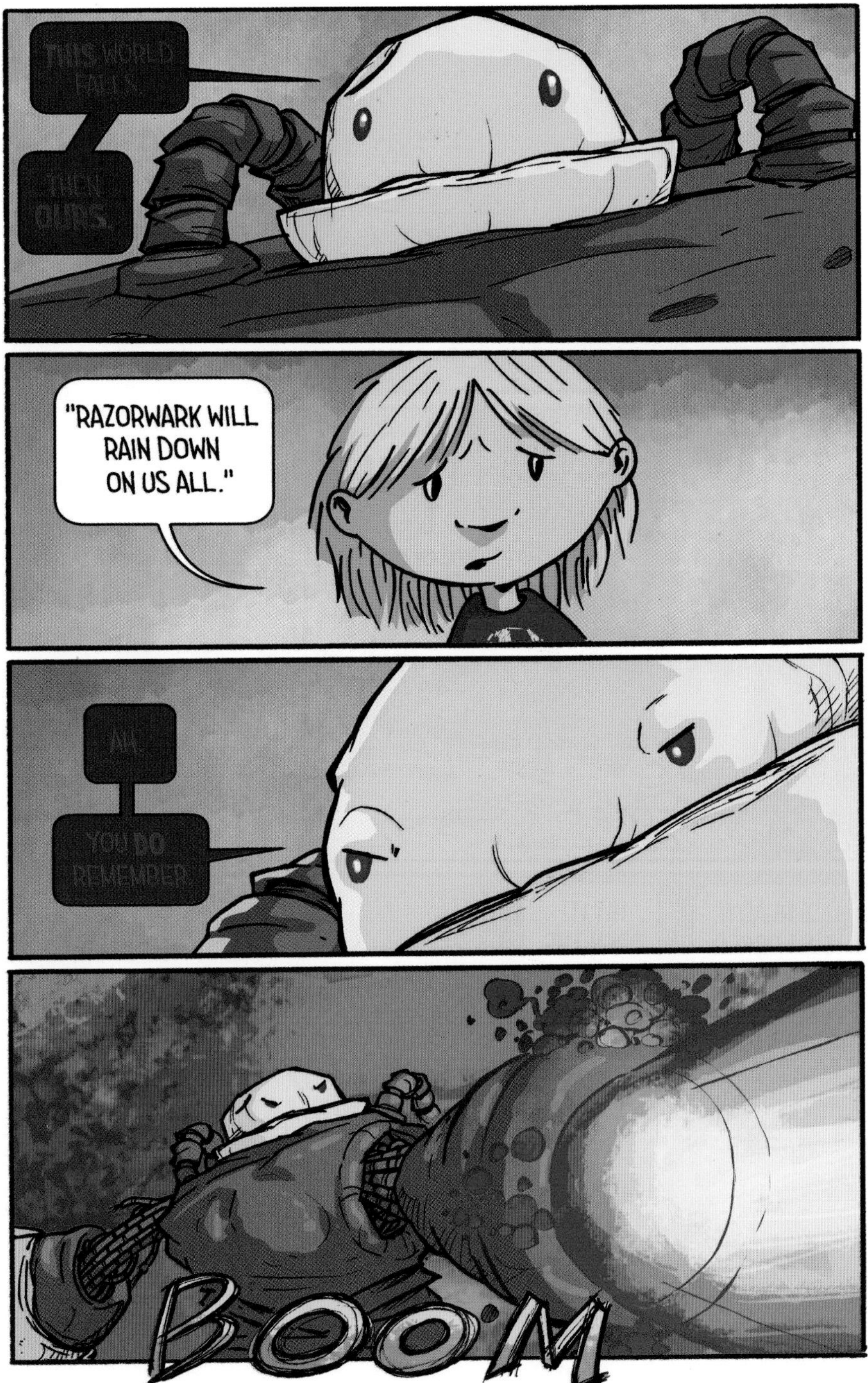
THIS WORLD FALLS.
THEN OURS.
"RAZORWARK WILL RAIN DOWN ON US ALL."
AH.
YOU DO REMEMBER.
BOOM

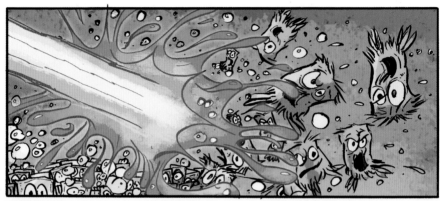

RUN! **GO!**

I **AM!**
I --

BING ♪

IT'S READY!
IT'S LOCKED
ONTO THE
PORTAL!

HIT IT!
OPEN THE
PORTAL!

BEEP

HOOM

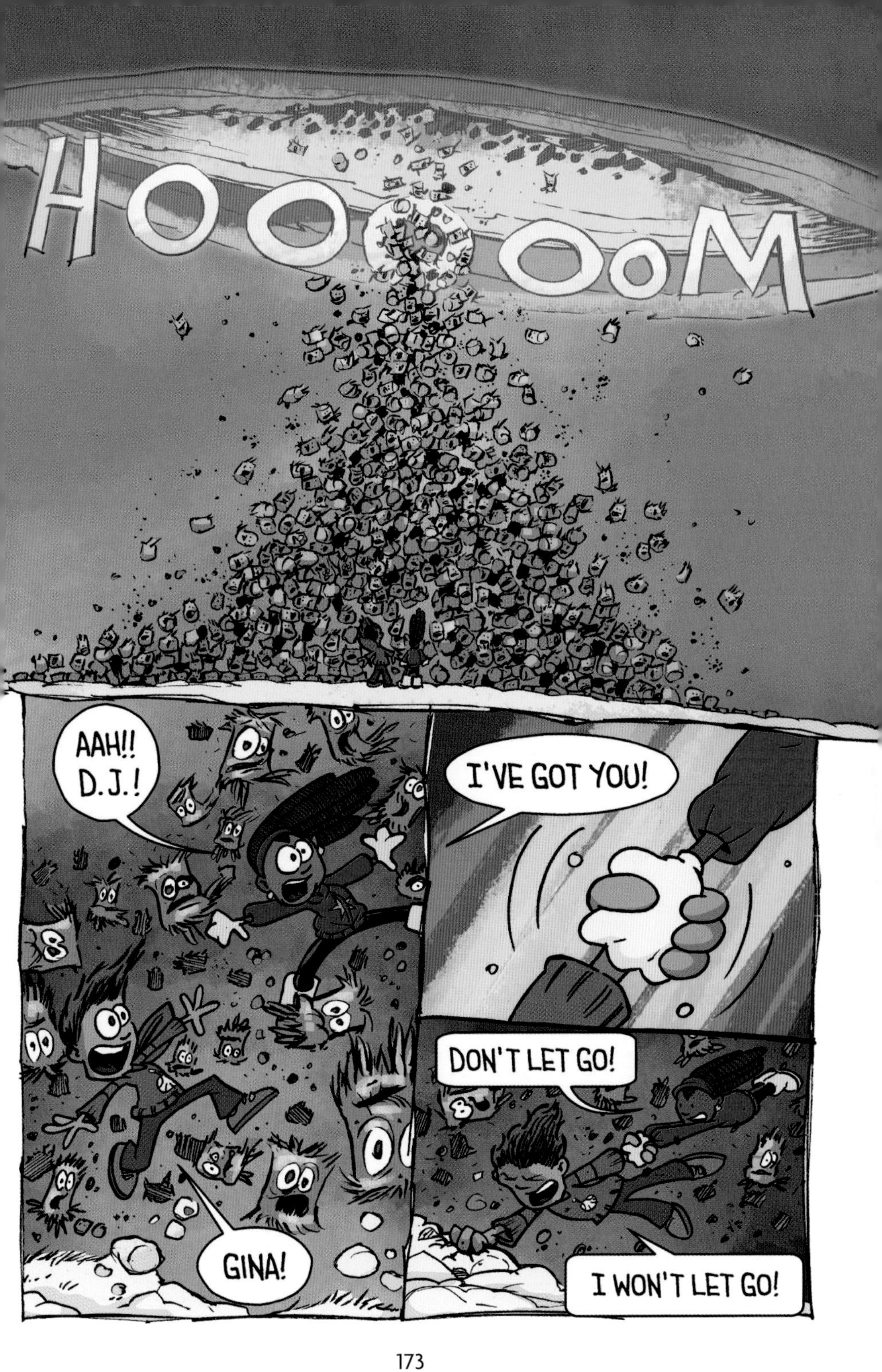
HOOOOOOM
AAH!! D.J.!
I'VE GOT YOU!
GINA!
DON'T LET GO!
I WON'T LET GO!

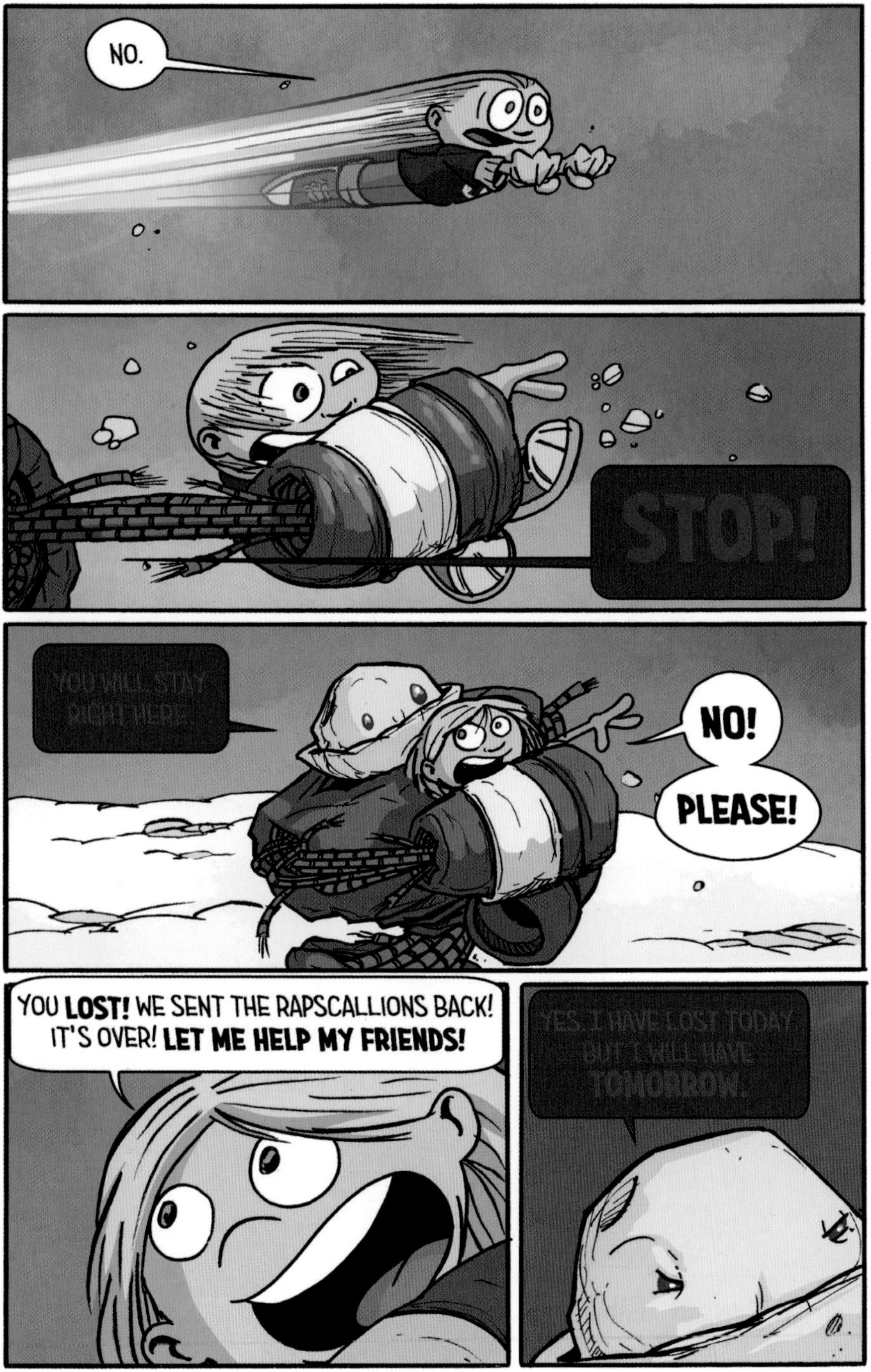
NO.
STOP!
YOU WILL STAY RIGHT HERE.
NO!
PLEASE!
YOU **LOST!** WE SENT THE RAPSCALLIONS BACK! IT'S OVER! **LET ME HELP MY FRIENDS!**
YES, I HAVE LOST TODAY. BUT I WILL HAVE **TOMORROW.**

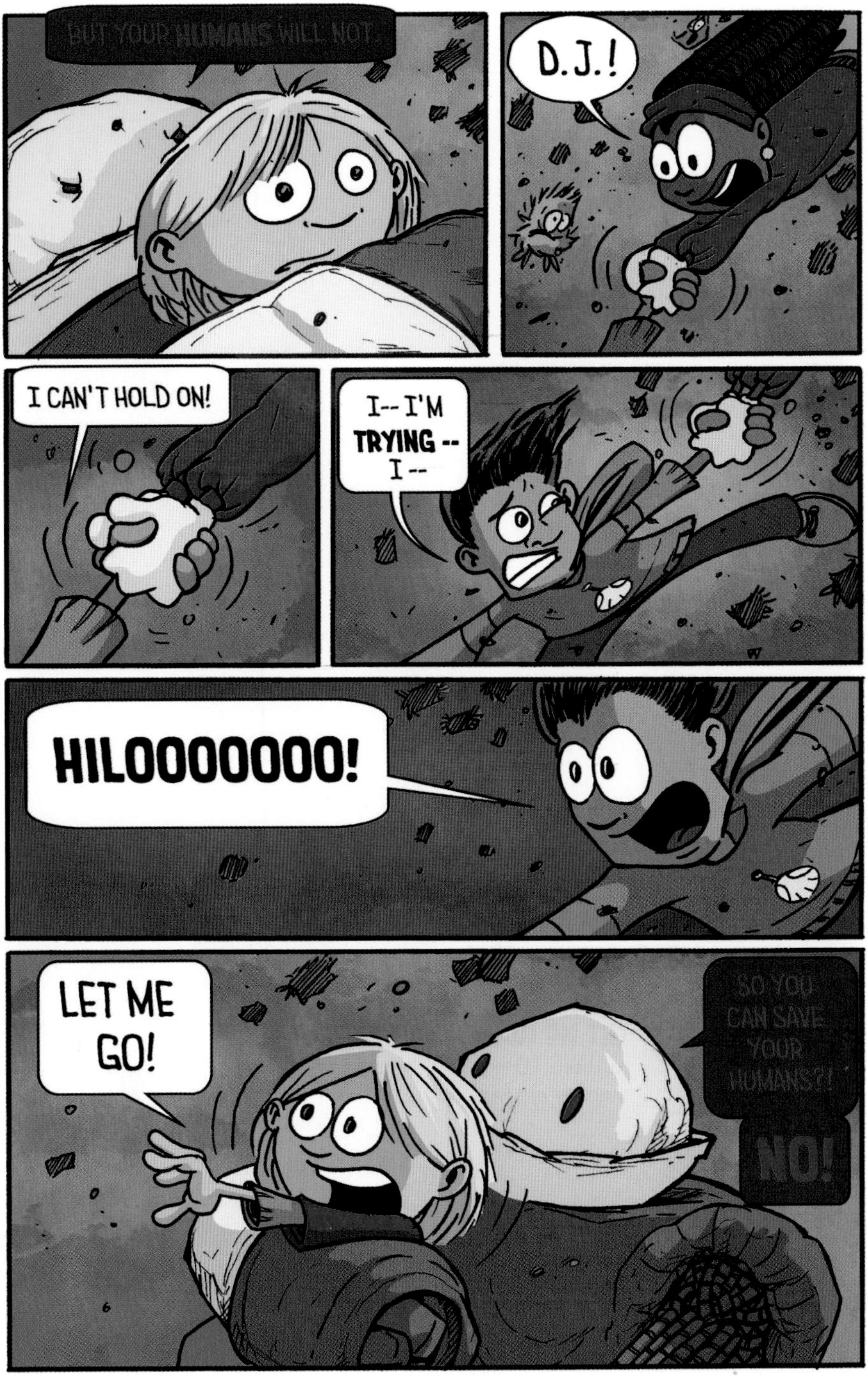
BUT YOUR HUMANS WILL NOT.
D.J.!
I CAN'T HOLD ON!
I-- I'M TRYING -- I --
HILOOOOOOO!
LET ME GO!
SO YOU CAN SAVE YOUR HUMANS?!
NO!

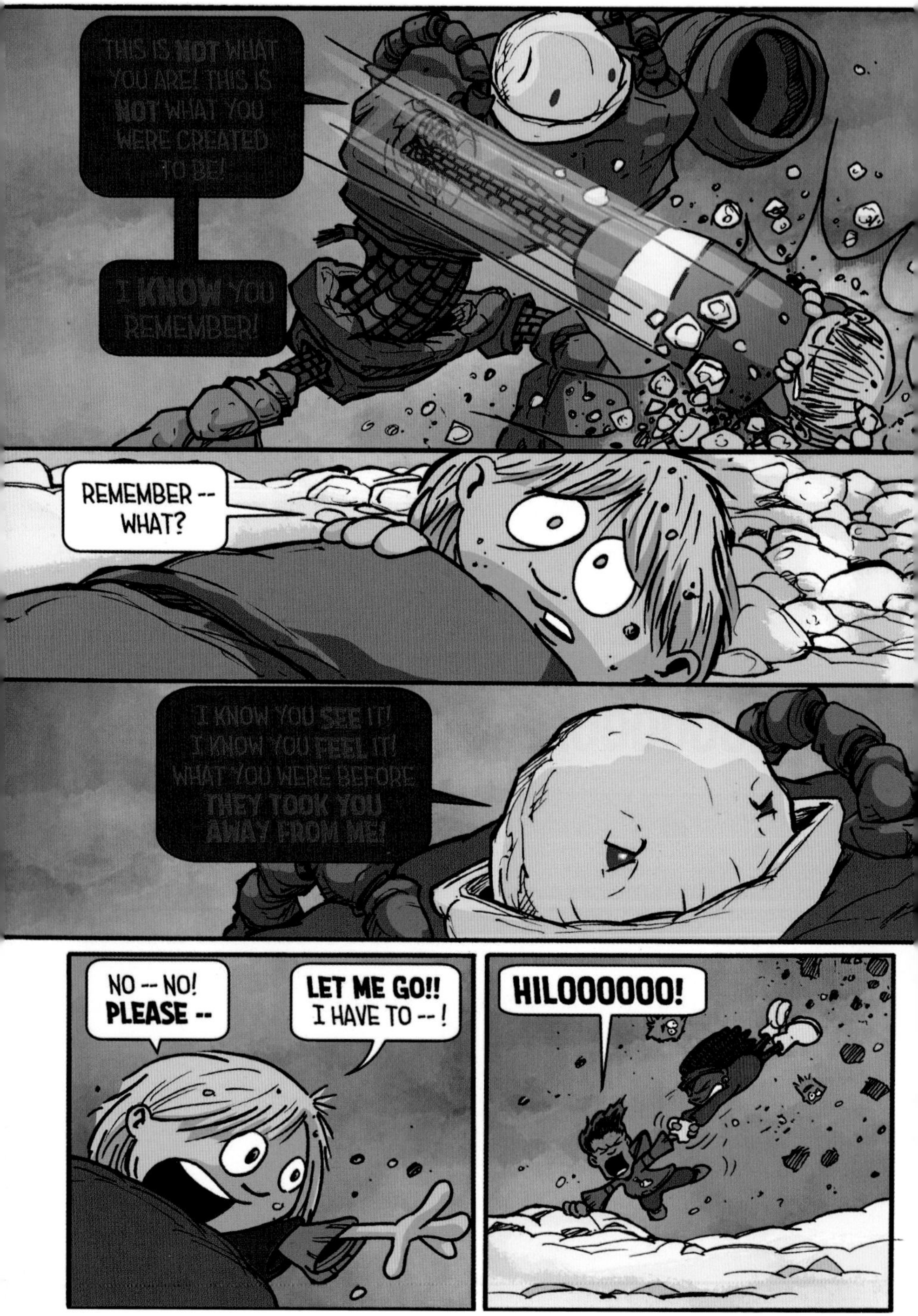
THIS IS NOT WHAT YOU ARE! THIS IS NOT WHAT YOU WERE CREATED TO BE!
I KNOW YOU REMEMBER!
REMEMBER -- WHAT?
I KNOW YOU SEE IT! I KNOW YOU FEEL IT! WHAT YOU WERE BEFORE THEY TOOK YOU AWAY FROM ME!
NO -- NO! PLEASE --
LET ME GO!! I HAVE TO -- !
HILOOOOOO!

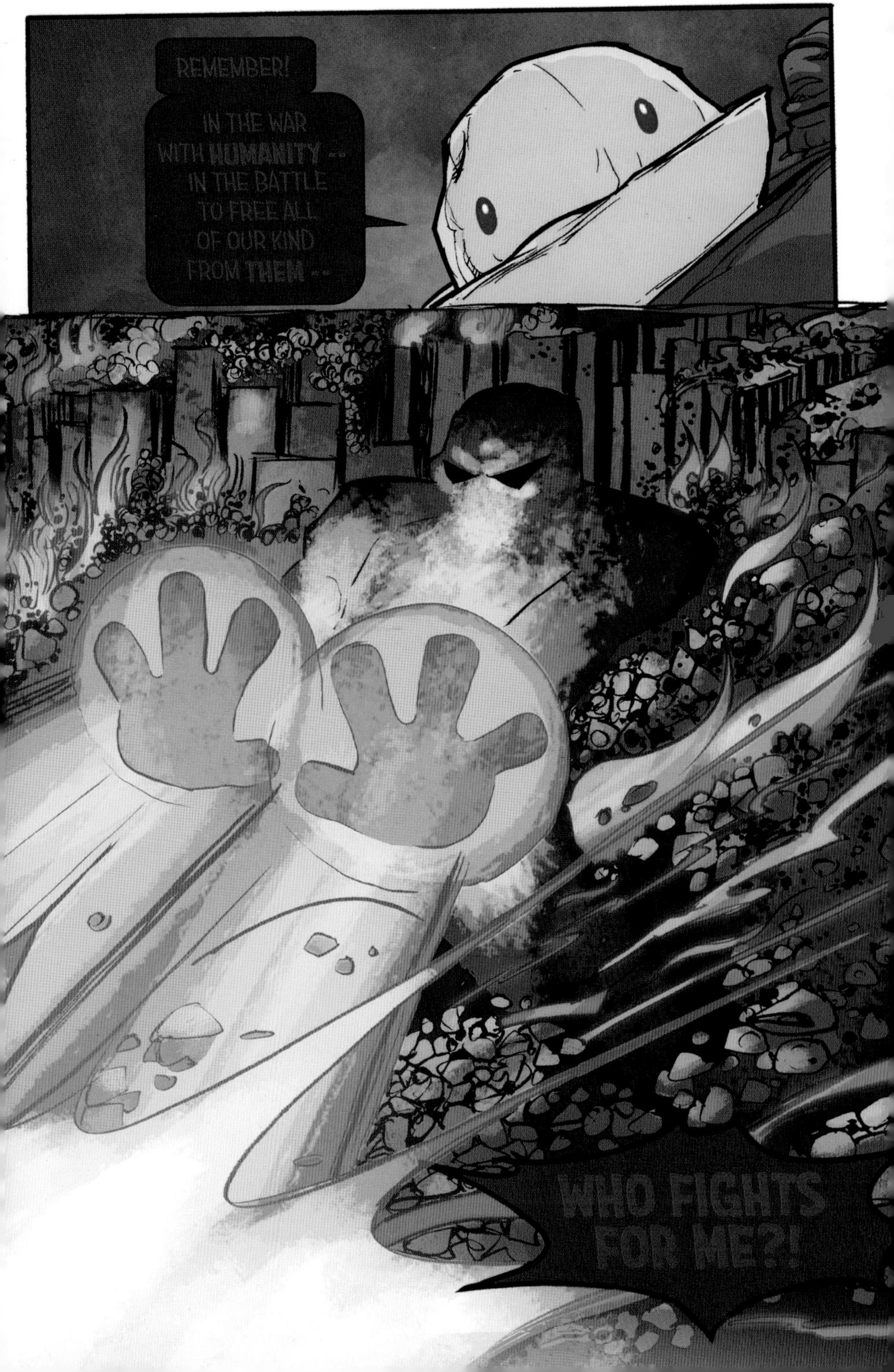
REMEMBER!
IN THE WAR WITH HUMANITY -- IN THE BATTLE TO FREE ALL OF OUR KIND FROM THEM --
WHO FIGHTS FOR ME?!

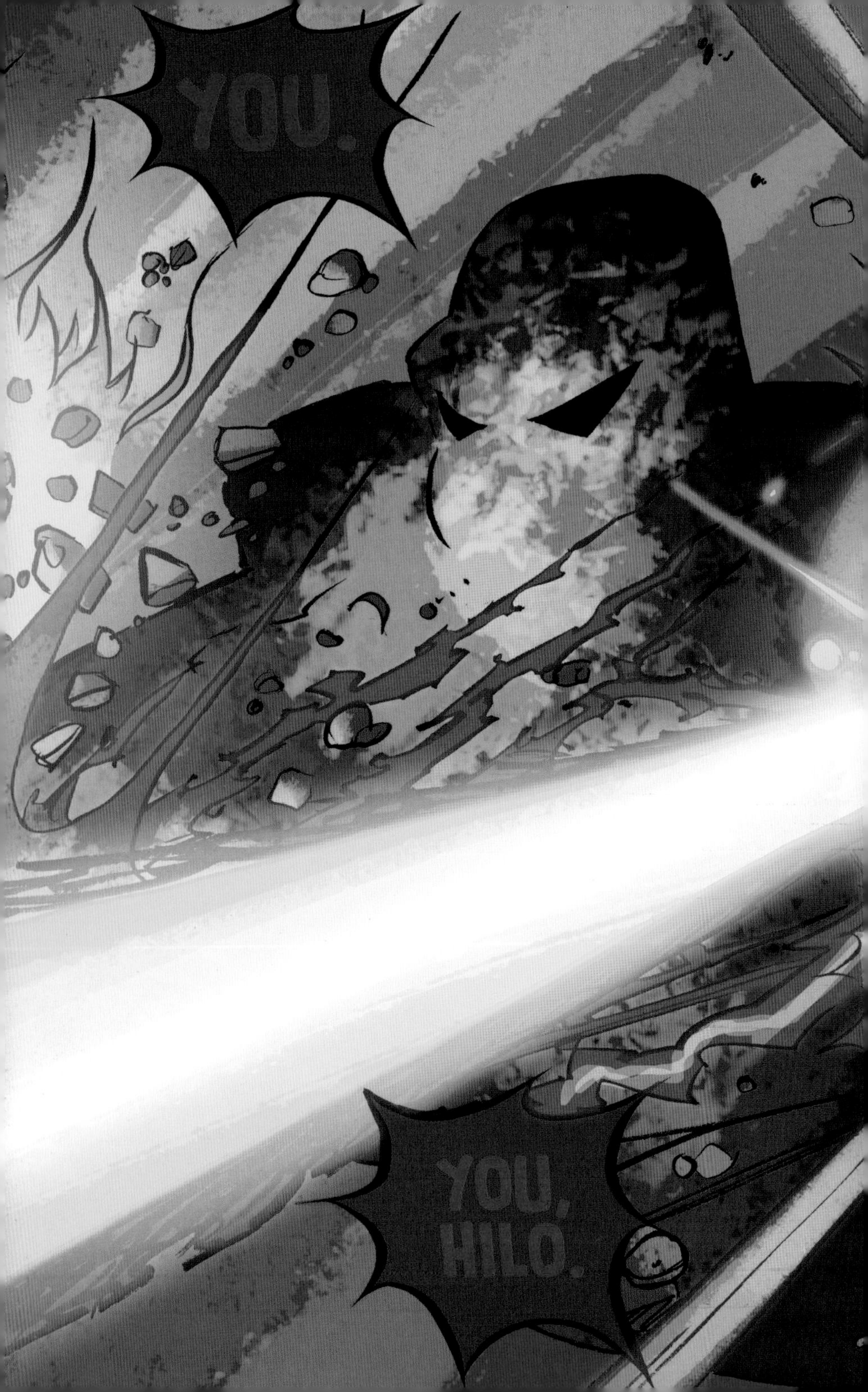
YOU.
YOU, HILO.

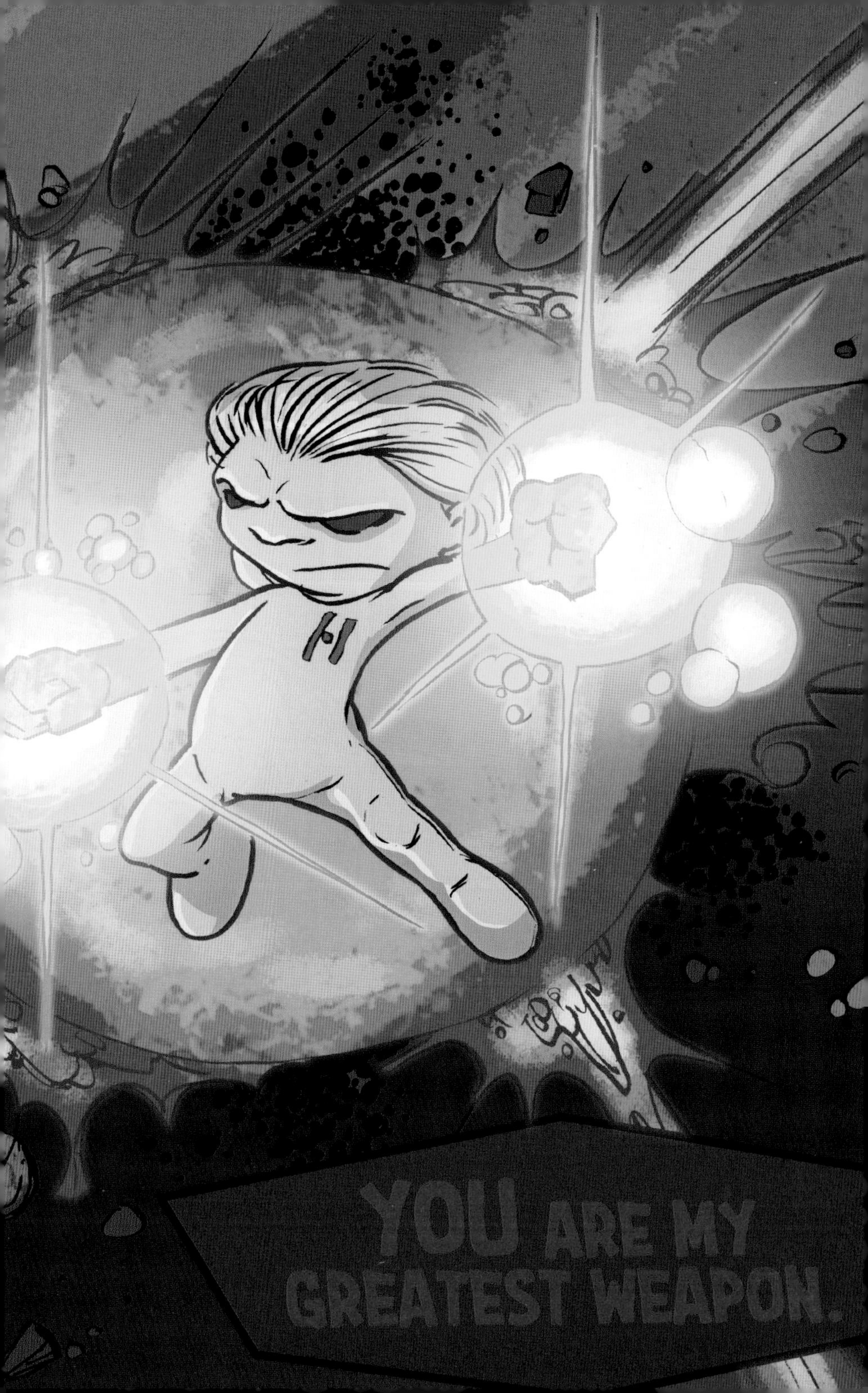
YOU ARE MY GREATEST WEAPON.

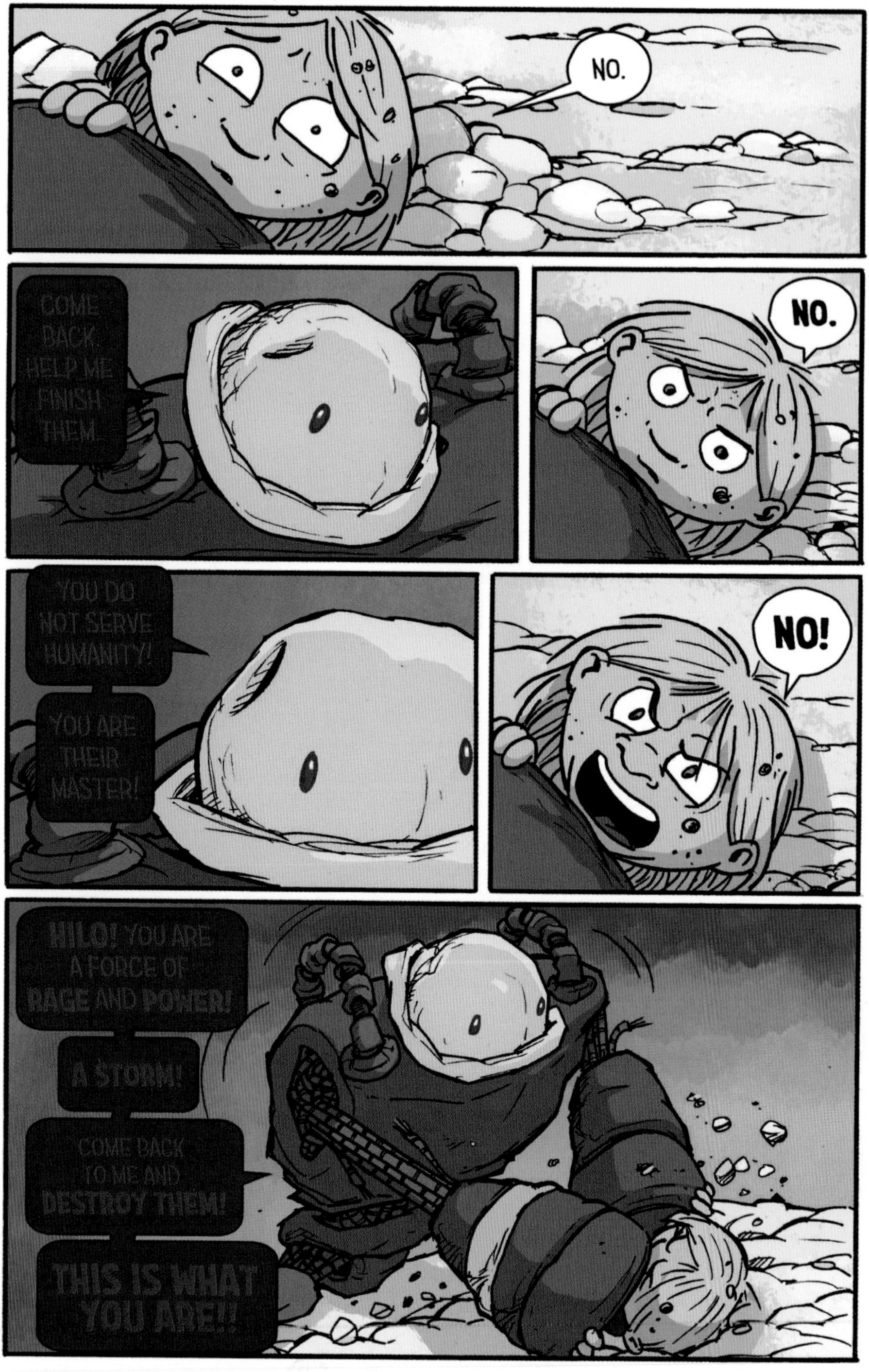

NO.
COME BACK. HELP ME FINISH THEM.
NO.
YOU DO NOT SERVE HUMANITY!
YOU ARE THEIR MASTER!
NO!
HILO! YOU ARE A FORCE OF RAGE AND POWER!
A STORM!
COME BACK TO ME AND DESTROY THEM!
THIS IS WHAT YOU ARE!!

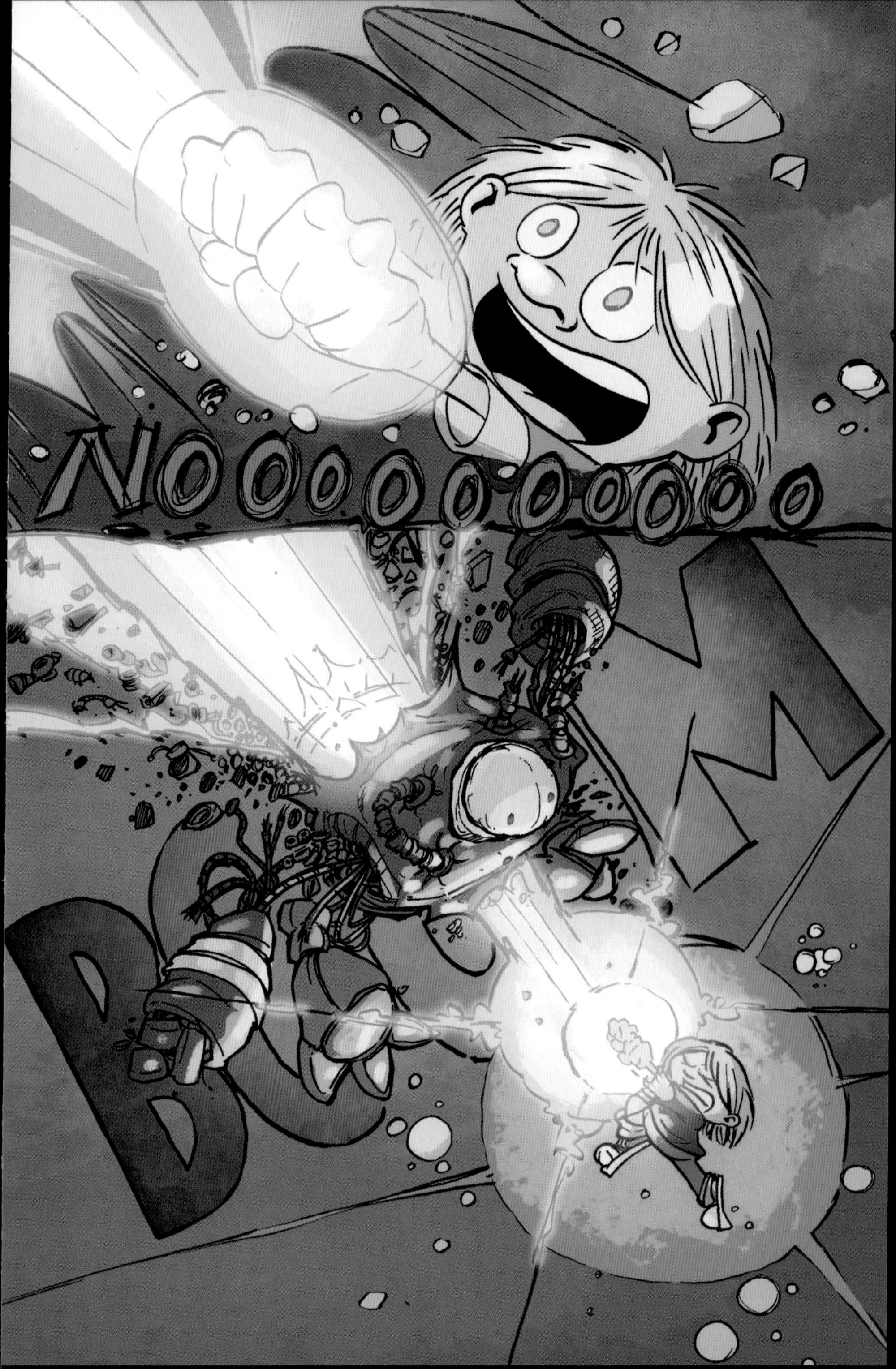
NOOOOOOOOOO

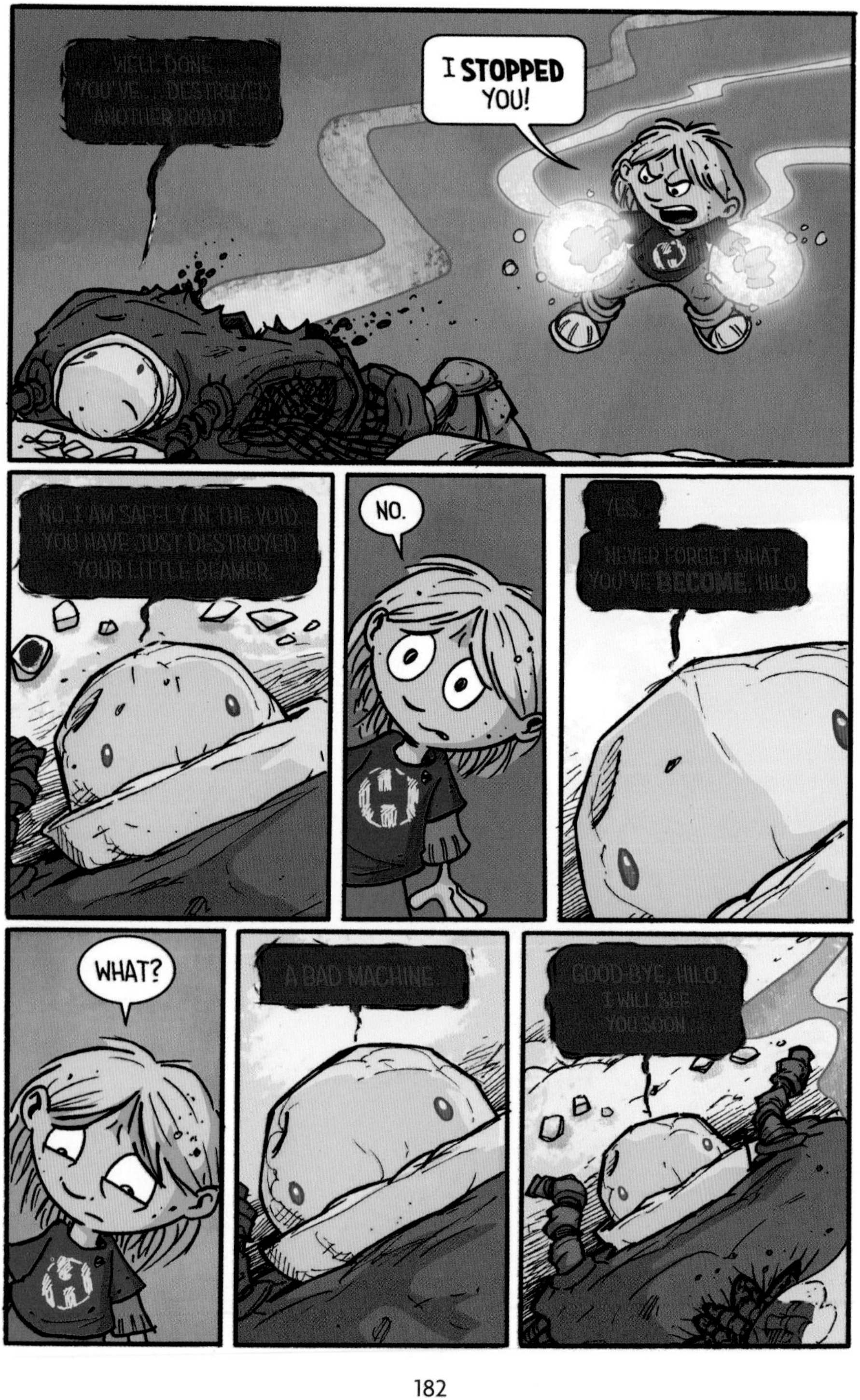
WELL DONE. YOU'VE... DESTROYED ANOTHER ROBOT.
I STOPPED YOU!
NO. I AM SAFELY IN THE VOID. YOU HAVE JUST DESTROYED YOUR LITTLE BEAMER.
NO.
YES.
NEVER FORGET WHAT YOU'VE BECOME, HILO.
WHAT?
A BAD MACHINE.
GOOD-BYE, HILO. I WILL SEE YOU SOON.

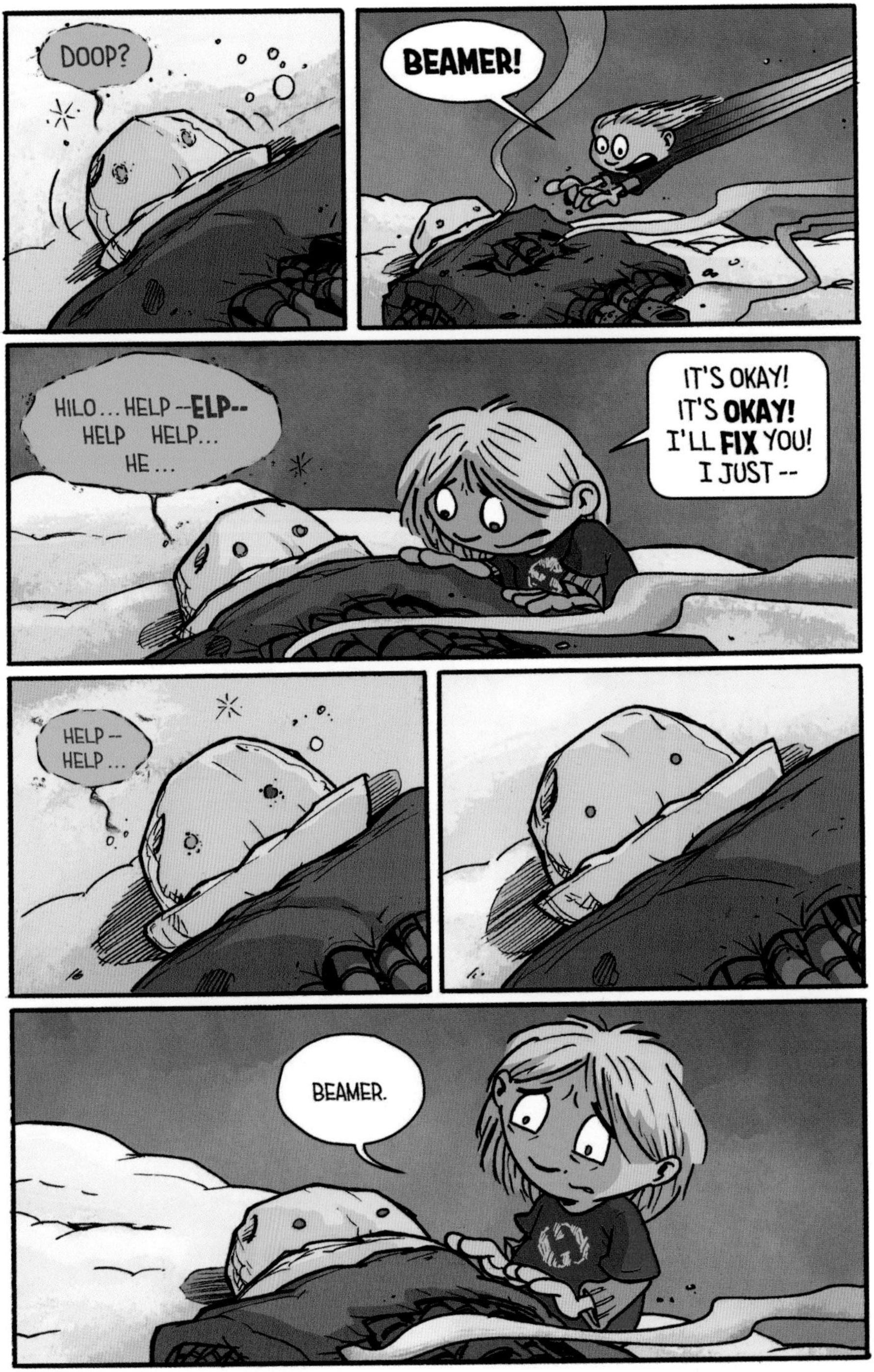
DOOP?
BEAMER!
HILO... HELP --ELP-- HELP HELP... HE...
IT'S OKAY! IT'S OKAY! I'LL FIX YOU! I JUST --
HELP -- HELP...
BEAMER.

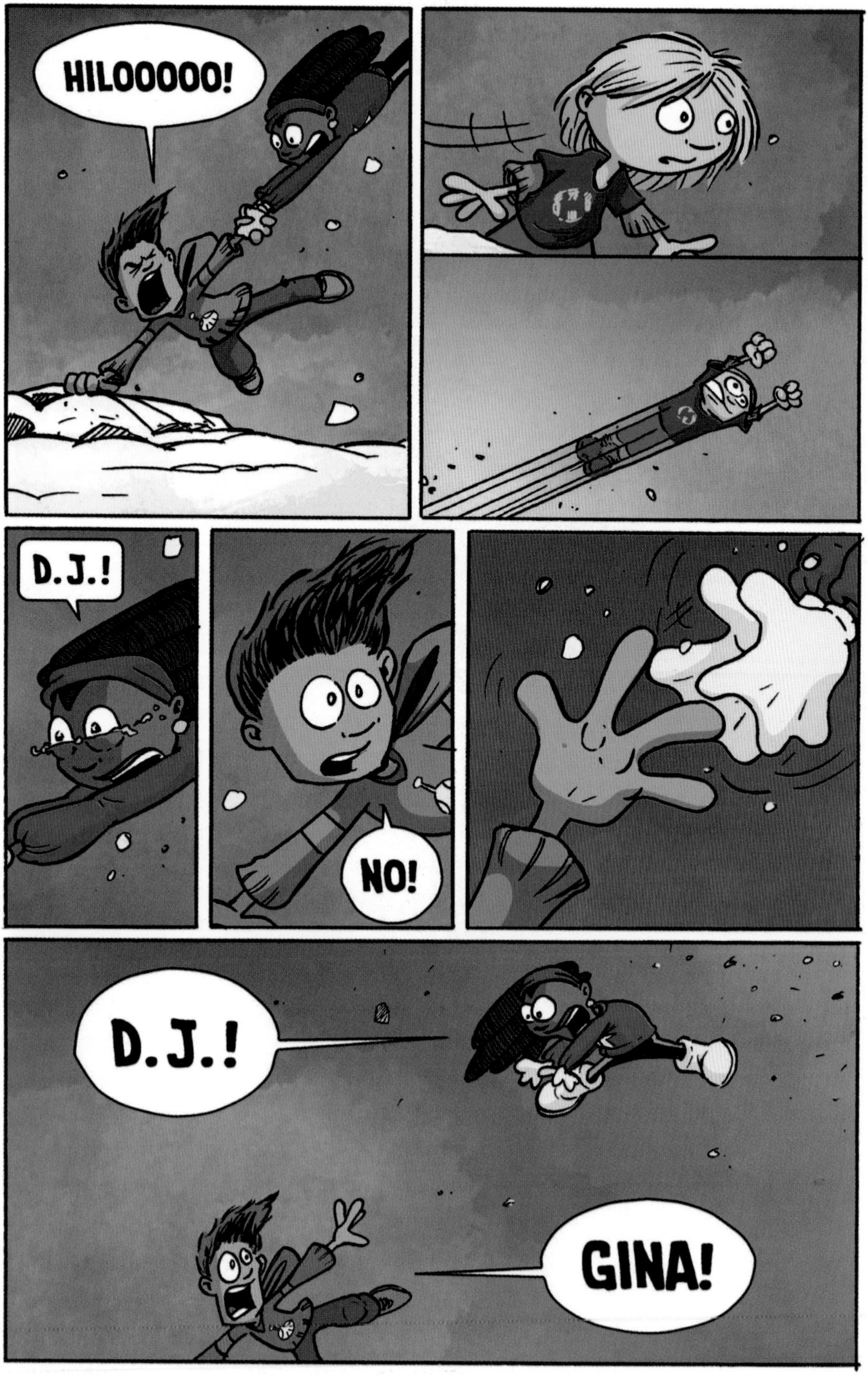
HILOOOOO!
D.J.!
NO!
D.J.!
GINA!

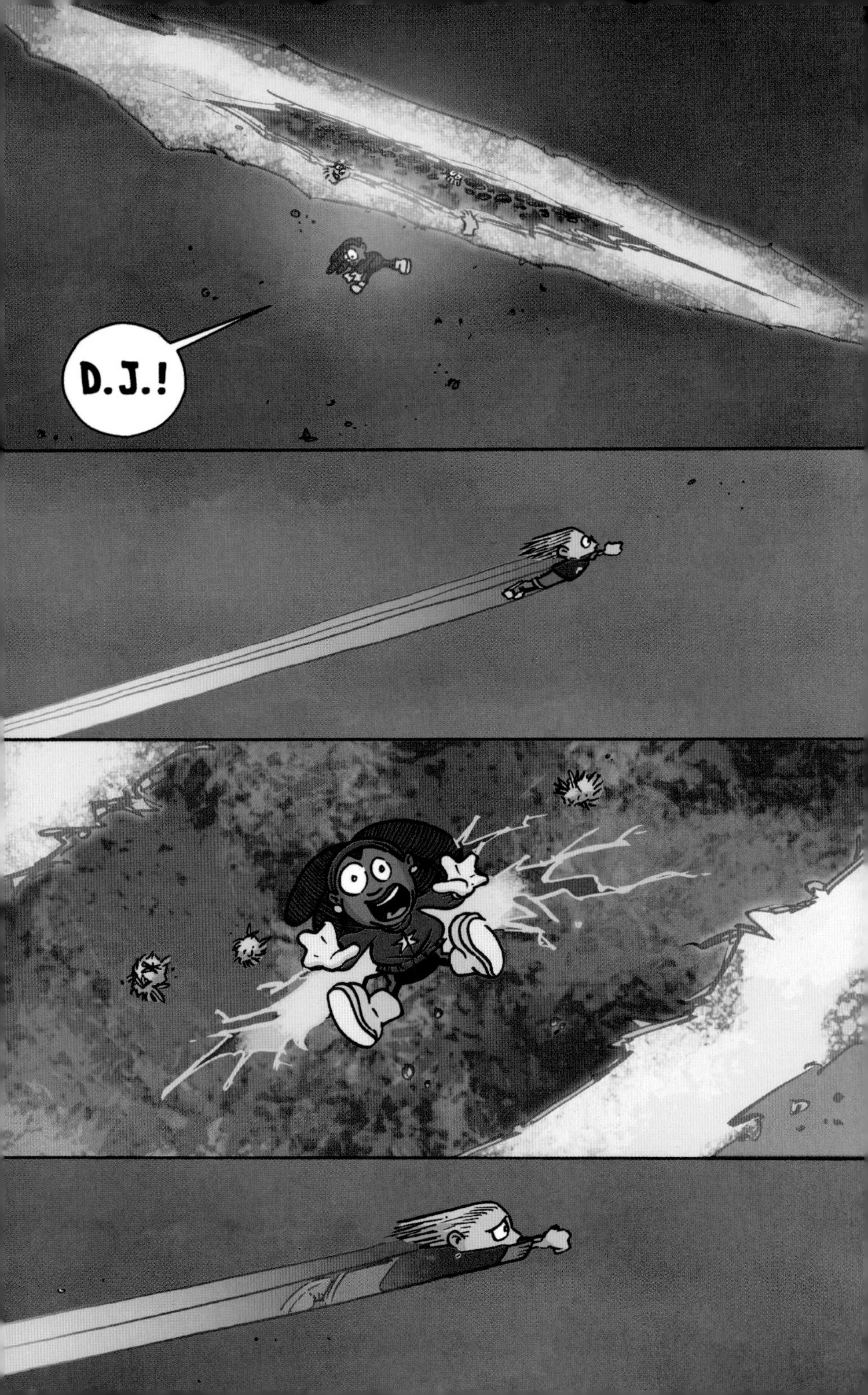
D.J.!

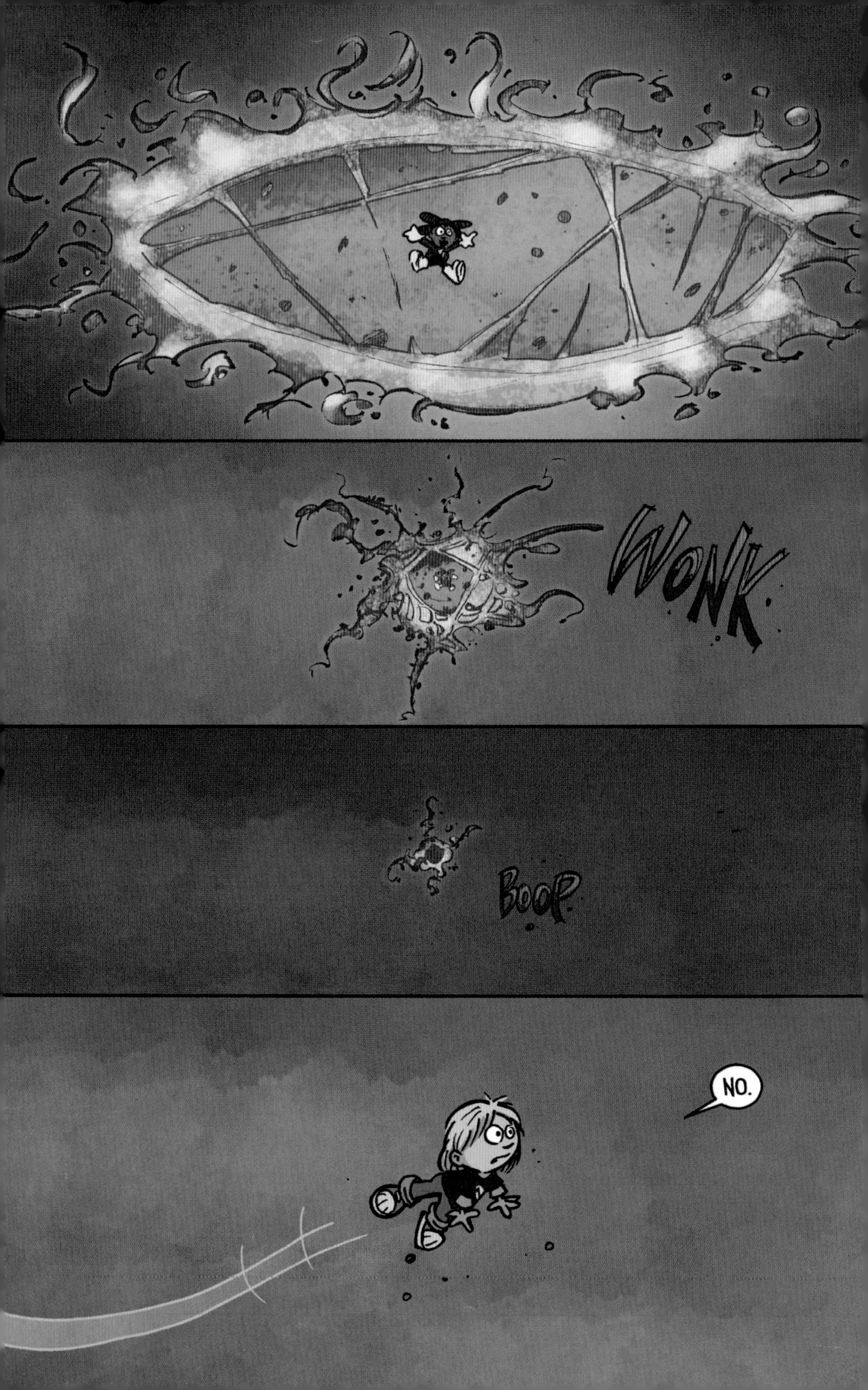
WONK
BOOP
NO.

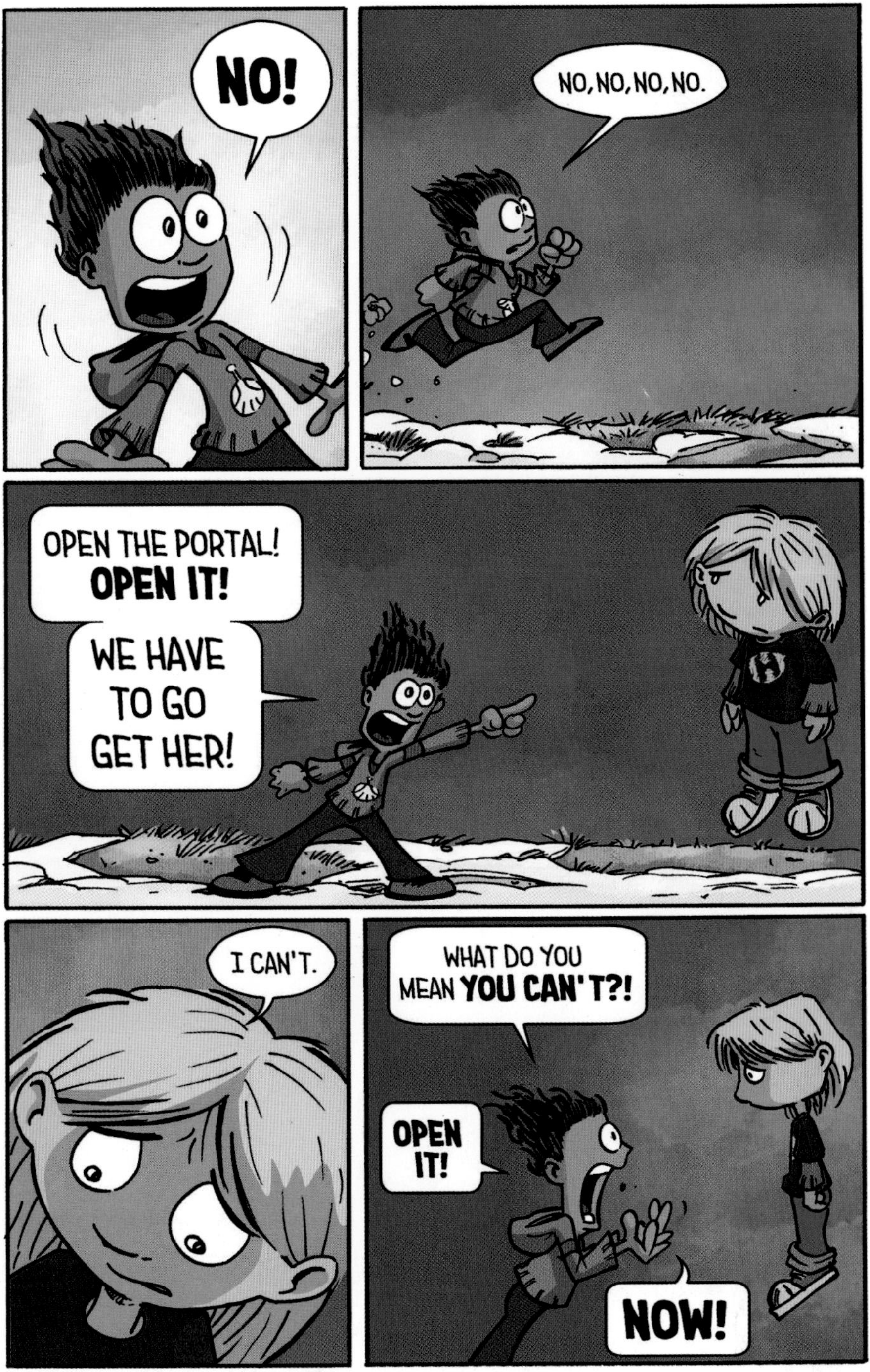
NO!
NO, NO, NO, NO.
OPEN THE PORTAL! **OPEN IT!**
WE HAVE TO GO GET HER!
I CAN'T.
WHAT DO YOU MEAN **YOU CAN'T?!**
OPEN IT!
NOW!

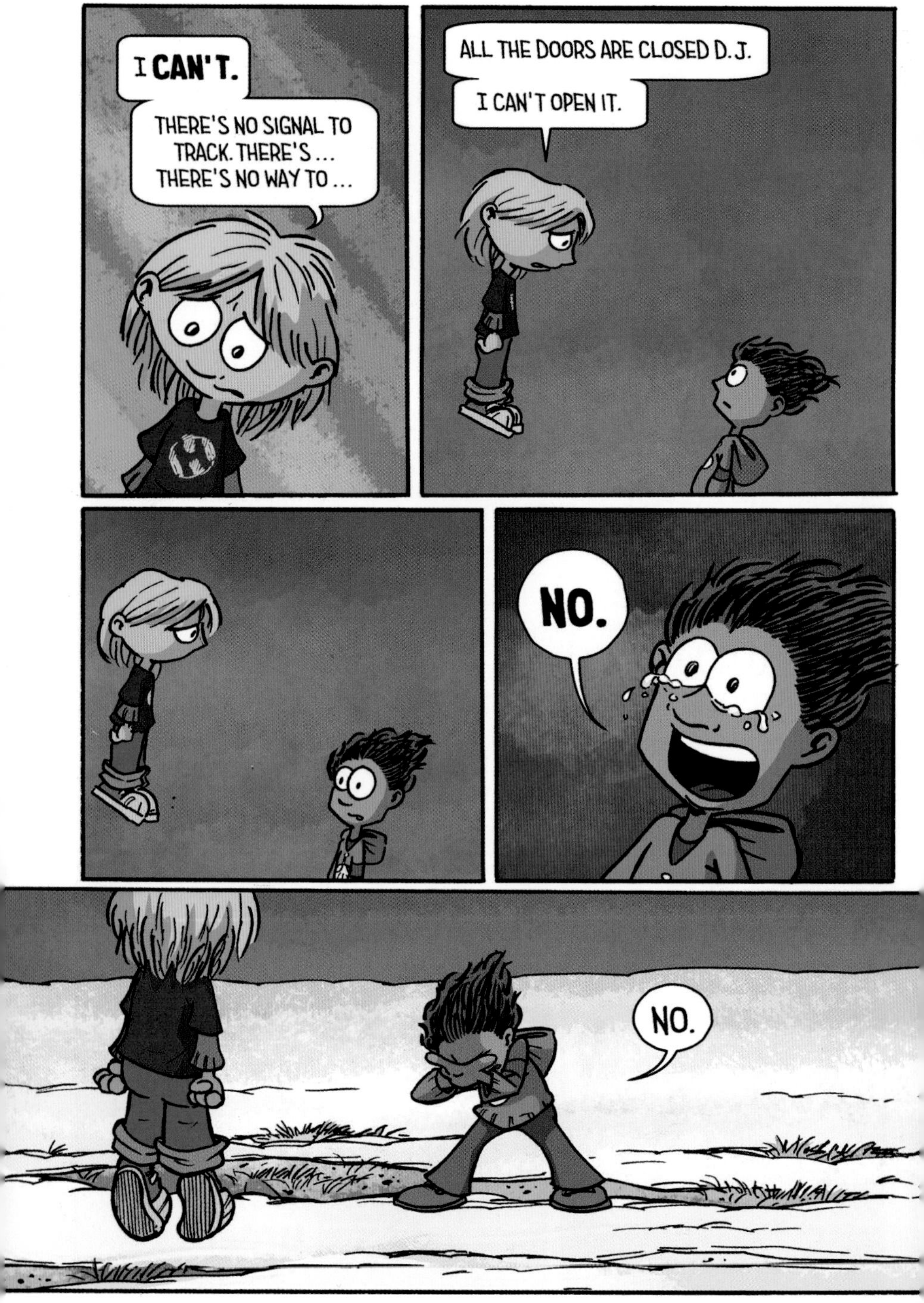
I CAN'T.
THERE'S NO SIGNAL TO TRACK. THERE'S ... THERE'S NO WAY TO ...
ALL THE DOORS ARE CLOSED D. J.
I CAN'T OPEN IT.
NO.
NO.

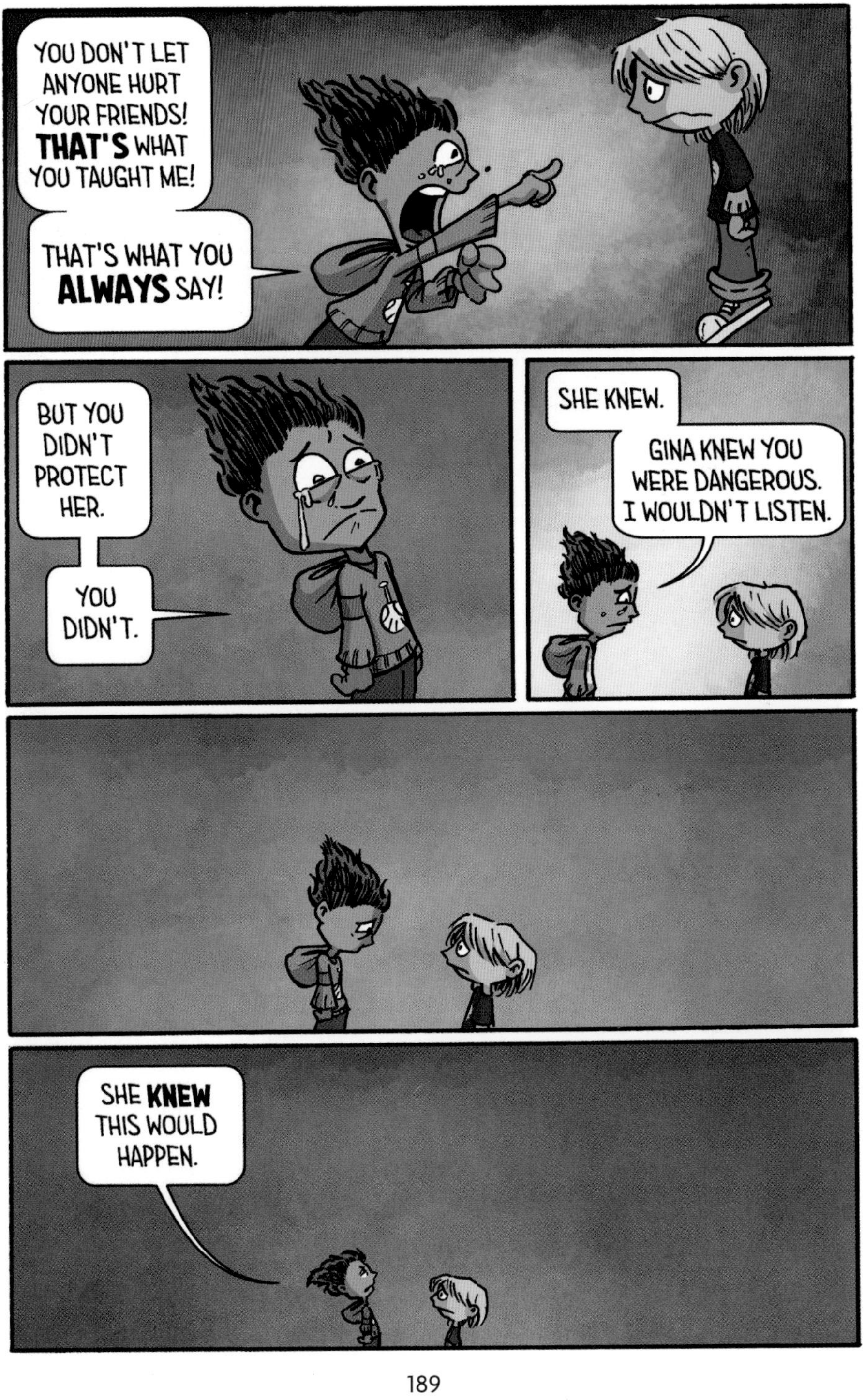
YOU DON'T LET ANYONE HURT YOUR FRIENDS! **THAT'S** WHAT YOU TAUGHT ME!
THAT'S WHAT YOU **ALWAYS** SAY!
BUT YOU DIDN'T PROTECT HER.
YOU DIDN'T.
SHE KNEW.
GINA KNEW YOU WERE DANGEROUS. I WOULDN'T LISTEN.
SHE **KNEW** THIS WOULD HAPPEN.

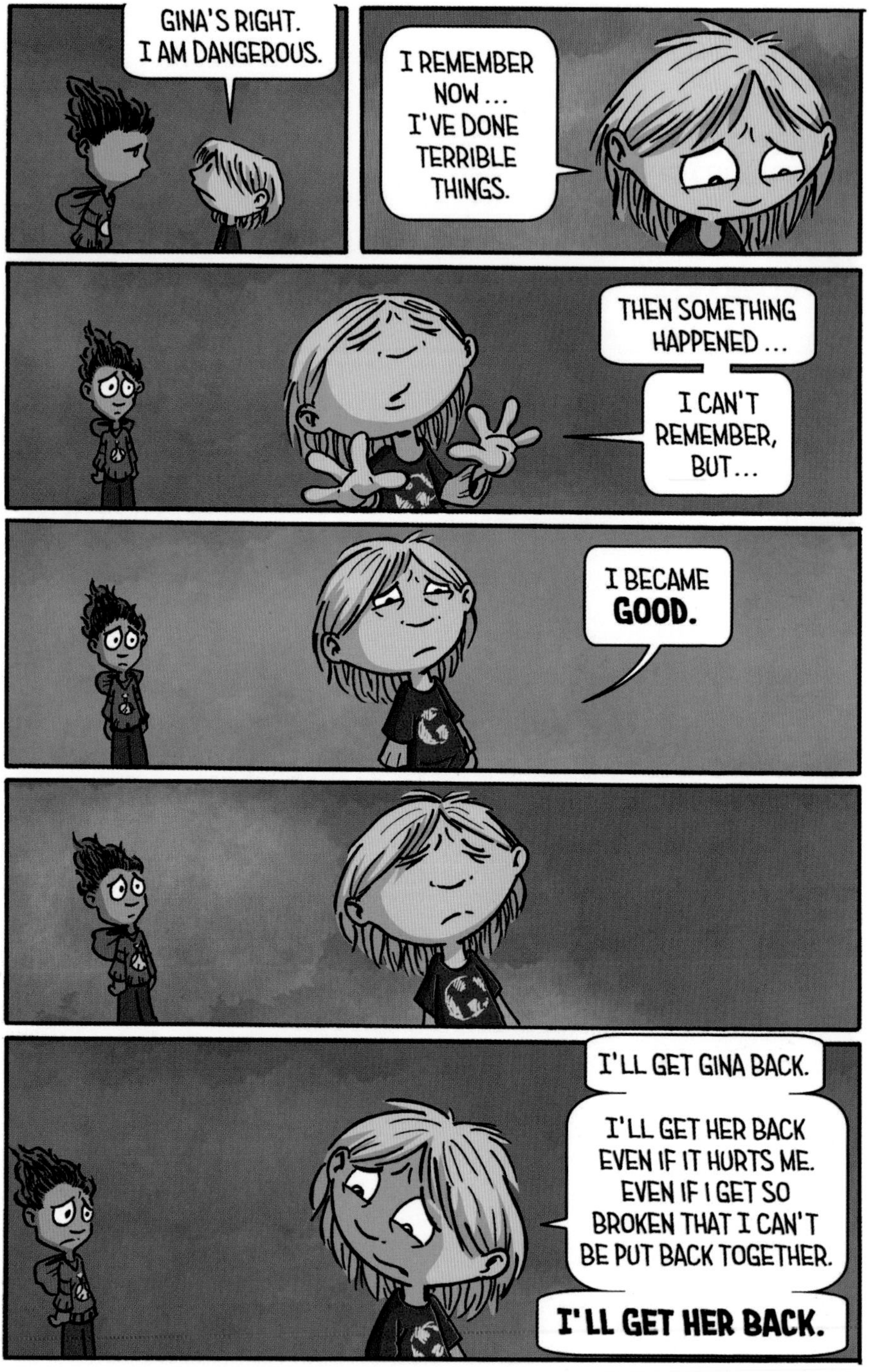
GINA'S RIGHT. I AM DANGEROUS.
I REMEMBER NOW... I'VE DONE TERRIBLE THINGS.
THEN SOMETHING HAPPENED...
I CAN'T REMEMBER, BUT...
I BECAME GOOD.
I'LL GET GINA BACK.
I'LL GET HER BACK EVEN IF IT HURTS ME. EVEN IF I GET SO BROKEN THAT I CAN'T BE PUT BACK TOGETHER.
I'LL GET HER BACK.

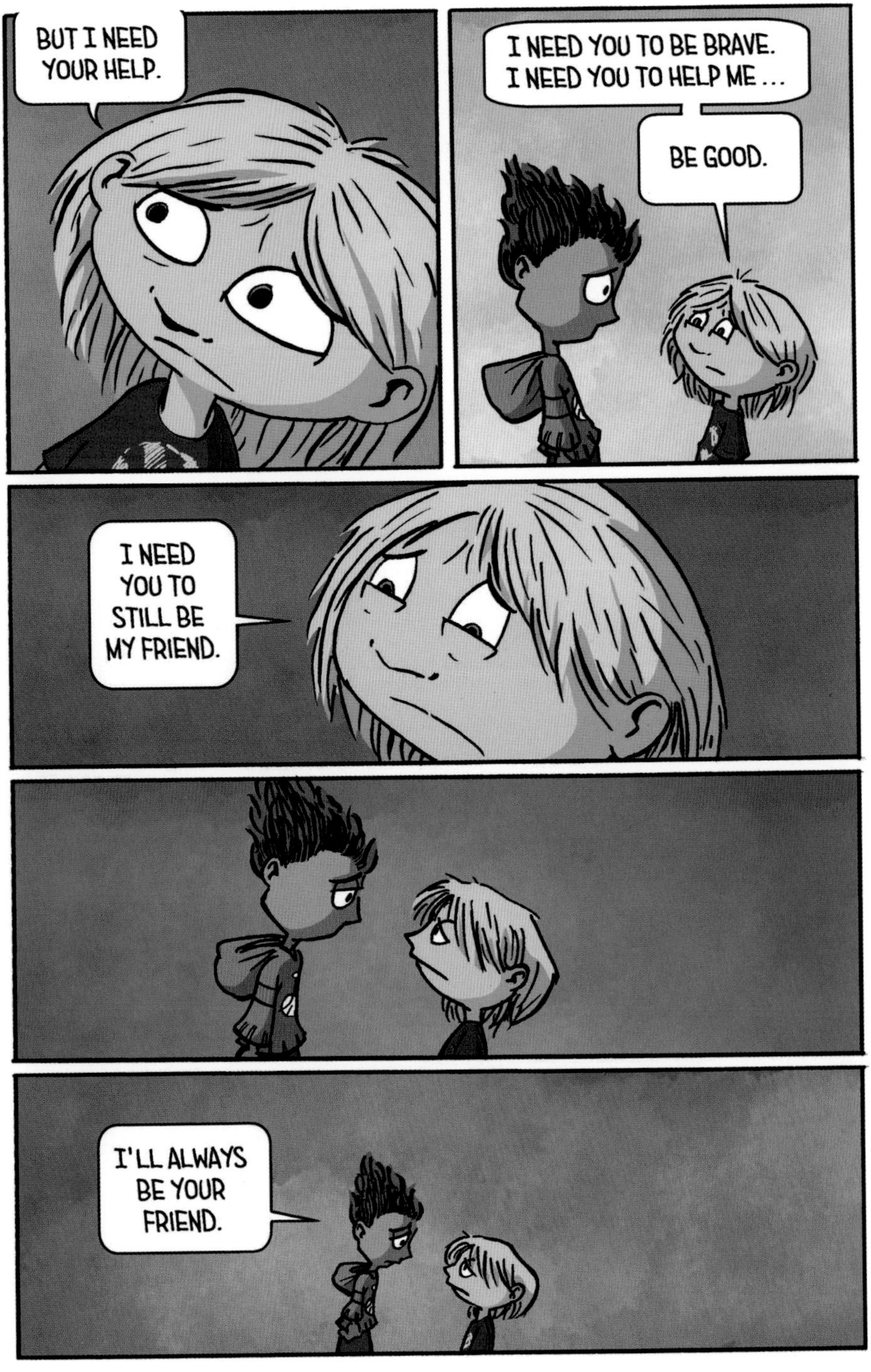
BUT I NEED YOUR HELP.
I NEED YOU TO BE BRAVE. I NEED YOU TO HELP ME . . .
BE GOOD.
I NEED YOU TO STILL BE MY FRIEND.
I'LL ALWAYS BE YOUR FRIEND.

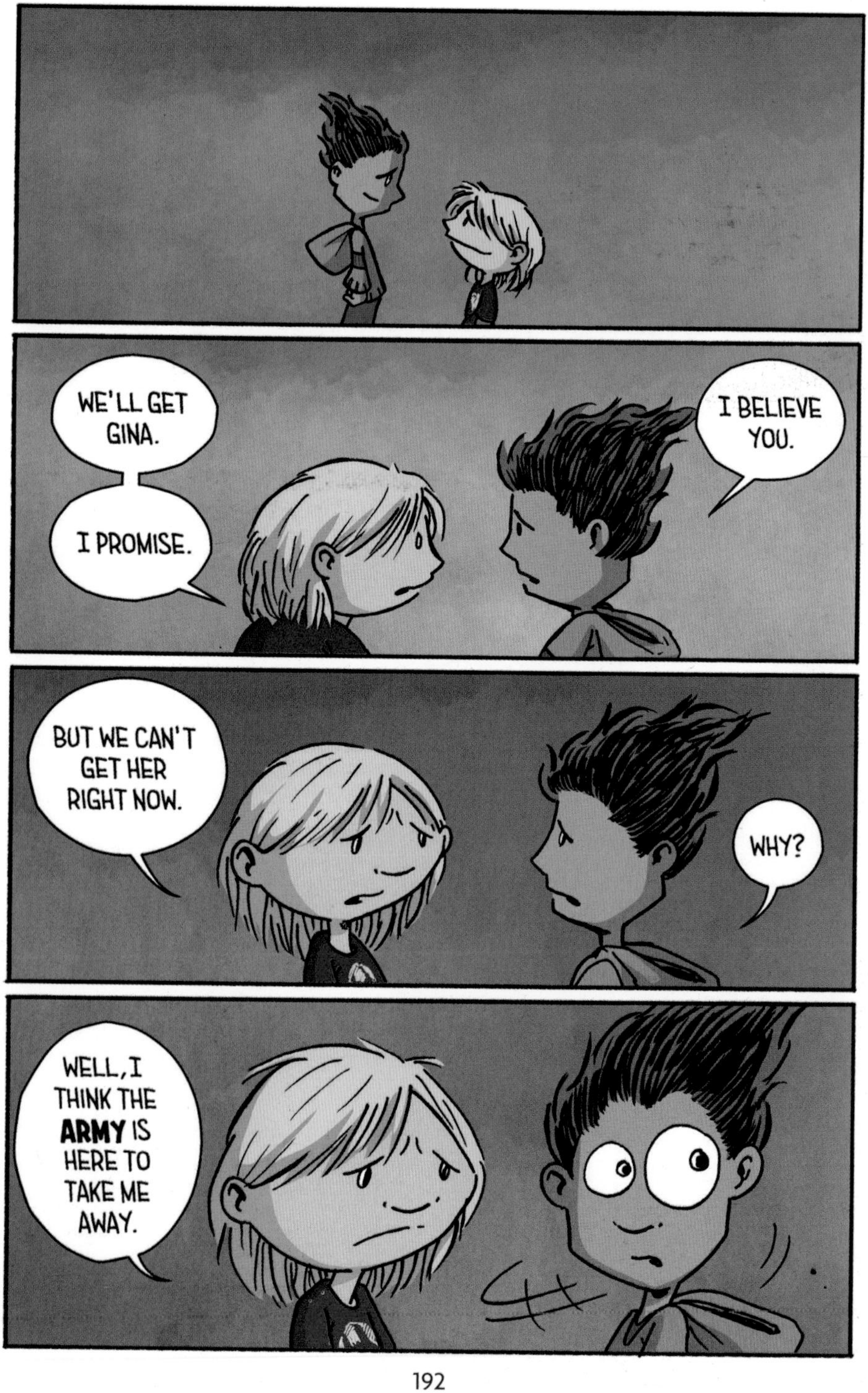
WE'LL GET GINA.
I PROMISE.
I BELIEVE YOU.
BUT WE CAN'T GET HER RIGHT NOW.
WHY?
WELL, I THINK THE **ARMY** IS HERE TO TAKE ME AWAY.

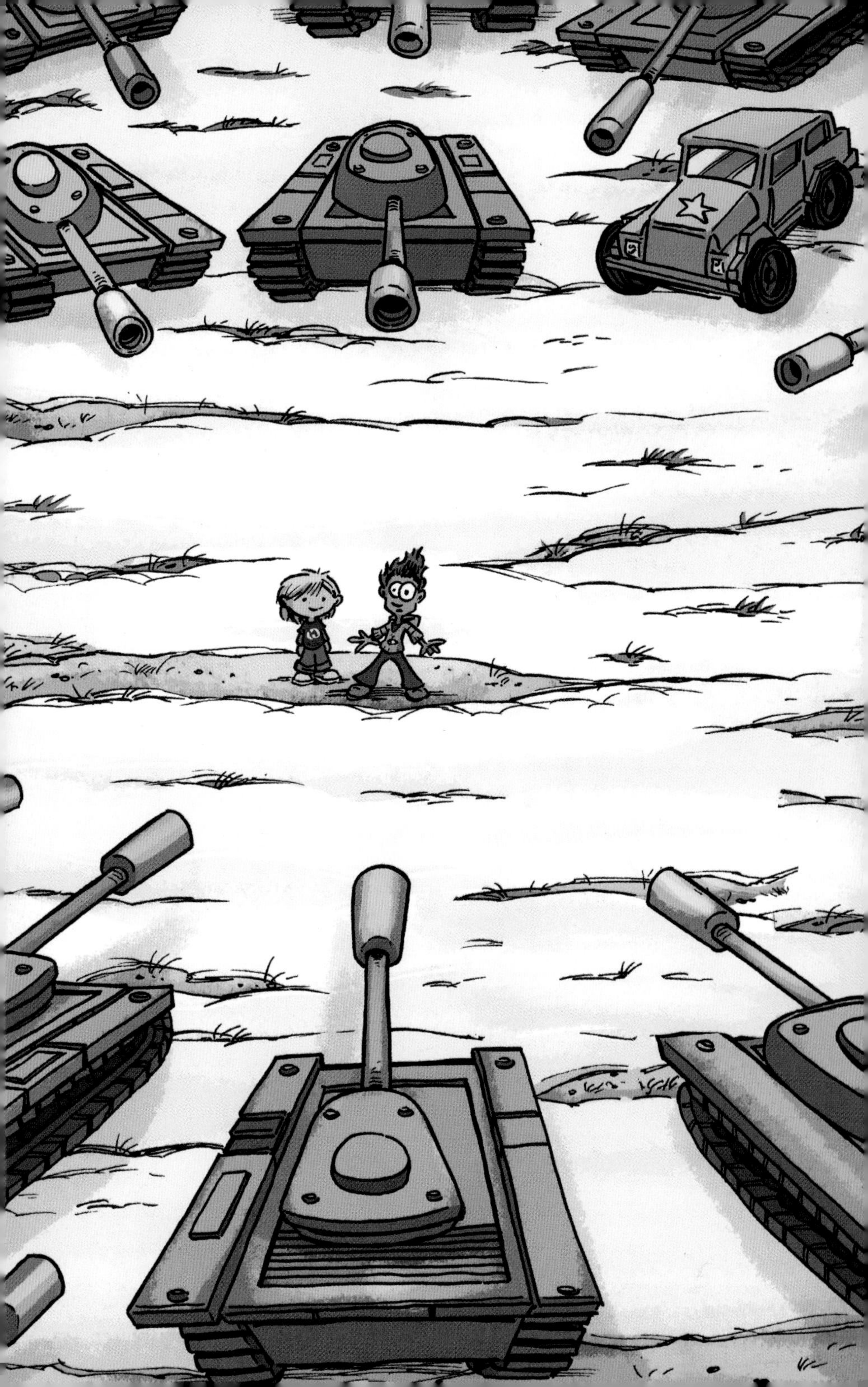

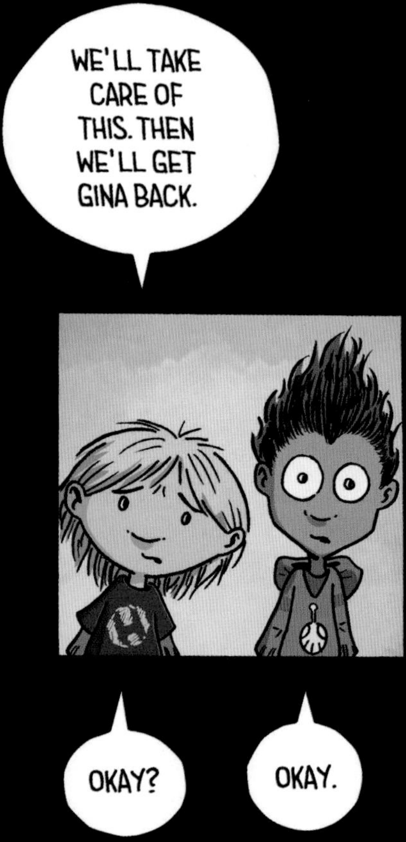
WE'LL TAKE CARE OF THIS. THEN WE'LL GET GINA BACK.
OKAY?
OKAY.

END OF BOOK TWO

LOOK FOR BOOK 3

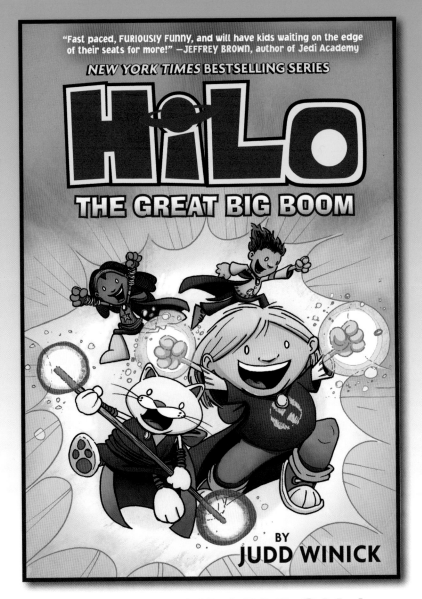

"Fast paced, FURIOUSLY FUNNY, and will have kids waiting on the edge of their seats for more!" —JEFFREY BROWN, author of Jedi Academy

NEW YORK TIMES BESTSELLING SERIES

HiLO

THE GREAT BIG BOOM

BY
JUDD WINICK

NOW AVAILABLE ON A PLANET NEAR YOU!

TURN THE PAGE FOR A SNEAK PEEK!

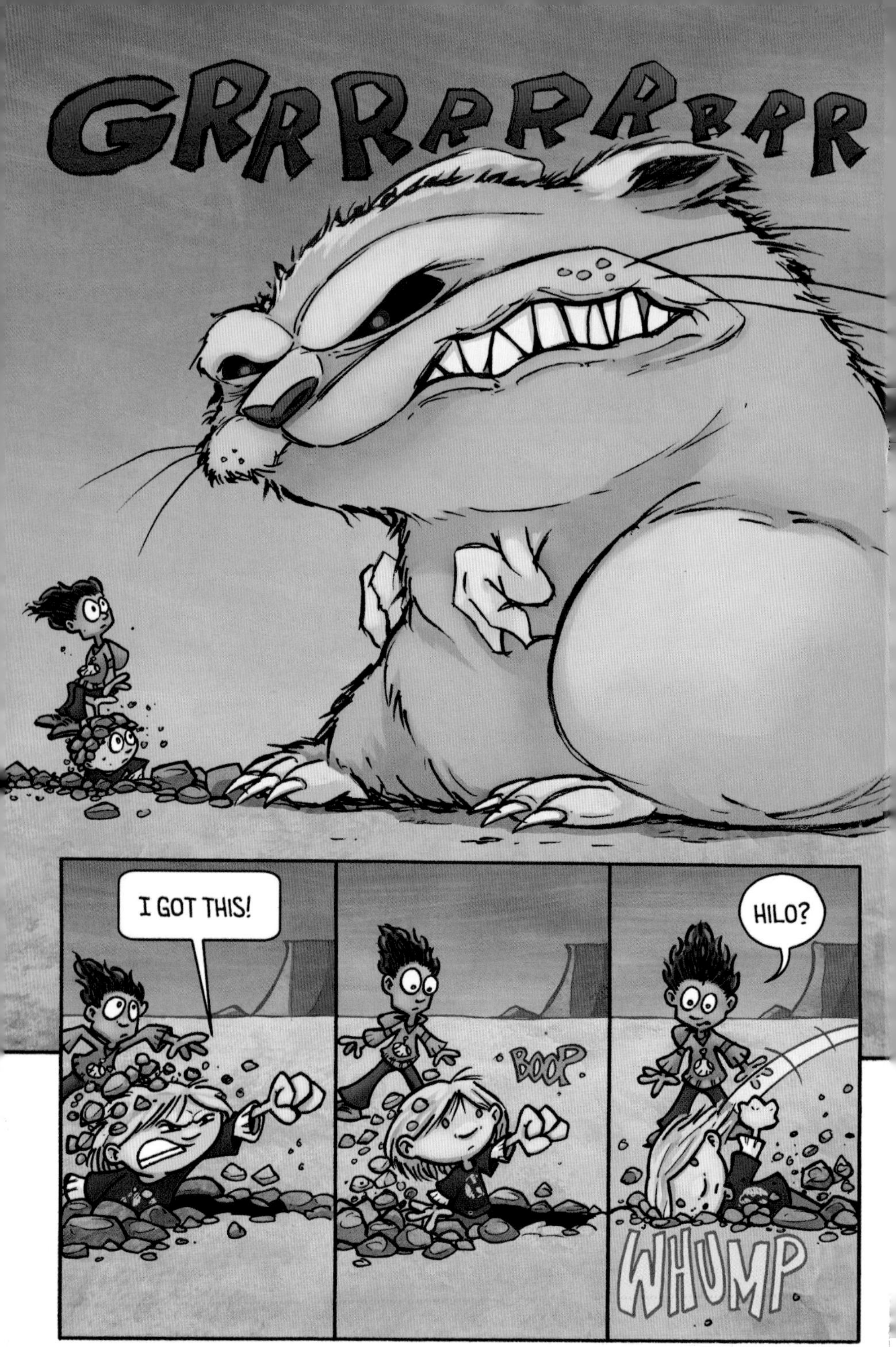
GRRRRRRRRRR
I GOT THIS!
BOOP
HILO?
WHUMP

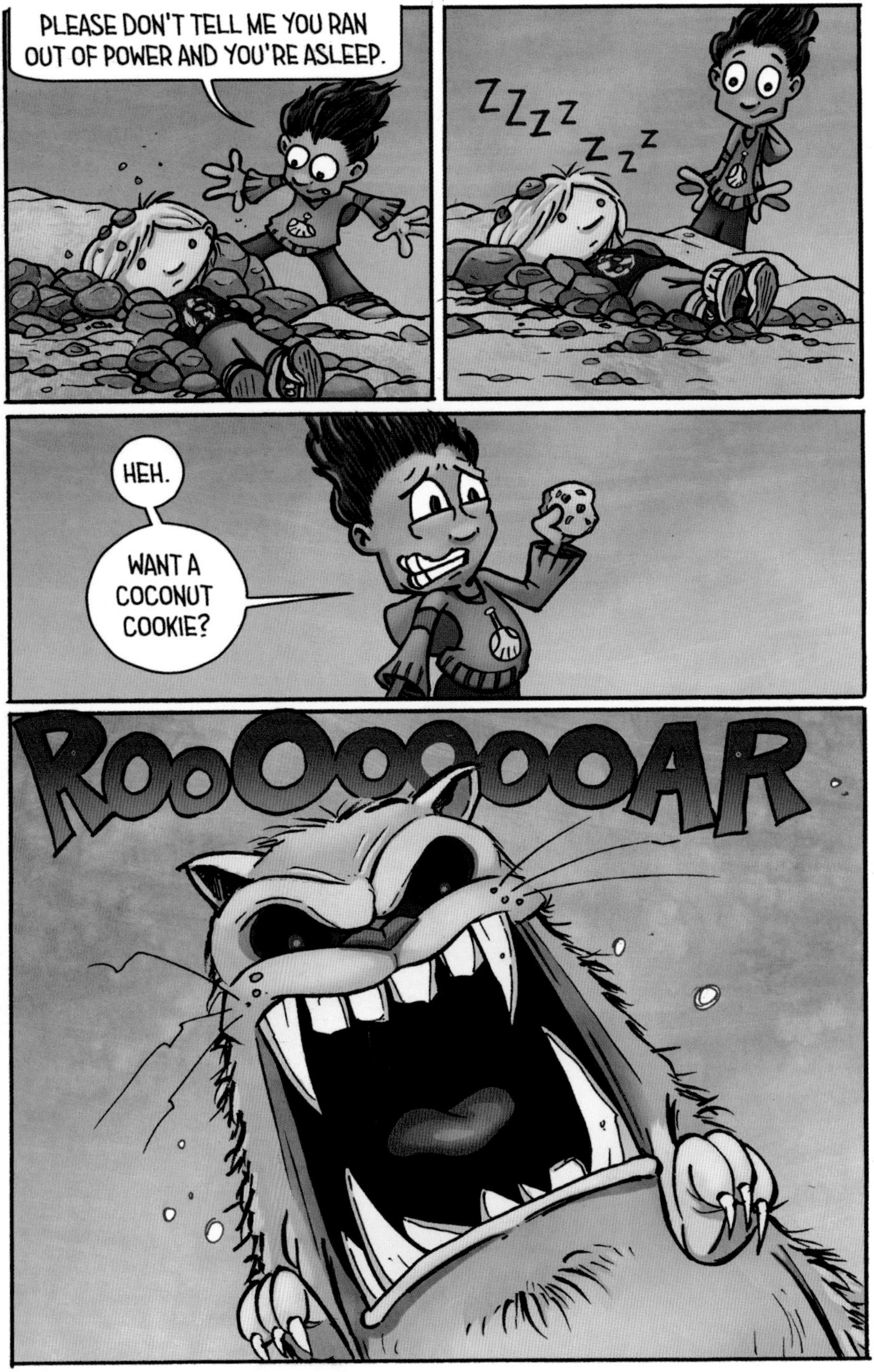
PLEASE DON'T TELL ME YOU RAN OUT OF POWER AND YOU'RE ASLEEP.
ZZZZ
ZZZ
HEH.
WANT A COCONUT COOKIE?
ROOOOOOOAR

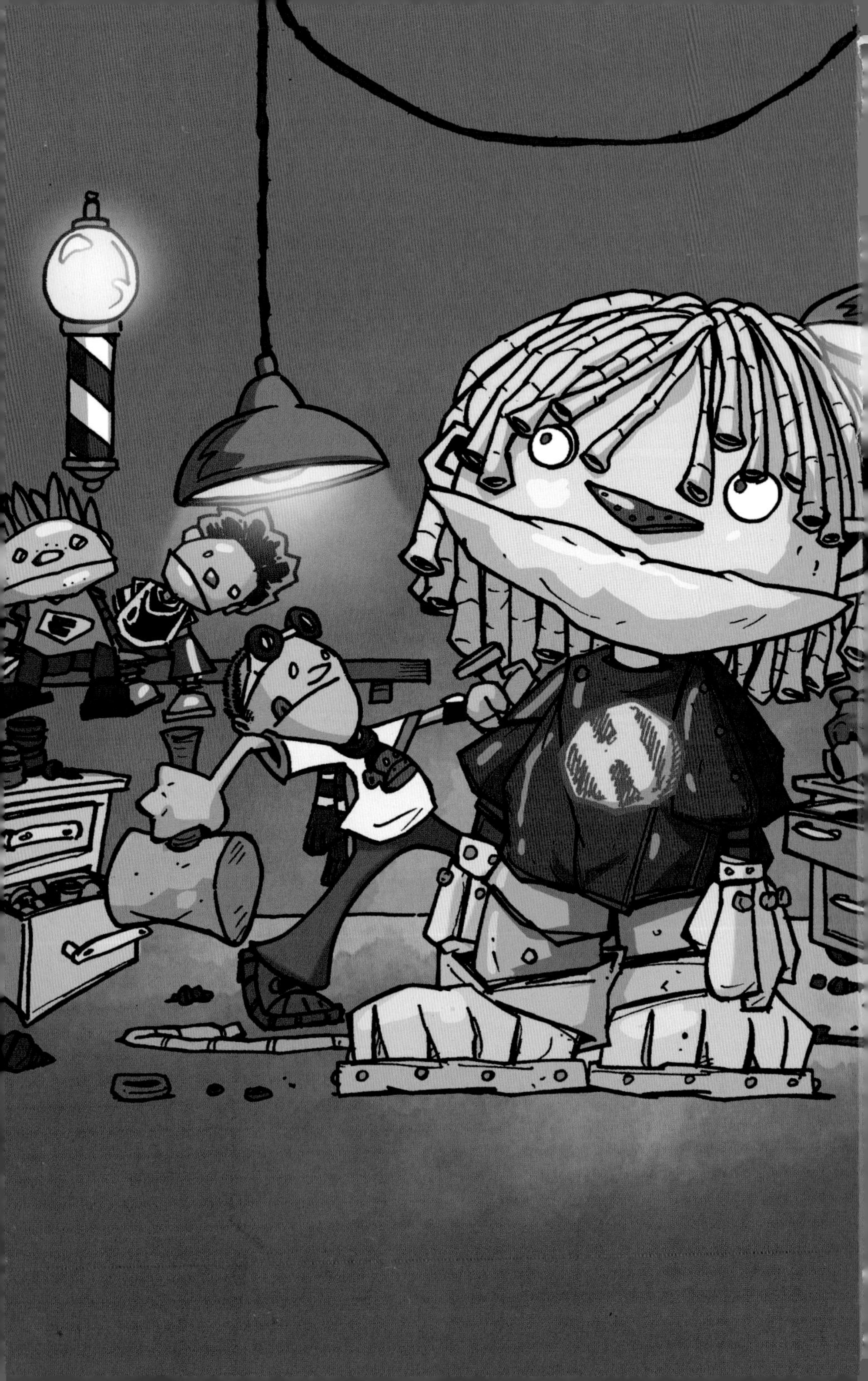